THE PRINCIPESSA

Christie Dickason lived as a child in Thailand, Mexico, Switzerland and the US. Harvard-educated, and a former theatre director and choreographer (with the Royal Shakespeare Company and at Ronnie Scott's among others), she lives in London with her family.

For more information, visit www.christiedickason.co.uk and for exclusive updates on Christie Dickason, visit www.AuthorTracker.co.uk

D0066715

CHRISTIE DICKASON

The Principessa

This novel is entirely a work of fiction.
The names, characters and incidents portrayed in it are
the work of the author's imagination. Any resemblance to
actual persons, living or dead, events or localities is
entirely coincidental.

Harper
An Imprint of
HarperCollins*Publishers*
77–85 Fulham Palace Road,
Hammersmith, London W6 8JB

www.harpercollins.co.uk

Published by HarperCollins*Publishers* 2007

3

A catalogue record for this book is
available from the British Library

978-0-00-723039-6

Set in Meridien by Palimpsest Book Production Limited,
Grangemouth, Stirlingshire

Printed and bound in Great Britain by
Clays Ltd, St Ives plc

For My Beloved Josh

Acknowledgements

My warmest thanks to those without whom ...

JOHN FAULKNER, my very own personal Google, expert in (among other things) languages, ancient warfare, political history, quirky anecdote and unexpected connections.
JOHN CEDERHOLM who introduced me to the Italian Dolomites and eastern Alps.
STEPHEN BASHFORD, for technical advice and helping to devise the Sky Monkey fuse.
STEPHEN WYATT, as ever, thrower of creative lifelines.
JEREMY PRESTON, source of research information and continuing support.
TOM FRENCH, for IT support and my website.
SUSAN SOLT for infusions of energy.
JAYESH PATEL, and his infectious enthusiasm for old Arabic manuscripts.
SYLVIA PIATEK, for helping me with Catholic prayers.
LEONARDO GIANNINI and GIUSEPPE GIANNINI for help with Italian vocabulary.
SANDRA HEMPEL for medical advice.
TESS, for her sharp but loving eye.
The late MICK TOBIN, stage carpenter, original source of my information on how to fire-proof fabric.
JOY CHAMBERLAIN and SUSAN OPIE of HarperCollins, for their enthusiasm and support – both of whom will find themselves in the book if they look carefully enough.
ROBERT KIRBY, my agent.
And, as always, the staffs of The London Library and the National Archives.

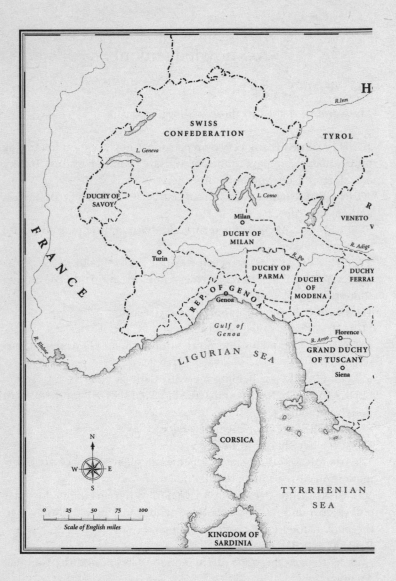

SWISS
CONFEDERATION

R.Inn

TYROL

H

L. Geneva

DUCHY OF
SAVOY

L. Como

Milan
○

VENETO

V

R

DUCHY OF
MILAN

R. Adige

Turin
○

R. Po

FRANCE

DUCHY OF
PARMA

DUCHY
OF
MODENA

DUCHY
FERRAR

DUCH

REP. OF GENOA

Genoa
○

*Gulf of
Genoa*

R. Arno

Florence
○

R. Rhone

LIGURIAN SEA

GRAND DUCHY
OF TUSCANY

Siena
○

D

CORSICA

N

W ✦ E

S

TYRRHENIAN
SEA

0   25   50   75   100

Scale of English miles

KINGDOM OF
SARDINIA

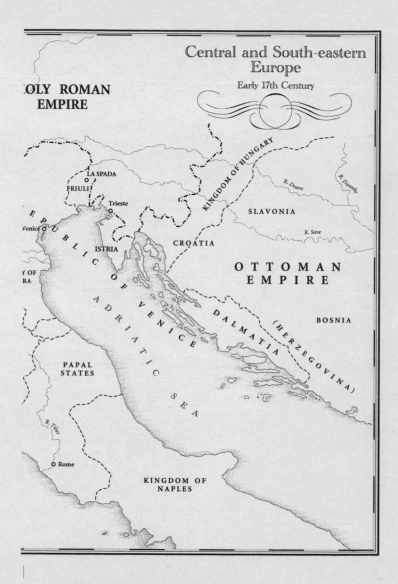

Central and South-eastern Europe

Early 17th Century

HOLY ROMAN EMPIRE

KINGDOM OF HUNGARY

LA SPADA

FRIULI

Trieste

R. Drave

R. Danube

SLAVONIA

R. Save

REPUBLIC OF VENICE

Venice

ISTRIA

CROATIA

OTTOMAN EMPIRE

Y OF RA

ADRIATIC

DALMATIA

BOSNIA

(HERZEGOVINA)

PAPAL STATES

SEA

R. Tiber

Rome

KINGDOM OF NAPLES

A la nature si comande dome obbedinle.
If you hope to rule the power of Nature, you must first
obey her.

(Friulan folk saying)

PART ONE

1

SOFIA'S RULES FOR SURVIVAL

Trust no one
Threaten no one
Hide your feelings and thoughts
Become a good liar
Avoid notice
Distrust your own desires
Smile
Keep your eyes open
Try to see with your enemy's eyes
Take special care when things go well
Be agreeable
Appear blind to the failings of others
Do not attach your heart
Be patient
Think ahead

Want to survive.

2

LA SPADA IN FRIULI, NORTH-EASTERN ITALY, MARCH 1607

'Stay!' shouted the *principessa*.

She kicked. Her horse leapt forward under her. As her attendant riders milled in confusion, her new young husband sat uncertainly on his placid mount. He was not a man for galloping.

Imagine her, at the moment that impulse seized her. Wearing the dark red boots and full split skirt of the Hungarian horsemen of the plains just to the east of La Spada, she could clamp onto the saddle like a man. She kicked again. Her black Barb mare unleashed a burst of the sudden speed for which the horses of the Barbary coast were valued. Together they flew up the slope of the mountain meadow between two flanking walls of jagged peaks, through a bright afternoon at the beginning of spring. The ground was heavy with melting snow. The cold air smelt of damp earth.

The mare had once won races carrying the *principessa*'s own colours of red and gold. Now it caught her urge for freedom and ran for the sheer joy of it.

At last! it seemed to say. Sedate for too long! At last! Whoopee!

The meadow rushed beneath the princess in a blur of pale green and gold, streaked by blue-grey patches of the last snow. The wind sucked tears from the corners of her eyes and forced cold fingers into her chest.

Flying. Flying.

She had not ridden like this since she was a child. Then, at the age of eight, she had been beaten for risking the life of the prince's only surviving legitimate heir.

All changing, all changing, all changing, said her horse's hoofs. Her thoughts scattered behind her, snatched by the wind, skimming over lurking rabbit holes, loose rocks, ice, anything that might bring horse and rider crashing down.

She heard hoof beats behind her and snatched a backward glance.

Her new husband of just two days, his face alight with ecstatic terror at his own daring, raced pell-mell after her up the meadow.

Yes!

Another glance showed her the attendants still in the distance at the bottom of the slope, still obedient to her order but stamping about in alarm at her unexpected flight. If anything happened to her, they would die.

Sofia leaned forwards, gave the horse its head entirely. The mare stretched its sure-footed stride to the very limit. Its power coiled and released under her. She floated on the glorious speed like a fragment of leaf on a snow-fed stream. She forgot rabbit holes and loose rocks. No longer *Principessa* Sofia, that sad heavy mass of ambitions, frustrations and fear, she was a light hollow shell filled only with the rush of blurred earth, the beating wind and the rhythm of her mare's hoofs.

A single thought rode with her, lightly, at the top of her mind.

Follow me! Follow me!

Her new husband, her sweet, timid, wealthy Baldassare, her unexpected gift from fate, had mastered his fear and galloped after her.

He would follow her again in other things and help her when she told him how. She had a new ally, with more life in him than she had feared on their wedding night.

Escape or rule.

Possible now, possible now, possible now . . .

Mare and girl soared to the crest of the meadow where it turned downwards and narrowed towards a mountain defile. A horseman came out of the defile and trotted lazily towards her. Sofia was already collecting up her mare and pulling it back from their shared ecstatic flight, when she recognized him. Her older half-brother, Prince Ettore.

Bad omen . . . rabbit hole.

She swung wide and cantered past him. Then alarm caught up with her. The hair rose on her neck. She reined in hard and turned in time to see the close brush of horses and Baldassare's fall. She heard the thump of his landing, saw him roll, lie winded. Then one hand waved feebly to tell her that he was still alive. His startled horse thudded back the way it had come, dragging his blue cape under its hoofs through the spring grass.

Ettore was off his horse before Sofia could reach them. He knelt beside Baldassare.

'Don't touch him!' Sofia screamed. She flung herself from her saddle.

Tenderly, Ettore lifted the younger man's head in his hands. Then he gave the head a short abrupt twist. Sofia heard a crack as if someone had stepped on a dry stick.

Ettore looked up and met her eye. 'My condolences, *principessa*. He seems to have broken his neck in the fall.'

A roar of despairing rage rose from her belly. With teeth bared and fingers turned to razors, she threw herself at him. Both of his cheeks were bleeding before the attendants could pull her off him.

3

LONDON, MARCH 1608

Francis Quoynt watched his golden fire rain down on the duke's guests packed into the formal garden on the north shore of the Thames. Black smoke swirled in the torchlight and slid between silk skirts and velvet shoulders like the probing fingers of an arriving fog.

Ashes, thought Francis. It all ends in ashes.

Glumly he watched a flight of his rockets shoot up into the night sky and explode in perfect unison, flinging out interlaced ribbons of falling stars. Well-born women gave little squeaks of mock terror and clutched at silk-clad male arms. Jewels flashed in the torchlight as soft clean hands applauded his work. He heard his name floating here and there in the hubbub of well-bred, approving voices, as clean and sharp-edged as an oak leaf. 'Quoynt!' 'Quoynt!'

He flicked a fallen smut of ash from his starched lace cuff. Melancholy sat coldly on his heart. His costly new boots pinched.

'Good evening to you also, my lord.' He ducked his head civilly to a passing figure who trailed a miasma of civet and orange water. 'Thank you for your kind words.'

He backed a little out of sight into a dark arch in the tall yew hedge.

Where had his passion gone? Even the special challenge later this evening did not excite him.

Misery had come upon him by degrees in the midst of his greatest success. He did not understand it – nor would he tolerate it. Self-pity was an indulgence for men with nothing better to occupy them.

He had no excuse for self-pity. He was above usual height, well-proportioned and still young, at the peak of his male strength. He also had the uncommon good fortune of still having all his teeth, digits and limbs. He had a fine head of fair hair like his father and, so far as he could judge, most of his wits. War had neither killed nor crippled him. He had succeeded beyond all imagining at this new peacetime trade. And if he had lost the woman he most wanted, there were others, even here in this privileged mob, who would have him if only he would take the trouble to woo. He had seen enough true misery to know that his own was a baseless fraud.

He looked down at his hands, trained to light fuses and to feel the most subtle changes whilst grinding together the ingredients of gunpowder. They looked unfamiliar now in jewelled rings. And far too clean.

The alien silk of his doublet gleamed like coal in the light of torches planted around the gardens. Pearls stitched around the cuffs of his sleeves glowed like tiny moons. His long legs were encased in yet more silk. He did not know himself any longer. He brushed another fallen smut of ash off the back of one hand.

Misery was not for a man who now had more money than he knew how to spend. It was wicked ingratitude to pine to return to leather and wool, but he did not like the price he had paid for silk.

11

He frowned up at a shower of white stars.

Empty show! This whole wasteful, pointless display did nothing but prove the wealth and status of his latest patron. Only two years earlier, after a youth spent in destruction, he could imagine nothing finer than to give innocent joy. But joy loses its point when you're short of it yourself.

As for innocence . . .! He scanned the crowd. There might be a faithful wife or devoted husband or betrothed virgin in that crowd, but he couldn't see any of them from where he stood.

'There you are, Quoynt!'

He had not hidden well enough. The duke's Master of Music jabbed a forefinger up towards Francis's face. 'Your bangs are drowning my music, which I composed especially for tonight! I insist that you make them quieter!'

Francis looked down at the little wriggling lapdog of a man. Hit him! Go on! Why not? His fists clenched. Why must he always behave well? Why must he always be civil to fools?

'Bangs and fireworks generally go together,' he said with a mildness that amazed him. 'I did suggest that you use drums.' Very soon, he feared, he would give in to that growing hunger to clout someone. Please God, it wouldn't be a duke. Or Cecil.

Twelve rockets fizzed up into the night sky, followed by a shock of thunder that rattled the trees and entirely drowned out the string quartet on the terrace behind the big house. Again, women screamed in false terror and clutched the nearest male arm. Again, applauding hands flickered against the unsteady orange torchlight. Rings and jewel-edged sleeve cuffs flashed.

'Stop your ungodly pyrotechnics now!' the Master of Music shrieked, rising onto his toes in fury. 'You import the reek of Satan . . .'

'By your leave . . .' Francis turned away towards one of his assistants who was waving urgently from the raised terrace behind the house. Silently the youth mouthed, 'He's here!'

Francis lifted his hand in acknowledgement, then went to alert the rest of his men, who lurked with soot-blackened faces, wearing coats of green leaves to protect them against sparks.

As their green-clad forms darted into place in the darkness beyond the torch-lit walks and central grassy promenade, a ripple passed through the guests like wind over water. The Master of Music felt it, turned and raced back to his musicians on the terrace.

With his right hand raised, holding a white handkerchief, Francis let the man have his fanfare, as far as those watery strings could ever manage a fanfare. He curled his lip. Feeble! Feeble. His ears craved the stout metallic shouts of trumpets crying 'Onward! Onward!' He let hand and handkerchief fall. Even now, after so many years, he held his breath.

In the next few thumps of his heart, Lady Gunpowder would decide whether to obey her would-be masters or to turn on them. She might rebel and set fire to hair and fry eyeballs like eggs, if she didn't kill outright. In this moment, repeated again and again, he and his men risked their lives to give frivolous pleasure to men and women who did not understand what a godlike force, cousin to earthquakes and thunder, was condescending merely to entertain.

The din of battle exploded around the garden in a harmless wreath of smoke and thunder. Tonight, the Lady had obeyed. Francis breathed again.

Serpents of light twisted and writhed in a carpet of earthly fire in the flowerbeds. Squibs leapt and crackled amongst the skirts and legs. There was a blinding flash of white light.

Into this glorious mayhem, at just the right time – just as the last squib died – King James the First of England and Sixth of Scotland arrived on the terrace, revealed as if by magic after the flash, at the top of the garden steps, his arms spread to embrace the heaving sea of bowing, curtseying, cheering subjects below him.

'Good man,' muttered Francis. In spite of his black humour, he felt a small stab of satisfaction. It couldn't have gone better. Like a seasoned playhouse actor, the king had found exactly the right spot on his stage at precisely the right time.

The two torches placed by Francis lit the royal face clearly and made the king's black pearl-and-diamond embroidered suit twinkle like a clear night sky. A shower of falling stars from a trio of rockets now threw a rippling light onto the gem that lay over the king's heart, the size of a thrush's egg, visible testimony to the king's infinite wealth and power. Nested amongst the glittering constellations of royal sleeve, cuff and stocking edge, set in an intricate nest of enamel and gold, and wonderfully lit by Francis's fires, hung the King's Great Pearl.

The crowd of guests still cheered, voicing their surprise at the flattering condescension of this impromptu royal visit, for which everyone had been feverishly preparing for the last three weeks.

As he allowed the homage, his majesty studied his still-foreign subjects with a cold, assessing, intelligent eye. His protruding jaw worked slightly as if he were chewing on his tongue. Graciously, he allowed time for everyone to admire the splendour of his attire, the number and size of his rings and the many chains hanging across his chest, and to murmur how the price of the King's Great Pearl could, on its own, finance a war.

The royal eyes met Francis's, saw the fire master nod, and moved on with a gleam of gratification. Then the king leaned to mutter into the ear of the small lop-sided man beside him. The short figure of Robert Cecil, the Earl of Salisbury and English Secretary of State, stepped out of the shadows behind his royal master and beckoned for Francis to approach. As the cheers dwindled, the *viola da gamba* player could be heard choking on the smoke.

On the terrace, Francis nodded and smiled but could not take in the king's words of praise. He was blind to the glares of the Master of Music and deaf to the whispers and murmurs of the crowd as it noted the signs of royal approval. He knew, even before Cecil asked him to wait at the water gate, that the moment he had feared for the last two years had finally arrived.

4

They sat in silence while the boatman pushed Cecil's private wherry off from the duke's water steps. They rode face to face on velvet cushions, their kneecaps almost touching, Francis with his back to the bow. As the night was fine, the sailcloth sides were rolled up and tied to the frame of the wherry's arched roof.

Francis eyed Cecil in the faint shifting light reflected off the water. The thick wool fabric and fur collar of his cloak smoothed out Robert Cecil's twisted, uneven silhouette. The high domed forehead and intelligent eyes caught orange glints from the wherry's lantern as the little man seemed to study the river. Francis felt sure that his patron could hear the pounding of his heart above the faint splashing of the oars.

'I've quite missed our evening jaunts on the Thames.' Cecil's tone suggested that this meeting was entirely social.

'I can't say that I have,' replied Francis. 'If you'll forgive me, my lord.' For two years he had been dreading the moment when Cecil would again ask to speak to him in absolute secrecy. He had known better than to hope it might never come.

'I won't say that I've missed the need.' Robert Cecil, the most powerful man in England after the king, leaned back and became a mere small lumpy shadow under the wherry's canopy.

Francis wiped damp palms on his silk-clad knees.

During those two years of waiting, they had kept up the cordial public relationship between patron and client. A relationship based, for Francis, on distrust, a degree of terror, and absolute knowledge that the little man had not done with him in his other, more hidden uses.

The rising tide tugged at the wherry as they turned upriver. Slowly, they left behind them the lights of the big houses lining the north shore of the Thames above London Bridge. With the houses, they also left behind the rich stink of the sewage that lapped at the riverbanks and sea walls.

In darkness, the flat muscular surface of the water felt infinitely wide. Beyond the leisurely comet of their own lantern, the stars of other lanterns wove an undulating net of light, from bank to bank and up and down stream.

Speak! Be done with it! Francis wiped his palms again.

They stared silently at the net of lights flung across the water. On the far shore, the lanterns hanging outside the Southwark inns raised a frail barricade against the dark void of the Lambeth marshes.

'I beg you, my lord. Spit it out!' Francis burst out, at last. 'Two years is a long time to torment a man . . . waiting for the axe to fall.'

'And why do you think you might deserve the axe?' Cecil sounded friendly enough.

'My lord, it was a mere metaphor.'

Francis glared down at the dark water that slid past the low side of the wherry and clamped his mouth shut. Cecil had that effect on most men – unsettling them into letting slip words they would rather keep mewed up.

'Most men would have swooned at the praise you had from his majesty just now on the duke's terrace,' said Cecil severely. 'I've kept my part of the bargain, Quoynt. Given you success, the chance to glut yourself on praise and acclaim. But you don't wish to feast, it would seem. A different patron might consider you ungrateful.'

Francis lifted his head sharply. 'Is my loss of appetite so clear to see?'

He knew Cecil by now. This was the prod meant to unsettle him and leave him open to the stiletto blow from an entirely different direction. But Cecil's usual dry relish for his games seemed missing.

'My lord . . .'

Cecil raised a small shadowy hand. 'Spare me polite protest, Quoynt. I know very well what I've done for you and your family.'

Whatever else you might have done, thought Francis. And however unhappily I may have earned your favour.

For many at court, a hint from Cecil was as good as an order. For the last two years, he had been unstinting in his praise of Francis and had recommended him amongst the nobility. Under the little man's patronage, Francis had been transformed from a military fire master, unemployed after the new peace with Spain, into an acclaimed artificer of civilian fireworks.

'With your help, my lord, I have prospered beyond my imagining.'

Cecil snorted.

'We are all grateful for your protection.' By 'we' Francis meant himself, his father Boomer, suspected of Catholic sympathies during the horrors of the failed Gunpowder Treason, and the lovely, still-vulnerable Catholic Kate, known by Cecil to have once committed the treason of hiding a Jesuit priest. Oh, Kate . . .!

Francis thrust her from his thoughts. With such a debt, and two such hostages to the little man's pleasure, how could he grudge Cecil any service?

'My lord, please don't mistake my loss of ambition. Blame my ignorance.' The wherry rocked with his fervour to explain. Cecil gripped the sides. He could not swim.

'As a soldier,' said Francis, 'I only ever knew dukes and knights man-to-man on the battlefield. I didn't foresee how working amongst them and their ladies in their leisure at court would twist me into a false courtier.'

'You make a passable imitation of one. Is it so painful?'

'I feel like a dancing bear dressed up in a petticoat and ruff.' Too late, Francis remembered whispered gibes in Whitehall that Cecil resembled a performing monkey dressed in court robes.

There was another silence while they continued upstream, swaying gently forward and back with each surge of the oars, headed for the tiny sparks of Whitehall ahead on their right.

'I can't save you from being a courtier,' said Cecil at last. 'But I can at least offer you a very different court.' He turned again to look at the water.

Francis also pretended to stare at the water. 'Where is this court?' he asked at last.

'Patience, Quoynt.'

Francis clenched his fists on his knees in sudden rage.

Dear God, don't hit Cecil!

Cecil's manipulations swilled together with the Master of Music and all those false screaming women and perfumed, over-prinked gentlemen who deigned to permit Lady Gunpowder to perform for them like a six-penny bawdy-house whore.

'My lord, haven't I proved my loyalty and discretion? If I am to serve you again this other way, I beg you, no more tormenting, no more toying! Just tell me what you want of me. I'll do it if I can. I'm sick to death of civil games!'

Let Cecil have his head off if he wanted it. Francis could take no more. He yanked at his starched ruff, snapped the ties and threw the accursed thing into the river. Both men watched it melt into a mess of pale floating weed.

'I had not intended to torment you, Quoynt.' Cecil sounded surprised.

And how does it feel? thought Francis viciously. To be surprised for a change?

'I merely save words.' The Secretary of State let go of the gunwales and began to gather his robes around him. 'What I will now show you would need a three-hour sermon to express.'

The collar had drifted out of sight. The oars splashed gently as the wherry began to turn. Francis heard faint cheerful shouts exchanged between two distant wherries. Dogs barked far away in the City. A fish jumped near their boat. On the closer shore, a woman's laugh could just be heard. Francis turned to look over his shoulder. They were approaching the lantern on King Henry's water stairs at Whitehall, which was the residence of the king and true seat of power in England, however much the men who sat in Parliament at Westminster might deceive themselves.

5

A large battered sea chest sat in the centre of the floor of Cecil's private office, incongruous against the gleaming waxed panelling, Turkey carpets, the silver and gold of Cecil's inkpots and pens. It was made of salt-stained leather, bound together with studded iron straps. It might have carried guns, pewter flagons, or coins. The domed lid was propped a little ajar with small blocks of wood.

'Open it,' ordered Cecil. 'With care.'

The attendants waiting at the landing had helped the Secretary of State ashore from the wherry and up the steep slippery water steps. Then he had waved them all away. By the time he and Francis had entered the small, self-contained city of Whitehall, walked a short way up the central avenue and turned into Cecil's private apartments, a groom had already lit a dozen beeswax candles, stirred the coals in the fireplace and left. Francis and Cecil were now alone in the wood-panelled office that smelled sweetly of honey and beeswax.

Francis raised the heavy lid. Startled, he looked at Cecil in question.

In the shadows of the bottom, a small boy lay tightly

curled, knees to his chest, arms wrapped around his head to hide his face. He looked no more than ten years old.

Cecil nodded.

Francis leaned down and lightly tapped the bony young shoulder, which was just touched by the candlelight.

The boy erupted from the chest. He clawed his way past Francis, flailing in panic, eyes blind with terror, and dived behind a tapestry hanging of David and Goliath. Francis sucked a scratch on his hand.

'He's lost his tongue,' said Cecil. 'But I believe he's the cabin boy from a ship found adrift in the north-east Adriatic, just off the coast of Istria. A privateer sailing under the English flag.'

The boy behind the tapestry reminded Francis of the lump of a mouse in a snake's belly.

'He's part of a message from that other court I mentioned.'

'I confess that I don't yet grasp the message,' said Francis. 'In any of its parts.'

'When found and taken in tow as salvage, the privateer was a ghost ship. No crew, no cargo . . . blood on the decks but no bodies. Except one – flying from the mast where the English ensign should have been. And the boy, too terrified to leave his hiding place in the chest.'

They watched the bulge in the hanging move deeper into cover, away from the edge. The boy's eyes had not seen Francis as he clambered from the chest. They were still seeing past horrors.

'There was a sealed letter in the captain's cabin,' said Cecil. 'Addressed to me and sent on to me, along with the boy, by Sir Henry Wootten, the new English ambassador in Venice.'

Francis watched the chief minister, puzzled. Something in Cecil's manner was askew.

'In this other court, they don't conduct their business as we do.' Cecil's voice took on a grim irony. 'The taking of the ship, and the manner of it, is the reply to my own very civil request to repay a loan taken out on behalf of the king at the time agreed in the contract, not before.'

Francis frowned. 'What objection can there be?'

'The prince of La Spada in Friuli, who made the loan, is dying. He wants his money back now, two years early.'

'Even though the loan contract says that he must wait?' Francis was not a lawyer, but even he could see that it was the prince of La Spada who wanted to break the terms of the contract, not England or the king.

'It seems that a dying man cares little for the finer points of law.'

'The nature of the message still seems extreme.'

'The loan is very large.' Cecil swallowed audibly. 'It's fortunate that the letter was addressed to me. For many reasons, I would like to resolve this matter without having to disturb the king.'

'Can't England simply repay the loan?'

'With what?' Cecil crossed to the window and seemed to stare at his fractured reflection in the dark diamond panes. 'King James was necessary for England, but he was a very costly necessary.' He leaned his forehead against the glass as if to cool his thoughts. 'You saw what he wore tonight. Just one suit of clothing, one night's jewels. And the Treasury is drained by the war with Spain.'

Francis was flattered, in spite of himself, by this unusual frankness. At the same time he felt alarm. Cecil did not usually explain so much. Cecil did not explain at all.

When James took the throne, Francis had been skulking at his family's home in Sussex, near Brighthelmstone, newly unemployed. He had not seen the new king's magnificent progress south from Edinburgh to London, but he had heard the tales. The feasts, the gold coins showered on ecstatic crowds, the music commissioned, the musicians paid. The generous gifts made to sweeten the many powerful men who had not entirely welcomed a foreign king trailing a noisy pack of equally foreign followers, all of them speaking English with a barbaric Scottish roll.

'He made up two hundred and thirty-seven new knights between Berwick and London,' said Cecil to his reflection. 'Before he had even arrived in London, all of them expecting lands and licences.'

In his two years at court, Francis had also heard about the allies bought, and the secret intelligencers. He had heard the English grumbling that their lands and taxes were being given to uncouth foreigners who brought nothing to England in return.

Everyone was, of course, as delighted as Cecil at the large royal family, which promised dynastic stability after two barren queens and a sickly boy. But officials muttered about the cost of the grand new households needed for each of its members – the king, his queen, Henry the Prince of Wales, Princess Elizabeth, the little Prince Charles, and of course, the infant Princess Mary, the first living royal child born on English soil since Edward VI, two generations ago.

'The early days of his reign were not the time to preach frugality to the king,' said Cecil.

Most certainly not the right time for the man who wished to curry favour and remain as chief minister, thought Francis.

Francis stared at the chest and then at the boy behind the tapestry. A plundered ship and butchered crew still seemed an extreme reply to an offer of financial negotiation.

'The proceeds from several trading voyages to the East Indies will cover the loan,' said Cecil. 'But one can never be certain how long any voyage will take. Or even whether it will escape the growing curse of pirates and corsairs.'

'I'm the wrong man for this envoy, my lord! This prince is clearly a mad brigand. You need a devious, practised, smooth-tongued eel. You must have one or two of those in your pay.'

'Are you telling me how to manage English affairs of state?' Cecil's voice was suddenly dangerous. 'Don't presume on my inexplicable liking for you.'

'My lord, you've told me often enough that I'm a bad liar. Why the devil send me when you will need . . .?'

'Enough!' Cecil unleashed the full force of his authority. His small size compressed his power, just as a modest shell contains the potential for a devastating explosion. 'You're a far better liar than you think! Even so, I agree that you're the wrong man. I would not send you neither, if I had a choice! But the prince of La Spada asks for you.'

'For me?' asked Francis incredulously. 'By name?'

The uneven shoulders of Cecil's silhouette rose and fell in a shrug. '"The acclaimed English fire master Francis Quoynt" to devise his funeral fireworks. Can't be plainer than that!'

Francis laughed. 'The prince is jesting at our expense. He would never ask an Englishman to devise fireworks!'

'You don't see yourself in that "acclaimed English fire master"?' asked Cecil curiously.

'Honour would never allow such a thing! After the Chinese, it's the Romans, Florentines, Venetians, and Milanese who are the great masters of explosives and pyrotechnics. The world travels to study with them.'

Francis could not understand why Cecil seemed not to grasp his argument.

'The French hire Italian fire masters to devise their fireworks,' he insisted. 'The Germans hire Italian fire masters. The Austrian Hapsburgs hire Italian fire masters – even the Great Turk hires Italian fire masters. Why the devil would a prince of Friuli want to hire an Englishman?'

'Nevertheless, he wants you.' Cecil coughed to clear his

throat, then explored one sleeve with a shadowy hand and extracted a pale handkerchief. He wiped his mouth.

Francis watched him with every sense now alert. Cecil's unease was unsettling him deeply.

'In return, he will write off the loan.' Cecil busied himself with making the handkerchief disappear again.

'Entirely?'

'Yes.'

Francis stared. 'No, my lord! Not possible! His proposal defies all reason! You must see that!'

'If Francis Quoynt the acclaimed English fire master goes to La Spada and devises his funeral fireworks, he says that he will write off the entire loan,' Cecil repeated with a touch of truculence.

'I tell you, it's impossible! You say that this loan is so great that it would bankrupt England to repay. But the cost of my hire is tiny! Insignificant! The King's Great Pearl alone – that one single star in that whole sky full of stars his majesty was wearing tonight – could buy me together with an army of sappers for a score of lifetimes. The prince wants something else!'

Cecil looked at the chest.

'The prince's offer stinks,' said Francis. 'It violates all reason, any way you look at it.'

Cecil folded his hands tightly in front of him. Francis had never before seen his patron look so unhappy.

Cecil never lost his composure. Cecil never lost his grip. Cecil in possible difficulty was more terrifying than Cecil in complete control. Francis was suddenly ambushed by memory.

He was five. His mother lay dying.

'Make her better!' Francis had begged his father in uncomprehending rage. 'Why won't you make her better?'

Boomer had turned away. Francis saw his father's tears and froze in terror. His mother was really going to die. His magnificent, awesome, all-powerful father could no longer put things right. His safe universe spun out of control. At the age of five, Francis had understood how vast and invincible was the darkness that waited to ambush him. He could never feel entirely safe again.

He shook off the memory. Why remember it now, here? He had never felt safe with Cecil.

'His funeral fireworks are clearly a ruse,' said Francis with growing conviction. 'The prince may simply want to lay hands on the English fire master – the former military fire master, not the present court pyrotechnician. To rack out information about what weapons the English could field in case of renewed war on the Continent. Or to kill me as a favour to the Spanish. I will be a hostage against your loan. You must see that.'

'Yes.'

'Even then, the best fire master in the world would not be worth so much,' said Francis. 'And I am not he. It's mad.'

'Mad both in principle and in truth,' agreed Cecil. 'My agent in La Spada writes that the prince has entered the last stages of the Great Pox. He's dying of the Neapolitan disease, and his mind is going.'

'Refuse his offer, my lord. Find some other way.'

'I can't.'

Francis again felt the five-year-old's chill at the helplessness in Cecil's voice. At the same time, he did not believe him. It was not possible that the most powerful man in England – and perhaps one of the most dangerous in all of Europe – did not dare refuse an absurd request by the ruler of some little principality no one had heard of, on the far fringes of the north Adriatic in that last tapering tail of the great Alps. The barbaric message of the ship was the work of a coarse and violent mind, no match for Cecil's deep understanding and quick, devious wits.

He eyed Cecil with a new suspicion. 'If I am to risk my life, my lord, do I know all the reasons?'

'To risk your life is your duty!' Cecil loosed a lightning flash of rage.

'So long as the risk is reasonable!'Francis shot back.

They hung suspended in the balanced struggle of wills that Cecil, at times and for private reasons, permitted with Francis.

'There is a little more to it than the loan,' said Cecil at last.

With difficulty, Francis suppressed a snort.

6

LA SPADA, MARCH 1608

That same evening, while Cecil in England explained how to find her, the *principessa* sat up late writing at a table in one corner of the *sala*. Her ladies – Germans, Florentines, and French alike, whom she employed in order to learn their languages – gambled at the game of *biribissi*, stitched, embroidered, tugged gently at drawn-thread work. They tried new pomades and traded the silver pins that held together the parts of their clothes. They flirted with their male companions and negotiated with their eyes. A young Spanish waiting woman, just added to the court, sat in the window niche with a single candle, pretending to read and not to mind being left out.

Sofia sealed a letter. Then she slipped a blank page from under the rest of her papers. She had torn it from the back of a poetry book belonging to the new Spaniard and hidden it with other scraps of paper and parchment that she acquired wherever she could without being noticed. The bottoms torn off old love letters, which her women had carelessly left lying on stools. Lists from the panterer, the backs of inventories, the sheets used to keep score in games, invoices from tradesmen, anything that could not be traced to her.

Pressing down hard on the goose quill pen, she wrote six words in a heavy, stuttering hand. The slight wobble of the strokes suited both the message and supposed agitation of the writer. She did not sign this paper.

With her little finger, she hooked a loose strand of hair out of her eyes, trying not to smear the ink on her hands onto her face. She waited for the ink to dry, careful not to glance about her as if anxious that someone might be watching her. One of the women was bound to be.

She was certain, for example, that Da Monte's daughter watched her, that creature who looked like a fish with her sloping forehead, large nose and weak chin. It was a pity she didn't resemble her handsome father as well as spy for him. And the two Florentines, whose spoken Italian was the model for everyone else, always watched her like a pair of cats eyeing a caged bird.

She tested the ink with a finger, then folded the paper and slipped it into her sleeve. 'Signorina Isabella,' she called to the new girl in the window. 'Will you sing to me? Your lovely sweet voice lifts my spirit.'

The girl blushed, leapt up and ran to fetch the ebony inlaid guitar that Sofia had given her when she first arrived in La Spada from Valladolid.

Prince Alessandro, Sofia's father, had not called for her yet tonight. Please let him sleep, she begged whoever listened. Let me sleep one whole night in my bed.

'Something from your Spanish song book so that I may learn the words,' she told Isabella.

She must wait for a moment alone, a thing more precious to her than all the gold chains and pearls hanging around her neck and twined into her hair.

Let the cats around the table look daggers at Isabella, if

they liked. In the three months the girl had been at court, Sofia had never heard her say an unkind thing about anyone, not even when overheard by the lions.

Her chance came at last, in the bustle of heading off for bed.

'I will take air in the gardens first.' She took only Isabella with her.

'I'm cold,' she said when they stepped into the *logetta* that opened onto the gardens. 'Spring is not here yet.'

'Shall I go fetch a cloak, your highness?' The girl was off almost before the *principessa* had replied.

In the darkness, Sofia hurried through the blacker shadows of a long terraced arcade, set with chairs and open to the gardens on one side, the *loggetta*, where they could walk under cover when it rained, as it often did in La Spada. At the far end was a snarling bronze lion mask set into the wall. Sofia slipped her piece of folded paper into the open jaws and stepped out through one of the arches into the black scrolls of the flowerbeds to wait for Isabella's return. Though it could not be read in this light, the plaque under the lion said: 'For the reporting of speaking ill against the ruler and the state.'

7

'La Spada lies north-east of Venice in the *Alpi Giulie*,' said Cecil. 'The Julian Alps, named for Julius Caesar, as the Romans named far too many places.'

He began to search among the documents in one of his chests. 'At a crossroads of imperial ambitions – Roman, Lombard, Venetian, and Hapsburg, who have only just ceded the region back to Venice. These mountains are all that keeps the Catholic German Hapsburgs and the Austrian Archduke out of western Europe.' He took a long paper roll from the chest. 'They also hold off the Ottoman Turks pressing upwards from the south. Let me show you.'

He unrolled a map on his writing table, placing silver-edged inkpots on two of the corners. Francis held down a third.

'Here is Venice and its *Terra Firma*, the Veneto,' said Cecil, his finger moving eastwards from Venice. '. . . Their solid ground, which provides that watery city with everything but glass and fish.' His finger traced across the top of the Adriatic to the Balkans. 'The Republic of Venice holds these lands but does not always control them. In truth, it's uncertain how many different peoples live there.'

He half-smiled. 'There's a story that the Venetian envoy to the counts of Gorizia once had to call for a translator before he had gone twelve miles from Venice, to ask directions from a farmer.'

Cecil pointed to the top corner of the northern bulge of the Veneto. 'And here is your destination, the Julians and Friuli. There's the Val Canale, the great valley in the Julians through which the barbarians rode from the east to sack Rome.'

Francis dug for half-remembered school-boy lessons.

'La Spada is scarcely in the Veneto at all,' said Cecil, 'but part of this uneasy Balkan region where allegiance and politics shift with each new invasion. The Val Canale . . .' he drew his finger through the mountains '. . . is now a rare land trade route into Russia, Hungary and Asia Minor.'

Trade, thought Francis. Now we come to it. Trade is at the centre, always.

'The water-logged Venetians don't know what to do with their mountains,' said Cecil. 'All hunters and bandits. They're still suffering from the surprise of ruling Friuli at all. Some Hapsburgs think it should still be theirs, as do the Slovenes and Turks.'

'And England?'

'Would merely like an ally in the Adriatic.'

'"Merely?"'

'It's time to ship you back to Sussex,' said Cecil with mock severity. 'You grow too sharp. English trade with the east is under threat. Though we're at last at peace with France and Spain, there's still an undeclared sea war in the Mediterranean and Adriatic, with increasing attacks on English ships.'

Francis had turned courtier enough not to retort that English privateers were the most feared of all the Mediterranean and Adriatic raiders.

'The West Indies may be all the rage amongst our merchant

venturers,' said Cecil, 'but it's our trade to the east, with the East Indies and the Levant, that underpins English finance.' A sharp glance probed for a sign that Francis understood. 'We must protect this trade if there's to be any chance of rebuilding our former prosperity.'

'I feel a courtier's collar tightening around my throat again.'

Cecil smiled thinly. 'You'll never persuade me that it doesn't fit. You're right. England needs even more than trade routes to the east. We also need safe harbours and re-provisioning ports. We need refuge from the Spanish and Barbary corsairs.'

Cecil glanced at the boy hidden behind the hanging and lowered his voice. 'In short, we need not just a nominal ally in the region, secret or otherwise, but a reliable friend in the north Adriatic amongst all those Catholics and Turks. In addition to the settlement of the loan, I must know where the prince of La Spada stands and which way his legitimized heir, Prince Ettore, leans – towards the Great Turk in Stambol who shares the English fear of the Catholic Hapsburgs, or towards our enemy, the Pope in Rome. But the prince also has both a legitimate daughter and a distant male cousin, the Duke Da Monte, who already plays a large part in ruling La Spada. Either of them may also aspire to the throne.'

Cecil looked reflectively at the map. 'Now that Spain has signed to peace with England, I most fear the double-headed eagle of the Hapsburgs. It could tear out England's heart. The Sack of Rome could be replayed in London. Hope won't stop it. Intelligence might. I need to know who would best be England's friend – the heir Prince Ettore, his sister, or the cousin Duke.'

'It's a daunting mission, my lord, half-mad and half beyond me.'

'I thought you'd jump at a chance to escape the tedium

of success. I've not only forgiven your ingratitude for my patronage, I offer you a new land to explore and new problems to solve. What more can you ask? You'll even feel the warm glow of duty done.'

Cecil looked up at Francis's height. Francis looked down at the tiny frame of the most powerful man in England.

'La Spada in Friuli,' said Cecil, sounding a little more like his usual serpent-tongued self. 'The Sword of Friuli, ruled by jumped-up brigands who call themselves princes because no one dares to disagree. And though they claim to have a court, I suspect your sword will serve you better there than the smoothest tongue. The place should suit you perfectly now that you've grown tired of London and Whitehall.'

He seems to forget that I will also be the hostage of a dying madman, thought Francis.

'Will you risk disappointing me?' The bottom of Cecil's long, odd face twitched in a chilly smile. He vanished for a few moments into his own thoughts.

'To tell the truth, I won't force you,' he said at last. 'Your best service comes with a willing heart.' He found his handkerchief again. 'But I won't plead, neither. Only to say that this embassy is more important to me and to England than you can possibly imagine.'

Your best service comes with a willing heart? When did the Secretary of State ever have a chance to make that observation? wondered Francis savagely.

He was in many minds at the same time. The prince's offer made no sense and therefore held unknown danger. Boomer and Kate continued to need Cecil's protection against the anti-Catholic fervour that followed the Gunpowder Treason two and a half years earlier. And England was in trouble. Cecil lived only for England, so Cecil was in trouble. A bankrupt England invited invasion. It lost its leverage in trade.

Unless Cecil was lying – which Francis had known to happen.

'What will become of the boy?' asked Francis after a moment. For the first time, he noticed the water jug and crusts of bread on the floor by the chest.

'You deal with him.' Cecil waved a small impatient hand. 'It's just as well that he won't speak. Just don't let him blab.'

'I won't harm him, my lord!' said Francis fiercely.

'I didn't mean for you to slit his throat! But in the past, you have shown a soft heart and a dangerous taste for rescue.'

Again their eyes met.

'I've ordered one of my secretaries to find a household to take him in, but so far no one rushes to oblige.' Cecil glanced again at the trembling bump behind the hanging. It was now shorter and fatter, as if the boy had sunk down onto his heels and hugged his knees. 'You can see the difficulty. I suppose I must increase the small endowment I'm offering to cover the costs of lodging him.'

'Greed doesn't guarantee kindness,' said Francis. 'Kindness is what the boy needs, and patience.' He stopped for fear that Cecil would think he was lecturing him.

'Am I unkind and impatient?' Cecil asked unexpectedly.

'Impatient for sure, but kinder than you pretend, my lord.'

Cecil cocked one brow but flushed slightly.

He's pleased, thought Francis with astonishment. Surely all those swarms of court flatterers must have numbed him to compliments – particularly one that's half insult.

'What will the boy do when he's alone again?' Francis asked.

'Climb back into the chest, most likely.'

'My lord, set your endowment aside to grow until his majority.' Francis had never seen the point in hesitating once he saw the right thing to do. 'I know where to send him.'

Cecil nodded absently and returned again to the window. He was still waiting for Francis's answer to his greater question.

By nature, Francis abhorred uncertainty. Every moment in his work, whether military or civilian, moved towards the absolute. A fuse would light, or it would not. The propelling charge of a rocket would fire, or not. A shell would explode, or not. He would continue to live, or not. For him, uncertainty was a black shell that sat inertly, unexploded, nursing death inside itself, waiting to surprise – maybe I'll kill you, maybe I won't.

He circled the room on his long legs, trying to shake his thoughts into order. Cecil ignored him as he passed, still standing face-to-face with his reflection in the dark window.

He was tormenting himself with a false sense of choice, Francis decided. Both reason and feeling told him that he had no real choice to make. At once, he felt his spirits lighten. The world rearranged itself more comfortably.

'This embassy, my lord . . . which part of it is the most urgent? Intelligence about a possible alliance or settling the loan?'

'If you feel that statesmanship is beyond you, why then, you'd best try for the loan. If the prince's second reply is as unreasonable as his first . . .'

. . . and I survive it, thought Francis.

'. . . then steal the bond. I feel certain that you could rise to a little theft.'

'I'll go, my lord. But you must take my heart as you find it.'

If Cecil felt relief, he did not show it. 'I will have someone watching your back.' Then to Francis's terrified astonishment, he added, 'I trust you, Quoynt.'

8

After leaving Cecil, Francis shouted from the water stairs for a public wherry to take him across the Thames to his house in Lambeth. He had bought it the year before from the survivor of two unwed sisters who could no longer manage the small estate. Cecil had offered lodgings in Whitehall, but Francis refused. Though his modest manor was only a short boat crossing away from both Whitehall and Westminster, he needed the protecting moat of the Thames between himself and the worst of court follies, to say nothing of himself and Cecil.

'I trust you, Quoynt.' He kept hearing those alarming last words.

Cecil had his balls in a vice. Of course Cecil could trust Francis! Francis owed him the continuing safety of his family, owed him worldly success, owed him the new life he had thought he craved. For Cecil, Francis was about to put his life into the hands of a murderous foreign madman who was dying of the Great Pox. How the devil could Cecil not trust him?

Even before the wherry pulled up to the water steps near the comfortable thatched manor house, Francis knew that he would never sleep. He stepped carefully over his man-servant snoring on a pallet in the antechamber and entered his own bedchamber. Unaided for the first time in many months, he changed his court silks for slim-fitting wool venetians, a coarse linen shirt without a collar, a padded wool jacket and an old leather jerkin. With relief, he swapped the pinching kidskin boots for an ancient pair made of heavy cowhide softened by wear. He stepped back over the sleeping manservant, again greeted the startled night watchman at his gate, and flung himself back out into the night.

With Lambeth Palace behind him, he marched beside the river towards the sea, along the track on top of the river wall. Ahead lay the miniature city of London Bridge spanning the Thames, now locked for the night to protect the owners of the fine houses on the northern shore from the suburb sinners and lowlife of the Southwark Bankside, where Francis was headed.

In the sweaty noisy crowds outside the inns that lined the riverfront, he felt again like his former self, the unemployed fire master just back from the Low countries, made redundant by the new peace with Spain. In The Bear near the foot of London Bridge, he bought a jug of ale and a pipe of the new Virginia tobacco. He nodded to several half-remembered faces, hailed a few old acquaintances and then leaned against the outside wall of the inn, gazing down St Olaf Street, shaking his head at the whores. But he could not settle. He left both ale and tobacco half-consumed, to be leapt upon by beggars, and began to walk again.

With every step, he grew more certain that Cecil had played him once again. 'Willing heart,' indeed! His long legs sliced the air like sword blades.

Head hunched into his shoulders, he prowled the familiar streets and alleys, growing more and more angry, with himself even more than at Cecil, for being such a soft fool. Cecil had been too clever to threaten. Francis had been flattered and seduced by apparent frankness, by that faint hint of respect and, even, comradeship.

You had no real choice, he reminded himself. As a soldier, he had often been sent without choice into places from which he might not return.

But why did Cecil pretend to ask? Why play on Francis's better nature, with that helplessness? Why flatter? Why hint at respect and comradeship? Why pretend that Francis did have a choice instead of giving him an honest order? Where were the respect and comradeship in that?

Back on Bankside, a pickpocket sauntered up out of the crowds, took a closer look at the size and evident evil humour of his intended prey and quickly dropped back into the shadows.

Walking north along the Thames, Francis passed the Little Rose, an inn with lodgings above, where Kate had once lived. He looked up at her window, now dimly lit. A shadow moved across it and disappeared again.

Leave it! he told himself. It's done.

He walked on angrily towards Paris Gardens, a country house turned brothel. From time to time in the last two years, he had tupped a woman there, who was clean and well-schooled enough to take the cold commercial edge off their coupling. He stopped and stood at bank edge staring down into the dark rubbish-filled river, now sluggish at high water and the turning of the tide. The white belly of a dead fish was turning into the current as slowly as a galleon.

He would not off-load his anger onto a woman, least of all one with so little real choice in having him.

He heard the thuds of a game of bowls being played by torch-light in the street behind him, and the shouted wagers. Sweet tendrils of tobacco smoke twisted towards him through the night air, cutting through the stink of middens, fish, alcohol and rotting waterweed. A woman leaned against his side.

'It would be a real pleasure to go with you, sir.' He felt the soft interesting pressure of her breast against his arm. 'I'll give a special low price to a man with those shoulders and legs.'

He shook his head but nevertheless felt a small hum of pleasure at her compliment, calculated though it might be. Even so, he checked the contents of his pocket.

This exchange then made him remember Cecil's unexpected flush at his own compliment. He felt a rush of unwanted compassion. Whilst he could at least pretend that the whore's words were sincere, Cecil would always know that any physical compliment was a lie.

Had he been tormented as a child? Francis wondered, anger ebbing. Because of his twisted back and odd little face? How old had Cecil been when he learned to fight back? Or had people always feared him because of his powerful father?

He looked back down at the water. The dead fish had been sucked into the quickening current.

How had Cecil felt when he first had to uncover to bed his wife? A powerful father couldn't help you there. Francis now remembered other glimpses of the little man's solitude, carrying alone so much of the responsibility for making England work.

A fist fight broke out on the nearby water stairs but ended quickly when one combatant was knocked into the river. Francis turned back to the indescribable mass floating on the water – tangled rushes, wood chips, bedraggled feathers, frayed rope, a linen garment turned green with slime, the end of a broken oar, a lump that might be a drowned water rat, paper, fruit peelings, lumps of solidified fat.

Cecil believed James to be the only choice among the many pretenders to the English throne, the only one who

41

could bring England the peace she needed in which to heal after years of war with Spain. For Cecil, the welfare of England came before all else, even his own. He expected others to feel the same. Cecil did whatever he had to do. The end, for him, justified the means, as Francis knew to his own cost. At times, Cecil had half-persuaded him to agree. To his credit, Cecil had never said that such a course would be without pain.

Pity for Cecil had nothing to do with his choice to go to La Spada, Francis decided. Pitying Cecil would be a capital offence. And you can't pity a man who would make you the hostage of a madman, even when you flatter yourself by imagining that he might like you as well.

To his astonishment, he found that he didn't care that Cecil was sending him off to possible death. As the Chief Minister had said, La Spada offered escape from both Whitehall and his melancholy. Once in La Spada, he'd have no time for such indulgence. He'd be too busy watching his back and trying to make sense of a mad commission.

For several strides, he reflected on the small value he placed on his life at the moment. Cecil could well have seen the dark truth that Francis did not much care if he lived or died.

Francis would rather go to La Spada, no matter what waited for him there, than stay at the English court and flatter fools with fireworks. His only other reasonable choice was to go back to war as a mercenary fire master.

His stride faltered. A door in his head threatened to burst open. He pressed back at it, trying to shut out the screaming horses running with their hoofs tangled in their own entrails, the charred lumps that his skills had made of living men, women and children. He pressed back against human screams, roaring flames and the earthquake rumble of collapsing walls.

He had purpose now, an illusion of clarity. He wedged the door shut with his new purpose.

He strode north again along Narrow Wall with the dark river on his right. He would collect the boy in the morning, then give some thought to those funeral fireworks, however unlikely. Be prepared, he thought wryly. The honour of English pyrotechnics may be at stake!

As he greeted the night watchman for a third time, his spirits were higher than they had been for at least a year. He felt a little drunk but exceedingly cheerful. Clearly, he was as mad as the dying prince of La Spada.

As he stripped off his shirt for sleep, he caught a sharp dark musky whiff from his armpits and understood precisely what he was feeling. It had been so long since he had been a soldier that he had not recognized this blend of cold fear, intense interest, anticipation, heightened senses and cool steadiness. This falling away of minor concerns, like a war horse before a charge whose blinkers close off all distractions but the way ahead. The feelings of the moments before going into battle.

Once again in his life, he was fortunate beyond his deserving. He felt alive again, reunited with his former self, rescued from a sleeping life in silks, yet spared the price of spreading destruction and death. Against all expectation, he slept well.

9

LA SPADA, 1608

'They are vile and obscene!' Prince Alessandro shuffled around the walls of his *scrittoio*, his intimate study where he had once entertained his closest male intimates. This was also the room where men from warring powers had met in secret, with only the prince as witness, pimp to their illicit temporary union. Here, German Hapsburg had talked to Turk about secret terms not written into their Treaty of Zsitva-Torok. These walls had overheard negotiations between English and Spaniard that, so far as the wider world was concerned, had never taken place. The figures painted on the walls had seen impossible handclasps and the signing of private trading contracts. They had watched bribes, threats, clandestine sales of weapons and all the other means by which the affairs of men progress.

Now the prince pointed at the mute witnesses on his walls. 'The Englishman must not see these abominations!' he said to his physician and to his confessor, Father Daniele. 'He must not be tempted by lusts of the flesh! He must fix his eyes only on God!'

'These abominations' had once been the prince's delight. He had paid a fortune to an acclaimed Florentine to have them painted. With his head dropped back against his chair, he had let his half-closed eyes wander over them while women were pleasuring him. He and drunken comrades had spilled their seed while they imagined themselves to be taking part in the painted scenes.

The frescos covered three walls of the *scrittoio*. They were titled '*In silvis*', '*In urbe*' and '*Rure*'. In the woods, in the city and in the countryside. In each of them, every living thing was copulating.

On one side wall, in the city, the whores and beggars, shop-keepers, street-sellers, porters, boatmen and their fares, stall holders, dogs, cats, doves, house flies, even horses abandoned by their lustful riders, were conjoined, copulating, swiving, sheathing the sword, treading, covering, mounting and beating the leather – on doorsteps and rooftops and in every corner, carriage, market stall and alley. Half-seen through painted windows, fine ladies bent over tables with their petticoats above their waists while fine gentlemen serviced them.

On the opposite wall, in the countryside, bare-buttocked shepherds lay on half-naked shepherdesses or pushed them with raised skirts against hedgerows. Behind them, cattle, sheep, swans, geese, goats, field mice, rabbits, chickens, even snails, all mated.

But the prince's favourite panel had been '*In silvis*' on the end wall. Here, in the forest, lay the most sensuous bare flesh, a party of twelve satyrs and naked nymphs writhing and twisting together on the leafy floor of a glade with intent, ecstatic faces. In the distance a stag could be seen mounting a hind. In the foreground butterflies and dragonflies mated on the wing. Rabbits coupled in one lower corner. At the bottom of the opposite corner were two copulating mice.

Over them all, sitting on a boulder with sinuous nonchalance, an ivy wreath on his head, presided the ancient god of abandon, Dionysius.

The prince stopped in front of the nymph who had once roused him the most swiftly. She was caught at the moment of her climax, eyes wide and intent, ecstatic but with a hint of fear.

'Whore! Why do you look at me?' The prince unsheathed his dagger and stabbed her painted left eye, gouging away the plaster. 'Shameless!' He dug out her right eye, then hacked ferociously at the wall until only the nymph's nose and chin remained. 'Cover them all!' he shouted. 'Hide their shame before the Englishman can see them.'

He turned on his manservant, Yuri. 'You heard what I said! They must be covered!'

'Highness!' The man ran from the room.

'They will be covered, your highness,' murmured his physician. 'Be patient for a few moments more.' He poured a tincture into a cloudy glass goblet and stirred in wine from an enamelled Moorish-style ewer. 'Drink something now to ease your pain.'

When the manservant returned with a large brush and slopping bucket of terracotta wash, the prince seized the brush. As furiously as he had hacked out the nymph's eyes, he now splashed the wash across bare buttocks and joined genitals. He painted out male hands clutching female breasts.

'Lascivious whore!' He splashed a great sweep of wash across a nymph's hand on a satyr's cock.

He worked feverishly until he began to stagger with exhaustion. 'Enough!' He threw the brush on the floor, ignoring the paint that splattered across his ankles, and stepped back to view his work.

Now the intent ecstatic faces seemed to sprout from damp

terra cotta clouds. From behind patches of paint already drying to a pale dusty pink, taut hands groped the air.

'I make room for thoughts of God.' The prince collapsed into his heavy, high-backed gilded chair. Yuri, short, bald-headed and nimble, leapt to lay a silk-lined wolf skin rug over his master's knees.

The prince stroked the thick grey fur for a moment. 'I killed him myself,' he said. 'A big male with a white snout. I can remember that day clearly. Every detail.'

Then he looked back at the ruined walls. 'Where is my daughter?' he demanded. 'Where is the *principessa*? Why does she leave me? Find her and bring her back to me! She must see how I make this place fit for the great work I shall undertake with the English fire master.'

The princess was on the battlements, throwing a knife at one of the heavy wooden doors. The knife itself was a beautiful thing, of a shining steel almost as bright as silver. Perfectly plain, perfectly balanced, it lay in her palm and along her middle three fingers like an offered crucifix. Each time it bounced off the door and clattered onto the paving stones she cursed under her breath. Then, it flew straight and stuck, but not far enough. The weight of the handle pulled it out of the wood. It rang on the stones.

Distant voices, as faint as gnats, called her name.

She threw again, missed. In the distance, she heard men's voices coming closer. She blanked them out and threw once more. This time the force of her suppressed fury drove the point so far into the ancient wood that the blade stuck and held. She levered the knife out and slipped it into its sheath she wore under her overskirt.

The voices were very close now, on the battlements.

'*Principessa!* Your father calls for you!' '*Principessa?*' 'Your highness . . .!'

She could imagine him now, snorting and gasping for breath as he roused from afternoon sleep. She knew he would at this very moment be shouting, 'Where's my little bowl of cream? My golden bird? Where is she? Find her! Bring her back!' Sometimes, she had only stepped into the antechamber or gone to relieve herself on a close stool. Sometimes, like now, she was hiding.

Today, she made his Uskok guards work. She did not answer their calls but stood silently against the outer wall, in the shelter of one of the towers. Hungrily, while she still could, she breathed in the fresh cold air and stretched her gaze over the valley. Clouds lay on the floor of the plateau below her like a lavender lake.

'Your highness?'

She could hear the fear begin to enter their voices. The search was taking too long. If her father grew too impatient, he became angry. When angry, he became dangerous. With resignation, she stepped out into view.

'Highness . . .'

'I know,' she said sharply. 'I'm coming.'

10

The prince raised his craggy, ruined head. 'Where did they run you to earth this time?' He pointed at the walls. 'See what I have done! I show God how I am changed.'

You had no choice but to change, she thought, but she smiled and nodded. The ragged hole of the nymph's blind face chilled her.

'Sit here by me again.'

Sofia pulled her stool close to him and leaned even closer to smoothe the wolf skin rug over his knees. She held her breath so she would not have to inhale the awful smell of his decay. 'You'll feel better now,' she said. She glanced at the moist empty tincture goblet.

'My elixir of life.' He stroked her cheek.

She smiled up at him, then let his large bony hand lie on her smooth wrist like an iron lock. He always touched some part of her, even when asleep.

'You're my best medicine,' he said. 'Never leave me!' Then he frowned at her hand lying trapped by his own.

Quickly, she closed her fingers to hide her nails. Though of a delicate pink and as shiny as agates, they were bitten to the quick. She could not help herself. The nails found themselves being torn by her teeth without her volition.

'Let me help you to some hot spiced wine,' she said to distract him from this imperfection in her being. Imperfections in her made him uneasy, and therefore angry. She warmed the wine with a poker. Then she held the jewelled cup to his cracked lips and watched the golden liquid made from their local grapes dribble down his chin. Then she sat again, while he groaned and sank at last into a doze.

She knew better than to try a second escape so soon. Sometimes he pretended to sleep just so that he could catch her trying to slip away. Fortunately, he demanded only her presence, not her conversation. This left her free to think.

She thought often about the future, twisting it this way and that, deciding whether she liked what she saw. Sometimes, she brooded on her half-brother Ettore. When he came to the throne – which must be soon – he would almost certainly have her killed, as easily as he had killed Baldassare. Or marry her off to one of his confederate counts who would strangle her soon after the wedding night. Or he would bury her in a distant convent with an endowment rich enough to ensure that she never breathed free air again. Sometimes, she took refuge from darker thoughts and whispered to herself the poetry or orations she had learned from her books. Whenever she could, she slipped out a book from under her skirts and read.

Recently, she had spent a great deal of time thinking about the new cipher that her father, with her encouragement, had written into the life of La Spada. Francis Quoynt. Fire master. English, like that loutish steward at her father's hunting lodge in the mountains above La Spada. She knew that this Francis Quoynt could not be the same man who had massacred so many at Udine. This man was the grandson. But he bore the same name, and with it, in her imagination, he wore the face of that earlier ruthless foreign mercenary about whom she had both heard and read. That man had promised safety and delivered death. She was counting on his grandson to do the same.

This afternoon however, as she often did, she passed the long hours sitting at her father's side by imagining all the different ways he might die . . . she saw her silver crucifix knife flying into his throat . . . magically, by itself. As if an angel had thrown it. When he died, however it might be, she knew beyond all doubt that he would burn for ever in hell.

In defiance of his daughter's secret musing, Prince Alessandro Hugo Uskoki di Pirati, ruler of La Spada, was determined to escape hell. He had studied the different requirements for salvation and damnation. He therefore knew that when he died he would most certainly be cast down into the eternal flames. He concluded that he had two choices. He could escape death, which the realities of his failing body made increasingly unlikely. Or he could negotiate with God.

For all of his life, the exercise of his will had given Prince Alessandro everything he wanted. He had not learned to accept the possibility of defeat. How could he?

Along with a throne, birth had given him commanding height, a dark-eyed handsome predator's face, natural ruthlessness, quick wits, and the certainty that he was always right. Nature had also given him the wit to recognize those times when it was advantageous to change his position and be right in a different way. On the rare occasions when the force of his will alone was not enough, he was willing to negotiate in order to get his way. On this matter of hell, he was willing. His wits had grown too curdled to argue against his intention. Nor did he any longer see irony in the fact that his power had also been his destruction.

Like most powerful men, he had had strong sexual appetites, which he satisfied without restraint. Reason, cowering silent before appetite, had not warned him of infection.

He treated the inevitable bastards well, dangled hope of advancement in front of their noses, and discouraged them from uniting against him, on the premise that his own blood were likely to prove more loyal than any get of strangers. He had killed the two of his whelps who had proved him wrong.

His only surviving legitimate child was, alas, a female, Sofia (whose similarity to himself he did not recognize). As grandson of the brigand who had made himself the first prince of La Spada, Prince Allessandro cared intensely about preserving the fragile, royal Pirati line. Therefore he had legitimized his oldest surviving bastard son, Ettore, and made him heir to the throne of the small mountain principality of La Spada.

As the great-granddaughter of a brigand, Sofia understood her own blood. She had known better than to protest but had privately set about getting her own way.

The prince now peered at his daughter through crafty half-closed eyes.

Still there . . . his lovely girl . . . letting him feed on her youth and strength.

He stroked her astonishingly smooth skin, like an angel's wing. He reached up to grasp a lock of her bright deep gold hair, then gripped on it as if it were a golden rope that might pull him back to health and former power.

She sat frozen, a mouse still alive in the jaws of a cat.

Then bitterness rose into his throat. How dare she sit there, so useful and yet useless at the same time? Female. The throne could, in certain circumstances, pass to a woman, that was not the difficulty.

But no woman . . . He tried to remember his reasoning, which had grown foggier in the last weeks . . . Not even you, my sweetest little fish . . . no woman can take my place . . . He clutched her hair as if it could haul him back into his lost memory.

No woman . . . he caught the thread now . . . no woman, however wily, not even his own blood, could successfully oversee La Spada's most important commodity. In his experience, it depended on man-to-man exchanges and oblique masculine understandings. It needed the male traits of a tight mouth, blind eye and the ability to hold your drink.

He let go of her hair and leaned back to study her.

Women talked. Women noticed things and had to blab what they had seen.

He frowned.

Women lacked the grasp for handling his realm's chief commodity, far more important than smoke hams or wine. Just as important as the iron mined and smelted for guns and cannons. As important even as the silver. It was the brokering of deals, both commercial and political. Perched here at the collision point of several warring empires, the prince offered the world a diplomatic free port.

If an envoy (or merchant) urgently needed to speak to his opposite number in a state with which his own state was at war, Prince Allessandro di Pirati always knew someone who could bring them together. At the highest levels, he had done this himself. The two enemies would meet secretly in La Spada for the true dealings that resolve most wars, political or commercial.

'I tell all foreigners they can bring in whatever politics they wish,' he said suddenly to his daughter. 'So long as they export them onwards to somewhere else. "Never try to sell your cause on the local market," I tell them.'

She smiled and nodded.

The flow of memory felt good. His back straightened. He gripped the arms of his chair as he had once done when granting audience to petitioners. Muscovites. Chinamen. Musslemen. French and Germans. English. Austrians, of course. Even the arrogant Portuguese.

Sometimes his warning was not enough. He had suspended more than one pro-Hapsburg German rabble-rouser, two English spies and several Turks in a small iron cage from the castle walls, with a dizzy view into the valley below until thirst and the ravens finished them off. In the clear sight of the population of . . .

He swallowed. In the clear sight of the population of . . .

He could not remember the name of his own realm.

. . . that perfect place from which to meddle in international politics . . . standing at the most important crossroad on the Continent. He could see it clearly on a map, but not its name. With Spain, France and Italy to the west, the Holy Roman Empire and Russia to the north, and the Balkans, the Ottoman Empire and rest of the Levant to the east and south. All of those names of places slid smoothly into his memory, so why not . . .?

'Water!' he croaked.

Sofia held his cup to his mouth.

The prince tried again, fighting terror. It – that place whose name he could not remember – lay in the armpit of Austria . . . which the Romans had called Noricum. If he could remember that ancient name, why not . . .?

He squeezed his mind, like a sponge in a fist. The name he wanted would not drip out.

. . . that place, where I rule, he thought wildly. At the farthest north-eastern edge of Italy. His principality. It controlled the Val Canale (no problem remembering that!) one of the only two open routes through the vast curve of mountains that split Europe in half, north from south.

He could see the mountains in his head, those great sharp teeth of the civilized world biting their way eastward from the French Alps to the Swiss Alps. Then curving down through the Dolomites, the Carnian Alps and the Julian Alps, before following the Dalmatian coast of the Adriatic, all the way down into Greece.

Greece.

He didn't want Greece! He wanted that place, which the steep, splintered limestone mountains made so easy to defend even though navigable rivers flowed to within two days' ride of the capital.

He did not even try for the name that time. Like a crafty hunter, he circled around it to attack from a new direction. Like the barbarians attacking Rome through the Val Canale . . . through the Val Canale from the plains of central Europe to sack Rome. They had ridden past the foot of the very mountains on which stood the Castello of . . . He clutched the arms of his chair to hold himself upright against an attack of giddiness.

'If I had been on the throne then, of . . .' He glared at his daughter. ' . . . the throne of . . .Where am I?'

Take care, she thought.

'In your *scrittoio*, sir,' she offered.

'No! Where is that accursed *scrittoio*?'

She did not meet his eye. 'I believe it is in Castello La Spada, sir.' She looked to see if she had yet guessed the answer to his riddle. 'In the *Alpi Giulie*.'

'La Spada!' he said triumphantly. 'If I had been on the throne of La Spada the barbarians would have been stopped at La Spada!'

He had often made that boast at state dinners, just to remind foreign visitors how things stood. He had now forgotten the foreign envoy he had expelled for murmuring

55

that his highness would more likely have joined the looters in Rome.

'La Spada,' he repeated, lest the name escape again. Nail it down. Bang. La Spada . . . bang!

'Easy to defend, hard to rule,' he said to Sofia. 'Tell that to your brother. He's most eager to get on with ruling.'

She lowered her eyes to hide any spark of triumph. Her secret work was having effect.

'Do you know why it's so hard to rule?'

Here was opportunity for herself, if only she could guess the answer the prince wanted. She tried to remember what he had told her in his ramblings and conversations over-heard when her father and Da Monte, his *Camerlano*, had believed she was thinking only of her needlework.

Outside the fortified administrative capital of La Spada itself, and a small spa town to the north offering hot springs, she knew that their realm, though beautiful and rich in resources, was also wild and inhospitable. Farmers speaking many different tongues worked isolated pockets in the valleys and uplands of steep jagged mountains of splintered limestone. Bandits of all nationalities and religions found easy lairs.

Recently, she had overheard agents reporting to Da Monte that cross-border raids in both directions, for livestock and slaves, had recently grown even bolder now that the prince could no longer lead punitive counter-attacks. The Hapsburgs, having temporarily defeated the Ottomans, were eyeing La Spada along with the rest of Friuli as a possible route into western Europe. The principality's mixed population might swing its allegiance in any one of many different directions.

'There are many possible answers to your question,' she said.

'You grasp it at once,' he said.

That stopped her for a moment. Then she saw what he meant.

'La Spada is hard to rule because we are like a great chest of mixed jewels.' She watched him. He nodded encouragement.

'Immensely valuable but challenging to keep in order.'

'Clever dove!' He seized her hand again. 'Now name me some of these jewels.'

This was more difficult.

'Tarviso?' she hazarded.

He frowned.

Not towns, then. What other resources? Buildings? The prince's own collection of paintings and sculpture which challenged the opulence of the Pope himself?

But none of those made governing difficult. What had he been speaking of just before he forgot the name of La Spada? The foreigners . . .

'Germans and Austrians,' she said tentatively. 'Both Catholic and Reformed.'

'*Gut. Bene.* Name me the rest.'

Confident that she had chanced on the right thread, she went on quickly. 'Venetians, Italians, Slavs, Magyars, the local Ladins . . .'

The prince was still nodding.

'Jews and Levantines,' she said. 'Musselmen from our neighbour Bosnia or from further south.'

'And the most precious jewels of all?'

She stared at the challenge in his eyes. Then she understood. The jewels that kept the rest in order.

The prince, one-quarter German, was descended on his mother's side from the Uskoks, from whom he took his name. They were a fiercely Christian tribe who had been driven northward out of their lands by the Ottomans in Turkey until they dug their heels in among the maze of little islands off the Dalmatic coast south of Trieste. They were angry, ruthless and trusted no one but others of their clan. The prince protected himself with a small army whom he trusted as kin.

'Uskoks,' she said.

He pressed her hand to his lips. With difficulty, she let him and did not yank it away.

'And now, clever girl, why is this treasure chest always at risk?'

If she were speaking to the remnants of his reason, there might be a drift to follow. 'Its very richness invites trouble,' she said, watching him again nod encouragement. 'Thieves and bandits of course . . .'

The wrecked face waited.

'Counterfeits . . .' she hazarded.

He smiled.

'And forgeries,' she said. 'Fraudulent gems can so easily be introduced and overlooked.'

Its geographical position as a crossroad gave La Spada a mixed population into which spies, dealers, intelligencers and agents of all sorts could slip without attracting notice.

'I wish to God that you had been born a boy,' he said. 'You have quick wits but such delicate little hands. Whoever rules . . .' He hesitated.

'La Spada,' she said quickly.

'I know the name of my own realm!' he shouted. 'I don't need your insults! I need a pair of strong hands, not these feeble paws!' He flung her hand away and raised his own. She slipped from her stool before he could strike her.

'Arrest her!' shouted the prince. 'She has insulted the prince! To insult the prince is treason! She betrays me with her weakness!'

His manservant wavered, uncertain what to do. Sofia pretended that she meant only to go fetch the scented salve she rubbed into her father's feet each day.

'Do it!' bellowed the prince.

The man ran from the bedchamber and returned with the captain of the Uskok guards.

'Arrest her!'

Sofia left him. In the antechamber of the *scrittoio*, she stopped and gestured for silence. 'He'll soon forget,' she whispered.

The captain nodded, sheathed his sword, bowed and returned to his post.

With thoughtful eyes, she watched him go. If she could enlist all the Uskoks on her side, she might stand a chance against her half-brother Ettore. But while they stopped short of injuring his daughter, they remained loyal to their prince.

Through the closed door, she heard her father now snoring. She listened a little longer then slipped through a door in the panelling into a narrow staircase that led to her own apartments. Again, she had survived his furious whims.

In the height of the prince's prime, only four years earlier, reason had begun to desert him. At first, it stole away, like an army melting away a few men at a time, taking with it names, the memory of his dead mother's face, the breed of his favourite hound. He would find himself staring at a hard, sweet russet globe in his hand, and at the white scar carved by his teeth, straining to remember what the thing was called. The most terrible months were those when he could still think clearly enough to understand how much worse it was going to get, and how he would finally die.

At the very beginning had come the single chancre. Weeks later, the fever and rash arrived in spite of dosings with mercury salts, decoctions of *lignum vitae*, and tobacco smoke baths. Then came the bone ache, the loss of appetite, the swellings. His thick dark hair thinned. His head throbbed. Irregular lumps heaved up under his skin and broke through as weeping ulcers, small fiery volcanos leaking away his life force. His strong right sword arm weakened. After that came a long deceptive truce. But it did not last.

As his thoughts began to desert in legions, frustrated rage took their place, along with terror that stabbed his chest like a sword. In lucid moments, the prince knew that he would soon die from the Neapolitan disease, or Great Pox. There was no escape. The only chance left to him lay in negotiation. The last might just be possible, as his daughter, that clever little bird, his bowl of cream had pointed out. He would be able to negotiate his salvation, just as soon as he had the help of the English fire master.

11

BRIGHTHELMSTONE, SUSSEX

As always, Francis felt his spirits lift when he arrived at the crest of the southern downs and saw the sea opening out before him. The sight was different every time. Now, late on their second day on the road from London, a hot red line sliced the water from the western sky. The setting sun, half-gone, looked as dense and fleshy as a woman's over-heated cheek. Faint mist blurred the outlines of returning fishing hoggies headed for Brighthelmstone or Hove. Below him, gulls circled over their nesting places, wings flashing pink as they caught the light.

On the other hand, he was not entirely looking forward to arriving at Powder Mote.

He looked over his shoulder. The chest rode with its lid propped half-open, as softly as Francis could manage on the small horse cart cushioned by a thick pile of sheep skins, just as he would transport a barrel of gunpowder.

'I wish you were up here at my side,' he called. 'You should take a look at the sea.' Then he remembered that, most likely, it was horrors at sea that had robbed the boy of words. 'You'll have to get used to it. There's no escape from the water down here. That's why we Quoynts like it. There's more than enough of the stuff to put out any fire we might start . . .' He caught himself again.

Clumsy clot! Now he'll think he's being taken among looters and fire-raisers! He remembered a child he had found hiding in a cupboard after he had breached a city wall in northern Spain, crushed.

That's why I turned civilian fire master, Francis reminded himself. Silk doublets, itchy lace and mindless civility had been the price of not making any more memories like that one.

'Have a quick sniff of the breeze.' He turned, threw open the lid and got down from the cart. He had quickly learned that the boy was far more terrified of him than of Cecil. 'I won't hurt you,' he called. 'Sit up and have a look.'

After a long moment when nothing happened, he returned and closed the lid again. The boy seemed not to have moved. However, he had eaten the bread Francis put in with him that morning.

'I feel a fool talking to a chest,' said Francis as they moved off again, with his chestnut gelding on a lead rein. 'But not as much of one as I'll feel when we get to Powder Mote.'

He paused again at the top of the chalky track that curved down to the house where he had been born, where his mother had died and where, until almost two years ago, Francis had lived whenever he was in England, with his father, Boomer Quoynt. Looking down from this height across the gorse and rough grazing, he could clearly see the outline of the ruined church that had belonged to the priory before King Henry dissolved the religious house and gave it to Francis's grandfather.

How tidy and prosperous it all looked now. The smothering ivy had been cleared from the chimneys and missing tiles had been replaced. The water of the moat glittered, weed-free. A new quincunx of young trees had been planted at the far end of the old orchard. Barn roofs now sat straight in stead of sloping like a drunkard's hat. The western windows of the house wing, built on to the old priory, winked back at the setting sun. A new earthwork berm protected the mixing house, where he and his father performed the final dangerous marriage of the salpetre, charcoal and sulphur to make gunpowder. Two of the storage sheds near the far side of the moat looked altogether new.

Francis sighed. This new order owed much to Cecil's patronage. And even more to the arrival of Kate.

He flicked the reins harder than he intended. The carthorse jumped forward indignantly.

'It's too big for a chicken and too small for a bear.' Boomer Quoynt jerked his firm, clean-shaved chin at the chest. He had spied the cart and come to meet his son at the outer end of the moat bridge. 'You should have warned us you were coming, France . . . fatted calf, and so on. You've cheated Kate of making even a special pie.'

Cheerily false, to Francis's ear. Kate was not a woman for making pies so far as he could remember.

'Were you down at the stamp mill?'

'We're replacing the main beam.'

Conversation between them was still awkward. Francis felt it skittering from one thing to another as if afraid to alight for too long. Nevertheless, he swung down from the cart and embraced his father, a figure of awe for most of his life and from time to time a good friend. Now, however . . .

Gratefully, faces hidden from each other, they let the warm simplicity of strong familiar arms speak instead.

'It's good to see you, unexpected or not.' Boomer stepped

back and eyed his son. 'By God, you're clean! Is that what London does to a man? All that hot water and bathing . . .'

From a distance it would have been hard to tell them apart, both lean, and broad-shouldered, of roughly the same height, though Francis might have been a finger's width taller. Only a very slight thickening of Boomer's torso and the colour of their hair identified them. Where Francis had a bright pale golden thatch like warm moonlight, Boomer's hair was silver, as it had been ever since he was nineteen.

'And what have you brought us that needs sheepskins layered eight deep?'

'Wait.' Francis led horses and cart across the moat bridge, under the gatehouse arch and into the forecourt of the house.

The front door stood open. A tall, dark-haired young woman in breeches suddenly filled it.

'Francis!'

He thought for a moment that Kate would drop the infant she held in the crook of one arm while clutching a bundle of linens to her side with the other. Then she released the linens, held on to the baby and ran out into the courtyard.

'Hello, Kate,' Francis said carefully. He leaned and kissed her in a brotherly way. 'You're still blooming, I see. Powder Moat hasn't crushed you yet.'

Boomer looked on, smiling broadly but with eyes as keen as flints.

'Greetings, oh Wailer.' Uncomfortably, Francis allowed himself to be given the newest male Quoynt, now six months old, last seen at the christening.

'Doesn't wail at all,' said Boomer with satisfaction. 'A calm, steady sort . . .'

'. . . like me,' hung in the air unspoken. Even Boomer would not push his son that far on such delicate ground.

This could have been my son instead of my half-brother. Francis shifted the infant to the crook of his other elbow. A quick glance showed the same thought passing through Kate's eyes.

For Francis, nothing was ever gained by circling around a difficult matter. A shell either exploded or it didn't. And then you knew. 'At least he'll have the same looks either way,' he said, with another glance, but at his father this time.

'But a different temper,' Kate retorted.

Why, wondered Francis, does no one prepare a man for the way he'll feel when his mistress marries his father?

12

Before her marriage to Boomer a year and a half ago, Kate had looked both her husband-to-be and her former lover in the eyes and said firmly that she had no intention of becoming the serpent in Eden. If either of them – looking at Francis – was unable to accept her presence at Powder Mote, she would leave.

'No!' both men had cried in one voice. Then they had looked at each other and laughed ruefully.

'That's settled then,' said Kate, unable to hide her relief. 'From now on it's just a matter of working out how to live with the truth.' She gave Francis a wicked look. 'Is that definite enough for even your taste?' Then she had returned to whatever task filled her hands at the time.

He had no choice then but to behave well.

Now, supper in the great hall, once the canons' refectory, was good-humoured. Francis leaned back in his familiar high-backed chair-of-grace, wrists hanging loosely over the ends of the arms, breathing in the honey smell of beeswax polish, watching Boomer and Kate, the two people he most loved in life. He turned his eyes to Richard Seaborn, his new-found nephew, the son of Boomer's dead bye-blow, whom he was learning to love.

Then he looked at the basket of the tiny scrap that he must come to love but who filled him, just now, with an excruciating jumble of feelings – the natural affection stirred by any small creature with large blue eyes, a cap of duck down fuzz and whole-hearted, gummy smile that convulsed his tiny body with good-will. Francis felt a fitting pride in the arrival of another male Quoynt to continue the line and a guarded pleasure in the open delight of Boomer and Kate. But the baby also made him feel suddenly replaced. No longer the youngest son. Shoved out.

I'm almost thirty, he thought with bitter self-mockery. Time to grow up. He was old enough to be the child's father, after all.

He stiffened slightly in his chair. When had he last made love with Kate? As he tried to remember, his normal clarity of thought deserted him. Then he looked up and caught his father's eye.

The serpent doesn't always bend to our will, he told Kate silently. He shouldn't have come to Powder Mote after all. Should have devised some other way to get information and materials, and another way to deliver the boy.

Kate, who had changed into skirt and petticoats for the occasion, shooed a wandering hen out of the hall and pressed on Francis another slice of roast pork with herb-stuffed prunes that were the last of the previous year's plums. Then she went to adjust the wrappings of Petty France, as she and Boomer had taken to calling the child.

The brat takes even my nickname, muttered an ignoble, internal voice (surely not his own).

Kate had set the baby's basket beside the boy's chest, lid open against the wall between kitchen door and table. Each of them glanced at it from time to time but the boy stayed put.

'Of course you should have brought him,' Boomer had said when Francis first explained. 'We'll soon have him out of there.'

'But gently,' said Kate. 'Leave the poor child to me. You're both too soldierly and fierce. Put him there, where he'll smell the food . . . do take care!'

'Do you imagine that you're not fierce?' Boomer had asked affectionately.

Now she picked up Petty France from his basket and held him over the open chest. 'Look there, my darling – a new friend for you. When he wakes up, he might play with you.' She replaced the baby in his basket and made an unhappy face at the three men at the table, wrapping her arms around her head in imitation of the curled boy.

'When we go to bed, I'll leave your supper on the table,' she said to the chest. 'Roast meats, sardines and some watered wine . . . and an apple tart.'

'Best leave a chamber pot too,' said Boomer, loudly. 'That chest stinks like a jakes . . . Down, girl!' he called to the hound that had been sniffing curiously at the chest and now stood with forepaws on the rim, looking in. 'She's a friendly soul,' he called to the boy. 'Wants you to play. But I'll lock her out of the hall tonight all the same, if you prefer.'

No reply came from the chest.

Francis sat listening to the echo of Kate's voice calling the baby 'my darling'.

'I feel a fool talking to a chest,' said Boomer. 'Do come out! No soldiers here, my boy. Not any longer, no matter what she says. We've all given it up.' Kate glared.

'I have another reason for coming,' said Francis. He leaned on the table, eyes on the walnut he was cracking. 'I'm off to the Veneto.'

He took shameful pleasure in the sudden fear in Kate's face.

'I'd like to come with you,' said Richard Seaborn in one of his sudden, surprisingly authoritative darts out of silence.

'To study?' Boomer leaned forward with interest.

Francis shook his head. 'To devise fireworks for a royal funeral.'

'An Italian has asked an Englishman to devise fireworks?' demanded Boomer in scornful disbelief.

Francis shrugged. They were mirroring his talk with Cecil, except that he had changed roles. 'So it seems.'

'The Little Toad is sending you!' Boomer exclaimed. 'Of course! What took him so long?'

'He's been good to us!' Francis was surprised by his need to defend Cecil.

'Because it serves his deeper purpose. Don't ever make the mistake of believing the man to be generous.'

But your own continuing safety rides on his generosity, Francis wanted to protest. And Kate's! 'Perhaps he needs someone he can trust.'

'You?' Boomer snorted gently. 'He trusts you because he can read you, France. Not because he likes you.'

Francis drew a deep breath. There was no way he would admit to his father that he had, for one moment during that evening at Whitchall, as they looked past their reflections at the river, imagined that Cecil was lonely and might want a friend. He could make a fool of himself well enough without his father to lay it out for him.

Silently, he cracked another walnut between his fingers and picked out the crumpled meat.

'How long will you be gone?' asked Kate quietly.

He considered a reassuring lie then told the truth. 'I don't know.'

Boomer pushed himself back from the table. 'Come take a pipe with me.'

They spent longer than needed in filling and tamping their

white clay pipes, then lighting them with coals from the fireplace. Kate watched them fuss, picked up the baby and left the hall.

Though the early spring night was still chilly, they settled on the familiar bench outside the great hall, with their backs against the old honey-coloured stone, gazing out into the dark void of the sea far below them. From this narrow, south-facing terrace that ran the length of the house, the lights of the fishing village of Brighthelmstone were hidden by the fall of the down.

Glancing out of an upstairs window, Kate saw only two shadowy shapes and the gentle pulsing glow of their pale clay pipes.

They smoked for a time in silence.

'She swears that the boy is mine,' said Boomer suddenly out of the dusk. 'Kate doesn't lie, any more than you do, France. We must both believe her. Settle our hearts. We owe it to her. Too cruel to her otherwise, and she doesn't deserve that.'

Francis swallowed against a rush of unexpected feeling. 'I agree. I missed my chance. It's as simple as that.'

Boomer tapped his pipe against the edge of the bench to shake out the dottle. 'Not so. She saw me, most accurately, as the stuff of husbands. And she saw that you're still in flight. At your age, I already had a wife and two children.'

'Whom you left behind when you went to war.'

'Often. And I suffered for it.' Boomer began to refill his pipe.

Francis fought off irritation at what might have been a rebuke. His father was right. He had wanted Kate but he did not want to settle. After the wedding of Kate and Boomer, there had been two possible matches for him in London, both women lovely, both rich, both a step up in the world for a humble fire master. One of them was still eager to lower herself to the match. La Spada would solve that problem at least.

'In time,' said Boomer. 'In time. In the meantime, you're leaving us again. The truth now, France. Are you coming back? Do you expect to return at all?'

'I don't know,' Francis said again.

'Whose choice will it be?'

'Not mine.'

'I had hoped not. But that's terrifying in another way. Can't you refuse to go?'

After a long silence, Francis answered, 'Why should I?'

'I thought you'd made a success of your new life in London.' Boomer's pipe flared briefly as he lit it again from the little bowl of glowing coals he had brought out with him. 'Your reputation reaches us even here in darkest Sussex. Even this far from the seat of power.'

'I'm merely a civilian pyrotechnician. It's all empty show.'

'But using the Quoynt skills, nevertheless. Better than letting them moulder in peacetime.'

'Skills or not, I loathe such success,' Francis heard himself say, with the grateful release of lancing a boil. 'I detest those pompous, smooth-tongued dandiprats who presume to tell me, a Quoynt, how to harness fire. Merely to make their wives and mistresses squeak with feigned terror and clutch at their protecting arms. You have a wife who can fire a musket. You can't imagine . . .' He veered away from treacherous ground. 'And now you've got another son who will surely make a better fist of the family trade than I've done.'

'We don't want to lose you,' said Boomer levelly.

'Nor do I want to lose any of you . . . not even my new half-brother, once I grow accustomed to him. But there's no purpose for me here any longer.' Francis raised a hand against his father's huff of protest. 'I know I've played my part in

71

saving the place. But it's for you and Kate now, and Richard. And the Squib.'

'Have we driven you away?'

Francis evaded the answer, noting his new-learned courtly slipperiness. 'There's no more risk in La Spada than when I was a mercenary at war in the Low Countries.'

'That risk was never acceptable!'

'But surely, it's more acceptable now that you have another Francis Quoynt to carry on our name and trade.' He felt his father go rigid.

Boomer puffed once more, then snapped his pipe and threw it down onto the stone terrace. Francis heard the soft clay grating under his father's boot.

'If it wouldn't upset Kate so much,' Boomer said softly, 'I'd clout you so hard for those words that you'd fly to La Spada without wings.'

Francis sank back against the still-warm stones of the house wall, astonished at the flood of gratified joy caused by his father's rage.

'So,' Boomer went on, '. . . you might as well ask whatever it is you came for.'

Francis found himself grinning in the thickening darkness. 'Have you been to Friuli?'

'Is that where the Little Toad wants to send you?' Boomer's voice rose. 'Why not just tie you in a sack and dump you in the Venetian lagoon with the other condemned men . . . forgive me, France . . . not a time for . . .' Boomer's voice trailed off. 'Friuli, eh?'

'The principality of La Spada, in the Julians, northwest of Trieste. You know it?'

'Too many mountains,' said Boomer. 'Too many places for bandits to take refuge. Too many different peoples bumping together – Germans, Turks, Ladinos, Bosnians, Slovenes, a few Venetians, all speaking their own tongues.' His hands moved as if searching for his pipe. Then he remembered that he had crushed it.

'Did you serve there, then?'

Boomer leaned forward restlessly and propped his elbows on his knees. 'Hellfire and damnation . . . and throw in all the saints besides! Why Friuli?'

'I feel I'm missing your drift.'

'The English have history there as mercenaries,' said Boomer. 'As they do in all of northern Italy. And the local memories are as long as their swords.'

'Our family runs this risk wherever we go on the Continent.'

'How far will you be from Udine?'

'North,' said Francis. 'If Cecil's man there is right. Just south of the Val Canale. Why Udine?'

'The English were blamed for a massacre there. Your grandfather was their fire master. It's in the *Liber.*'

Francis decided not to tell his father that the prince of La Spada has asked for him by name. 'Grandfather was a long time ago,' he said.

'Their blood feuds can persist through six generations. Can you truly not refuse this mission?'

Francis remembered the crack of desperation that he had imagined in Cecil's voice. 'Not with any honour.' He considered his next words carefully. 'Father, for many reasons, I don't wish to refuse. I want to go.'

'That's it, then. What can I tell you to help keep you safe . . . so far as possible in that bandit-ridden wilderness.'

They spent the next three hours and all of the next day discussing information and formulae from the *Liber Ignium*. This was the record, kept for six generations by the Quoynts of their secret recipes for gunpowder and the machines of war that used it. Francis scribbled notes furiously but wanted

73

many more than he had time to make. Meanwhile, Richard Seaborn assembled and packed the items on their growing list.

'I'd be happier if you took Richard,' said Boomer. He had moved on to writing letters of introduction to some of the many English who still held high positions in Tuscany and the Veneto.

'You'd put both of us at risk?'

'Richard has languages, and experience of the wolf-packs that roam European courts.'

'The English court is hardly a pen of sheep,' said Francis tartly. 'I won't risk another of your male spawn.'

Boomer thought that over without comment. 'France,' he said at last, without lifting his head from his letter to an English lord in Trieste with whom he had once served. 'Let's not spar in your last hours here. That was for when we had all the time in the world.'

Suddenly, Francis did not want to leave after all. 'Perhaps I'll find myself another Richard in Friuli,' he said lightly. He did not say whether he meant another apprentice or another piece of the family from the wrong side of the blanket.

'Nothing to do with me this time, if you do,' said Boomer. 'Though there's nothing wrong with a good Quoynt bastard. But whoever the mother is, just beware of her father and brothers.' He sprinkled sand on the letter, then shook the sand onto the floor. 'Come with me now to my bedchamber. I have one or two trinkets I'd like you to take.'

13

Boomer gave Francis a stoneware bottle. 'Don't let it break, and don't mistake it for ale. It holds a liquid with the appetite and bite of a serpent.'

Francis took it gingerly, with raised brows.

'A vitriol bought from a Musselman apothecary in London, to make trials of its appetite for dissolving different metals . . .' Boomer shrugged. 'I had hoped that the resulting residues might have useful qualities.'

Francis slipped the bottle back into the padded, silk-lined wooden box from which his father had taken it.

'Its possibilities still tease me,' said Boomer. 'You go into the unknown. I send with you a gift of unknown discoveries still waiting for your wits to tease them out. Who knows?'

Francis kept his eyes on the box. He did not like the valedictory tone of this gift. Boomer was handing over to him as the first begetter of invention. Boomer was still at the peak of his prime.

'I don't mean to die just yet,' his father said dryly. 'Don't get your hopes up too soon.' He busied himself in a cupboard. 'But I admit, I am losing my taste for danger.'

Francis nodded but was not convinced.

'Now sit at the table,' said Boomer, still buried in the cupboard.

Francis heard suppressed delight in his father's voice.

'Cover your eyes.'

Francis obeyed, suddenly feeling eight years old once more. A New Year's gift. His name day. He remembered the gifts. His first saddle. A hawk, complete with jesses and a hawking glove. A Chinese book, which he could not read, but which was filled with marvellous woodcuts of different sky patterns for firework explosions.

'Look now.'

On the table lay a book, newly bound, still smelling of glue and the pigments that decorated its cover. The size of a small paving stone. He opened the cover.

Liber Ignium. The Book of Fire. The title was written in letters of gold.

'As it's best not to risk the family's only *Liber,* I had this copy made for you. You must take it with you.' Boomer's delight was as great as his son's.

Francis turned over the pages in disbelief. He did not need to scribble hasty notes. Here was a brimming treasury of all his family's knowledge, the record of the fire master Quoynts. Begun by his great-great grandfather, the first Quoynt fire master, and continued for five generations. The secrets of their deadly trade, filled with ingenious ways to destroy, to bring down walls, horses and men.

He had studied it hungrily as a boy, covertly, at night, while Boomer pretended not to know that Francis had discovered its secret hiding place.

Here were the familiar recipes for fireballs, to fling or shoot from a mortar. The countless mixtures of burning pitch and oils. Here were page after page of gunpowder recipes. The slow and the fast, serpentine, mealed, and corned. Here were the different powder compounds for blasting in mines, firing muskets, lifting rockets.

All of it was written in the Quoynt family cipher, which Francis had learned to read at the age of eight along with English, Latin and Greek.

'Whose hand is this?' he asked curiously. It was square and forthright, not the elegant work of a court scribe or practised clerk. And it wasn't Boomer's. His father's hand had grown coarse many years earlier, after he lost the tips of the fingers on his right hand in an explosion.

'Kate made the copy and I corrected the cipher. I had her begin it as soon as you went to London.'

After you two were wed and suspected I would not wish to return to live here again, thought Francis. Tangled emotions tightened around his heart. Kate and Boomer had done this together. They had laboured for two years to make this wonderful thing for him.

He turned the pages: secret ingredients, alchemical trials, both successful and failed, with notes on both. Here too, laid out in the diagrams and formulae, was the history of warfare. First came his great great-grandfather's diagrams of mines and counter-mines, both zig-zag and forked, that would be driven up to the enemies walls, together with his trials of slow and fast mixtures to bring those walls down.

There were clean copies of the cramped faded recipes originally written in his grand-father's hand, for cannon mixtures, and for fire-arrows, fire-lances and other incendiary devices to set the enemy ablaze. Here was a record, too, of his grandfather's service as a mercenary in Italy, with diagrams of siege engines, and his passionate pursuit of a reliable exploding shell, in place of cannon balls made of iron and stone. An explosive shell which could be fired without blowing up the gunner.

He read his grandfather's notes yet again. The difficulty,

which his grandfather had not overcome, lay in the propelling charge that projected the shell at the enemy. The first, smaller propelling charge most often set off the second, much greater charge meant to explode only when it reached its target.

His own father's notes continued this pursuit of a breeding shell. Then came notes made by Francis himself as he wrestled with the same problem while also devising his own rockets. Here were notes on different delayed fuses to run between the initial propelling charge attached to the bottom of the shell and the second explosive charge at its heart.

He turned another page. And here was his father's warning against the price a mortal man must pay for daring to play God.

Be prepared for that great difference between God and his feeble Image. Man cannot escape his conscience. Having been in the service of princes does not acquit us. The ends of our lives must be spent in search of a peace we have not earned.

Discovering those words two years earlier had given Francis the courage to tell his father that he could no longer be a soldier. That he wanted to betray the tradition of his forebears. He wanted to stop being a military fire master and turn artificer of civilian fireworks. This unexpected permission tasted bitter-sweet now. He had betrayed them all for nothing.

'This is a gift beyond all my expecting or deserving,' he said. He closed the *Liber* and held it in both hands. Between his palms lay the lives and knowledge of five generations of Quoynts. He held their accumulated power. The *Liber Ignium* was a fuse that burned through time to end with him . . . and one day Petty France, who might make a better fist of things than he had done. The *Liber* in his hands felt like a talisman that would keep him safe.

Boomer, moved by his son's rare show of emotion, nodded briskly. 'And I've a few words to add to it, a nothing – mere words.' He looked at the ceiling and then at the floor. 'It's only the devout wish to see you again. Having raised you this far against the odds, I could not bear to lose you now.'

Not 'we' but 'I', Francis noted. That was a gift indeed.

14

LA SPADA

'Your hands have lost their magic today.' Irritably, Prince Alessandro jerked his naked foot from his daughter's lap.

Sofia rose to her feet, eyes down. The manservant Yuri leapt forward to cover the mottled flesh of the prince's bare foot with a knitted blue silk stocking.

'May I go, then?' She looked at the faint pinkish stain on the marble floor where the prince had thrown down the paintbrush. The smoke from the herbs burning on the brazier near the prince's chair was making her head swim.

'GO?' The prince trembled suddenly on the brink of one of his violent rages. 'Where else would you rather be? Eh? Sit here beside me again. You might do me some good yet.'

As she sat on her padded stool covered in red silk damask, Sofia had to close her eyes. Otherwise, she knew that her gaze would crack the marble floor.

'That's better.' Just as suddenly calm again, he picked up one of her hands, which she was covertly wiping on her skirt. 'Young skin,' he said thoughtfully. 'Young life . . .' He pressed her hand against the quilted silk over his heart. His stumbling heartbeat thumped at her palm.

She shaped her lips into a smile. Not to smile was to wish her father ill. To wish him ill was treason. Castello La Spada was filled with smiling people and unsmiling ghosts.

'You're my best medicine.' He pressed her hand harder against his heart. 'Pour your strength into me. You have more than you need, and I have so little.'

You took all of my mother's strength, thought Sofia. Then her life. And much good it brought you!

He set his hand beside hers and contemplated: one hand slim, long-fingered and smooth, the other the broken wreck of a swordsman's hand, a hand that had once seized power by the scruff and held it fast. It was a hand that had cut throats and signed warrants for executions. It had cupped more female breasts than its owner could remember and parted the way for his member as it took yet another citadel, not always after a surrender.

'I'm going to die,' he said. 'Soon. Then hell will have me.'

Stop smiling. To smile now would be treason. Her head ached, as many other heads in the Castello often ached, with the effort of getting it right. Her mother had got it terribly wrong, just once, but fatally.

Sofia risked a quick hungry glance at the rectangle of bright blue outside the closed window. The top of a sweet chestnut tree in the gardens bulged upwards like a green cloud.

Outside the walls of Castello La Spada, young women of her age sat with their dying fathers from love, not fear. They lay with young husbands and stroked swelling bellies as they sat in the sun in gardens on this rare bright gift of a day. Or they rested by the side of roads where they were free to walk as far as they liked. Or they galloped up the slope of a mountain meadow imagining that they had finally escaped.

'Hell will have me,' her father repeated to reclaim her attention. He clutched her hand. 'Hold me!' he cried. 'The flames are reaching for me!'

She stayed silent. Once, when she had protested, he had slapped her for daring to argue with him.

The truth of the prince's health was kept secret from most of his subjects with the help of his High Chamberlain and cousin, the duke of Da Monte who handled the day to day running of the principality.

But Sofia heard the secret whisperings, like rats in the walls. She paid certain of her women to gossip and report back. She put her ear to the lions and overheard men plotting. The lions spat out fears and rumours.

The nobles and soldiers of La Spada weighed the risks of rebellion. Was it too soon? When would it suddenly become too late?

They weighed the advantages of backing Ettore, the male heir, against those of backing her, who was legitimate but female. The man who might swing the balance, Da Monte, could also lay claim to the throne if he chose. As far as Sofia could learn, he had not yet made up his mind what to do. She even heard it suggested that the family might be brought down altogether.

She weighed Da Monte as a possible ally. By all reports as well as her own sense of the man, he still seemed content enough to wield the true day-to-day power and more than happy, therefore, to go on disguising how ill and mad the prince had become.

The prince's orders were still obeyed. Documents bearing his signature and seal emerged from his apartments. No one had yet dared to move against him and his ferocious Uskok guards, not even Ettore, who had already proved that he would murder to become the next prince.

In the long hours spent at her father's side, Sofia had

turned the future over and over in her mind. Even a mere trading commodity like herself, if clever enough, could shape what was to come.

'God forgive me for all those I burnt!' The prince broke into her thoughts. He staggered up from his chair to the brazier that always burned to keep him warm. He thrust his sword hand into the flames.

'Your Highness . . .!' cried Yuri.

'Leave me!'

Sofia stood and stepped back.

The prince growled in pain through clenched teeth. Sweat burst out on his forehead. 'I did this to them . . .'

Then his sleeve caught fire. The starched lace flared like dry grass. His resolve broke. He screamed and staggered back. The serving man flung a cloak around the burning sleeve. The prince sobbed like a terrified child.

'The fires decreed by God burn even hotter . . . than these earthly flames,' he gasped. '. . . Eat us eternally with an infinite, exquisite agony! God must forgive me! I must not go to hell! I will not!'

As Yuri helped him back into his chair, the prince stared at Sofia without recognition, breathless and quivering with terror. Faintly, she smelt the urine that he had voided into the padded depths of his clothes. 'What shall I do?' he begged his eighteen-year-old daughter.

'Have courage,' she said. 'The Englishman is coming. Remember? You sent for him. No one refuses your invitation. He'll be here soon to help you.'

When the prince fell abruptly into a breathless sleep, Sofia fled to her *camera* to scrub her hands with pumice. Then she inhaled the smoke of the sage and rosemary that burned night and day in a brazier beside her bed. Though the prince's last mistress had already died, blotched and raving, and Sofia detected early signs of the disease in the manservant, she herself seemed still clean. She had not tended him in the first stages of his illness when he seemed to have infected the others.

With a reddened hand, she marked off another day on her record. One month and two weeks ago, on the prince's instructions, she had written the letter that her father believed to be his own idea. If she calculated correctly, the English fire master's ship should be somewhere between England and the southern tip of Italy.

She sent for Isabella to sing to her. Music helped make the waiting more bearable.

15

'Leave me!' Dressed for bed that night, Sofia held herself tightly in control while her ladies curtsied and backed from the royal bedchamber, taking with them their sharp prying eyes and ready tongues. From the age of eight, when her old nurse died, the *principessa* had banished all sleeping companions from her bed. She knew that her women murmured vile suggestions about her unnatural desire for solitude, even the chief lady-in-waiting who was meant to teach the others how to behave. Sofia did not care. She had good reasons for wanting solitude.

The last lady went. The last maid turned back the coverlet on the bed carved to resemble an arbour of grapevines. She checked the coals in the pierced brass bed warmer, scooped up Sofia's linens for laundering and left.

Sofia unlocked the double doors of a small private cabinet of ivory and sandalwood. She took a heavy iron key from one of the inner drawers and opened a low, narrow wooden door set into the thickness of the stone walls. The cavity behind the door was just tall and wide enough to hold her if she had still been wearing her wide Spanish farthingale and stiffened skirts. To her left, at waist height gaped a square hole in the wall large enough to admit her head and shoulders. The lion's belly.

She reached into the hole and felt for the folded papers lying on the bottom, fallen from the hungry jaws on the floors above. She took the papers back out into the candlelight to read them.

'*Sr. Corsari has lied to his wife's father about gambling away . . .*'

Nothing to do with her father or the threat of rebellion. She tossed the paper aside and opened another.

'*Bembo writes in secret to his relatives in Venice and may be plotting to join the Son in an uprising against the Father.*'

She read that one again, refolded it thoughtfully and put it into a drawer in her cabinet.

She read through the rest of the *denunziones*, which were the moral and civic duty of all good subjects of La Spada. Some were signed, as the writers hoped for a reward in the Venetian way. Others, like the suggestion of Bembo's treason, were anonymous.

She put two more pieces of political gossip into her private cabinet. She kept one denunciation to show as a private warning to the object of its bile. Three exposing adultery she threw onto her fire.

Hers was not the only belly in the Castello. She knew that her half-brother Ettore controlled the access to the information from at least one other, which was located in his quarters in the Castello. So far as she knew, her father, Da Monte, and the Inquisition controlled the rest.

Her belly, like the others, had many mouths. These were open slots, set into the walls of the Castello as the mouths of bronze lion masks – the *bocce di leone*. An engraved bronze plaque above each mouth invited a different sort of confidence. The *bocca* in the public piazza in front of the Castello, for example, gaped hungrily for news of financial crimes – lying to avoid tax, embezzlement, bribery, theft.

The information that fell through the walls into Sofia's hands mainly concerned moral crimes and politics, although any subject might arrive if an informer merely thrust a *denunzio* into the nearest mouth in order to avoid detection.

Some days the lions feasted. On other days, they swallowed only a tidbit or two. But over time, the intelligence they disgorged added greatly to the ease of ruling, as the Venetians, too, had learned. Even so, as helpful as such intelligence might be, it was not Sofia's chief use for the lions.

When she had finished with the denunciations, she went back into the little stone closet and put her head into the hole. She held her breath so that her nightgown did not rustle and waited for the pulsing of blood in her ears to settle. Then she listened. The lions told tales that no one could imagine, unless they could enter one of the bellies. Faintly, fragments of voices reached her through the channels in the walls. Some came from the chamber where several of her ladies slept.

By eavesdropping from the age of nine, ever since she had first discovered the indiscretion of the lions' mouths, Sofia had lost all expectation of kindness and friendship from those she ruled.

'*What does she do in there all alone?*'

'*. . . glimpsed the inside of heart her father's grisly cabinet . . . she didn't know I was peeping . . . all manner of strange things: manikins, toad stones against poison . . . why would she want those if she did not mean to poison someone's . . .?*'

'And who might that be? Can anyone not guess?

'. . . Alone?' Who says that she remains alone? Just because she banishes us . . .'

She could have arrested or dismissed most of her women, but who could replace them who would be any different? One night soon after Baldassare died she had begun to listen.

'. . . young widows never sleep alone for long . . .'

'I'm quite certain she knows how to pleasure herself.'

'Lucky her! . . . wouldn't mind if my husband met a similar accident.'

She could not bear to listen any longer or she would have killed them all. She did not return to the lion's belly for a month.

Then one evening, as they all gambled over cards in the *saleta*, something in the voice of one of her women had alerted her. Sofia drew her next card and tried to think what she had just heard. A reference to riding and to accidents . . . she had caught only the end of that snatch of gossip. That night, she finally returned to the lions.

Trembling with cold and apprehension, she had then listened night after night. She endured endless complaints about monthlies and facial blemishes. And about her own coldness. And Ettore's latest noble whore. She heard male courtiers being anatomized from eyebrow to ankle. She listened to breathless confidences about groping and kisses and to sobering tales of marital brutality that made her miss the gentle, wary Baldassare even more keenly. He had been that miracle of political marriages, a sweet boy of great good will, who wished to love his new young wife. She would not be so lucky the next time she was sold in exchange for lands, an army or a trade treaty. Night after night, she resisted the drops of poison that seeped through the walls.

*

Tonight as they undressed for bed, the three Florentines began to mock a love poem one of them had found under her plate at dinner. A pitiful imitation of poetry, they agreed, but the would-be poet was not unattractive.

'. . . *somewhat resembles the late Count Baldassare . . . the same fine leg and hopeful eyes. What a shame that was!*'

Sofia heard a thoughtful silence. She imagined sighs, but they might have been no more than air currents in the walls. The women lowered their voices, but they were standing very near the lion's mouth. There was a murmured question that she could not hear, then the reply:

'. . . *but how can there be any doubt? The Bastard Elect would never risk letting his sister conceive a legitimate heir! Count Baldassare was too mild and . . . ever to pose a military threat, but what if he had fathered a son on the princess?*'

Sofia pushed her head as high up as she could into the wall but heard nothing more than commonplace exchanges and murmurs of goodnight. She left the little closet and locked the door.

Agitated almost past enduring, she hauled off the heavy lace-collared night gown they had imprisoned her in and threw it on the floor. Why hadn't she seen it? She had spent enough nights and days thinking about the murder. If her women were right, she herself had unwittingly played a part in bringing about Baldassare's death.

Naked and shivering, she took from the bottom drawer of her cabinet a small folded piece of fine old linen. She shook it out and dropped her old shift over her head, prickling with pleasure as it floated lightly down over her naked skin. She had rescued it when one of her ladies meant to give it to a beggar.

She let none of her women touch this shift. She washed it herself in secret, taking pleasure she did not understand in the gentle softness of the fine worn fabric. It comforted her to feel the garment settle on her shoulders and whisper against her legs and belly. The shift did not battle against her like the steel-stiffened bodies she wore by day, nor scratch like gold lace. There was nothing hard and glassy about it like her jewels, no weight. In its barely perceptible embrace, her body felt as free as that of a cat or dog, able to stretch and curl at will, to seek the position that most soothed and eased, not one that dignity or duty decreed.

From another drawer in her cabinet, she lifted a man's embroidered silk glove, only a little larger than one of her own, which she pressed to her nose, hungry for his last fading scent. Then she took out a ragged square of velvet cut from a woman's gown, its black now faded and the silver tarnished long ago to a dull dark grey. She carried both into bed with her, wrapped the glove in the velvet and lay down curled on her side. With the little bundle held under her cheek she looked like a young girl cuddling a doll to comfort her in sleep, but there was nothing childlike about her thoughts.

She was a general waiting for war to be declared. As a general, she gave herself odds no better than half on winning. To her advantage, she knew who her enemies were and where they had dug in. She had already begun a secret war that Ettore did not suspect.

Against her was the loss of her greatest ally. But she had survived before she had Baldassare; she would continue to do so without him. Her apparent weakness and smaller forces were not necessarily a disadvantage. Ettore feared her, but for the wrong reasons. His intelligencers had infiltrated her household to try to uncover schemes for raising a rebellion.

He must think her simple!

She fell asleep beneath the delicately carved bunches of grapes that framed the canopy of her bed, trying to decide how best to deal with the English fire master when he arrived and make sure that he jumped in her direction. Judging by her father's behaviour today, he was now certain that the idea she had plucked out from his mad ravings and nursed into reality was entirely his own.

16

DOVER

His bags had disappeared. Francis cursed. He had piled them aft and turned to look over the rail at the activity on the dock as his ship prepared to sail for Venice. He might have noticed the loss sooner if he hadn't been thinking about his father's parting gifts.

He scanned the dock, saw no one making off with his bags, then hailed the quartermaster who, by chance, was walking towards him.

'If you had taken the trouble to tell anyone,' said the man before Francis could speak, 'I might have been able to arrange a suitable berth for your manservant.'

'My manservant?'

'He'll have to sleep on the floor of your cabin...which, I must say, you occupy only by chance, as the previous occupant suddenly cancelled his passage . . . or he'll have to sling his hammock among the ordinary seamen . . . if they'll have him.'

'Did he take my bags?'

'Who else?' The quartermaster looked at Francis as if he were simple.

'And where is this man of mine now?'

'Making your cabin ready, of course. As we're about to get under way, there's no chance to stock any extra rations and I won't have my . . .'

But Francis was already headed aft, towards the high poop deck and the officers' quarters under it. He found his cabin . . . there was no mistaking it . . . and closed the door.

'You dunder-headed ninny! I said that you weren't to come!' He kept his voice low but his rage could have ignited the ship's lantern swaying gently in its swivel three inches from his face. They stood almost nose to nose in the tiny cabin, with the lantern between their faces, both fair heads brushing the wooden ceiling.

'You'll need my help in Friuli,' said Richard Seaborn. 'And, like you, I've nothing left to lose.'

Francis stared, temporarily speechless. 'You impudent pup!' he wanted to say. How do you know what I do or don't have to lose? He wanted to box the young man's ears, but the level blue Quoynt gaze stopped his hand.

Because Francis had moved to London soon after Seaborn arrived at Powder Mote, he did not yet know this new-found nephew well. But he had already noticed that the quiet young man had the knack of achieving his will without any sign of effort – as when he had decided to live at Powder Mote. He just went ahead quietly and did it – as now. Francis did not like him any better for it. How the devil, short of cracking him on the head and bundling him over his shoulder, was he going to get Seaborn off the ship before they sailed?

Richard shuffled sideways politely, so that Francis could sink down onto the narrow bunk. 'I think you'll find the bunk so short that you'll need the floor for yourself. I've found a corner for my hammock on the gun deck.'

'Is my father part of this?' Francis asked. Gun deck, he

thought. Not fit for carrying dogs. Even the ship's pigs and chickens at least had light and air before they were eaten.

'He loaned me the cost of my passage.' Seaborn stooped down and pushed Francis's riding boots under the bunk. Then he hung Francis's heavy oiled wool cloak on a peg on the back of the cabin door.

'What are you doing?' Francis demanded.

'I'm your manservant.'

'God's Balls . . .!' exploded Francis. 'Stop this mummery!' Seaborn was the son of a bastard half-brother Francis had never known, much older, born during Boomer's early days as a mercenary and dead only a few years after Francis himself was born in lawful wedlock at Powder Mote. Though Boomer kept a tight mouth on the subject, Francis knew that the mother, though not English, had been nobly born. His new manservant out-ranked him socially by a good many degrees. 'You can't sleep on the gun deck!'

'I have already slung my hammock,' Seaborn smiled at his furious uncle. 'Between two cannons. They have very strong mounts.' He turned his attention to a saddlebag.

'Leave my stockings where they are!'

'You'd best start to accustom yourself to being my master.'

And you'd best stop enjoying yourself so much, thought Francis.

Crack him on the head and overboard with him into the harbour!

In Seaborn's favour was the knack for explosives he'd shown from his first days at Powder Mote, and a great willingness. Without his help, Francis could not have carried out his masterpiece firework display, designed for the wedding of Kate and Boomer. This display, paid for by Cecil, had also made his new reputation and turned him into the pyrotechnician every nobleman and merchant wished to employ, instead of an unemployed military fire master. And he did not doubt the young man's cool head and quick wit.

'What languages do you have?' Francis himself spoke good, schooled Latin. He also had soldier's Italian, a few words of Dutch, could order ale in German, Flemish and French but lacked the words to address a lady in any of them, barring Latin.

'Latin, Greek and Hebrew, of course, from my tutors.' Seaborn looked briefly into another time and place. 'Spanish. *Como no?*' He stretched a long arm and crouched to tuck Francis's stockings into his riding boots. 'I can dine, flirt and debate in Italian and French. And English, almost.'

'How are you with a sword?'

Seaborn hesitated, uncertain for the first time. 'Well-schooled but never tested in battle.'

Francis sighed, still uncertain what to do. He heard the shouts begin up on deck and the boatswain whistling instructions.

Seaborn stood up, seeming to fill the tiny cabin with his young male body. Though slighter than Francis, he was almost as tall, with narrow shoulders that had been proved stronger than they looked.

He was large enough to be useful in a fight. Francis stared up at that face, just familiar enough for him to believe their connection. Most convincing was the stubborn set of the mouth and the coolly amused gaze he had seen so often in his father's face. A Quoynt, sure enough. Time and need would tell whether he also carried the Quoynt streak of ferocity under his gentle manner.

If not, thought Francis, I'll have both of us to defend.

The ship quivered. Francis felt the faintest hint of a lean, a loosening of motion that told him they were pulling away from the dock. Only then did it occur to him that Seaborn had stood up at exactly the right moment, and yet again had got his way.

'It was a mistake to come,' said Francis.

'For you or for me?'

Now Francis stood up too. 'Richard, as my new man-servant, you must learn that I will not tolerate insolence.'

For a moment, Seaborn held his eye. 'Forgive me, sir.' Then he smiled. '*Bene!* Very good!'

And the greatest danger you're going to face in La Spada, dear coz, Francis replied silently, is very likely to be me.

PART TWO

17

NORTHERN ITALY

Francis lifted his head. He glanced at Seaborn, riding at his side, and saw his own uneasiness reflected back. The two men escorting them drew long-barrelled pistols and laid them across their pommels. While their horses stamped and stretched their heads down for grass, they all watched the track ahead of them and listened.

Since sailing from Dover, Francis had fed hungrily on the novelty of being on the move again. At the sight of Venice, floating delicately but stubbornly on the surface of the sea, he felt a leap of an excitement that had eluded him for more than a year. A representative of Sir Henry Wootten, the first British ambassador to Venice, had been rowed out to meet their ship when it dropped anchor in the ships' pool at the bottom of the Grand Canal.

To Francis's disappointment, they did not go ashore but transferred directly by boat to the small oared galley that would take them onward to Aquileia on the north Adriatic coast. Francis had handed over a letter on state affairs from

Cecil to Sir Henry, along with an English cheese, and had taken Sir Henry's letter for the prince of La Spada. Then he asked the Englishman if he might go ashore for an hour or two to explore Venice, but the galley captain was in a hurry to get underway.

'It's just as well that a dangerous fellow like you is moving on,' Sir Henry's man had said with a friendly laugh. 'The Venetians might not welcome you. They still talk of the last explosion at the *Arsenale* forty years ago. Broke windows as far away as the mainland, they say.'

Instead, Francis sat under the canopy on the galley's high sterncastle where they were berthed, asked questions and gazed curiously at the delicate alien façades of the floating palazzos just across the water. And at the dense packing of churches. Everywhere he looked, another curving dome or triangular façade and bell tower sprouted amongst the curious cone-topped chimneys: the odd pointed double domes of the doge's chapel of St Mark's, the new church of San Georgio Maggiore solid and male-looking on its own island, San Zaccharia, almost straight ahead of him, near his own personal place of worship, the *Arsenale*. Almost a small town in itself, it was one of the world's greatest ship-yards and armouries.

He noted the national ensigns of the moored ships and watched the little single-oared boats the Venetians called *gondole*, which reminded him of wherries. He watched sailors furling the sails on the great war galleys which the Venetians still used.

As they left Venice, past the islands in the Lagoon where little egrets perched like white flames on the top of mooring posts, he gazed back with longing at the vast sand-coloured front of the *Arsenale*, near the bottom of the main island of Venice.

On my return voyage, he vowed. If he survived to make it.

He would have liked to take with him some of the fabled *arsenalotti*, the craftsmen of the *Arsenale*, renowned for the speed and fineness of their work.

As they sailed east along the Adriatic coast, he leaned for hours on the stern rail, studying the shallow misty waters of the coastal marshes, watching geese, ducks, purple herons, diving cormorants and the gulls that circled their galley and perched on the single mast. He talked with the sailors, who included two Hampshire men, and learned from them a few words in a number of different new languages, including Ladin and Friulan.

'*Un, doi, tre, cuatri, cine . . .*' he repeated. '*Omp.*' Man. '*Femine.*' Woman.

At Aquileia, he asked again if he might explore this old Roman City of Eagles at the far end of the Veneto, which had once rivalled Rome itself.

But the urgency of the galley captain was repeated here.

'No time!' said the pilot of the riverboat in a barely recognizable dialect of Italian.

Behind the man, Richard rolled his eyes and made a throat-slitting gesture.

Francis noted the badge on the man's cap and nodded agreeably. A castle superimposed on a long-bladed sword. Castello La Spada, the badge of the dying prince who wanted funeral fireworks so costly that they could bankrupt the English treasury.

For six days the shallow-draft boat carried them from the flat marshes of the northern Adriatic coast up into the narrowing funnels of alpine river valleys. From the warm early spring of the coast, they followed the retreating hem of winter into the mountains of Friuli.

Ribbons of human endeavour followed the rivers and floors of the branching valleys. Streams fed by melting snow crashed down over waterfalls to swell the main rivers and drive mills and forges. Higher in the mountains, people lived in small hanging valleys or on minute pinpoints of land, balanced above crevices – splits in the earth that seemed to open into the underworld. Farmers gazed at each other across dizzy chasms, almost within earshot but separated by a hard day of descents and climbs.

On the sixth night, the boat set them down. Francis and Seaborn slept in a tiny hamlet protected against bandits by a wooden stockade, in a farmhouse heated by the warm bodies of the cows below them. The resinous scent of the surrounding pines and firs helped to sweeten the odours of the cows. The waterfall that powered the village forge crashed in their ears all night, along with the mournful clanging of cowbells.

Before leaving the village, Francis bought a steel hunting knife of finer workmanship than any he had seen in England. After breakfast, two new escorts arrived, leading a pair of bristle-maned horses with short backs and sturdy haunches for them to ride. Their luggage was loaded onto half a score of heavy-footed packhorses with thickly feathered legs, as if the animals wore fur coats against the cold.

As their procession rode out of the village, Francis cried, 'Wait!' He looked up to watch a heavy bucket roll past on a cable just overhead.

One of their escorts pointed uphill at a pulley system in three stages lowering iron ore in swinging buckets for half a mile to the hamlet from the dark mouths of the mines high above on the mountainside. Then he waved them on impatiently. 'No time!'

Only two hours later, Francis had reined in his mount and lifted his head to listen. Horses.

'Bandits?' Francis asked.

Their escort shrugged. Francis drew his own pistol and held it across his thigh.

Something flashed like a mirror through the trees. The steady beating of hoofs grew louder. Now he could also hear the dense jingling of harness, the clatter of metal striking metal.

The two escorts watched the track, pistols raised in their hands.

More bright flashes flared between the trunks of the tall dark pines. Then a river of silver began to pour through the gap of the track. Men in shining cone-shaped helmets and fish-scale armour that shattered the light like thousands of tiny mirrors, rode towards them, their half-hidden faces impassive, mouths stern under black moustaches. The steady pounding of their horses made the dust quiver. The jingling of harness and clashing of metal filled the air. The silver river flowed around Francis and Seaborn and closed behind them. Six, eight, twelve, sixteen, twenty . . . They carried swords, muskets, saddle maces. Some carried upright spears.

The light reflecting from their armour confused the eye and made them seem to be everywhere at once. It was hard to count their true number. Francis and Seaborn held their own horses steady in the centre of the bright swirling current of men and horses.

A sudden shout brought them all to a halt in two ranks of miraculous order.

'Signore Cointo?'

It took Francis a moment. 'I'm Quoynt,' he said in English. He repeated it in court Latin.

The captain, or so he appeared, sat on his horse in the centre of the track ahead of them. His troop stood ranged on either side of the track with Francis and Seaborn between them.

The captain gave an instruction in a language that sounded almost familiar.

'I believe that he said to put up your gun,' murmured Seaborn.

The man made a tiny move of his head. The nose guard of his helmet flashed in the sun.

'These don't look like any bandits I've ever seen,' said Francis, with his pistol still in his lap.

One of the cavalrymen said something and the captain laughed. In Latin, the cavalryman translated back his commander's reply.

'The prince sent us to protect you from bandits. You're safe with us.'

Francis doubted that but nevertheless put away his gun. With these numbers it would be mere posturing to do anything else. Particularly as their own armed guide seemed to have vanished.

The captain turned his horse and set off at a trot back the way he had come. Francis glanced at Seaborn and kicked his horse to follow. The translating cavalryman fell into place beside Francis and another man rode with Seaborn. The rest dropped back to guard the packhorses. Like their language, these men were almost familiar but strange at the same time.

After trotting for some time in silence, except for the metallic clatter and blowing of horses, Francis asked Seaborn loudly, 'Who do you suppose these splendid fellows are?'

'Uskoki,' said the cavalryman. 'The prince's own guard.' He clamped his mouth shut again and stared straight ahead.

Francis glanced at the stern, half-metal profile and reined in his curiosity for the moment as to just who the Uskoki might be. In appearance, they might be Greeks, or Arabs, or simply mountain men from the east, from some strange part of Muscovy or Hungary. His own experience did not reach that far.

The terrain soon grew steeper and slowed their pace. Along with watching red squirrels leap from tree to tree, and hawks circling above, Francis memorized the route – easy enough to follow back, on well-established tracks. For the rest of the day, they climbed north and east away from the river, through thick forests of different pines, silver fir, black fir, oak and larch, climbing deeper and deeper into the Julian Alps. Once they rode for a time beside a long lavender-grey ribbon of snow in the deep shadow of a bank. Small white crocuses pushed up through the dripping edges. The occasional stand of fringed long-stemmed violet-coloured bells nodded gently in the air disturbed by their passing.

Francis pointed up at the snow on the highest peaks. 'Even in summer?'

The man at his side nodded curtly.

For a time after that, Francis contented himself with looking.

They passed descending caravans of loaded mules and draft horses hauling iron, cannons, small arms and silver, down to the boats.

After a couple of hours, Francis hazarded another question. 'When do we arrive in la Spada?'

'Tomorrow.'

After another sideways glance, he decided that the man did not mean to be uncivil, merely to the point.

The country through which they now travelled seemed to have very little in common with the landscapes Francis had seen painted behind Florentine Madonnas or Venetian battle scenes. It was abrupt, grey, black and wet, covered with thick forests of firs and pines, not terracotta and gold pricked with orderly lines of spearhead cypress.

The village houses and the occasional small isolated farmhouses also looked to Francis more Helvetian or German than Venetian or Tuscan. In place of red tile roofs, they had wood or split rock shingles. Most had walls of wood with small windows shuttered to keep out the cold and wooden balconies for enjoying the sun. On most of the balconies, feather beds and pillows slumped over the balustrades. The pelts of wolves, foxes and bear hung drying on walls, reminding Francis how very different Friuli was from Sussex and London. Most, like the house where they had slept, penned the cattle at ground level, with the people living above.

That night, they began to hear the screams of foxes and the howling of wolves. Bear had left prints in the sand and mud on the riverbanks. Once, gazing up at the narrow slice of evening sky above a gorge, Francis spied the tuft-eared silhouette of a lynx watching them from a ledge far above the river.

When they stopped to make late camp in a mountain meadow, he took this unexpected chance simply to sit still, listening to the crunching of grazing horses, the crackle of the cooking fires, breathing a clear sweet-smelling air that Londoners would never know. He walked a little way from their campsite to a pale white carpet laid on the meadow floor and found a solid mat of the white crocuses he had seen earlier that day at the edge of the snow bank.

Richard was sitting by one of the small cooking fires, talking to two of the Uskoks in who knows what language. Francis gazed about him, listening to the varied voices of the river below them, letting his thoughts roam, hauling them back from too much speculation. Until he reached La Spada and learned what he must deal with, he refused to brood on uncertainties. As he rinsed his wine cup in the icy river, Francis saw the translator near by, doing the same.

'Who are the Uskoks?'

The man shook the last drops from his cup. 'Our name means "the people who have jumped away".' He shot a sideways glance at Francis. 'We see it coming and we're not there.'

Francis thought that this may possibly have been a jest, but to be safe, he merely nodded.

The next morning, they started out before dawn in a faint grey light that barely showed the course of the track. Sheer mountain walls crowded in on either side of them as if ready to clap together and flatten them like gnats. Then, about three hours later, suddenly, at the end of a long, twisting stony climb, the towering ridges of jagged rock leapt back to offer a high, wide rolling U-shaped plateau of fresh intense green that promised summer flowers as sweet and gently seductive as any man-made garden. The Castello of La Spada rose from the far end of this valley, as harsh and brutal as the mountains around it.

18

LA SPADA, FRIULI

That same morning, the *principessa* washed in a large marble tub in a private chamber in the royal baths. Back in her *camera*, she kept changing her mind, dropping puddles of silk on the floor, yanking off ribbons, trying a chain of pearls, a chain of gold and jet.

She saw her women lift their brows at each other.

I must make up my mind, she told herself, or they will talk. Avoid notice at all costs. Survival rule number four.

Still in her shift and under petticoat, she tried on a pair of emerald earrings, a wedding gift from Baldassare, to stiffen her will. She looked in the mirror of her *restello* on the wall beside her bed, with her belts and ribbons hanging from the pegs under the shelf.

Too matronly.

She rejected some coral earrings because they looked too much like gouts of fresh blood. She laid them back on the shelf of the *restello*. Picked up another pair.

'I'll have these,' she said. Pearl drops hanging from a golden bow – a virgin's choice.

She tried a tightly laced black and gold bodice, with padded sleeves. Then another bodice of cut velvet. Finally she settled on black silk brocade with pearls stitched along the top edge, then a tight black silk jacket over the bodice. She looked at her image in the glass. The narrow sleeves of the jacket showed off the slim length of her arms. She laid her fingertips on the exposed upper curves of her breasts.

Veil them, or not? She decided to leave them bare.

Her women bound the weight of her long hair into a net of golden wires of almost the same colour as her hair, to swing between her shoulder blades. One of them fastened on a heavy dog dollar of beaten gold.

At last, she was satisfied.

She dismissed them all and scented herself alone, her hair, her hands, between her breasts. In the air of his *scrittoio*, always filled with the smoke of burning herbs, her father would never notice. She chewed eight fennel seeds to clean her breath and tucked more seeds into the pocket hanging inside her skirt. She leaned close to the mirror to peer closely at her complexion but saw nothing to mar its smooth surface. She was ready to do battle.

19

A golden eagle circled far above them on splay-tipped wings. Francis tilted his head back. The fortress of Castello La Spada loomed above the eagle, its eastern face lit by the late morning sun. Made of the same stone as its pedestal, the Castello seemed to grow from the sheer column of rock on which it crouched, a final pinnacle jutting out from the end of a sharp-toothed ridge. The thick walls sprouted from clefts in the rock into squat towers and flowed along the changing levels of the peak. Only a few narrow windows pierced the walls.

Below the Castello, sheer cliffs fell almost to the valley, ending just above the steep-roofed *casones* of the lower town that clambered up the bottom slopes. Streets sat stacked one above the other, three or four deep. Above the streets, single houses clung to narrow ledges reached only by zig-zag flights of steps carved into the rock. Then the cliffs rose too steeply to allow even a single vine or row of lettuces. Below the Castello, the rock face was streaked here and there with the discharge of privies.

Not only would enemies have a hard time getting in, thought Francis. Once in, you'd not easily get out.

This was terrain through which he and Seaborn might need to escape. He snatched at details, trying to make a map in his head.

The Uskoks kicked their mounts into a trot as they passed the first of the outlying *casones*, so that they seemed to emerge from the cloud of dust they themselves had stirred up. Barking dogs began to gather in their wake. At first, Francis saw no other people. Then, in the corner of his eye, he spied someone slipping out of sight.

I'd hide too, he thought, if these men came riding past my door.

As their track curved towards the town, a narrow sloping ridge came into view, running between the grim streaked face of the old defensive *fortezza* on the summit of its jutting column of rock down to the the lower town on the level of the plateau. The rocky shoulders of the peak narrowed sharply at the top of the ascending ridge. Together the shoulders of the mountain and the descending ridge formed the guard and blade of *la spada* – the sword.

In the Castello, a watcher on the battlements left his post and ran to relay the news that the Uskoks were back, and that they were escorting two men and a half-score of pack-horses.

They clattered and jingled through a gate in the outer wall near the tip of the blade. The first curious faces appeared in windows and doors.

'*Di sotto*,' said the cavalryman suddenly. The Lower Town.

Even the smallest houses were in good repair, even those with only oiled parchment in the windows instead of glass. Francis noted large stores of stacked firewood. Not only feather beds but fine red and blue Turkey carpets hung over balconies. Glimpses into fenced-off yards showed large, well-kept stables.

They passed several forges, making tools and blades ranging from skinning knives to swords.

Near the bottom of the rising ridge, Francis saw a pair of gates and a pounded earth carriage drive that led through the pines to a Venetian-style villa framed at the far end, its façade an arcade of delicate columns and spires of stone lace. Here in La Spada, waves of stony outcrop lapped at its foundations instead of the sea.

'The duke,' said the cavalryman, following the direction of Francis's gaze.

Francis nodded as if he grasped the significance of this information.

Everywhere he saw signs of prosperity, but surely not enough to allow the ruler of La Spada to make a vast loan to a foreign power. He wondered again about Cecil's motives in sending him here. If Cecil wanted intelligence on how to take the Castello, he would be disappointed. Francis could also see why the Hapsburgs, with all their numbers, might hesitate to invade.

Seen from down here the Castello's protecting cliffs seemed to overhang the town. Sappers couldn't reach the walls to undermine them and couldn't tunnel through that solid rock, in any case.

Francis imagined Cecil, listening intently, sitting absolutely still on his stool behind his desk, his feet barely touching the floor, like a schoolboy. Moving only to scribble a note.

Any cannon close enough to breach the walls with iron or stone balls – he continued his imagined report – would also be within range of those guns poking their snouts through the tops of the Castello walls. Staying out of range of the Castello guns would lengthen the attacker's range too far for his cannon to do serious damage, given the height of the peak and the resulting angles of trajectory.

He knew what was needed to take a fortress like La Spada.

But his grandfather had failed to devise it. Boomer had failed. Francis himself had so far failed. For all his experimenting, he had never made that crucial, elusive step from mere fireworks that burst harmlessly into a scattering of stars, to that dark, elusive miracle that would penetrate a distant enemy stronghold and explode only when it reached its target. Neither too soon, uselessly, in the air, nor too late, so that it could be thrown back at the attackers.

The Uskok riding at his side saw him looking up. 'Never taken,' he said.

Francis heard both pride and warning. As they entered a long open market place, he left off musing on destruction to turn towards the smell of baking bread. They had eaten nothing but a tough mouthful of dried meat shortly before dawn that morning.

Abruptly, he reined in his horse. 'What is that?' he exclaimed.

'*Piazza Erbe*,' said the Uskok at his side. 'In the summer, they sell fruit and vegetables.'

'No.' Francis pointed past the stalls selling dried apricots and dates, sponges from the Adriatic, dried beans and chick-peas, crocks of preserved fruits and vegetables, baskets of limp green foliage, stoneware bottles of dyes with sample banners of scarlet, purple, green and blue flying from poles. 'The creature being unloaded over there.'

'*Camelus*,' said the Uskok. Camel. 'We often use them here for carrying heavy loads. From east of the mountains. They carry twice the load of a horse.'

Francis now saw four more couched camels being unloaded. He stared across the marketplace. 'May I ride closer?' He had seen pictures of camels, but these lumpy nose-in-the-air animals looked very little like the rather worried and delicate creature he remembered from a bestiary.

'No time.'

'France, do you see the camels?' Seaborn was so excited that he forgot his manservant role. 'You'd think we were in Stamboul, not Friuli!'

The Uskoks trotted through an avenue of aromatic cedars along the top of the marketplace, then through a stone-paved piazza with a central fountain which might have been in Florence or Rome. The spouting marble dolpins Francis glimpsed between armoured shoulders were startling after both the camels and the wildness of their journey.

The Uskoks turned onto a rising stone-paved causeway that climbed the sword blade ridge to the gates of the Castello. Heavy stone balustrades lined the sides to guard against falling over the sheer edges.

Four abreast now, they rode towards the two culverins that pointed the dark eyes of their barrels down the causeway from the stocky gatehouse at the top. Francis felt his horse tighten under him as it felt for footing on the ridged stone paving of the slope. Up here, a brisk, chilly mountain breeze scoured away the stink of the middens and left behind the scent of pine.

He looked over the parapet. A cavalry troupe was exercising on the plateau, arms and armour flashing in the midday sun. Beyond the soldiers, the plateau curved smoothly out of sight around a distant mountain range. The north east seemed to offer a gentler and more generous approach than their own climb up into the Julian Alps from the south.

La Spada might be remote from its nominal overlords in Venice and from western Europe beyond Venice. But Francis now understood Cecil's concern about alliances. The plateau would make for easy travel to and from the Hapsburg cities to the east and the kingdoms of eastern Europe. And for easy invasion. From the farthest edge of his known universe, La Spada now leapt to just off-centre in a strange new one.

And in case he ever forgot this new truth, there were always the camels to remind him.

As they rode up the causeway, the sun edged behind cloud. A curtain of mist began to slide over the tops of the nearest mountains. Wispy fingers crept down through the pale grey rocks into the dark green of the pines on the lower slopes. The wind begin to rise.

The troupe clip-clopped through the portcullis gate into the sloping cobbled piazza beyond. The Uskoks stopped.

'Please dismount now,' said the cavalryman, whose name, Francis had finally learned, was Venturini.

Francis and Seaborn obeyed. Their swords and horses were taken.

'Your belongings will follow you, and your swords.' Or so Francis thought the guard had said. The man's words were a mix of Latin, Italian and German.

With Seaborn a respectful two paces behind Francis, they were led on foot across the sloping piazza and up a ramp through a long arched tunnel between two damp stone walls.

It was difficult to know whether they were inside or out. On either side, sets of stone steps doubled back and disappeared through gateways or ended at wooden doors studded with iron. Or they led sharply up to higher levels which they themselves might or might not reach if they continued their more gradual ascent. Feral cats gazed down from ledges and doorsteps high above their heads. They turned and turned again.

Suddenly, they emerged from an alley lined with goldsmiths and jewel merchants into another piazza, much larger than the first, which was centred on the low circular wall of a *cisterna* or public well.

'Holy Mars!' said Francis. This was not what he had expected.

Ahead of them, just beyond the *cisterna*, on a wide pedestal of marble steps taking up the entire width of the piazza, a Greek temple looked down at them across the sloping cobbles, its lofty, delicate arcade of fluted limestone columns pale and gleaming.

'The new *Magno Palazzo*,' said their soldier guide proudly. The great palace of the prince of La Spada.

'He's here . . . dismounting . . . walking here now.' 'He's here!' Unknowing, Francis followed the gust of news as it blew through the streets and corridors. His own footsteps lagged only a little behind the running feet of the messengers who carried word of his arrival to the prince.

20

MAGNO PALAZZO, LA SPADA

'I had not expected to find the latest Jesuit style here,' murmured Richard. 'I daresay it rivals the most extravagant flowerings of the notorious Papal luxury in Rome.'

Francis gazed at the high arching hall into which they entered, at the creamy fluted marble columns shaped in the ancient Greek fashion.

Broken pediments flanked high doorways. Balustrades with the delicate contours of a woman's body guarded high galleries. Along the length of the hall, marble statues of pale grey, dusty pink and white faced each other in two lines like courtiers waiting to dance.

Francis had expected more of the green-stained stone nooks, brutal arches and damp heavy shadows of the outer Castello. Here he saw only air and light. Sounds winged crisply through the spaces and bounced off frescoed walls. The air smelled of fresh plaster and paint. High windows around the domed ceiling let in the sky.

'Signore Cointo!' A dark wiry man trotted towards them between the lines of statues. 'His highness, The prince of La

Spada, commands your presence at once.' He spoke Latin, the shared language of educated men and women everywhere from Edinburgh to Istanbul.

Francis looked down at his muddy riding clothes, unchanged for a week. He had not changed his linen for three days. 'I must make myself more fit for his presence.'

Nor have I eaten since dawn, he wanted to add.

'Come now. That is his command.' The man, wearing the sword and castle badge of La Spada, gave Francis a pleading look.

Francis handed his filthy riding cloak to Seaborn. 'Go find yourself refreshment while I'm gone. And fetch some for me. This doesn't sound like an invitation to share a pot of ale.'

Smelling of horse, sweat and wood smoke from the last night's fire, he followed the sliced and quilted green silk back of his guide. His thirst was almost equalled by an intense curiosity. For the first time on this journey, he might be about to know more about La Spada than Cecil did.

Mad or not, this prince clearly made his people jump.

Francis felt for the letters to the prince from Cecil and Sir Henry, and began to rehearse his prepared formal speech of greeting.

He still could not imagine what pyrotechnical effects could be extraordinary enough nor what number of paper and timber castles, floating fireboats, and flame-spouting monsters could be large enough to equal in cost a debt too great for the English Exchequer to repay.

In his new Roman palace, Prince Allessandro Hugo Uskoki di Pirati kept magnificent court, *alla grande*, in the Spanish fashion. The Castello officer rushed Francis up a broad flight of marble stairs and through a long *enfilade* of rooms on the high-ceilinged first floor, each one leading into the next. Each new room, Francis soon realized, was reserved for people more important than the ones received in the room before.

Very much like Hampton Court, he told himself, reassured by this faint sense of familiarity.

Armed guards wearing the badge of La Spada, stood at each new threshold. A succession of ushers stepped forward, saw Francis and his guide and stepped back at once to let them pass.

More fresh plaster, more frescos, and more gilding than Francis had ever seen. Paintings in heavy gold frames, inlaid cabinets, tables topped in onyx, porphyry and marble . . . He snatched on the wing at whatever sights he could. Moorish porcelains, Chinese vases . . .

First they passed through the two lowest levels of privilege, in the largest and most ostentatious rooms, where ushers stood ready to deny access to the unworthy. He noticed an ornately framed notice board with the names of the Castello officers on duty that day.

'*La sala . . . La saleta,*' his guide replied to Francis's questions, leading him through a press of bodies as thick as in a busy market place.

Both of these chambers were crowded with petitioners clamouring to achieve an official ear. The crowd stared curiously at Francis as he was escorted past them into the exalted glory of the *antecamera*. A rustle of whispers followed him.

'Who's that?' 'Who the devil does he think he is?'

He heard German, Latin, Venetian, and what he now was beginning to recognize as Ladin and Friulan.

The door to the next room had already closed behind Francis before he realized that the final querulous voice had been speaking English with a Cornish burr. But there was no time to turn back and learn more.

Now two black-robed Jesuit priests were frowning at him and murmuring together. Francis avoided their eye uneasily.

119

Cecil had executed the leader of the English Jesuits very nastily, only two years earlier.

A third man, small and wizened like the last grape on the vine, squinted at him as if memorizing every hair in his eyebrows.

Cecil's back-watcher? Francis wondered. But the man gave no signal of recognition.

Here, also, the chief usher greeted him and led him onward. In none of the chambers was he offered refreshment after his long journey.

With each new threshold crossed, Francis felt his station rise. With each new threshold, the waiting crowds diminished. This prince was holding his subjects at a distance, he thought with interest. Dying monarchs were more often attended by a solicitous, ambitious flock of well-wishers hoping for death-bed favours.

His head began to swim with frescos and tapestries, with inlaid tables, ivory cabinets and still more statues. The *antecamarilla*, where the prince received bishops and ambassadors was altogether grander than its equivalent at Hampton Court. The great study beyond the *antecamarilla* was heavy with gilded swags, the final frontier for visiting cardinals and viceroys. Apart from the usual ushers, it was empty. Of living people, that is.

Entering the *camarilla*, Francis stared at a pair of Herculean twins shouldering the brass balls at the tops of a huge pair of firedogs. Half-naked nymphs propped up either side of doorways. Satyrs held candlesticks. Human bodies knelt beneath heavy marble tabletops, reached out towards each other along chair backs, buttressed the chimney pieces around fire places.

In the next room, the prince's grand *camera*, or sleeping chamber, Francis would have expected to find the truly important visitors who were paid the compliment of royal informality. No one waited there under the gilded ceiling, apart from a small page asleep in a corner. Almost the size of a small galleon, the royal bed stood vast and empty, centred against one wall, a miniature temple with fluted columns for bed posts and a gilded arcade marching around its heavy solid base. In spite of its feather pillows and damask curtains, it looked more like the work of an architect than a joiner.

Then gilded gesso and fresco gave way to polished wood and painted leather in another antechamber, which was in fact a good-sized retiring room. They had entered the realm of close acquaintances, trusted friends and informers.

Still no sign of the prince, thought Francis. Anything began to seem possible. Perhaps the man did not exist at all.

Having passed through the antechamber, the Castello officer knocked on yet another door.

'*Scrittoio,*' he explained. The private study of the prince, the end of the line of rooms. This was as far as anyone could go.

The door swung open. The craggy, ruined face of the prince of La Spada looked out from a huddle of wolf skins in a heavy high-backed chair. 'You came only from England, not the East Indies,' he said.

Francis smiled politely and stepped forward into a haze of burning herbs.

'What took you so long?' demanded the prince.

Francis forgot every word of his prepared speech, in Latin or any other language.

21

For flash of time, he thought that this room too was crowded with people. Then he saw that many were statues and paintings of the Virgin and saints. Others stared out from the walls with wide-eyed intensity, from behind curious blotches of terra-cotta paint that hide most of their bodies. Francis turned his attention to the only three living creatures in the *scrittoio* – the prince, a black-robed Jesuit priest and the girl who knelt at the prince's feet. Francis heard the prince's voice, forgot the priest and saw only the eyes of the girl.

He felt a sudden odd, urgent need to hold his ground. The gaze she lifted to him was both challenging and desperate, like the eyes of the young Spanish soldier whom Francis, equally young, had faced with sword in hand in his first fight to the death.

He looked back at her with a puzzled frown.

It was a straight animal gaze, without a trace of humour, civility, or graciousness. It held no hint of the formal courtesies you offer to a newly arrived stranger. He felt himself being anatomized, drawn in.

So there you are, her eyes said. Now what?

He waited in frozen stillness as if he had startled a deer

or she-wolf, held in place while the creature decided what to do next.

He could not have said afterwards what colour her eyes were. Their colour was a mere detail. Her look was so intense that, in meeting it, he accepted their shared leap, in an instant, from being complete strangers into a profound but unmapped intimacy. After a moment, he collected himself enough to offer the beginning of a smile.

Her lids dropped, delicate fortifications behind which she fled. As far as he could tell, she never looked at him again.

After the shock of her first quick look, Sofia kept her face down to hide her thoughts from those clear intelligent eyes. She would have said that they were green like seawater but would have to look again to be certain. Not yet, however, not until he had finished taking the measure of his surroundings.

This was not the man she had expected. This was not a brutish soldier, descendant of a man said to have massacred women and children after the promise of safety. Nor did he seem to be a court fop. This English fire master, descended from a long dynasty of military fire masters, was beautiful. A cool detached part of her noted that her heart was beating faster and harder than usual. She had not expected a beautiful man. She risked another quick glance.

Not quite beautiful, she decided. He had too much of a rough edge for pure beauty . . . even taller than her father, who had been magnificent in his prime. He was very fair, fairer than she was, like a Circassian from the Black Sea, or a northern German . . .

A chilling thought struck her. He looked a little like the Vranghi, her half-brother's personal guard of tall, fair or rusty-haired mercenaries from the mountains to the east of La Spada, descended for many generations from the ancient

Britons and Danish mercenaries. The English fire master might well feel a clan bond with such men. Ettore's mercenaries were not her friends.

A further glance told her that the broad shoulders were the Englishman's own, not a tailor's flattery of padded sleeves and standing rolls. And he was even taller than she had first thought. His way leaning forward slightly, as if in eager interest, had misled her.

She heard him inhale the heavy clogging scent of burning herbs, saw him glance at the brazier. His bow to her father, and his greeting, were easy and elegant in spite of his dirty travelling clothes that brought in the smells of an outer world of horses and active men.

Danger, danger, danger, thumped her heart. This man had an air of unthinking authority, which needed to be tamed. She might have to reconsider her strategy with him. When you mean to use whatever weapon falls under your hand, you must be certain you can control it.

Francis held his bow for as long as he dared, buying time to compose his face.

Forget the girl! Whoever she might be . . . think only of the prince, your new patron . . . the man who now controls the length of your life.

He saw now why the ruler of La Spada might hide himself away from his subjects. The same age as Boomer but looking twenty years older . . . No, Francis corrected himself. Boomer would never look like that, however old.

Where it was not covered with brownish scars, the prince's skin was tinged a bluish grey. Tufts of dry-grass hair bristled from under a knitted silk cap. A once-powerful frame hunched shivering under a wolf-skin rug.

The Great Pox, thought Francis, with a twist of revulsion. Cecil's agent had been right. Francis had seen the disease often enough among his men during his two years in Flanders. Death was indeed standing close behind the prince's chair.

The prince's left foot wore a curved Turkish slipper over a thick silk stocking. His bare right foot rested in the young woman's lap. A small pot carved from purplish stone sat open on a red silk napkin on the floor beside her, along with some linen swabs.

Francis could not resist another curious glance. Black satin billowed around her collapsed farthingale. An immodest expanse of creamy flesh set off several jewelled chains. The low, wide-cut neckline of her bodice was edged with pearls that matched her skin.

His hands could almost feel the tender softness of those half-exposed breasts.

A heavy dog collar of gold weighed down her slim neck. Her dark red-gold hair was unveiled but bound up at the back in a beaded net of golden wires. Not a serving woman, for sure.

He looked helplessly back at that creamy flesh.

Hell and damnation! He didn't need this. But he couldn't take his eyes off her neither. Dressed like a picture he had seen of a very expensive Venetian whore. Full court rig. And lovely neat ears, with more pearls reflecting warm lights from her skin.

The prince was speaking. Francis tried to listen.

She wore a ring on her marriage finger.

Francis felt sick at the thought of her in bed with this ruin. He could smell the man's putrefaction through the scent of pine and rosemary burning on a large shield-like brazier.

'. . . may already be too late, unless you can work fast . . .' the prince was saying, his voice rising in anger. 'Your predecessors have all failed even to begin!'

Francis sketched a second smaller bow to give his reason time to catch up with the sudden new question of predecessors.

Cecil did not say that he had sent anyone before Francis.

'I will endeavour to serve your highness in whatever you desire,' he began.

'Endeavour's not good enough! Can you? Yes or no?'

'I wish to be certain that I understand exactly what you want me to do,' said Francis carefully.

'Fire me up to Heaven. Are you simple or deaf?'

22

'To Heaven?' Francis repeated.

The prince glared at him. 'You are a fire master?'

'Indeed. I am.'

'You shoot rockets up into the sky and fire projectiles over long distances?'

Francis nodded agreement, beyond speech.

'Then I order you to project me to Heaven. I must ascend like the prophet Elijah, amid whirlwinds, in a chariot of fire, to the very foot of God's throne.' The prince fumbled amongst some papers in his lap. 'Look here! And here!' He waved two manuscript pages. 'I have it on good authority that St Paul himself was assumed bodily up to Heaven. Bodily! D'you hear? On good authority! The thing is possible!'

Francis swallowed. So much for Cecil's hopes of reasonable re-negotiation of the debt. The raided ship, the boy in the chest, and the English corpse flying from the mast made sense now. The prince was completely north by northwest, as addled as a year-old egg – but rather more dangerous.

'Your highness,' he began carefully. 'Your request finds me unprepared. I was told that you wanted me to create a firework display.'

The prince gave him a look of deep cunning. 'Of course, you didn't know my true purpose! State secrets, Signore Cointo. Where are your wits? Why would I hire a foreign fire master – and English at that – if I did not need absolute secrecy? A Roman or Venetian would be too close to home and surrounded by temptations to blab.'

Francis nodded in wry understanding. 'Of course.'

Oh, my lord, he said silently to Cecil. I did warn you!

'Do you imagine, for instance, that the Church would permit me to do such a thing if it knew?'

Francis glanced at the Jesuit priest sitting on a stool in a far corner beside a small altar, eyes on a book in his lap. The Roman Catholic Church. 'Not for a moment, your highness.'

The prince followed his glance. 'Don't fear Father Daniele. He's mine.'

Francis nodded, unconvinced. Even corrupted priests can overlook heresy only so far. And not at all if they are secretly agents of the Roman Inquisition. He looked again at the Jesuit.

Whether or not he was the prince's thing, the priest wore the black robes of men who sent other men to the stake for painting an angel's wing in the wrong way. He was invested with the authority of men who claimed exclusive right to interpret God's Will and to define heresy. To Francis, going to Heaven before you were invited sounded very much like heresy.

'Are you comfortable in your lodgings?'

Francis murmured politely. He did not say that he'd not yet seen them.

'I wouldn't stable my horse there,' said the prince. 'Tomorrow you will move to my hunting lodge just outside the city, where you can work in secret. No spies there except my own.' He raised his brows and gave a bark of a laugh to mark this last point. 'Not even spies of the Roman Inquisition, who would prevent me if they knew! They can't tolerate the thought that any man might speak directly to God without their interference!'

The girl kept her eyes on the floor. The Jesuit seemed not to have heard.

'The best lies are near-truths,' said the prince, leaning forward in confidence. 'Therefore, you must also make fireworks as cover for your true work. To explain your presence in La Spada, I have announced that you're here to devise my funeral fireworks. In truth you will be preparing my Ascension!'

So much for writing off the English debt, thought Francis, fighting the suck of despair. At least, he now understood the prince's terms. Funeral fireworks were indeed almost worthless to him, except as a distraction. Whereas, a flight to Heaven would be worth every penny of the English debt, however large it might be.

However great the debt, Francis thought, the prince would be buying me cheaply if I could do what he wants. Unfortunately for both of us, and for Cecil, and England, it's impossible.

He must find that watcher-of-his-back and let Cecil know the true circumstances of the prince's commission. He needed to know what Cecil wanted him to do now. The debt could not be written off after all. He didn't see much hope for Cecil's desired alliance either. He wondered, half in earnest, how far he would have to run to escape a disappointed Cecil.

The prince waved Francis closer, which was far closer than Francis wished. A cratered but still forceful hand closed on his wrist.

'The court is filled with those who want me dead.' The man's breath was a blast from an open grave. 'Move a little off, where you can't hear us.' The last was to the girl.

She removed from her lap the prince's foot, which he seemed to have forgotten. Then she rose and went to stand at a far window, looking out. She was as exquisite in motion as she had been in stillness.

Francis tried to attend to the prince's words, but kept looking sideways at the way the light outlined her shape. The heavy net of her hair pointed down at her hips hidden inside the black silk cone of her skirts. She raised one arm and rested it in a graceful curve against the window arch. Francis felt a dangerous tightening in his belly and groin.

Wife? Mistress? Slave? Men bought female slaves even in Venice.

'I am dying,' said the prince. He released Francis's wrist to raise his large hand. 'Don't waste my time with protests; I know the symptoms . . . when I can know anything at all. Time is short. We must be blunt. My past sins are killing me. And, alas, I can no longer even remember the pleasures that bought me this pain.'

Francis took a grateful step back.

'My sins will also condemn me to hell unless you can project me to Heaven.'

'Surely, God decides the direction of your journey after your death.' Francis glanced at the priest, hoping the man had noted these blameless words.

'You grasp it exactly,' cried the prince. 'You must send me to Heaven whilst I'm still alive!'

'But the journey would kill you for sure!' protested Francis, unable to believe that he was taking part in such a mad debate.

'That might be a difficulty,' said the prince. 'But surely not an insuperable one. In any case, you must arrange it so that I fly at the exact moment I begin to die.'

Francis looked at the girl for her reaction to this madness. She did not move.

'I must arrive at the foot of God's Throne at the exact instant that my soul parts from my body, before I can be snatched down to hell. Once there, I will convince Him to let me stay in Heaven.' The prince gave Francis another crafty look. 'I have considerable proven powers to persuade.'

Francis nodded in what he hoped was a thoughtful manner. He no longer dared look at the priest. This incredible scene was testing his playhouse skills to their limit.

'The vital point is that I must not die before I fly,' said the prince. 'If I die too soon, before I can reach Heaven, then hell will have me, without chance of appeal. My soul must leave my body only after I have reached Heaven. I must not die before . . .'

'Yes, your highness, I understand,' Francis said quickly.

'You must do it!' The prince's voice rose. 'Or I will burn for Eternity! Do you know how it feels to burn?'

All too well, thought Francis. And how it looks . . . and smells.

The prince clambered to his feet, dropping the fur rugs. 'If you dare refuse to help me, I'll have you burnt!' he shouted. 'So you'll learn how it is!' He staggered, tried to catch himself, but one leg rebelled. He seized the back of his chair. 'If you refuse the work I have hired you for, I will demand my money back from the English king himself! I will send him your charred corpse in place of an account.'

Francis leapt forward, grabbed him and began to lower him back into his chair.

'I can't! I must not . . .!' wept the prince.

'Father!' The girl turned from the window. 'Let me . . .!'

His daughter! Francis felt a relief that he didn't care to examine too closely.

'Go!' she ordered Francis, pushing him aside. 'He's past caring now.'

She gave off a delicious smell of jasmine and limes. Then

her eyes met his again. 'Welcome to La Spada.' Like her father, she spoke Latin, the universal language of European diplomacy.

As he left the prince's *scrittoio*, Francis noticed at the bottom of one blotched fresco a pair of copulating mice.

The prince intended a heresy far worse than daring to interpret God's Will for himself. He meant to challenge it.

Francis shook his head to himself in disbelief. He sat on the side of the canopied bed, stripping off his filthy stockings while Richard laid out his best suit of clothing.

The prince meant to make God change His mind, with the help of Francis.

He wriggled his bare toes thoughtfully. He could try to steal the bond now, then cut and run. Either retracing their journey from Aquileia. Or perhaps overland. He must learn as quickly as possible about any overland routes to Venice and the protection of the English ambassador, Sir Henry Wootten. He wriggled his toes again. It might be best after all to learn, if he could, what Cecil wanted him to do now.

The girl at least, was most likely sane. Francis could swear he had seen a gleam of amusement in her eye when she welcomed him to La Spada.

'Have our swords been returned? he asked.

'Not yet.' Seaborn knelt and opened a second travelling chest.

When Francis had at last found his way to his *camera*, Seaborn told him that there was to be a banquet that evening in Francis's honour. Wearily, Francis now prepared himself. Urgent as food had become, he would now almost rather sleep.

Their temporary lodgings were not in the new *Magno Palazzo* but in the old heavy stone *fortezza*, that they had seen from the outside. Francis's bedchamber, centred on a vast bed, the *cama*, made of gilded wood and heavily draped against the cold drafts, had the low ceilings and dark, damp stone walls that Francis had expected to find elsewhere. However, the transforming magic of frescos continued even here. The vaulted stone ceiling had been plastered, then painted a clear pure blue and illuminated with gold stars that winked and gleamed. This ceiling made Francis feel unstable, about to fly upwards, as he sometimes felt when he looked up for too long at real stars in a real night sky.

He watched Seaborn but did not feel ready yet to confide in him, nor certain where to begin, nor did he know how much of the truth to tell.

'My most urgent question,' he said finally, 'is how to make myself fit to sit amongst the nobles of La Spada. Have you discovered yet how we might conjure up a basin of hot water? Perhaps even a little soap?'

'Sir,' Richard sketched a bow, which may or may not have been ironic. 'I have already arranged for you to bathe.'

Francis stood up and shoved his feet into his house slippers, which Seaborn had already unearthed in a chest, wondering wryly how it was possible to ache so much to box the ears of a perfect manservant merely for being perfect.

23

Yet again, Francis did not find what he expected. To him the word 'baths' conjured up the old stews of Southwark, the public bathing houses with their huge, steaming communal wooden tubs, so frequented by prostitutes that 'stew' became the popular name for a brothel.

At the baths in Castello La Spada, in a pink marble entrance chamber, a page civilly stripped Francis of what remained of his clothes. He stepped naked through the next door into a hot cloud.

His lungs at once filled with heavy, steamy air faintly scented with lavender and roses. The steam was so thick that he could not judge the size of the room. The nearest wall, just visible, was covered in blue and white tiles, inset with ornate stonework grilles. Under his bare feet lay a warm chequer board of white, black, and dark red marble squares.

The cloud spoke. 'Signore, please sit here for a time.'

Then Francis spied a misty shape spreading a towel over a heavy carved stone bench. A good many other men could be hidden in here, as well he thought. But no one else spoke or leapt at him out of the cloud with a dagger.

'*Caldarium?*' Francis asked with interest. He had heard of

such places but never been in one. He might have been in Stamboul, or anywhere else in the realm of the Great Turk. 'How is it heated?'

His soldier's Italian and fluent Latin were equal to the answer – yes, the *caldarium*, heated by hot air in the spaces under the floor.

A Roman hypocaust, he thought with relief. At last, he had bagged something familiar. A known word to stabilize this slithering new geography in which he found himself. The Roman Empire, Rome in its glory days.

He then sat in silence on the towel, feeling his muscles soften in spite of his need to remain alert to face this banquet in his honour. The marble floor, which he would have expected to chill his feet, was very warm. Sweat rolled down his forehead and trembled on his brows. It gathered on his chest. Drops trickled down his ribs and the backs of his arms. He began to ache for a nap.

Take care, he thought. This seductive ease may be no accident, any more than the princess's carelessly raised arm had been an accident.

He sniffed the damp hot air. The sweetness of rose and the sharper animal fragrance of lavender masked any scent of soporific herbs. Then he decided that the urge to hide in sleep was a very reasonable response to his day so far.

A naked youth appeared from the steam to summon him onwards through a domed hall that was almost clear of steam, past a round hip-deep marble pool into which a leering dolphin on one wall spat a steady arc of water. Smooth stone benches lined the three other walls. The air here smelled of mountain pines. The walls wore many different complex patterns of russet, blue and clear green tiles, inset with lacy stonework grilles.

In a smaller side room, now giddy with heat, hunger and exhaustion, Francis let himself be soaked in a stone tub of steaming water.

Like an old rooster being gently stewed until tender, he thought.

But warm through and through, at last – and beginning to smell better.

Boiled chicken, he mused drowsily. With almonds. Perhaps. Soon.

The youth dried him with harsh linen towels, then laid him out on the marble slab of a central bench and rubbed him with scented oil.

'How much of the Castello is kept warm like this?' Francis asked, before surrendering entirely to the blissful pummelling of his aching shoulders and back.

'Fire under the floor,' said the youth, uncertainly.

'Hypocaust,' murmured Francis again. Roman. A word learned as a boy from his tutor in the Small Parlour at Powder Mote. Rome, the model for later empires everywhere. Still something familiar, part of his known world. He allowed a limp arm to be taken up for vigorous attention.

The usher who delivered Francis to the baths told one of Sofia's ladies of the wardrobe who told the maid of the wardrobe, who told Isabella, who slipped into the antechamber of the prince's *scrittoio* and told Yuri who gave a message to the princess. Sofia would reward each of them in time.

Her father seemed to sleep. She stood up quietly from her stool. The ragged pattern of his breathing did not change. He did not suddenly open his eyes and demand to know where she thought she was going. She took a careful step backwards, then another. Waited again. Then she slipped from the room.

Unattended, she went down a narrow staircase in the thickness of the wall – one of many in the maze of the Castello – to the floor where the baths had been built, three floors below the great rainwater tanks that pushed the arc of water out through the dolphin's beak. She let herself into a small closet, then stepped up onto the little dais where her father had often stood before he grew too ill. She pressed her face to the grille that had let him watch the palace women bathing naked and unaware of his eyes.

At first, the bath boy stood in her way. Then he stepped aside to refill his oil bottle. Sofia inhaled sharply. The Englishman lay naked, stretched out drowsily face down on the marble bench, his long limbs gleaming with oil.

Steamy air crept through the grille carrying the mingled scents of rose oil and purifying sage. Her heart drummed. It still warned 'danger, danger, danger,' as it had that morning, but she did not hear. Not even Baldassare had had such long elegant legs, nor such strong slim feet with such perfect, fine-boned toes. Her palm would fit exactly against the pale arch of his foot. The double mound of his indented buttocks and the wide, interlocking planes of his shoulders filled her with fascinated delight. She could not take her eyes from him.

What am I going to do? She had misjudged, badly.

The bath boy murmured something. The Englishman turned over onto his back. Sofia pressed clenched fists against the grille as she stared, shifting her head to get a better view through the stone lace. His genitals were as lovely as the rest of him, fair-skinned, not red nor creased with purple wrinkles. Golden fur framed them before climbing his flat belly to end in a point beneath his navel.

She was flushed as if caught herself in the steamy heat of the bath chamber. I've seen naked men before this, she reminded herself. And not just Baldassare.

Ever since her father's illness began to keep him away from this place, she had taught herself to spy through this grille to grow accustomed to the sight of naked males, so

137

that she could learn to despise them. She had studied them whilst they were off their guard, reduced to forked naked-ness without their furs, swinging cloaks, silks, velvets, bombast and rolls. When unprotected by their swords, spears, daggers or pens, their exposed wrinkles and potbellies, the narrow shoulders, bandy legs and flat feet helped her to fear them less even when they held so much power. It let her imagine that she might one day command them and be obeyed.

I have seen you naked, she would think as she looked a general in the eyes. I know as only your wife should know that you have the private parts of a small boy.

Her spying was not going to help her with this Englishman. Her eyes went back to his cock, lying in soft repose against his belly.

She was creased by sudden pain as she remembered her hopes for Baldassare.

That's gone, she told herself. Put it away. Put it away. Ettore will pay, in time. As soon as she could command the weapons and the power to punish him.

She watched the Englishman again. His hair was the colour of a bright harvest moon, neither silver, nor gold . . . like certain ducklings before they were fledged. His eyes were closed. His face wore an expression of sleepy pleasure that tightened her chest.

It was a terrible mistake to have spied on him. She would never be able to look him in the eye again, let alone despise him. Those eyes of his would be able to read her thoughts far too well.

The boy, now oiling his belly, leaned closer with a ques-tion.

The Englishman opened his eyes, gave the boy a level look and shook his head. Then he closed his eyes again.

Sofia unclenched her fists and wiped them on her skirt.

It should make no difference to her whether or not he chose to accept a matter-of-fact caress, or even more.

The first time she saw it, she had been shocked to learn that men did such things with each other . . . that people did such things. Now she shrugged. To most men it seemed to mean very little, whether with bath boy or page, even though it was held to be an abomination by the Church. If she wished, she could tell several of her waiting women things about their husbands or their intended husbands that might come as an unwelcome surprise. No longer shocked, she merely took note. It was always useful to know as much as you could about as many people as possible.

Perhaps the Englishman is one of their fervent Protestant prudes, she thought almost hopefully. It seemed necessary to find something unfavourable to think of him. She knew she should leave her spying place. There was nothing more she could learn.

But she stayed with her face pressed against the grille while the bath boy scraped the oil off that long lean body with a pair of seal skin gloves. She watched the Englishman stiffen suddenly when someone else came into the outer chamber and stay alert until he heard them splashing in the pool. She watched him sit up at last, flushed and tousled. He raised his eyes and stared straight at the grille. Sofia leapt back so abruptly that she almost slipped and betrayed herself by falling.

He can't possibly have seen me! she told herself. She had made certain of that herself long ago by bathing in that same chamber. Nevertheless, she crouched in the darkness of the closet, trying to breathe quietly, until she heard his voice leave the baths from the central pool chamber.

She had to keep a cool head. Make only the right choices. No mistakes. Her father failed day by day. Time was growing short before he died, or someone . . . Ettore . . . Da Monte

. . . decided to hasten his death and seize the crown. Or the Hapsburgs understood his true weakness and invaded to reclaim La Spada. Or the Great Turk presumed on the rumoured *entente* with England and pushed into Europe again. She sat on the edge of the little dais in the near dark, thinking hard about what she heard daily when Da Monte told her father about state affairs.

Sofia watched people closely. After watching Da Monte, she suspected him of ambition beyond his present title of grand *Camerlano*. A cousin of the prince, he served as unofficial regent during her father's decline. He was already the *de facto* ruler of La Spada, receiving envoys in her father's name, sending out documents bearing the prince's signature and seal. He consulted and informed her father from policy alone.

The lions told her his true feelings. He had confided in close friends about her father's growing madness and the threat that it posed to La Spada. According to one *denunzio* he had twice said that he feared the prince would have him killed on the spot for an imagined slight. He had not, however, suggested overturning the prince.

Da Monte was not an impossible ally, she thought. For the moment, the duke seemed loyal to her father, whatever his private reservations. He had been fond of Sofia's mother, might even have once hoped to wed her, though Sofia had never been able to confirm that rumour. He had a weakness for lovely young women. And he had clashed on several occasions with Ettore. He was also astute enough to know that Ettore might very well either kill or banish him. Best of all, after watching him step back from moments of crisis, Sofia suspected that he was, in truth, suited to being second-in-command.

As for her half-brother . . . She could still feel her nails tearing his cheeks, and the hands of the attendants who finally managed to pull her away. She could still hear his voice, falsely sincere, falsely forgiving, as he explained to the prince and anyone else who would listen. His poor half-sister had been so maddened by the loss of her new husband that she had turned her fury onto the nearest person, who had merely run to help.

I marked you! I will prevent you! she swore in the darkness of the closet. They won't be able to pull me off next time.

Unlike Da Monte, Ettore might well raise a rebellion against his father, as much from fear as from greed for power. A bastard could never feel entirely secure in a succession – look at that Lutheran queen of England, Elizabeth Tudor, a bastard in the eyes of the True Church, who had executed her closest legitimate rival, her cousin Mary. Ettore might already be feeling the effect of the small drops of poison Sofia was dropping with great care into the caldron of their father's mind through the lions. But slowly. Too much was as dangerous as too little. Neither father nor brother must be pushed too far before she was ready for the fight.

Only one thing was absolutely clear. If Ettore succeeded his father, she was dead. By apparent accident, like Baldassare, or as good as dead in some convent on a remote mountaintop. She could risk no mistakes with Ettore. Her half-brother would not give her a second chance. The Englishman must help her. That was why he was in La Spada.

Think ahead!

Who else must she fear?

Her father, of course. If anyone were safe with him, she was. But constant land slips changed the terrain of his mind every day. One day he might turn even on her – his little bowl of cream, his dove, his elixir of life – with more than a slap.

She drew a deep breath. Everyone was living in fear of

her father's rages. Therefore everyone was dangerous, like vipers fearing a careless boot.

She pressed her hands to her cheeks. They felt hot, as if she were starting an ague.

Think ahead – the most vital rule of all. But wasn't that what she was doing right now?

Be patient. That rule lived in her blood and bones. Every day tried her patience to breaking point, but she would not let it snap.

Try to think ahead, she told herself again. She had meant to use the Englishman to advance her cause. She had thought to enlist him with promises of money and eventual power. She did not need to watch him to know that these things were not his price.

Distrust your own desires.

She stood up angrily. There was no need to remind herself of that rule. She had no desires to be distrusted – only the knowledge that she must rule La Spada or accept death in one shape or another.

24

A splatter of applause brought Francis to an astonished halt just inside the door. The applause was for him.

He was back in the great *sala* through which he had passed on his way to meet the prince. The jostling petitioners were gone. Long tables had now been set up for the evening's banquet. At least eighty pairs of eyes stared at the two extremely tall, blond foreign visitors. Heads bent together in comment.

'The famous English fire master,' someone explained loudly in French. A man laughed.

Francis flushed. The edge was unmistakable. In any case, being at the centre of attention still made him flinch, even after two years of fame at the English court. He had grown up with secret tunnels and solitary danger in the powder mixing shed. His work attracted attention – oh yes, indeed it did. But he himself had stayed in the shadows, known only to the few other men he had trusted with his life.

A serving groom led him to a folding wooden chair at the table just below the royal dais. Having achieved his seat, Francis looked about him. Seaborn seemed to have disappeared.

A pretty woman with black hair and flushed bosom smiled across the table. The man next to her met Francis's eyes, warning him off.

Now that he had recovered from his surprise, his frank return gaze made the man's eyes slide away.

Blond hair sat next to black, fair skins next to brown. He could hear at least three different languages being spoken around him, in addition to Latin. An envoy from Portugal leaned across the table speaking accented French to a small elderly Jesuit. The man seated on Francis's left made no attempt to talk to him but harangued the man across from him in what Francis thought might be Ladin. His right-hand neighbour seemed to speak both Italian and French but neither of them as his native tongue. A plump, snub-nosed man who spoke Italian with what sounded to Francis like a very English accent gave him a curt nod, belched and turned away again to his neighbour a little way down the table.

Francis watched him for a moment, wondering if this was Cecil's watcher-at-his-back. The man did not look at him again.

The two Jesuits he had seen in the *antecamarilla* were sitting with two other members of the Congregation of the Inquisition. The taller of the two priests whom he had seen on his way to meet the prince now gave him a civil nod and continued his open study of the English newcomer.

Francis nodded back and looked next at the room. The great *sala*. The surprising sense of light and air was here too. Light falling through a band of high clere-story windows was caught and redoubled by mirrors and gilded surfaces.

All surfaces that were not gilded swarmed with frescoed figures. From the high panelled ceiling Roman gods and goddesses supervised four different battle scenes, one on each wall. The leaping torches and wavering candles that dispelled the early dusk made the armoured figures seem to move.

There's a fair bit of looting represented here, thought Francis, eyeing Greek statues in alcoves. Florentine mosaic tables holding Ottoman-style vases and gourd-shaped Chinese porcelain urns jostled for space amongst the crowd of waiting diners. He tilted his head back to look up at a false painted gallery he had noticed earlier, peopled with sharp-eyed, well-dressed women caught in mid-gossip, looking back at him, interspersed with fierce-looking soldiers and richly robed men.

'Art to glorify God and the Church, eh?' said his right-hand neighbour suddenly.

Uncertain of the man's tone, Francis merely smiled. He waited for a sign that this might be Cecil's agent, but the man turned away again.

Francis gazed about, looking for the small wizened man who had studied him so intently. He had not expected to need Cecil's help quite so soon, nor to have information that Cecil, for all his intelligencers, seemed to lack.

On the wall behind him, a carved green marble fountain the size of a large fireplace spat water into an ornate semi-circular basin balanced on a dolphin's snout. People gathered around it, washing their hands and wiping them dry on linen towels offered by waiting servants.

Francis spied Richard at a place near the bottom of the board, seated among the underlings who rated only benches.

He serves here voluntary, Francis reminded himself. It had been Seaborn's choice in the first place to let his new passion for fireworks suck him willingly down to the level of trade.

Cecil's back-watcher might very well be a servant, thought Francis. Or stable hand or mercenary soldier, who would not dine in the *sala*.

An invisible consort of strings, harps and cymbals began to play. There was a rushing and scraping like a wave breaking on a shingle beach. Those who already sat leapt to their feet again. First to enter were six guards, dark and stocky, marching two by two in blue and red livery with silver sashes. Uskoks – Francis recognized Venturini and two of the others. Then came a white-haired man, who was, whispered Francis's neighbour, the governor of the Castello. Behind the governor walked a short, dark wiry elderly man, richly dressed in dark blue velvet with a fur collar on his robe and skin like tree-bark. Francis glanced at his neighbour with raised brows.

'The Duke. Da Monte. The grand *Camerlano*.' He looked at Francis and repeated '*Camerlano*?' Then he waved dismissively. Too complicated to explain.

The Lord Chamberlain, Francis decided. Though what that title might mean here, he had no idea.

Behind Da Monte marched eight tall fair men with blond or russet hair. Two of them were taller than Francis. Three were of his height. All were built like fair ground wrestlers. Francis looked at his neighbour again.

'The Vranghi,' said the man. 'Prince Ettore's *bravi*. His Praetorian guard.'

A herald now raised his voice. A wave of bows and curtsies swept through the *sala* to greet the entrance of a dark slightly heavy young man wearing sober midnight blue that flashed with silver and jet. A layered collar of white lawn framed his face. His cap of soft black velvet carried a vast single pearl. As he passed, Francis saw a pale tracery of scars on his sun-darkened cheeks.

Francis bowed along with the rest. *Principe* Ettore Ferdinando San Sebastiano di Pirati. Legitimized heir to the throne of the principality of La Spada. Son of a dying madman, ambitions and intentions unknown. Handsome enough, though much shorter than his father, he kept turning his head in quick watchfulness, as if to catch a false move

146

or suppressed smirk. He was followed by six waiting gentlemen dressed almost as richly as he.

At a respectful distance behind her half-brother walked the girl with the questing eyes. *Principessa* Sofia Serafina Santa Catarina Adorata di Pirati, according to the herald. According to Cecil, the prince's only surviving legitimate child. She was followed by four ladies-in-waiting.

She wore black again.

Knows how well it suits her complexion, thought Francis. He had learned a thing or two from the English court ladies. Including how to ignore his own surges of a hunger to touch their flesh or to fill his nose with their smells.

Gourd-like puffs of silk sat just below her shoulders. Tight sleeves outlined the length of graceful arms and ended in turned-back cuffs of stiffened gold lace. A high pale standing collar rose behind her head but left her neck bare where an Englishwoman would have worn a ruff. In place of the chains and heavy gold dog collar she had worn earlier hung a single rope of Russian amber that flashed in the light. Her hair was now braided and wrapped around her head into a crown that glinted with tiny lights of exactly the same colour as those of her amber necklace. Where her brother was over-alert, she seemed deliberately veiled, cool and self-contained, moving a little as if in a dream. Then Francis saw the quick smile she launched at one of the men she passed.

He steadied himself, but she did not so much as glance in his direction.

After she took her place, everyone sat down. The Uskoks stood on one side of the royal dais near the *principessa*, the Vranghi on the other by Ettore. Their father, Prince Alessandro, did not appear.

Francis hauled his gaze away from the *principessa* to try to read the loyalties of the people around him as they in turn watched the royal pair on the dais. Here was where

Cecil excelled. Francis envied him his skill in reading the finest nuances of fervour in an eye. Cecil could detect argument in the silent compression of lips and treason in a raised brow or head bent to murmur.

Prince Ettore was staring at him.

Francis bowed his head respectfully.

The prince kept staring, deep in his own thoughts.

There's another one to try to watch, thought Francis. He was beginning to feel weary beyond description.

The royal brother and sister sat coldly side-by-side, speaking rarely, never smiling. As he speared a slice of roast duck off a central platter with the tip of his knife, Francis wondered whether the princess lusted for her father's throne. If so, it might prove an interesting duel. He glanced at the faces chewing on either side of him. There were bound to be factions in La Spada, divided over the succession. There were always factions in any realm with a dying ruler and more than one possible heir. But how was a stranger to read them?

It was hard enough to try to grasp the nature of La Spada itself. Sinking fast into his intense weariness, Francis smiled and nodded, content to make the most of his first solid meal in two days.

Welcome as it was, however, the food increased his growing sense of dislocation. The dishes were both strange and familiar at the same time. With the expected eight dishes of roast meats – roast beef, pork and lamb – and the eighteen dishes of eight pigeons, he was also offered pickled smoked pork chops with horse-radish, artichokes in a cream sauce, and cabbage stewed with bacon, spices and wine as well as a very solid, very German boiled dumpling the size of his fist and flecked with ham.

He tasted a strange vegetable stuffed with herbs and crumpled into a wrinkled oily heap of purple-black skin and greenish flesh. It made his tongue burn slightly as he mopped up some of the oil with a piece of flat bread more like a pancake than an honest English loaf.

Without warning or previous glance, the princess sent Francis a melting smile. He was so startled that he almost forgot to respond with a smile of his own.

Then he saw that Prince Ettore had noticed and was staring at him again. Again, Francis bowed his head respectfully. Then he kept his eyes safely on his food. He had begun to feel a dangerous and inexplicable urge to laugh.

At the bottom of the table, among those seated on mere benches, Richard Seaborn was chattering in who knew what tongue to a buxom older woman who kept nodding and reaching out to touch his arm.

Francis gave up any attempt to think. The music had begun to mix with the babble of voices into a single blur of sound.

After seven hours in the saddle, arriving in a strange place, meeting the prince and learning of the impossible, heretical absurdity he had been hired to devise, followed by a bath and then, at last, food and wine, he wanted only to fall onto his bed and pray that sleep would bring clarity. Suddenly, he was too tired even to eat. He dipped his greasy fingers in the offered bowl of scented water, wiped them on a fine linen towel. Then he balanced on his chair, trying to keep his eyelids up while he waited for the prince and princess to leave the *sala*.

'Signore Cointo?' The usher had to repeat the name twice before Francis remembered that this was his new Italian self. 'Prince Ettore commands your presence. Please attend him when he leaves the hall.'

Francis didn't understand every word of the Italian dialect, but he caught the sense.

Wake up! he told himself severely. This may be the most

dangerous man of all – most likely, the one who will inherit Cecil's bond, if you haven't managed to snatch it by then. In all that heretical nonsense about shooting a man to Heaven, don't lose sight of the debt. Cecil wants that bond put safely back in his own hands.

Did Cecil have any idea what he has got Francis into?

25

'What does my father want with you?' Prince Ettore sat in a high-backed chair very like his father's, in his own study. He had dismissed all his attendants and spoke in thickly accented but intelligible English.

Either he already knows and is testing my frankness, thought Francis. Or he truly doesn't know and is testing my loyalty.

'To devise his funeral fireworks.'

Ettore stared thoughtfully as he had at dinner. 'You've already seen that my poor father is no longer as he once was.' He re-crossed his legs. One hand wandered to his scarred cheek then rejoined its fellow in his lap.

From this distance, the scars on Ettore's face twisted like rivers across the plains of both his cheeks. Not the marks of a blade, Francis thought, but as if the prince had fallen through a tree and been torn by branches.

'Be sure,' said Ettore intensely. 'There's no the taint of madness in our family. Do you know the saying, *"Chi la fa, l'aspetti"*? "As you sow, you reap," I think you say in England.' He regarded Francis steadily. 'The prince, my father, has reaped.

151

Whatever he asks of you, it is the will of a dying man who no longer knows his own mind.'

An invitation to treason. Francis nodded as blandly as he could, pretending not to understand.

In the eyes of Prince Ettore, his father clearly deserved his fate. Not much filial gratitude there.

'It's not unknown to design your own send-off to the Afterlife,' said Francis. 'Many men pen their own epitaphs.'

In the last two years, he had learned that he found it easier to be devious where he disliked. He disliked Prince Ettore.

'The prince, my father, imagines that his fable of funeral fireworks will explain your presence here in La Spada. An *English* fire master! As if we didn't have enough of our own.'

Francis felt more than dislike, he realized. Ettore filled him with a deep animal desire to snarl and bristle the ruff on his neck. Even the young man's mad father had been easier to like.

'As you clearly know your father's wishes, your highness, I will not insult you with repetition.'

Prince Ettore's eyes flashed with pure malice.

It wasn't just the veiled insults and reined-in scorn. Francis saw nothing he recognized as a fellow soul in those cold eyes. It was like looking into the eyes of a snake.

'Let us speak directly, as befits two men of action.'

Francis nodded. Take special care when a prince troubles to flatter you, he told himself.

'I will be the next ruler of La Spada. In time, but not yet. Meanwhile, I must keep my father from doing too much damage whilst he still holds power. La Spada needs my steadying hand. I need the help of all who wish her well. Are you among them?'

'I hope to serve all your family, not just your father.' He forgave Prince Ettore another flash of irritation. In the young man's place, he would want to kick his own backside too.

'You are not the first foreign fire master my father has hired,' said Ettore tightly. 'You should know that both of your predecessors died.' He watched to see the effect of his words.

'Fire master is a dangerous trade.' Francis spoke calmly. But this news of predecessors shook him nonetheless. Two of them, and both dead. He must learn urgently how they died.

'Even so, it might be safer to work for me than for my father. He has many loyal followers who believe they still obey the man they remember. I don't murder just because I'm impatient.'

'Ah,' said Francis. 'My predecessors.'

'You understand me at last.'

Francis looked back at the dark, cold, angry eyes. He nodded. Ettore could know of his father's lethal rages, however, without knowing of his plans to visit God. The more Ettore spoke, the more certain Francis became that the prince had not trusted his son with his intentions.

'If, while employed by my father, you learn anything counter either to his safety or to the good fortunes of our state, you will tell me. Just as my father is no longer entirely himself, he is no longer entirely the ruler of La Spada.'

'I understand.'

'Good,' said Prince Ettore. 'I shall order that you be well looked after during your stay here. I reward those who serve me. That is all'

Prince Ettore was straightforward if treason could be straight-forward. He might even be granted some excuse for his treason. There was no doubting the quick wit gleaming in his dark eyes. He was right to believe that La Spada needed a steadying hand. Reason said that he could well become the final arbiter of the English debt.

A courtier would have sworn loyalty on his knees, thought Francis glumly. And squared his conscience later.

As he followed the usher into the lower passageways of the old *fortezza*, Francis pondered the nature and number of those 'loyal followers' who still obeyed the prince, including the Uskoks. He could understand why they might fear the heir apparent. In spite of his claim to be a steadying hand, Ettore was as unsettling as open razors inside a fine silk sack.

'The prince, my father . . .' Lest Francis forget that he was of the true royal blood, no matter how basely born. Hungry and uncertain.

Ettore was as dangerous as his father.

A snake or a madman, thought Francis. He must deal with one of them.

When he reached his *camera* at last, he found Richard sprawled in exhausted sleep on his wool-stuffed mattress on the floor. He had left a note for Francis on the bed, beside a pile of candles.

'Good tidings, master!' he had written in an elegant copperplate hand that would betray him instantly to any schooled eye. 'You are important enough to be given beeswax, not mere tallow. We may survive the night.'

26

Though his body screamed for sleep, Francis tossed in his bed.

Had his two unfortunate predecessors truly been killed by the prince, as Ettore had suggested? And who were they? Agents of another power? Unfortunate mercenaries who had accepted a well-paid commission? Or merely failed mountebanks caught out in their deceits?

He threw himself onto his side. If either had been English, surely Cecil would have warned him! Where was Cecil's man, who might or might not know the answers to these questions? He turned onto his other side.

'. . . then steal the bond.' He could still hear Cecil's voice. To steal the bond . . . first find it . . . how? Then escape from La Spada and flee to Venice . . . two tall fair men? . . . think about that later.

Need time to find the bond, therefore pretend to comply with the prince's demand . . . with a Jesuit priest sitting right there to hear every word?

He sat up and pounded his pillow into a different shape. He lay down again.

To buy time to find the bond, pretend to satisfy the prince

while . . . by doing what? What the prince wanted was both mad and impossible . . . but how else was he to get the bond unless he . . . Unless he did what? Fired the prince to heaven?

He flung himself onto his other side.

Ho, ho!

He heard a bell ring faintly in the night signalling one of the *horae canonicae*, the obligatory prayers of monks and priests. He groaned and turned over yet again. The bell reminded him that he was in a Catholic country, among England's natural enemies. Worse than mere Catholics – among Jesuits, agents of both the Spanish and Roman Inquisitions, whose leader in England Cecil had ordered hanged, cut down, then drawn and quartered while still alive.

Francis skipped like a stone over the surface of sleep but never plunged into the depths. Almost . . .

Another bell brought him sharply awake, cold with absolute certainty.

Cecil had sent him to La Spada in full knowledge. He didn't want Francis to return.

The mournful notes of the bell hung in the air, then faded. Francis climbed out of bed and wrapped himself in his cloak.

This mission was Cecil's punishment. The end of their two-year amnesty. Cecil was no longer prepared to forgive Francis for lies he had told in the past. For the failure to report certain facts. The successful end to the Gunpowder Treason had justified the means, for Cecil if not for Francis. The Secretary of State had seemed, therefore, to forgive Francis. But no longer.

Francis stepped around Richard and went to the window. Beyond the faint shadows of rooftops lay only a thick darkness. He pushed the casement a little open. The air smelled like rain.

He shivered inside his cloak. The stone floor numbed his feet. He went back to bed. He still did not sleep.

You can't serve a powerful man without learning some of his weaknesses, he thought. During the terrible events of the Gunpowder Treason, Francis had learned a great deal about Cecil. Cecil would not tolerate having his weaknesses known. He dared not. He battled every day for power and for his life against jealous enemies who hungered to see him fall, including his own cousin Sir Francis Bacon.

Cecil meant for La Spada to be a lost cause. Francis knew it now.

Francis knew too much. It was time to replace him with another innocent. He tried to swallow but his tongue stuck to the back of his throat. He knew at that moment, beyond doubt that Cecil meant to be rid of him.

But his sick heaviness was only partly fear, sinking in the claws it had sharpened in uneasy dreams. He felt betrayed – by his own gullibility even more than by Cecil.

I almost began to pity him! thought Francis viciously. That hint of desperation in the voice . . . feigned! The weariness and sagging shoulders . . . feigned! Cecil had played him.

He even told me as much, thought Francis in cold fury at both himself and Cecil. Mocked me to my face. '. . . a soft heart and a taste for rescue.' And Francis, deafened by a rush of good will, had not listened.

Then he thought about the prince and his mad request. The summons to dinner had interrupted him before he could tell Richard the entire incredible tale of the prince's intention. Then after dinner, Prince Ettore had summoned Francis and Richard had made himself busy among the other servants, asking where to find oil for their boots and more candles, and where he would find his master's breakfast.

How splendid that some of us can sleep! Francis turned back onto his other side.

27

He woke again to the crash of rain against the window. The glass panes flashed brilliant white, then went dark again. Thunder grumbled.

He rose and crossed to the window again. Lightning scalped the peaks above them. The stones of the Castello quivered under the blows of thunderclaps.

Francis pushed open the window and offered his face to the storm. The air smelled emptied, as if everything in it had been burnt away. The sky leapt with sudden flaring brilliance. Lightning bolts fell on the peaks and sliced into valleys. It would be easy to believe in angry gods. No matter how much gunpowder he used he could never achieve such magnificence.

A ball of lightning the size of a man's head seemed to hover just outside the window, cold and silent amongst the blazing sheets and bolts.

'Richard!' exclaimed Francis. 'Wake up! Come, look!'

Sleepily, Seaborn joined him at the window.

'How could we achieve that effect, d'you think?' asked Francis. 'So still and yet it's fire . . . see how it shimmers!'

Seaborn shook his head in silent wonder but Francis knew

that the youth's keen mind was already probing at the possibilities.

When the ball lightning wandered off and disappeared, they turned back to the chilly room. Francis wiped his face and hair on the corner of his quilt. Richard lit a candle, dressed and left in search of breakfast for them both.

Francis waited, sitting on the side of his bed. He had worn down his earlier cold rage at Cecil with too much repetition. The storm had taken the rest. It was almost dawn now. Too late to sleep.

But losing that clarity had left him with uncertainty again, on all counts: Cecil's motives in sending him. The English bond. Whether Cecil did in truth know what he was sending Francis into . . . or not. What he should do now. He was still thinking himself around in circles, lurching and juddering like a cart with a broken wheel.

He went back to the window. The rain now fell in rippling sheets. Beyond the lower rooftops where the shimmering power of the ball lightning had hovered, he could see the faint shapes of needle rocks and splintered boulder staircases that climbed to block out the sky. Dawn was coming, but it would be late in seeping through the clouds.

Uncertainty had led him into this mess in the first place. He hadn't known what else to do with his life.

He did not care for this realization in the least.

The rain eased. The light outside the window suddenly changed. Although barely brighter than before, it took on a thinner, fresher texture than night's blanket of dense shadows. Day had arrived. Distant cows and chickens began to complain. Tiny bells announced animals on the move.

Francis heard knocking from the wall behind him. And again. He lifted aside a wall hanging and saw a small wooden door set into the stone wall. Seaborn stood on the other side.

'The panterer gave me the makings of a posset,' he announced happily, holding up two eggs and a jug of steaming milk. 'Someone wants to build up your strength.'

Francis was never certain just how much to read into his nephew's apparently straightforward remarks. 'Where did you learn to make a posset?'

'From Kate.'

Francis could detect no hesitation or awareness in Seaborn's voice, only the youth's fondness for his young grandmother-by-marriage. Praise Jupiter! That particular family skeleton was still a secret shared only by Kate, Boomer and himself.

'How did you learn about that door?' he asked.

'In the kitchens. There's a whole second castello between the walls of the first. For the servants to use.' Seaborn cracked an egg on the rim of a metal cup.

'And did you also, by chance, hear any rumour how soon we might be moved to that hunting lodge?'

Seaborn shook his head and concentrated on beating together eggs, milk and wine.

Seated at a small walnut table covered with a Turkey carpet, Francis broke off some bread, which Seaborn had also brought back with him. Even after their journey together as man and servant, he still felt uncomfortable eating while Seaborn waited for him to finish before taking his own meals. He watched the young man's deft, confident movements. Seaborn had lost no time in beginning to unlock the details of life in the Castello.

A dog wandered into the room, sniffed at their legs, accepted a crust from Francis, waited for a time in hope, then wandered out again.

At his age, Francis demanded silently, why should he care if his father was most likely right about bringing Seaborn after all, and he himself was wrong? He put down the bread and brushed a crumb from the table carpet. Then he gazed up at the golden stars on the ceiling.

Two passing maids glanced curiously through the door, which Seaborn had left standing a little ajar, to avoid the impression of wanting secrecy. On the advice of a fellow manservant, he said.

Seaborn now dismissed the house groom who was sweeping up the last of the ash from last night's fire and gave the night soil pot to a second groom.

'What would you have me do with those?' asked Seaborn. Together, they regarded their travel chests and bags, still packed.

'Nothing for the moment. Though I won't lay very high odds that His Highness remembers his promise to move us.' Francis stood up and made a restless circuit of the chamber. There was no knowing how long they must wait. It wasn't a day for moving about in the open in any case.

'Richard, I need your advice.' There, he'd said it.

Seaborn looked into the passage and firmly closed the door.

28

Sofia knelt in the royal chapel in the new *Magno Palazzo*, head bent, eyes closed, but she wasn't praying. The chapel was the only refuge from which her father's retainers hesitated to summon her. She often fled there to clear her thoughts.

Early morning prayers, well before dawn, attracted few people who were not in Holy Orders. The demands of risings and breakfasts among the nobility kept them and those who served them far too busy, just then, to serve God. Sofia knew without looking that only two of her waiting women knelt behind her, hoping that the *principessa* would note their piety. They imagined that she cared.

She knew every Order of Service by heart. Between kneeling and rising and reciting the *Ave Maria*, the *Pater Noster*, the *Confiteor*, she was carrying on her usual silent but impassioned debate.

As always, she greeted both Father and Son civilly in their own house, then ignored them. They were male. Therefore she treated them with caution and guile. Neither had ever responded to any of her prayers, that she could remember.

Then she spoke with the Virgin Mary, who sat smiling

vacantly under a heavy gold halo in a niche on her left, about what troubled her. From time to time she had asked the Holy Mother to intercede, although none of the mothers she knew of had been able to save even themselves. She would never dare trust a confessional priest with her true dangerous thoughts. Sincere confession broke at least two of her rules for survival. Number one – trust no one. And number three – hide your feelings and thoughts.

I must begin today, she told herself now. She thought that she knew what she must do, but it frightened her. She would have liked another voice to confirm her decision and to tell her that she was strong enough.

She did not know whom she was begging to be given strength. Perhaps there was a safer way. She had practised patience and guile for so long that taking action terrified her.

She squeezed her eyes tightly closed and tried to recapture the way she had felt on the back of her Barb mare just after her marriage, flying up the slope of the meadow with the wind blowing tears from the corners of her eyes, filled with the belief that all would now be well. That young woman clamped to her saddle could have done anything she wished – uprooted pines with her bare hands or stood in her stirrups to snatch the sun from the sky.

That feeling had lasted such a very short time.

She tried to push away the images that now invaded her head. Ettore . . . a demon made flesh . . . the man who killed her freedom . . . kneeling beside Baldassare . . . the sound of a neck breaking.

That gentle young man didn't deserve to step between us, she thought. He deserved joy, not a Pirati. I killed him by marrying him. Her eyes filled.

She shook her head. It was done. Gone. She must think only what to do next.

She leaned forward and dropped her forehead onto her folded hands. This is my last chance, she thought. Time is running out.

Please let me survive my father's rages, she begged. Throw a cloak of invisibility over me so that he no longer notices me. Let him sleep so deeply that I have time to do what I must. Let Ettore despise me and believe that I pose no danger to him. Let my father live long enough for this English fire master to carry out my will. If he agrees.

And if he did not. If she failed. If Ettore survived to become the new ruler . . . she knew what she must do then. If she could not rule in place of Ettore, she must kill herself before anyone else could do it.

She raised her head at the sound of rustling silk. The Duke Da Monte was lowering himself stiffly onto his knees across from her.

He was not known as a pious man.

When he saw her eyes on him, he inclined himself gravely.

Had she imagined that he held her eyes a little longer than mere courtesy required? She sent back her best smile, then dropped her gaze demurely. A snatched glance showed a flush rising beneath his greying beard.

Yes! she thought. Things were on the move. The duke's flush was a good omen for the day.

29

Francis finished telling about his meetings with both princes.

'To Heaven whilst still alive?' asked Seaborn in disbelief. 'My best advice is to cut and run, now.'

They exchanged grim smiles.

The familiar breadth of Seaborn's brow and the set of his jaw made Francis feel – almost – as if he were confiding in his father. But Seaborn was not Boomer. Francis did not yet know if he could trust his new nephew with his life. It was safer for Richard not to know that Francis must not leave La Spada without the English bond, written-off or not.

'So what will you do now?' asked Seaborn.

It would not be prudent to betray Cecil's confidence.

'What do you need me to do, France? I forced myself on you knowing a little of the dangers. Don't fear to make use of me.' Seaborn gave Francis a direct look. 'What else do I need to know? Why did Cecil agree to send you? His intelligencers must have warned him that the prince is mad.'

Francis could not lie to someone who looked so much like Boomer. He told Seaborn about the bond.

'So, flight is indeed a serious likelihood,' said Seaborn thoughtfully. He seemed not at all surprised to learn of the

English debt. He held up one hand and lightly counted off the fingers. 'First we dye our hair. Second, we shrink to the common height. Third, I steal provisions. Fourth, we turn invisible to descend the causeway. Five, we steal horses . . .'

'First, I find the bond and steal it,' said Francis.

Francis had his letter from Cecil identifying him to Sir Henry Wootten in Venice. And Boomer's to his former military colleague, now a lord and living in Trieste. Francis had hoped never to need either letter.

Wootten could offer them a safe house if they reached Venice alive. But they knew nothing of local loyalties and alliances between that city and La Spada. They had only the small amount of local currency that Cecil had provided for the voyage.

'Venice may love the Pope no more than London does,' said Francis. 'But how close to Venice must we travel before we're no longer seen as enemy spies?'

They stared at the floor in a long unhappy silence.

Seaborn had forgotten his servile pose and now sat at the little table with Francis. Absently, they both chewed on the bread. 'You can't go back without the bond?'

'And fail Cecil?'

'You must pretend to accept,' said Seaborn at last. 'Tell the prince that you'll do it.'

'Gull him, you mean?' Francis set down a spiced bread roll half-eaten.

'Make a show of complying, for the moment. The prince wants to be deceived. He begs you to deceive him. If he already believes his venture is possible, all you need do is explain how.'

'But, Rich, It's what I do most badly in all the world! I'd make a far better thief than mountebank!'

'But I have enough experience at deceit for both of us.' Seaborn gave Francis one of his rare lovely smiles. 'You can devise sky rockets, why not devise the mere promise of a novel one? Devise an explanation of a fiery chariot to Heaven. Buy yourself time to think of a way out, France. You know that you will.'

Francis stared back thoughtfully. He did not acknowledge the compliment but in spite of himself, he was pleased by Seaborn's faith, misplaced as it might be in this case. He was never certain what the young man really thought of his suddenly-discovered uncle, who was only a little senior, less well tutored and much less elegant.

'If I pretend to comply – and carry it off plausibly – there's the problem of the prince's confessor, who won't leave his side and will hear every absurd lie I utter.'

Francis stood up and began to pace, tracking after his thoughts, trying to step on the hems of his next words. 'That priest is compromised up to his ears as a churchman and will do everything he can to save his own skin once his master is dead – which will include betraying me. Heresy or fraud, he can't fail. Or else he's an agent of the Inquisition. Either way we're in the fire . . . I'm in the fire, that is . . . for doing nothing but spin tales.'

They both knew that if Francis were arrested and executed by the Inquisition, Richard would be put to the sword. Almost certainly, he would first be racked for evidence against his master. Unlike England, neither the Roman nor Spanish Inquisition had qualms about using the rack.

'From what they say in the kitchens, the prince does not accept refusal,' said Seaborn quietly. 'Never did, even before the pox ate his wits.'

Francis made another circuit of the chamber, gazed out at the steady drizzle, then struck the wall with the side of his fist. And one for Cecil – he hit it again. 'I must escape from this luxurious cell of ours before I . . .' He hesitated. The ready phrase 'go mad' did not want to roll easily off his tongue. 'I want to study the battle terrain. You need not come with me.'

They donned hats and cloaks and went to explore.

'Where is everyone?' asked Seaborn. They were headed through the low, dark passageways of the old palace towards the high ceilings and airy gilded opulence of the new *Magno Palazzo*, or so they hoped.

'Drowned,' said Francis sourly. They entered a small parlour, still in the old palace.

Francis heard a faint moan. They both froze and listened, heads raised. The moan was not repeated. Instead, Francis heard a long deep exhale of air. They turned together towards the far wall of the parlour. There was another long sigh. Francis felt a chill brush past him.

A curious bronze plaque had been set into the stone of the wall. Bronze eyes with pinpoint pupils stared back at them above a snarling lion's mouth. Francis felt cautiously into the shadowed gap between the jaws and met only empty space. He knelt and pushed his hand in until his sleeve jammed on the lion's teeth. He felt nothing but cold air pushing past him out of the hollow wall.

With Richard's help, he untied his right cuff, unpinned, then removed his padded jacket sleeve. This time his hand slid through the lion's mouth until his fingertips touched a back wall. He reached downwards. Even with his arm inserted past his elbow, he could not feel the bottom. At his eye level as he knelt was a flat plaque, just below the bronze snarl.

'*Denontie Secrete contro chi occultera . . .*' The next few words were too worn for him to read. '*. . . o colludera per nasconner la vera rendita . . .*'

'That's not Italian I recognize. Can you read it?' he asked Richard.

Seaborn leaned closer. 'We need more light to see clearly . . . "Secret denunciations against witchcraft . . ."' he read

168

slowly. 'And then it says, perhaps, "the failure to disclose tax liabilities . . ."'

'Fetch me that button.' Francis pointed to a tiny gleam on the floor against the far wall. He dropped the button into the lion's mouth and listened. The button fell into silence within the wall. As any messages of betrayal would seem to fall.

Francis stood and waited while Seaborn reattached his sleeve. He studied the lion mask. The betrayer would see his or her own twisted snarling, secret face staring back.

'So, the walls of La Spada have tongues,' he said. And it seemed that anyone might serve as their eyes. Cecil, for all his agents and intelligence gathering, had missed a trick here.

30

With its old and new parts taken together, the Castello of La Spada was a small self-sufficient town on its own. The administrative offices for the principality were in one of the older parts of the original damp stone *fortezza*, the chief offices of the royal household in one of the new wings. Ducking through courtyards and along open alleys, Francis and Seaborn also found stables, barracks, kitchens, gardens, church, water tanks, butchers and a locked, heavily-guarded armoury. Although Francis from the age of eight had been taught by Boomer how to read and remember a building, and was quick to assess its strong points and its vulnerable cracks, he often found himself lost.

It makes a good defence against invaders, he thought. You can counter-attack while they're stumbling around lost in the kitchens.

For the most part, the watch seemed to know who he was and allowed them to pass freely from one part of the palace to another. After nearly two hours, they turned into a damp passage that ran parallel to the outer wall. As they walked, they peered out through low narrow arrow slit windows at changing slices of the misty plateau floor below.

The parts, when you could see them, would add up to a single field of fire.

With amusement, Francis touched the stone walls. Bored soldiers of any nationality filled the long hours of watch in the same way. Carved initials. A tally of lines marking off long hours or days. A crude drawing of a standing cock. The words, *'MISeRERE NOBis.'* And, less piously but with equal fervour, *'Ric. F. podex est.'* 'Riccardo F. is an arse-hole.' He squatted down and looked with particular interest at several inscriptions in German.

They lifted the internal bar on a small but solid door. (Would resist a ram, Francis noted. You would need explosives or fire to break through.) On the other side, they found themselves tipped out into the open space of the large piazza in front of the *Magno Palazzo*.

Curved arcades of tall arches with two floors of windows above them, embraced the cobbled expanse. Under the arches, shops and market stalls were beginning to reopen after the storm. Lengths of silk were flung back over poles like flags – scarlet, purple, green and gold. Between the shop fronts, narrow doors guarded a deeper privacy.

They strolled under the arches, out of the drizzle, among a growing press of shoppers, porters, vendors and merchants in rich robes, with perfumed beards.

Francis turned his head eagerly, trying the air: frankincense, orange water, sage. Civet. Leather. Rosemary and lemon. Jasmine. Honey. But no tang of sulphur. No trace of an apothecary selling this breath of the devil – brimstone, other men called it – or mercury, verdigris, iron filings, copper salts, amber and pitch.

It occurred to Francis that if he were to pretend to try to fly the prince to Heaven, he must also begin to make those covering fireworks. Real fireworks. That much, at least, he could truly achieve.

171

La Spada Alta was even more mixed in population than it was in architecture and perfumes. Francis spied men and women dressed in Venetian, German and Moorish fashion. The shop-keepers were German, Italian, French, Hebrew, Greek and Turk. There were goldsmiths, gem merchants, vendors of Turkey carpets, of silks and pearls, and of the fine steel-work and small arms that Francis had admired on their journey, precious goods too valuable to risk in the open market square below.

No apothecary, however. In spite of the ten pack-animal loads of materials they had brought from England, Francis would need more if he undertook the prince's funeral fireworks in earnest.

'Perhaps in the lower market,' said Seaborn. '*Di sotto.*' Among the dates, sponges, dried apricots, chickpeas and camels they had seen the day before.

After circling the arcades, they climbed a flight of wet stone steps onto a broad terrace on top of the walls.

After a glance along the wet stone paving and puddles of the terrace, Francis leaned on the wall between two of the towers. 'It needs a strong wind.'

The view into the valley was very different today. Instead of a heart-stopping plunge there was a soft grey wall that oozed water into the air. The trade route to the east, into Hapsburg lands had disappeared under fog. As Francis watched, tiny, distant horses and mules, passing eastwards below the Castello, blurred, grew indistinct, and then vanished like a wizard's trick.

'I need fog in order to transport His Highness,' he said under his breath. 'Fog! Al-kazam! Gone to Heaven!' He felt a sideways glance as Seaborn decided that he was jesting and that he, Seaborn, would not have to set about investigating the biddability of fog.

'How many people know what the prince intends?' asked Seaborn. It was a sharp question.

'How many do I have to gull, do you mean?' asked Francis between his teeth. 'I don't know!' But it was the first thing he must learn if he wanted to turn mountebank and lie to a dying man.

There was the prince himself, of course. The priest. The son, perhaps. Ettore had called his father 'mad' but didn't mention heresy. And the daughter? Francis considered. 'The *principessa* may hear everything . . . the prince seems to consider her no more than he would a canary. But she fears him.'

Enough to keep his secret?

Or enough to betray him?

Francis watched a single horseman do the vanishing trick.

He lifted his face. Fog above. Fog everywhere. At any moment, he would turn court poet and start to imagine that this fog has arrived entirely as an obedient metaphor for his own confusion.

'Signore Cointo!' 'Inglese?'

Three Uskok guardsmen took solid shape on the terrace.

'We searched everywhere.' Venturini sounded aggrieved, as if Francis had been deliberately hiding. 'The prince demands you, at once! *Subito! Schnell! Celerime!*' He thrust an arm in front of Seaborn. 'Not you. Just your master.'

31

'You fled yesterday without my permission.' The prince glared at Francis from his chair. 'Before you had told me how you mean to transport me to Heaven.'

'I don't believe that I had agreed to do it, sir.'

The *principessa* again sat at the prince's side, on a low stool, in a pool of black silk, silent, avoiding Francis's eyes. But listening, oh, how closely she was listening. The Jesuit confessor, however, was not on his stool. Francis kept his eyes averted from the ruined frescos where he had just noticed the rutting stag.

'Don't be coy,' said the prince. 'You're a solider . . . yes, I know all about you. Your name, Cointo, is well known here. Useful fellows for taking castles, if they're in your pay and not that of your enemy.'

Francis decided not to remind the prince that it had been his grandfather who made himself so useful in Friuli, not himself. He cared even less to ask whether an ally or an enemy of the prince's forebears had paid.

'Are your wages too low? Is Cecil a miser?' Before Francis could protest that the return of the bond would be wage enough, the prince grinned knowingly. He tapped his nose with a terrible, blue-nailed finger. 'It's not enough to serve, eh? Honour and gratitude fill no bellies? I know how poorly the mighty often pay those who do the true work. Fetch my purse.' The last was to his daughter.

'I don't need . . .!' Francis clamped his teeth shut. Bribes, he had almost said.

'Then what will satisfy you, if not riches? Do you want my daughter?'

She stopped dead, half-way to an inlaid cupboard.

Francis felt the blood climb his neck and flood his face.

'There she is – a widow, already spoiled. But lovely all the same. Take her for a night . . . or three. Her value to me lies elsewhere. Just be sure to give her back and keep your mouth shut.'

His ears burned hot enough to set fire to his hair. He glanced at the princess. She stood with her back still turned. 'I thank you, sir, but the princess is far too precious for the likes of me.'

'You can have whatever you need. No matter how much. Speak, man – it's yours! Give him the entire purse.'

The princess turned and held out an embroidered kidskin pouch crusted with gold braid. Francis did not take it. He could not look at her.

'Take it!' The prince's voice began to rise. 'I have others – all yours. Take whatever you need, but do as I ask! If you need workmen, ask . . . smelters, smiths, alchemists. If you need the blood of new-born babes, ask!'

'I need the English bond in my hand.'

Francis heard the prince's breath rasping in and out of his throat. The bloodshot eyes sharpened and went very cold.

'You mean to deceive me,' said the prince. He sounded suddenly in complete ownership of his reason again. 'I'm dying but not yet completely without my wits.' He leaned forward in his chair and grasped the arms as if he would break them off. 'If I give you the English bond, what will you do? I know! I'm not a fool!'

The princess half-raised a hand, then dropped it again. Francis felt her will suddenly beating at him like a wind but did not know which way it pushed. She made no further move to calm her father.

'You would steal the bond and escape without honouring it!'

'No, I would not!' Francis stepped closer to the prince and glared down at him. 'Haven't I just refused your bribes?' There, he'd said it. He eyed the battlefield of rage and naked desperation that was the prince's face.

'Sir . . .' Francis thought it now politic to bow ever so slightly. 'I want no more than you promised the English Secretary of State. If you were not the ruler here and I were not a mere foreigner who depends on your good will, I would call you out for the insult.'

'You would, would you?'

'And be thoroughly thrashed.'

'Once,' said the prince. 'Oh, yes. Once I would have had your heart out.'

But now you need me, Francis reminded himself. Just now, I have a little power. But fragile, fragile. He took a deep breath and prepared to follow Seaborn's advice. He wished the princess were not there to hear it.

'I will undertake to do as you wish.' He could not force himself to say 'fire you up to Heaven.' 'And I accept willingly all that you can give me to help in the endeavour. But it will be dangerous, and difficult. What if it proves impossible?'

He heard the rustle of silk as the princess moved, shifting her weight, taking a half step forward. Stopping. How long would she allow him to spout such nonsense?

'Impossible?' asked the prince. 'No, no, no, no! It must not be impossible! Swear that it is not impossible!'

'I swear to try with all my powers to overcome impossibility,' said Francis quickly. 'We will test its limits. And triumph!'

But, sweet Jupiter, how? And the girl now believed him to be a mountebank! How long did he have until she accused him?

'Such a thing has never been tried,' he explained. 'There are many questions to answer. Mistakes are possible. I must concern myself a little with your royal safety, for example.'

'You sound half-hearted.'

'No, sir. Merely modest about my own abilities.'

'All the resources of La Spada are yours to command! You are buoyed up by my will. You must send me to the foot of God's Throne! Challenge impossibility! There will be no mistakes. Tell me that you have no doubts!'

Francis hesitated for a fatal heartbeat.

'Yuri!' shouted the prince. His manservant ran into the room from the ante-chamber where he had been coiled to spring up at the sound of his name.

'Fly!'

'Your Highness, you know I can't!' The manservant looked startled.

'Do you disobey me?'

Fear began to glaze the manservant's eyes. 'I would do anything you ask if I could. You know how faithfully I've served you . . . through your illness . . . when others have . . . Highness, I beg you!' The man fell to his knees.

'I order you to fly!'

'But that's impossible!'

'Nothing is impossible,' shouted the prince. He rose to his feet, a little unsteady but imposing nonetheless. 'Anything can be done if a man has the will to do it!' He shot a look at Francis. 'Is that not true, English fire master?'

Francis hung suspended over the fires of hell. He saw now

177

where the prince tended. He swallowed. 'One should not assume the impossible.' It was the best he could do. He could not look at the man on the floor.

'There!' cried the prince. 'The Englishman puts you to shame. You assume that you cannot fly! Have you tried?'

Say 'yes', you fool! Francis urged silently. Can't you see his drift? Dear God, say 'yes'! Tell him that you've tried and failed.

'Of course I haven't tried, your highness . . .'

'And yet you assume that it is impossible? You refuse me on mere assumption? Before you refuse me, you should test the possibility.' The prince shouted for his Uskoks.

Three men ran into the room, swords drawn.

'Yuri wishes to determine whether or not he can fly. Take him up onto the walls and see if he can fly down to the valley.'

'Please, highness!' The man was now weeping. His mouth moved but terror swallowed his words. Two of the guards seized him by the arms.

'NO!' he screamed. 'I will die! I will die!' He writhed and twisted, drumming his feet as they dragged him towards the door. 'Help me!'

'Highness!' Francis could bear it no longer. 'Wait!'

The prince raised a hand. The Uskoks paused.

'You wish to make a test of possibility, do you not?' asked Francis.

'Is that not what you yourself recommend? Not to assume impossibility, but to test?'

Francis drew a long slow breath. 'The purpose of any experiment is to learn. It is not a true test, in the scientific way, if the experimenter cannot learn from his results.'

The prince nodded. 'That seems reasonable.'

'If his test should fail, the man Yuri will be dead. And therefore unable to learn from his own actions.'

The prince frowned thoughtfully, then nodded again. 'I

178

take your point.' He turned to Yuri who was watching Francis intently. 'Do you assert without trial that it is impossible for you to survive a flight from the walls.'

'Yes! Yes!'

'Then there is no point in making the experiment?'

'No, highness!' Hope crept into his voice. 'Absolutely none!'

Oh, you poor fool! thought Francis in despair. Tell him that you've tried and failed! It might, just possibly, deflect the argument.

The prince followed his logic now past the point of any possible hope.

'Therefore, because you fear this death without testing the proposition, believing without evidence that death is inevitable, you refuse even to try to obey me?'

Yuri threw a desperate look at Francis.

'Release him.'

The guards loosened their grip. The man staggered forwards and stood in confusion.

'Deliberate disobedience is treason,' said the prince. In a single clean movement, he took a sword from the hand of one of the guards, turned away. Then, with the full weight of his body behind the blade, he swung it in a wide arc and sliced off the manservant's head.

Francis closed his eyes, heard the thud of the head on the floor, the shriek as the weight of the falling corpse forced the breath from the man's lungs. The shocked silence.

'Either way, he was dead,' said the prince. For a moment Francis saw the formidable, terrifying general that Alessandro Hugo Uskoki Di Pirati had once been. 'Why draw the matter out?'

My fault! My fault! raged Francis. If only he had not hesitated . . .

'I haven't lost the knack.' With satisfaction, the prince

179

returned the sword and sank trembling into his chair again. 'Have I cured your modest doubts?' he asked Francis.

'I suffer no doubt, sir. Modesty is an empty custom in England, and I'm stupidly slow to learn your more honest manners here. I have no doubt at all.'

The guards dragged away the body. Then one of them returned for Yuri's head. While two grooms removed the small dripping carpet where Yuri had fallen and began to roll up the larger bloody grass matting on the floor, Francis covertly studied the princess. She had moved away to stand by the little altar in the niche, straight-backed, hands folded in front of her, pale against her black skirts, watching everything, with a white face but steady gaze.

'Get the agreement,' said the prince. He looked at the princess. She seemed not to hear. He repeated the order.

She turned her head away and went to a cabinet, from which she took two papers. She gave one to her father and one to Francis.

'We must have no suspicion between us,' said the prince. 'No more doubts like those you raised in me earlier.'

The princess meanwhile had brought a pen and inkpot to the little table by her father's side.

'You will sign, and I will sign,' said the prince. 'You will swear to send me to Heaven. I will swear that, if you do so, I will cancel the bond for the loan.'

Francis unfolded the paper in his hand. It was a contract undertaking to launch Prince Alessandro safely to the foot of God's Throne, at the moment his soul was preparing to leave his body.

He couldn't sign such a thing.

'Is there a difficulty?' asked the prince. 'Or does modesty plague you again?'

Francis looked at the servants who were still cleaning Yuri's blood from the floor.

'There's no difficulty, your highness.' Francis signed.

Prince Alessandro signed a second copy. Solemnly, they exchanged copies.

'Come tell me straight after breakfast tomorrow what progress you have made.'

It very likely made no difference for Yuri what Francis had said or done . . . he tried to convince himself. The prince believed that what he wanted was possible. Therefore, he believed that Francis could do it, if only he tried hard enough. The prince had always meant to terrify him into trying hard enough.

Unfortunately for Francis, trying hard would not be enough. If he wanted to return to England alive with the bond, he had to think of the way out, of which Richard had been so certain. Before tomorrow, straight after breakfast. Signing a mad contract made matters neither better nor worse.

'Go! Begin!' said the prince.

I need to get a message to Cecil, thought Francis. He felt an icy wind at his back. It would be good at least to know the identity of the man he could ask for help.

PART THREE

32

THE *CAMERA* OF FRANCIS, LA SPADA

Francis sat at his table and stared at the blank square of parchment in front of him. After a moment, he dipped his quill in the pot of oak gall ink and made a first line. Then a second line beside it. He paused.

This is mad, he thought. Far worse than anything he had had to do in the last two years.

Tomorrow, straight after breakfast.

He sat with his head in his hands until Seaborn returned from the kitchen with two stoneware jugs and a pair of red Murano glass goblets.

'*Birra!*' Seaborn announced triumphantly. 'Their local brew.'

'Drink up!' ordered Francis. 'I need your bladder full.'

Seaborn raised his fair eyebrows but obeyed.

Francis drained his beer and returned to his drawing. He joined his two parallel lines with two shorter ones, to make a long rectangle. 'I must study Astronomy. Can't lie about something I don't understand.'

'Ignorance doesn't stop most men from talking,' Seaborn

came to look over his shoulder, holding his own refilled goblet.

Francis wished that the rectangle did not look quite so much like a coffin. 'I propose that the prince will ride inside . . . just there.' He pointed to the rectangle, then he added a decorative scroll supporting another line. 'His seat.' Then he drew a blunt triangle on one end of the rectangle. 'A Heavenly chariot!' he announced.

'Your Heavenly chariot looks very like a rocket,' observed Seaborn.

'Stick with what you know, I always say.'

'Where's your propelling charge?'

Francis scribbled a cloud of smoke at one end of the rectangle, and some tongues of fire. Then he threw down the pen. 'Thus far, it's bollocks. An ordinary firework enlarged. At the size needed to carry a man, it would never fly. Even our mad prince will surely see that!'

'Have you also considered the difficulties of penetrating the Heavenly Spheres?'

Francis glanced up at his erstwhile apprentice. 'The old astronomy?'

'Stick with what you know.'

Francis could not tell whether Seaborn was mocking him or not. 'And where would you have me place the earth, then? Still in the centre? Or in its proposed new humbler place as a mere rotating suburb of the sun?'

'In the centre, still, I think,' said Seaborn. 'We're in the lands of the Inquisition. Best not to invite any more trouble.'

'On the other hand,' said Francis. 'I must be modern. I must be more than modern! For, don't you know, I possess new knowledge that has eluded all the other keen minds of the world. A *fantasia particolare*. I mean to tickle God's toes! Such a brave soul does not fear the puny Inquisition!' He held out his goblet for more beer. 'Such a man puts his earth in its proper place. I'm with Signore Galileo, Master of Mathematics in Padua. My sun goes in the centre. My earth is a mere suburb.'

'Shhhh.' Richard glanced at the door, but he had already closed it when he returned with the beer.

'No lions in here are there?' demanded Francis, a little giddy with lack of sleep and the madness of where he found himself. 'We've none of those blabbing lions in here, have we?'

Seaborn had never seen Francis in the antic humour that infected him when he was secretly terrified.

'Keep drinking,' said Francis. He took a closer look at his nephew's face and took pity. 'I'm neither drunk nor infected by the prince. I have a purpose, never fear. Drink!' He held out his own goblet again. 'But now I beseech you, coz. By your favour, most kindly, will you fetch a fresh page and help me draw a map of the Heavens? I've never before had to aim so high.'

The apogee of a shell's trajectory, the height of a city's walls, the distance to haul a canon, yes, often judged. The way to God's Throne, never.

For some time, they passed the pen back and forth, both fair heads bent close over the table.

Studying their work with his head tilted to one side, Francis wiped his pen on the velvet square, '*Bene*. That's done. Let's pray that it's enough to keep me alive for another day at least.'

He tested that the ink was dry, then folded the parchment so as to hide its contents and sealed it several times with wax Seaborn had found. As with a display of fireworks, unlike war, most of any effect lay in the showmanship.

While they worked on the map of the heavens, Francis had drunk steadily from his own goblet, distracted briefly by wondering what mineral salts had been used by the

Venetian glassblowers to achieve that fine shade of warm red. Now, while he was sealing the drawing, Seaborn, agleam with unvoiced curiosity, went to steal the liquid contents of several close stools.

Setting the map aside, Francis dug into his bag of fire master's materials and extracted a small sealed earthenware crock labelled 'Turkish Salts' which his grandfather had called 'burak' in the *Liber Ignium*. He shook the grey-white powder into his own close stool.

Seaborn returned carefully balancing a pungent leather fire bucket, three-quarters full.

'Now we turn alchemist,' said Francis. As a fire master, whose life depended on the accurate manipulation of different material substances, he was more at home here than he was with astronomy. He pulled his thickest linen shirt from a dressing chest and stuffed it into the close stool along with a glove.

'Let the Great Work begin.' He unlaced the front of his trousers and pulled out his cock. 'Come, help me marry two base substances.' He grinned at Seaborn. 'We must prepare for the next operation, *nigredo*, the blackening.'

Together they pissed onto the shirt.

33

While the shirt and glove dried, Francis left Richard to slip back into the tasks of a manservant. He headed back up onto the walls again, where an idea lurked, shadowy and elusive. A faint whisper heard earlier, before he was ready to listen to what it wanted to tell him.

The shirt was a beginning, but it was not enough.

He understood gunpowder, fuses, trajectories and the sizes of guns. He understood things he could touch and smell. How the devil do you propose an impossibility? How can you describe something that does not exist? What bricks do you use to build an imaginary castle?

The morning fog had lifted. When Francis looked over the outer skin of the wall, he inhaled sharply. The sudden, abrupt landscape struck him a blow beneath his ribs. On the far side of the curving green tongue of the wide valley below La Spada, terror had solidified into jagged mineral teeth. In the closest range, a little to his left, a mountain had been broken open like a loaf of bread by giant hands, spilling limestone crumbs larger than a house across the table of the high plateau. To his right lay the dark river cleft out of which they had climbed when they arrived.

He pushed back from the wall and studied the open terrace that ran between the inner and outer walls.

He saw three cannon, light and of an unfamiliar type, resembling falconets but larger. For use, he presumed, against any invaders who broke through the town walls. Guns big enough to threaten a besieging enemy on the distant valley floor would tear apart even walls as solid as these with their recoil.

Eyes down, he looked for that elusive thing he had only half-seen through the morning drizzle, just before the prince's men found him.

The stone paving had begun to dry. Between dark damp patches, puddles reflected the bright but opaque sky. Francis stopped to peer at a large puddle in the projecting angle of a tower. A solid mount of some sort rose through the reflected sky. Lines of heavy bolt tops lay just below the surface. Whatever had once been mounted there would have faced the valley through an opening in the tower wall.

It was too broad for a gun mount. He could not say what had stood there but felt that this was what he had come back to see.

What had he almost understood that morning before being interrupted? Clarity tickled with coy fingers, teasing him.

'Who's there?' he asked suddenly. A dozen strides took him to the corner of the next tower, where he had seen a flicker of movement. He rounded the corner and met the gaze of a cornered doe turning to meet the pursuing hounds.

'*Principessa!*' Standing with her back pressed against the outer wall. She was alone, unattended by any of her women. Her cheeks were flushed with chill and the end of her perfect nose was bright pink.

'Ah, it's only you,' she said.

Francis bowed, weighing the implications of 'only'. 'Whilst

I try to think best how to serve your father, I thought to stretch my legs.'

'A happy chance encounter then,' she murmured, with a glance at his legs. 'How do you find La Spada?'

He looked hard at her before he replied. He still couldn't say what colour her eyes were. A poet would call them green. She was waiting to hear his answer with an interest that was not entirely benign.

It was too late to pretend that they did not understand each other.

'After this morning? How do you imagine I find it?'

'Poor Yuri would have died in time,' she said. 'And less swiftly. My father had infected him.' She stared down at her hands, as if examining them for symptoms of infection. 'My father will die soon.' She looked up, daring Francis to make an empty protest. 'Whether you help send him on his way or not.'

'I know, madam.'

'And I know that you mean to gull him. He asks the impossible. And you know it.'

'And now that you know this?' he asked.

'What punishment do I intend for you, do you mean?'

'What punishment do you feel is deserved for deceiving a dying man?' He met her gaze coolly. Her eyes, he now saw clearly, had the dark-stained clarity of peaty water, glittering on the surface, with their true depths hidden under an illusion of transparency.

She blinked, then half-smiled. 'It depends on who is doing it. I believe your deception is kindly meant. His mad purpose comforts him.' She gave a tremulous sigh. 'Poor father. I haven't the heart to discourage him neither.'

A softer child than the son, thought Francis. Or so she would have me think.

'How far will you take it?' she asked.

'How far will you let me?'

She gazed over the parapet into the valley. 'To a successful conclusion.'

'And what is that?'

She smiled again. 'We'll come to it. I feel quite worn out by frankness now.' She continued to gaze out. 'I do so love these mountains.'

After a moment, Francis rested his folded arms on the high wall beside her and gazed in silence as well.

'Like it or not, you're going to need my help.' She did not look at him. 'You don't even have to trust me. I'm certain my brother is panting to be your secret . . . patron.' There was amusement in her voice now, but it was entirely dark. 'Be sure, Signore Cointo, I'm a far safer choice.'

'Were you lying in wait for me?'

'Stretching my legs.' She studied him again. 'Unlike my father, I'm not mad. But I do pray most fervently that you can satisfy him. As a dutiful daughter, I must help my father make his way to Heaven, if that's his will. What can I do to make the task easier for you?'

Francis searched for the best answer. She seemed to be little more than her father's prisoner, a coin to be offered casually in exchange for service. What true power did she have to help? On the other hand, she had also just seemed to say that she was willing to help him murder her father.

'Don't trust too much in appearances,' she said.

Francis looked at her sharply. Perhaps she was a witch, who could read minds.

'Do you believe in the power of will, signore?'

'To tell the truth, the power of will is my only resource, just now.'

She smiled up into his eyes. 'Then we are alike. We have no choice now but to be friends.'

Take care! Francis struggled to take a firmer grip on himself. Take care, my boy! She's dangerous.

'Your favour would be a gift beyond price,' he said at last. 'But, *principessa*, I have a soldier's needs . . .' He stopped in confusion. 'The help I need may be military,' he corrected himself.

'And, royal or not, I'm a mere woman?' She shook her head with a mock frown. 'Oh, signore! I pity your English women if you expect so little of them.'

Francis pushed away the memory of Kate lighting a fuse and diving for cover . . . Kate with a musket at her shoulder and a powder burn on her cheek.

The *principessa* put out her hand as if waiting for a supporting arm. Francis freed his arm from his damp cloak and let her take it. Her fingertips were cold on the back of his hand, which looked twice the size of hers. With a lurch of pity, he noticed that her nails were bitten to the quick.

This is the first time I've walked arm-in-arm with royalty, he noted wryly. He would never have imagined these circumstances. Through the wet sheep stink of their cloaks, he could smell oil of jasmine. He was most aware, not of her rank, but of her slim body moving beside him inside its carapace of silk and wool.

'Where do you take me?' he asked.

'What would you say to the gift of a library?'

Astronomy! thought Francis with relief. In the astronomical works of a library, Heaven would surely tell him exactly where it could be found. The prince was certain to ask whether Francis knew. Like most people, Francis had a general sense of where the Heavens were – up there, somewhere beyond the clouds and stars. Most likely.

But 'most likely' was not good enough for constructing a hypothetical navigation chart for an imaginary journey to the exact foot of God's throne. Not if he wanted to convince.

'You are pleased?' She sounded truly eager to know.

'More than pleased.' He stepped back to let her precede him through a small door back into the Castello.

In a library, he would find scientific manuscripts. Volumes on Mathematics, Philosophy, Alchemy. A library would cough up the sonorous, weighty words he needed to impress the prince. It would provide flashes of illumination to blind the prince to Francis's pitiful ignorance. In a library, he might find the bricks for building an imaginary castle, enough formulae and figures to stack up all the way to the foot of God's Throne.

34

She could feel his awareness of her. She told herself that the desire to take his arm had been mere curiosity and had nothing at all to do with the unexpected pleasure his presence gave her.

See him only as a challenge. Be agreeable. Be agreeable. Hide your feelings and thoughts. Think ahead.

'As we will pass it on our way to the library, shall I show you the shirt of fire that once belonged to Hercules?' she asked.

He stopped and pulled away his arm. 'Why do you ask about a shirt of fire?'

'You have an air of eager intellect.' Though startled by his intense response, she gave him her prepared answer nevertheless. 'I believe that you enjoy seeing and learning new things.'

Francis watched her unlock a long shallow ebony chest inlaid with ivory in an intricate pattern of bird-like women sprouting into coils of leaves and arabesques. The hinged front dropped down into a writing desk exposing the filled shelves behind.

'*Ecco*. Here it is.' She pulled a green onyx box onto the table top and lifted the lid. Inside was a folded bundle of very ordinary-looking linen. The princess watched him in what seemed like proprietary pleasure.

'No! Don't touch it!' she exclaimed when he extended an exploring forefinger. She replaced the lid.

'How do you come to have this shirt of fire?' Francis would have liked to try to identify the substance with which the shirt had been treated. He had learned long ago that such miraculous objects could almost always be explained.

'My father bought it from a holy man in Dalmatia.' She reached a slim arm into the back of a shelf.

Could it be mere chance that she should talk of shirts of fire? he wondered, watching the line of her arm. Or was there a way that spies could listen in his *camera*? She had replaced the shirt innocently enough.

'What do you think this is? The label is too faded to read.' She offered a flask.

Francis sniffed cautiously. 'It's not safe to keep,' he said.

'*Bene*. Danger is the point. This chest is my father's *memento mori*. To remind him that life is both short and cheap.' She sighed. 'He doesn't need such reminders now.' If she could be said to be shy, she seemed shy as she showed him the rest of the dreadful treasures in the chest: poison rings and books, a glass dagger filled with venom. He examined them all curiously but carefully, disturbed by her matter-of-fact acceptance of their purpose. He noticed that she wore a dark toad stone ring herself, against poisons.

She opened the shutter and went out onto a covered balcony. 'Come,' she ordered. 'I'm sure you will disapprove of this one too.'

'Why do you imagine I disapprove?' he asked, a little ruffled.

She flicked a glance at him and lifted off the perforated

wooden lid of a stoneware jar. Francis gazed down at a coiled reddish brown snake drowsing in the bottom.

'An Egyptian asp,' she said. 'Cleopatra's way out. My father and brother control almost every moment of my life.' Her lips tightened. 'You've seen how he keeps me by him. But I shall deny them both the final pleasure of ending it. In La Spada you either rule or die.'

He felt dizzy with this sudden swing.

'There's no middle way for me.' She looked at him. 'How should I think instead? Advise me.'

'You must have allies here in La Spada, who will defend you.'

'That is my most loyal ally,' she said, looking down into the jar.

'There must be others. You are the prince's true child! Your brother was a bastard . . .'

'You are impertinent!' she said. 'All tales of the coarseness of English manners are correct.' A tear escaped to contradict her furious tone of voice. 'You are cruel. An English barbarian.'

'Forgive me, lady.' He cursed his own lamentable lack of tact. 'But I can't believe that in all La Spada you don't have a better champion than a snake!'

'Where?' she cried. 'Who? Do you see him anywhere? Do you see anyone mad enough to risk my father's jealousy or my brother's bile?'

'There's me, madam.' It was out before he knew it.

'You, my champion? Why?' She slammed the lid back on the jar. 'Now you mock me!'

Pretend that she's right. Give a rueful laugh. Take back the offer now!

But her vulnerability and need, her evident despair under the rage, broke through his good sense. Reason deserted him.

197

Her huge eyes, brimming with tears, gazing wildly into his own, the soft heaving bosom . . . Even as he noted the wild, excessive theatricality of it all, his cock was stiffening, even as reason still begged, albeit faintly, for him to flee. He reached down and picked up one of the small white-knuckled hands that still rested on the wooden lid of the snake's jar.

She froze for a moment, staring at their joined hands. Then, with a small whimper, she stood up and dived against his chest. Her arms gripped him like the hoops of a barrel.

How did we arrive here, all of a sudden? Francis thought in astonishment. His arms tightened, feeling the delicacy of her ribs. As he looked down, holding her, fighting a fierce need to bury his face in her fragrant, silky hair, he could not see the small smile of triumph pressed into his upper sleeve.

'Forgive me,' she said after a moment. She straightened and laid her hands to her cheeks, framing her lips, like a painting of Modesty Confused. 'I did not mean to press you so far.'

It was the gesture that did it. He suddenly saw it. She was acting. Had been acting ever since they met that day.

Francis felt a sense of 'ping', as if a tightly-stretched wire had snapped. Whatever had bound them slackened.

He saw Cecil standing at the dark window, a picture of power in defeat. His anger at Cecil stirred again and included her. He stepped back.

Not this time, madam, he thought. Spare me the maiden in need of a champion! Spare me the hints of being forced to take your own life. My pity has hardened. I'm not so easy to twist into compliance as I was once. I learned my lesson with the last one.

He looked at her coldly, observing his own steadiness. He was angry with himself and still aroused, but free. Master of himself again.

Thank you, my lord, Francis told the absent Cecil. For this timely rescue.

But if she wasn't mad . . . and he was now more or less certain that she was not . . . then what the devil did she want from him? Not a lover. The moment she began that game, the extraordinary frankness of their earlier understanding had disappeared. So, what was her game?

If a surfeit of surmise could kill, he'd be a dead man.

He still wanted to kiss that delicate, devious mouth.

35

Sofia felt him retreat. The air around her seemed to chill. She felt sick. He was looking at her with such distant displeasure that she wanted only to run away and hide under the coverlet of her bed.

'And now we will go to the promised library,' she said brightly. 'It belongs to my father, but he has forgotten it since he became ill. It's his private fiefdom to which only a favoured few may apply for access.'

He did not respond.

She had lost control, she thought. Begun to chatter like a fool.

She wished, just then, that the Englishman would pretend to be more courtier-like, less open, so she could pretend that all was still well. That she had not in some way made a terrible mistake and made a fool of herself and lost his good opinion, which she had not known until just now that she wanted so much. He accompanied her politely but the warm connection running under all their earlier words and acts had vanished.

She tried to think what to say next but felt only a cold, bereaved confusion.

If this desire to die of misery might be a symptom of love, as the lions had suggested, then she must not love . . . why was she even thinking of love? Love had nothing to do with her intentions for him.

One died from poison or steel, or from thirst while hanging on the walls. She could not afford even to feel love, let alone die of it. She must refuse to love. 'We have scrolls here that were rescued from the library at Alexandria,' she offered.

'I follow you like a pilgrim to a shrine.'

I had him, she thought with despair. I felt him in my grasp. And he tightened his arms around me. He was with me. Where did I go wrong?

She opened a door in the inner wall and led him into the gap between the walls. Ahead of him, she went down a narrow flight of zig-zag steps, then along a series of narrow corridors. Then she led him down again, spinning around and around down a steep spiral staircase. She had hoped that he would be admiring her waist and the back of her neck. Now she was certain that he was not. Though it was not among her rules, Sofia did not lie to herself, even though she lied to almost everyone else.

She had begun to lose him when she pretended that the snake was hers, when it was really kept to eat the mice. It wasn't even an asp but a mountain viper.

It had been a stupid lie. An impulse, not even part of her script.

He had begun to hate her when she began to lie.

I lost him when I began to act what I did not feel, she thought. She had not regretted putting her arms around him. On the contrary, she could have stayed like that forever.

She stopped outside a small door and made herself smile up at him. Perhaps his pleasure in the library would recover some of the lost ground.

*

Francis watched her slim form spinning down and down below him on the stairs. And the way one raised hand brushed the wall to steady her. He had never met a woman like her, not even Kate. Kate was warm, generous, passionate, high-spirited and straightforward. This one made Lady Gunpowder seem straightforward. This one was a tangle of golden threads. She had thorns. This one had already, somehow, embedded herself in his being, and he did not have the least idea how to deal with her.

Whereas, she seemed to have a very shrewd idea how to deal with him. Knowing to offer him books from Alexandria after the desperate maiden had failed . . . She terrified him even more than her father did.

'The House of Wisdom,' she announced over-brightly.

At least she seemed to know that she had played him wrongly. He ducked his head under the low lintel and followed her through the door.

While she watched him expectantly, he gazed about him in disappointment. He didn't know what he expected of a House of Wisdom, the refuge of lost books from the great library at Alexandria, but, on first look, this was not it.

36

THE HOUSE OF WISDOM

Dusty light from a single narrow window seeped into the corners of a room not much larger than the bookstore on the upper level of the Gate House at Powder Mote. The simple shelves were only partly filled. The north-facing window slapped a sharp-edged beam of brighter light across a pine table set just beneath the sill. The man at the table was already pushing aside a scroll and pulling a piece of blank parchment across his work. He leapt to his feet.

'Sofia Sultana!' He bowed.

'Signore Rabac Albona, our guardian of all wisdom,' said the princess in Italian. She translated into Latin for Francis, in case he had not understood.

A grand title for a modest role, thought Francis. Given the small size of his fiefdom.

'Here's an English pilgrim, for you, Albona. You must be kind to him. He wants wisdom.'

Francis detected a definite edge to her voice. He noticed a sleeping pallet on the floor, the coverlet tossed carelessly into a heap.

Albona wiped his hands on a scrap of silk. The fingers on his right hand were stained yellow and green as if with unnaturally vivid bruises.

Here was yet another face of La Spada.

The librarian, tall and lean, wore a long, loose belted linen robe in the Moorish style that stopped just short of a pair of yellow slippers. A white turban covered black hair, which escaped to curl excitedly around his ears. These organs, fleshier than the rest of him and protruding slightly were the only disruption of his otherwise lean and harmonious lines. Wired spectacles rested on a long straight nose in a dark-skinned, handsome face. Apart from the hair and ears, there was something neat and pointed about him, like an otter or ermine.

He seemed genuinely pleased to see the *principessa*. However, the expression of the eyes behind the spectacles also revealed a suppressed irritation at being interrupted.

The princess looked about as if pleased to be there. 'I like your new prison for the Ancients.' She went to inspect more closely the polished steel grilles protecting two sets of floor-to-ceiling shelves.

'I'm happy that you're pleased.' His eyes flicked to the table.

On it sat three stoneware crocks, a bowl filled with a milky liquid, scraps of torn silk and two soft brushes. There was also a half loaf of torn bread, sitting in a scattering of crumbs and of little grey balls like those children make from bread when they've finished eating, to throw at each other on the sly. Francis could not detect an odour from the liquid in the bowl.

'Sultana.' The librarian gestured to his chair beside the tale. 'Please sit.' He used this invitation as an excuse to roll up the open scroll and push aside his working materials.

'Not today.' The princess turned away from the shelves. 'Thank you,' she said, accepting two small books, which Albona had waiting for her. 'I will give Signore Cointo a key so that he may come and go as he pleases.'

Francis nodded amiably and wondered why the man would not meet his gaze.

'What wisdom do you seek?' asked the librarian, sliding from Italian into Latin.

Francis looked at the *principessa*.

'You can trust Rabac,' she said, gifting the librarian with a flash of the bright clear eyes, which Francis had not seen since she had dived into his arms. 'Or so I believe. Just don't burden him with more than he wants to know.' She left them.

'Astronomy,' said Francis with less hope than when he had been offered the library.

With a key from a small bunch hanging on his sash, Albona unlocked one of the new steel grilles and opened his hands, palms up. 'I give you the Universe, pilgrim. Please. Make free . . .'

Francis disliked the man's tone now that the princess had gone. 'With respect, Signore Albona, that's no Universe there. Merely the words of those who have pondered it.' And only a very few, at that, he added silently.

'If a wise man writes it down, does it not become the reality?' The edge sharpened in the librarian's voice.

'What becomes of truth, then, when wise men disagree?' Francis retorted.

'It takes refuge in a library,' Albona tossed back. 'Where contradictions happily lean against each other like lovers.' He gestured impatiently at the books. 'I can only show you where the arguments lie. You must find wisdom for yourself.'

'Her highness was mistaken. I don't want to become wise, merely plausible.'

Albona had been turning away. Now he swung back to Francis. Behind the glasses, a cautious interest sparked. 'That's all you want? To be plausible? You've no greater philosophical ambition than any aspiring rogue or swindler?' He might even have been a little amused.

'I must become the King of Mountebanks,' said Francis with a frank smile. To his relief, Albona snorted. In his two years at court Francis had learn that, often, when he followed his natural inclination to tell an awkward truth, he was disbelieved and given credit instead for a sharp wit. Yet again, this seemed to be the case.

'Plausible astronomy . . .' Albona went to the unlocked bookcase and seemed to search with his hands. 'Here's Astronomy . . . but is it plausible?' His fingers roamed, resting briefly on each leather spine, feeling its pulse, probing its warmth or chilliness. 'Do you read Greek?'

'And a little Hebrew, so long as I can mouth the words silently to myself.' Francis had grown accustomed in London to the astonishment caused in certain court circles that a tradesman, even one as particular as a fire master, might be as well tutored as a gentleman.

'Have this one then,' Albona said, pulling a thick volume from its shelf along with a small shower of dust that further thickened the dim light of the corner. 'And these.' He took the two books to the table and dusted them with a piece of silk. 'Have these as well.' He handed Francis three more from the shelves. 'There's as much plausibility as you could possibly need, whatever your purpose.'

Francis chose to ignore the insinuation. 'I may take them?' he asked in astonishment. 'But these are volumes you keep locked away!' He gazed at the precious enamelling and gilding of their covers, the silver rims, the gold leaf of their title pages, the dense thickets of their contents.

'Her Highness vouches for you. Take them . . . take them!' Albona had already returned to his table, chafing to get back to his work. His eyes kept returning to the half-hidden scroll. His fingers already tightened on the brush handle.

206

It seemed clear to Francis that the gift of books was not the mark of any special privilege or trust. Signore Rabac Albona wanted to get rid of him as soon as possible, so he could carry on with his mysterious work.

He hefted the books, each weighing as much as a three-week old piglet, and settled a hip on the table edge in a friendly sort of way. 'Are you a Persian?'

'Turk.' Albona looked up in resignation, seeming to understand that he was now to pay a little for his earlier incivility.

'Albona sounds more Italian than Turk, or is it "Al-Bona"?'

'I name myself after Rabac and Albona, two neighbouring villages on the Dalmatic coast south of Trieste, where I was born and lived for three short years before an Uskok raiding party removed me and sold me to the di Piratis for forty ducats. I am now a free man.' He crossed his arms. 'Have you any further questions?'

Francis wondered how far to push.

'Please. Ask anything you want to know, but without delay,' said Albona. 'Your time may be short. The mountebank before you survived only two weeks. But, then, the man was not an aspiring astronomer, merely a tout for flying carpets.'

Albona puzzled Francis. He was either a possible ally or a dangerous enemy and it was too soon to know which.

Francis stood up, books stacked in his arms. 'Thank you for this plausibility. And for your conversation.'

'I'm yours to command,' said Albona dryly.

Francis looked down at the jewel-like books. A small inspiration began to tickle his mind – not a large inspiration, not a way out, but a touch of showmanship. He must think like a pyrotechnician – all showmanship and effect – not like a military fire master setting real charges to bring down real walls. 'On second thought, I need more plausibility than I can carry. May I return with a small chest?'

37

That evening, the prince ate some pickled melon. It was too much for his stomach and made him vomit. 'Call my guards,' he choked. 'The cooks have poisoned me!'

'In a moment, father.' Sofia wiped his chin with a scented towel while the royal physician took the basin away for assessment. The hem of her skirt trailed over the streaks of Yuri's blood still staining the floor.

How many more would die before her father finally set them all free? Yuri this morning and the cooks this evening. The death of Yuri was causing enough rustling among the rats in the wall. To kill one or more of the cooks on the same day because some pickles had disagreed with him would make the prince's madness clear beyond all doubt. You could not stop so many mouths. Word would flood out from the kitchens. Give Ettore the excuse he needed to seize the throne at once, an excuse he must not have if she could prevent it.

The lions had been silent, of course. No one was fool enough to denounce the ruler to himself or to Da Monte, his *Camerlano*, his Lord Chamberlain. But that day, after Yuri's death, Sofia had felt a new reluctance to enter the prince's presence.

'Call my Uskoks!'

'Father, look!' Sofia ate two pieces of the melon from the half-empty plate, then another. 'Wait to see if I am poisoned too.' It was possible that Ettore might try to poison both of them, but the royal taster was still alive and flirting with a page in the antechamber.

She could scarcely contain her impatience to be able to think undisturbed about her encounter with the Englishman. She had been so certain that he was captured. That she had done enough. It should have been easy. He had been netted from almost the first moment he entered her father's *scrittoio*. She had seen it in his eyes, which were frighteningly transparent to someone used to living as she did. How did he survive with such truthful eyes?

His withdrawal had been just as clear as his interest. He did not trouble to hide his sudden coolness that had made her want to weep.

To deal with him, she was going to have to act in a new way. She had lost him with lies. Therefore, she must woo him with truth. Her habits of a lifetime, her rules would no longer serve her. She was a novice at truth. In her experience, truth most often killed you.

The prince sank back into his chair at last. 'Sit down.' He closed his eyes. One of his hands felt for her arm, stroked it, then clamped tightly onto her wrist. 'I feel better. Perhaps I'm not poisoned after all.'

'No, father.' Was it safer to smile or to frown?

'Let Father Daniele say the Rosary for me.'

Sofia closed out the murmur of the priest's voice and rehearsed her personal commandments, which she kept locked in the secret book of her thoughts.

Trust no one. That scarcely needed to be said. Not even this Francees Cointo! Him least of all. A foreigner, who did not know how games were played, who humiliated her when he should have been flattered . . . How could she employ the truth with a man like that?

Threaten no one. Ettore had driven that lesson home.

Hide your feelings. Lie.

Hiding her feelings and thoughts led naturally to becoming a good liar. Lying had never caused her any difficulty, until now. But now, with the Englishman, this rule had betrayed her. As for the rest,

Avoid notice. It was too late for that.

Appear blind to the failings of others. Every day.

Keep your eyes open. Smile. Distrust your own desires . . .

She kept her eyes open, always. She smiled, and knew very well the effect she could have when she did – except with the Englishman. More than ever, she distrusted her own desires.

Want to survive. Her will to survive grew sharper and more urgent by the day.

Take special care when things go well. That rule did not apply just now.

Be patient. The time in which she could afford to be patient was running out.

Do not attach your heart. Never again. Never again.

Think ahead. Always!

But since the English fire master had arrived, Sofia had felt things going on beyond her sight, hidden dangerously from her understanding. New possibilities shifted in the shadows at the edge of her eye. She could not think ahead about what she did not yet know.

It had suited her more than her father could have guessed to send for the English fire master in the letter she had written over his signature, now grown so jagged that she would soon have to forge it altogether, like Da Monte. She wished, almost, that the Englishman had been what she expected. A knowing courtier. A swaggering soldier who flirted with death in public and had grown used to adulation. A man who enjoyed causing fear, like the late fire master of La Spada.

Instead, she had looked up into the startled interested eyes of this near-giant of a man, who cut through the crowded *sala*, not seeing how other people, even self-important Castello officers and head ushers, fell back from the force of his purpose, not noticing the speculative looks of the women over their fans. Or how drowsing dogs pricked up their ears and fell into step at his heels as if sure he must be going somewhere of greater interest than where they were at present.

Silently, she tried to get her tongue around the barbaric abruptness of his English name – 'Francis Quoynt . . . Quoynt!' It ended like an axe blow on a block. Whhhoooi, thump!

'*Try to see with your enemy's eyes.*' That was all very well, but what if you could not see even whether he was an enemy or not?

'Francees Cointo,' she murmured, listening to the breath struggling in and out of her father's chest. 'Signore Cointo.' This small transformation of his name seemed to strip him of a small piece of armour.

The prince was now asleep in his chair, his head thrown back, mouth open, one hand clamped on her wrist. His time was running out, and hers with it.

The Englishman was her last chance. But if she read him rightly, she must act with him as she had never acted before. Openly. She must convince him that she acted openly.

Tonight, she decided. So that the sudden galloping of her pulse might not rouse her father, she pulled a book from her skirts, held it in her free hand, and tried to concentrate on an essay concerning hereditary principalities. 'The hereditary prince,' she read, 'will be more loved . . .' Not new jumped-up princes, like Ettore.

She would act tonight.

Her father's hand jerked in sleep, jolting her hand. Carefully,

211

she unlocked his fingers from around her wrist . . . paused. Placed his hand on the wolf skin rug across his knees. Waited.

His breathing still sucked and whistled.

She took a careful step backwards, towards the door. As always, Father Daniele ignored her. She nodded at the prince's new manservant, who was dozing on a stool near the wall. The man leapt up to open the door for her, silently, on hinges Sofia had ordered to be oiled.

'Your highness . . .' he whispered.

Sofia backed slowly out of the room.

The door closed. She was almost safe. Tonight she could not sleep close by, as her father often insisted, in the little bedchamber that opened secretly into that of his own, or on her stool.

No shout called her back.

The young Spanish waiting woman Isabella and a maid both curtsied and followed her from the antechamber. They should have been attending her in the prince's *scrittoio* but Sofia wanted as few witnesses as possible to his true condition. The young women, for their part, were happy to stay as far as they could from possible contagion.

'You may announce that the prince is doing well and now sleeping peacefully,' Sofia told the Castello officer who was staring listlessly out of a window in the *camarilla*. With chilly dignity, she walked on through the *enfilade* of public rooms.

'The prince is doing well,' she told Da Monte, who was holding his own court in the *antecamarilla*. Feeling the press of ten speculative male eyes on her back, she passed on into the *saleta* and then into the *sala*, which was almost free of petitioners so late in the evening. She nodded graciously here and bestowed her dazzling smile there.

As she walked, she read eyes, watched for the pursing or relaxation of lips. He's for me, she thought, smiling, and him. The count over there by the fountain will support my brother.

And so will he. And these sluts . . . She smiled with measured warmth at a clutch of women by the fire of the *sala*, who rustled to their feet, playing cards still in their hands. '. . . they'll curtsy wherever their husbands tell them to bend their knees.'

She dropped one of her finest smiles onto an ageing grandee from whom she would have almost certain backing, as her half-brother was rumoured to have raped the man's oldest granddaughter.

At last she turned into the long damp corridors that led through the old *fortezza* to her own *camera*. Here, at last, away from the press, while Isabella and the two Austrian German speakers from the Carniche laid out her night things and brushed out her hair, she could think again.

Reason still told her to strike tonight. Nothing would be gained by waiting.

Tonight, she repeated silently.

She began to plan, thinking ahead in a new direction. Mulling over the details distracted her from the full reality of her intent.

'Hang my house gown ready on a peg of the *restello*,' she ordered one of the Carnians.

Do what you must, she told herself. You can even take some pleasure in it . . . the right course need not always be unpleasant. But never lose sight of what you know. Do not, ever again, attach your heart.

'Leave me,' she told the maids when they had finished preparing her for bed. Her gown and slippers were ready. She settled down to wait.

Then the call came.

'Your father wants you again!'

Not tonight, then.

Be patient! Be patient! Smile. Seem agreeable.

She must survive to twist the future or else there was no point in thinking ahead.

38

Francis was still eating a breakfast pasty when the call came.

Seaborn leapt to fetch him their drawing of the Universe while Francis gathered together a clutch of other papers. He also took the shirt and glove. The prince's page called another page to help him. The two of them staggered away with a chest.

'Wish me well.'

The prince leaned forward hungrily. 'What news? What progress?'

The pages dropped the chest with a thud.

Let the comedy begin! thought Francis. He felt like a novice actor suddenly thrust on stage in his first performance.

He bowed to the prince, then to the *principessa*, who stood at a small table warming a cup of wine with a hot poker. Her glance collided uneasily with his then slid away again.

He offered the prince his first drawing. His heart thumped. Most playhouse actors needed to fear only shouts of derision and thrown apples or nuts. Actors were not beheaded for forgetting their lines.

The prince unrolled the map of the Heavens. 'What is this? An onion? Do you mock me?'

'It's no onion, sir!' said Francis quickly. 'But a map! Those lines show the heavenly spheres nested one inside the other. See! It says there that it is a map for your journey. *Mappa itineris Coelestis principis.*' Francis felt like a man trying to run on ground littered with round lead shot, but at least he was not yet telling outright lies. Not about the universe. Most of the books he consulted, whilst agreeing on little else, had agreed on the onion.

'Surely, you would not trust me to send you somewhere if I could not tell you where it might actually be?' he asked the prince.

'But how I will travel? Answer me that! You waste time like the others. There's no time left.' The prince sank back against his pillows, his large frame limp with despair. He closed his eyes. 'A map! What good to me is a map? I need pitch to mend a water pot. I am cracked by my sins. Nothing good can stay in me. I feel everything leaking away – my thoughts, my memories, my vital force.'

Francis glanced again at the princess. He would have preferred not to have her as witness again, in spite of her reassurances on the battlements. Her performance with the cupboard of poisons had unsettled him. The painted eyes on the walls watched him incredulously.

The prince had once been a soldier.

'Would you set off blindly into battle?' Francis asked. 'Ignorant of the terrain where you were to fight. Not knowing whether it was desert or sea?'

He tried to judge whether he had caught his audience yet. He was beginning to fear that he might have underestimated the lingering sharpness of the prince's wits. Or else, he had overestimated how much befuddling pain-killing tincture the man had taken.

'I have been your heavenly intelligencer, your highness. I have been your scout who maps the terrain for you.' After a night spent with Albona's books and endless re-copying, he had improved greatly on the first rough drawing he and Seaborn had made.

He knelt and smoothed the map across the prince's knees. 'The Heavens do indeed resemble an onion, as your highness said. Like an onion, our universe is made of concentric spheres. But unlike an onion, each sphere is of a different substance. At the very centre, in the heart of the onion, sits . . .' he glanced uneasily at the prince's confessor, who was kneeling today before the little altar, apparently at prayer. '. . . the sun,' said Francis firmly. 'As postulated in the new astronomy of Masters Copernicus, Galileo, and others.' He drew a deep breath. 'Not yet widely published but known to a select few.'

No outcry followed this first heresy against the Catholic orthodoxy. He continued, pointing with his finger. 'This first sphere outside the central sun, Sol, is that of Mercury. Then we have the sphere of Venus. Then comes our own, that of *Terra, cum orbis lunari*, with the orbit of the moon lodged in it like a pearl set in a ring. Then . . .'

'When I sail on a ship,' the prince interrupted. 'I trouble myself only with where I will arrive and what I mean to do when I get there. I leave it to the captain to chart the course. Where is Heaven? I don't see Heaven on your map. Where is God's throne? How will you chart my course to His Throne?'

Francis said a silent prayer of thanksgiving to the books of Albona, his reluctant ally. 'A keen question, your highness. Your course? Yes. Where exactly is Heaven?'

'You repeat the question. What is your answer?'

I wish that you were madder still, thought Francis. 'Do you ask which way must we aim, your highness?'

The prince glared impatiently, not stooping to respond.

Francis could delay no longer. He told himself that he was merely on the stage at the Rose, or Blackfriars, or in a private hall. He spoke lines written by Masters Dekker, Jonson or Shakespeare, not lies.

'That very question kept me from sleep last night. Instead, I studied with compasses, measured declensions. I filled pages with calculations. I threw them into the fire. Endless pages like these!'

He took a bundle of papers from his pouch and waved them in front of the prince, papers scribbled with diagrams copied from Copernicus, Brahe, and the French royal mathematician, Jean Pena. 'All asking, at what compass point does Heaven lie?'

He put the papers away again before the prince could ask to examine them more closely. Showmanship, he reminded himself. King James appearing in a flash of light. Smoke and thunder. No one sees the men in their cloaks of green leaves.

'Near dawn, in despair, I at last remembered the final aim of our work – God Himself, and I began to pray. He sent me a revelation.'

The prince was at least listening now. There was a rustling as the princess bent to return the poker to the brazier.

'I saw that I had been going at matters from entirely the wrong direction.'

'Get to the destination,' said the prince.

In the corner of his eye, Francis saw the princess sit down on her velvet-cushioned stool and settle to listen.

'My revelation – that Heaven is not a common earthly destination!' He wanted to turn his back on those intent, knowing eyes. 'Heaven can't be steered for in the same manner as the Bermoothes or Samarkand. My revelation was also this – wherever God is, there, too, will be His Throne.'

He cocked his head in question.

'I could have told you that.' But the prince was still listening.

Francis drew a deep breath and careered onward. 'Insofar

217

as God Himself is All-encompassing, then it follows that the Heaven where he resides must also be All-encompassing.'

He faltered. The argument had convinced him in the small hours of the morning. Now it felt as slippery and insubstantial as the prince's flight. 'And this All-encompassing Heaven,' he resumed, gesturing, 'must therefore form a kind of greater sphere encompassing the Heavenly spheres. Entirely.'

The prince frowned. 'To the point, Cointo.'

Francis laughed lightly as if the prince had made a witty quip. 'You have it! There is no point, your highness. You grasp the truth faster than my tongue can speak it. There is no point at all. No compass point. You have hit the mark! You can travel in any direction and still reach a destination that is all around you, can you not?'

'Bravo,' said the princess quietly. Her father continued to frown.

'Imagine,' said Francis a little wildly, 'that the air in this room . . .' He swung an all-embracing arm. '. . . is that part of Heaven which is wrapped most closely around our own nested spheres – encompassing it, as I said. All around the onion. And this . . .' he held his clenched fist in front of him '. . . represents those seven nested spheres. If I were to move in this direction . . .' With his other forefinger, he drew a path in the air away from his fist. '. . . I penetrate the air. But, look! If I fly off in this direction . . .' He repeated the gesture to the opposite side of his fist. '. . . I also penetrate the air! Likewise, in this direction. And this. And this! It matters not at all in which direction I move, I must always enter that all-encompassing infinity!'

Strictly speaking, none of what he had just said was a lie, except perhaps the words 'beyond doubt'.

The prince looked thoughtful but still not wholly convinced. 'I can't dispute what you say. But why did you not realize this before?'

Francis found that he was breathing hard, as if he had just run a race, or climbed a particularly steep cliff. His face burned. 'I have always thought it possible, your highness, but I could not risk your safety with mere possibility.'

He dragged the chest across the floor to the prince's feet and lifted the lid. He took out two books, three books, six more books. The gold and jewels of their covers flashed. He built the books – decorated and plain – into a low wall around the prince's feet. He produced still more books. The jewelled and gilded covers gleamed as testimony to the corresponding value of their contents.

'Sir, I could have brought a dozen chests and still not brought more than a tiny part of all the different answers offered by scholars and wise men to the question of where Heaven lies. I am a fire master. I never pretended to be either a scholar or wise. A sleepless night showed me that none of these wise men and scholars . . .' He allowed the faintest edge of derision. '. . . could give me a certain answer. That certainty could come only from God.'

And may He forgive me! he thought.

'I might have died last night while you were studying and scribbling and waiting for Heavenly guidance! I'm slipping, Cointo!' The prince gazed at him now with haunted eyes.

'I pray that your Highness may live still for many years . . . but I accept your judgement,' he added hastily.

Francis prepared to talk wisely next about trajectories and the downward pull on a cannon ball.

The prince stirred in pain. 'Give me a drink!'

The *principessa* stood and offered him the heated wine, which she still held. The prince pointed at her silently. She drank from the cup.

They all waited, motionless. After a moment, Francis realized that the prince was waiting for his daughter to show signs of poisoning.

After the prince had drunk and the princess had wiped her father's chin with a silk napkin, Francis found himself being studied like a captured enemy while the prince was deciding whether to execute or enlist.

'You sound plausible, Cointo, but it's all sound! Words, words, words . . . goose droppings! Give me something beyond dry scholar's words and a map of an onion! Show me some tangible proof of your powers!'

Francis abandoned trajectories. He raised the lid of the small gold coffer that Richard had borrowed from the chapel treasury late last night (Francis did not ask how). A stink of urine rose from the coffer to blend into the foetid air in the closed room. He lifted out the linen shirt, carefully dried in front of the fire, then the glove covered with mica that gleamed like silver scales.

'I must, above all else, keep you safe on your journey, your highness. You must be in a fit state when you arrive, must you not? With all your powers to persuade still intact.'

The sincere ring of his voice astonished him. He glanced now at the burns festering on the prince's right hand.

'There will be great heat on the way to Heaven. First, from the ignition of the rocket that will propel you upwards. After that, you must travel past the heat of the sun and through the burning stars. You must be kept safe from this heat.'

The price began to rock very slightly in his chair. 'No fire,' he moaned. 'No fire. You must launch me without fire!'

'Of course,' said Francis quickly. 'But you will still face the heat of the Heavens.'

He removed his doublet and put on both shirt and glove. Then he crossed to the brazier.

'Your highness, behold!' Francis bent and thrust his right hand in its silvery glove into the flames.

The prince screamed and held his own burnt hand to his chest.

Francis turned his hand in the flames as if rotating a joint on a spit. The prince leaned forward, mouth open, eyes wide in disbelief.

Neither shirt nor glove caught fire.

Francis clenched his teeth. He thought his arm would begin to roast like a suckling pig, but the shirt still did not catch fire.

The princess opened her mouth as if to protest but closed it again.

Francis endured a moment longer. Then the heat became too much, even through the padding tied around his wrist under his own shirt and sewn inside the glove. He removed his hand from the fire. Took off the shirt and held it up in triumph, a little scorched, perhaps, but not blackened.

'You will have such a shirt to wear on your journey, your highness, and such gloves.'

'Let me try them now!' The prince reached out.

'They can be used only once before their virtue melts.' Francis watched the prince for signs of doubt as he folded the shirt back into the coffer. It seemed impossible that the man would swallow such flummery. He could not let himself look at the princess. 'You shall have your own, in time, to test if you will.'

And may you forget!

As Boomer's apprentice at the age of eight, Francis had been delighted to learn this method for preparing one of a fire master's many forms of protection. But he had also learned that it was designed only to keep sparks from setting your clothes alight, not to withstand prolonged exposure to flames.

'Tomorrow, I will show you my design for your heavenly chariot,' he said. 'And demonstrate how it will carry you to your destination.' With luck, he might by then have worked out a few more plausible lies, including how to lift a rocket without seeming to use fire.

The prince glared down into his lap. 'Why has no one else been concerned with my safety?' He sounded plaintive.

'Because no one else knew what to do.' My lord Cecil, he thought, behold what serving you has brought me to! 'I am the first.' The silence lengthened. Then Francis saw that the ruler was weeping.

'I begin to believe it possible.' The prince held a silk hand-kerchief to his eyes for a moment, overcome. 'Oh, Merciful God! For the first time, I begin to believe it to be truly possible.' He blew out a huge shuddering breath. 'When this thing is done, you must have whatever you like . . . marry my daughter if she takes your fancy. Help yourself to my treasury . . .' He began to gasp with the force of his emotions. 'Call my man . . . call the *principessa* . . . where is she?'

'I'm here, father. As always.'

'Let me touch you. I need to touch young flesh . . . to eat a hatching chick, drink lamb's blood, anything to maintain my vital force. Signore Cointo, I must survive to enjoy your gift of hope.'

I have ascendancy, thought Francis with astonishment. For the moment at least, he had won some small ascendancy over the prince's unsteady mind.

Standing beside her father, the princess gave Francis a look of approval mixed with something much darker, which he could not read.

'Go!' the prince ordered. 'Don't waste another moment, signore. Work every moment between now and tomorrow! Come back tomorrow to give joy to my soul again.'

39

'I almost pitied him.' Francis leaned on the wall and looked down into the lower town. As long as they stayed within the walls of La Spada Alta, it seemed that they were fairly free to roam unaccompanied. The top of the walls seemed a safer place to talk than inside the Castello. 'He wept for joy.'

'He deserves no pity.'

Francis glanced at his nephew. 'You sound absolute in that for such a gentle soul.'

'I have the advantage over you of being a mere servant. I can move freely in the places where people gossip. And where they suffer.'

'My very own *bocca di leone*,' said Francis. 'So, spit out the morning's news.' In England, he had not foreseen this use for Seaborn.

'It's no secret that the prince is dying of the Neapolitan Pox. Most of the maids and grooms know. It can hardly be hidden. Two serving women he once bedded are also infected.' Richard's mouth twisted. 'Bedded after he knew that he was infected. He told one of them that she need not fear because he was dosed with mercury. He gave the other no choice. It was not rape, but her great privilege.'

Francis cocked his head at the bitterness in the young man's voice. A sign of the steel that he knew lurked in the tall, gentle and very earnest youth.

'And besides,' said Seaborn, 'Does the prince never think that the women who wash his linens might have noses and eyes?'

I'm not the only one forced to learn fast, thought Francis. 'What's the pantry opinion of Prince Ettore?'

'Ruthless, clever and over-careful of his position. Take care never to remind him of his base birth.'

'Did he never hear that England was ruled until lately by a bastard queen, as all good Papists must deem her?'

'I hear that he's just as fearful of the legitimate princess as the old queen was of her legitimate cousin, Scottish Mary.' A moment of private thought followed, on each part.

Francis wrestled a moment longer with his conscience, and lost. 'Can you wriggle higher than the maids and grooms in your gossip?'

Seaborn took a very long time to reply. 'It may be possible.'

'Take care,' said Francis, now urgent with guilt. 'Don't be taken for a spy.' He wanted to snatch back his question. 'You hesitated. Is there danger you haven't told me?'

'What do you want me to learn?' Seaborn gave Francis a suspiciously direct look. 'No. No danger, I swear. On the contrary.' Francis waited, but Seaborn offered no explanation of 'on the contrary'.

'I need to learn the factions in La Spada,' said Francis. 'And their strengths. How many back Ettore? Does the *principessa* have followers? And what of Da Monte?' If Cecil wanted an ally for the English, Francis must not choose the wrong side.

Silently, he begged Boomer to forgive him for turning his grandson into an English intelligencer and putting him at equal risk with his son.

'I must go devise another impossibility,' said Francis. 'The prince demands a launch without fire! And wants the design for his fireless chariot of fire by tomorrow.' He breathed in the air, which still carried traces of the winter chill. Spring came late in these mountains.

'There's snow, still.' He pointed at the peaks across the plateau. If all went well tomorrow, he would ask the prince if he could ride outside the walls. Apart from seeing those grey-white crocuses growing through the snow bank, he had never ridden from spring flowers into snow.

'In particular, learn all you can about the Lord Chamberlain, Da Monte,' he told Seaborn. They trotted down a staircase discovered by Richard that morning, which led directly back into the old *fortezza*. 'A distant cousin to the prince. Learn the specifics of his title and position. Is he loyal to the prince or ripe for a rebellion?'

Seaborn nodded seriously but Francis felt his eagerness. A hound let off the leash, waiting to begin the chase.

Francis closed the door firmly. Suspicion, however dark, would be far better to have abroad in the *Castello* than the truth. Seaborn had disappeared with the remains of their afternoon meal to pursue his intelligence gathering in the kitchens. Francis had not been able to face yet another performance, this time as a courtier in the great *sala*. Nor did he want to remind Prince Ettore of his existence.

He spent the rest of the daylight searching through the books in the chest for inspiration for his Heavenly chariot. He leafed through and set aside books on astronomy, theology, mathematics, medicine, law. Books written in Latin, Greek, Hebrew, German and Italian. He found nothing that would fly better than a rocket.

The prince was mad only in parts. He would have Francis's head off like poor Yuri if he believed himself insulted or that

Francis meant to pull the wool over his eyes. On the other hand, as Seaborn had said, deceit is made easier when the deceived wants to believe.

Francis studied the woodcuts in a volume on the lives of the saints, hoping that one of them might suggest a vehicle for ascension. He found nothing better than assorted gaggle of helpful angels.

Then he retrieved the sketch of the giant rocket he had made the day before and laid it on the table. The books were no help here. He knew as much about rockets and the firing of them as any man, ancient or modern.

How might such a thing fly? Even if the prince could be persuaded to agree to a powder propelling charge, no amount of gunpowder would send it higher than the highest of the surrounding peaks. He tried to imagine what questions the prince might ask.

He dipped his pen and leaned forward with concentration. He drew another rectangle. He paused, waiting for impulse to guide his pen again. Something in his experience must surely suggest an answer.

How do I get there? he heard the prince ask. How will you propel me so far? How do I penetrate through the Heavenly spheres?

He heard the man moaning 'No fire! No fire!' It was impossible to fire a rocket without applying fire.

Suddenly, he dipped his pen. Hitting the spheres might be very like running into a wall. He drew a pointed ram on the nose of the rocket, like a military battering ram.

He studied it. Perhaps a borer might serve better . . . No, he decided. The necessary turning of the screw might make the prince dizzy . . . can't have that . . . he'll need all his wits to debate with God . . . Ram, it is. I can't believe I'm doing this . . .!

Ram.

Hit by sudden inspiration, he then drew a small arc of two parallel lines. 'Handles!' he exclaimed. The saints were assisting him after all. 'There.' He cocked his head and considered the drawing.

Then he began to draw short, quick curving strokes, in parallel pairs, one inside the other, again and again all along the outsides of the rocket rectangle, like the handles on a jug. He was beginning to enjoy the madness. As it would never happen, he could devise whatever he liked. Freedom from Reason made anything possible.

'Now it no longer resembles a mere firework,' he said with satisfaction.

Richard had returned and now gave him an uneasy look from the floor, where he had begun to cut out shell casings from sheets of vellum.

'It's mad enough even for his highness.' Francis added two more 'handles'. 'What a pity one can't draw an infinite number.' He squeezed in a final double arc. 'I hope to represent the concept at least. Congratulate me! I believe I may have solved the problem of propelling such a great weight straight up over such vast distances. Without fire, if I can.' He bared his teeth in a wild grimace and rolled his eyes. 'Poor Tom's a'cold. Spare a penny for poor mad Tom!'

Richard swallowed. Then risked a smile. English was his second tongue. Even now, after two years in England, he was still sometimes uncertain whether words were spoken in jest or not.

Francis dropped his pose of madness. 'It's as well that it's all just talk. "Words, words, words – goose droppings!" as his highness put it. I don't know how the devil to lift the bloody man more than a foot, let alone far enough to convince any witnesses that his highness is off to Heaven. Even if I could use fire, one of my rockets might make him twitch, but not much more. Firing him from a bombard might do the trick, but I fear the prince would smell a rat if I proposed such a thing. He's mad sideways, and not always as you'd expect.' He pulled the drawing back to look at it again, squeezed in one more tiny jug handle. 'I'm glad I never met him in the field when he was in his prime.'

Seaborn worked silently while Francis stared down at his drawing.

Francis put down the pen and stood up. He should be thinking how to steal the English bond. He must not let the prince distract him from his chief purpose.

'This is mad play, but I can't think what else to do. Let's pray that his highness won't notice what I leave out.' He felt in his pouch and found the iron key, which had arrived with breakfast. 'Did you know that the librarian here was once a slave? Perhaps I'll go make faces at Signore Albona. He strikes me as a man skilled at surviving in La Spada.'

40

When Francis opened the door, Albona looked up in alarm.
As before, he pulled a piece of stained parchment over what
he had been doing, then sat back with a look of weary resignation. The bread, brushes, silk scraps, stoneware crocks,
and bowl of milky liquid again stood on the table.

'Signore Cointo, who else? Back for still more plausibility?'

'I need more than plausibility tonight. I need revelation.'

Albona leaned forward over his work, elbows on the table.
'I'm only a librarian, not one of your priests.'

Francis let the reference to priests pass. 'Do you have any
works on guns and munitions? Any histories of warfare?'

Albona shook his head. 'I believe not.' He waited for
Francis to leave again.

'I believe that you do.' Francis bent to peer more closely
at a volume behind a locked grille. 'Signore, would you be
kind enough to unlock its cage?'

Albona hesitated, then stood up with reluctance. As he
left the table, a corner of his sleeve caught the parchment
hiding his work and shifted it. Francis saw his hand begin
to move to replace it, then stop. Francis stepped away from
the bookshelf. While the librarian was turning his key, Francis

moved closer to the table. He saw the corner of a book. He pushed the parchment aside altogether and stared down, appalled.

The book lying open on the table had once been an illuminated Catholic Psalter. Now the remains of a large gilded letter 'N' hung raggedly above a pale smear that once had been the text. A prickly green rose stem, missing both leaf and bloom, undulated snakelike across the top of the page towards the severed brown head of a nightingale that was no longer there. The image on the preceding page remained only as a single cloudy smear flecked with gold.

'Why are you destroying that book?' Feeling sick, Francis imagined the *Liber Ignium* destroyed in the same way. The work of generations wiped out, quite literally. His own history and his present knowledge destroyed together.

'Is that how it looks to you?' Albona went back to the table and laid his hands on the Psalter protectively.

'"One of my priests" would certainly see it that way.'

Francis looked at the stains on Albona's hands – the softened pigments he was removing from the page. He picked up the bowl and sniffed. Milk, just as it had seemed. He leaned close enough to see, just above the man's fingertips, the ghost of a rose bloom. Albona had removed all the paint and was just beginning to rub away the underlying outline with a ball of bread dough.

Albona watched him warily. 'I feared last night that I saw a determined curiosity in your eye.'

'Why?' demanded Francis, eyes still on the ruined pages. 'The *principessa* honours you with the title of guardian. Does she know how you treat your charges? How many others have you destroyed?' He stared around him at the shelves. 'Are there any books left intact here? Or are all those pages completely blank? Have you stripped away all of those contradictions that might lead a searching mind to wisdom?'

He imagined the poetry, philosophy, mathematics and astronomy all wiped away, leaving unborn thoughts trapped forever inside the fleshless skulls of men long dead.

'Signore Albona, I mistook you for a scholar. But you're a murderer.' He stared back down at the ravaged book on the table. 'You're as much a barbarian as the men who burned the Alexandrine library! You murder thought!'

'And I mistook you for a man of curiosity and understanding. You are arrogant and ignorant, after all.'

Francis watched Albona tighten, then stop himself. He noted the direction the man did not allow his hand to move. 'Do you attack only Christian texts, or do you wipe out the wisdom of the Ancients as well?'

'Only Christian, as it happens. So what do you mean to do now? Denounce me as a despoiler of religious texts?'

Albona's hand almost moved again.

'To whom?'

'One of your priests might wish to know. Or the Inquisition.'

'My priests?' Francis laughed. 'Even buried in here you must know that England broke with Rome before you were born. And is no friend of the Inquisition, neither – Spanish or Roman.'

'But the prince summoned you to La Spada. He employs you.' Albona was still as wary as if they were circling with swords. 'A man's a fool if he presumes to guess the loyalties of a mercenary.'

Francis flushed with anger. 'I'm no mercenary now. I serve only England.'

'By serving the mad prince of La Spada? What dangerous whim of his do you encourage with your plausibility?'

'And where are your loyalties?' Francis demanded. 'Why does a man who has given his life to books also destroy them?'

231

'You ask me to explain?' Albona barely suppressed a sneer. 'Are you willing to listen to my explanation? Can such heathen abomination be dignified with an explanation?'

'God's Balls! I wouldn't have asked otherwise!'

Albona looked startled by this outburst. He pressed the fingers of both hands to his mouth while he thought, rocking slightly from side to side. His glasses winked in the light from the window. 'Oh, me,' he said.

Francis saw thoughts chasing each other through the dark eyes.

'Am I a fool?' Albona asked aloud. 'Perhaps.'

'I don't serve the prince,' said Francis more quietly. 'I need plausibility in order to survive him.'

Even after that peace offering, Albona hesitated. 'I'm not the destroyer,' he said at last. 'The true destruction took place long ago. Let me show you.' He held out his stained hands. 'No hidden weapon. It's safe to come near.' He bent over the table and turned the Psalter towards Francis.

'Not until you remove the dagger below your knee,' said Francis. 'Use your left hand.'

Slowly the librarian raised the right side of his hem and took the small needle-like knife from the soft flat sheath strapped to his leg. He pushed it across the table to Francis. 'I meant to use it on myself if ever I was discovered, before the Uskoks set to work on me.'

Francis picked up the stiletto and weighed the likelihood of a second hidden weapon.

Albona pulled open the neck of his robe. 'I beg you, either let me explain what I've been doing or kill me at once. If you think I mind dying, you're quite wrong. In truth, I would prefer your soldier's cut to lying suspended above the valley in an iron cage too weak from Uskok questioning to keep the ravens from eating out my eyes.'

It was a pretty speech. It struck Francis yet again that the residents of La Spada were given to pretty speeches. Even the prince, with his weeping and joy.

'You asked, why?' Albona pushed the Psalter across the table towards Francis. 'Look there, where I have removed all of the pigment. Do you see what lies beneath?'

Francis could not resist. He leaned closer and squinted. Beneath the cloudy smear, he could just make out a delicate tracery unlike any writing he had known, full of arabesques and strange kinked tails.

'You see knowledge older even than that of the Greeks,' said Albona. 'Lost knowledge. Lost to copy a psalm. Painted out to save money. Truth was hidden so that some *scriptorium* monk could reuse the paper to make this pedestrian copy of a copy of a mongrel version of some verses from a Bible of uncertain origin and dubious authority. That frugal monk and his fellows were the true murderers of knowledge, not I. Successful murderers, I must say.' His long fingers stroked the edges of the pages. 'I am grateful to be blessed as the midwife of the rebirth.'

A little flowery still, thought Francis, but the man sounded sincere. 'Is it Arabic?'

'An old form of the script, from Persia. I first make this fair copy . . .' Albona showed Francis a clean page of similar writing in his own hand. '. . . then I strive to translate it into Latin.'

'What's the subject of this book?'

'It's your scientific treatise, on warfare and munitions among much else – that's why your earlier question startled me. But my ignorance of the subject makes translation slow. Many words are unfamiliar to me, in any language.' He extracted a second paper from the pile. 'Here are some earlier passages, which I have already translated into Latin.'

Francis read with rising excitement. 'How much more have you finished?' He laid the stiletto back on the table.

Albona offered the pile of papers. Francis read intently.

'Do you grasp the content then?' asked Albona.

'Yes.' Francis continued to read, brows arched, eyes leaping across the words, breath quickening.

Albona watched him in speculative silence.

At last Francis set the papers down on the table, holding the final one suspended in the air. 'It breaks off here . . . I recognize much that we also have in our books at home in England. But here are also some new and strange attempts and ingenious conceits I've never before met.' He leaned eagerly over the table to the Psalter. 'So, how much farther have you advanced?'

'So impatient to learn!' Albona half smiled. 'You've read all I've uncovered so far. Are you truly hungry to read more?'

'How fast can you work?'

Albona squared the corners of the pile of papers, deep in thought. 'Contrary to your fears, I've not "destroyed" any of the volumes you can see on those shelves. But something once stood in those gaps you can see works I have restored fully, and translated. Books and scrolls both alike.'

'Where are they now?'

'What would you give to see them?' There was a teasing note in the librarian's voice.

'Your unconditional release from arrest.'

'I think I had that when you set down my blade.'

They exchanged guarded smiles.

'You understand that most of them would be deemed heretical by both the Roman Church and Lutherans as well,' said Albona. 'The work of infidels. Often contrary to the accepted scientific orthodoxy and the teachings of the Christian Church, both Catholic and Protestant.'

'You may be sure that I'm not an agent of the Inquisition.'

'I am,' Albona agreed. 'Chiefly because there's no room in La Spada to squeeze in one more.' He spread his stained fingers on the papers possessively. 'If I'm to risk showing you the other translations, you must make a fair trade. Tell me – what use do you mean to make of what I will show you?'

'None but delight.'

'Not entirely frank,' said Albona. 'But I suppose I must forgive the natural caution of a stranger in an unfamiliar place. And you have an honest face.' He walked three steps to the nearest wall, caressed the panel of a shallow arch and leaned.

41

Francis stood at the bottom of a dark well. It was a pit in which prisoners lay until forgotten

'Here is the true library of La Spada,' said Albona's voice. He vanished long enough for Francis to fear that he might have fallen into a trap after all. Then Albona reappeared with a lighted lantern.

'Look up.'

Francis tilted back his head. Now he understood the full scale of the *principessa*'s gift. A shadowy cliff of books, shelf above shelf of them, rose upwards, gallery by dim gallery before fading into darkness beyond even the last hint of lantern light. He turned. The well was six-sided, with books on all six sides. The narrow encircling galleries left the centre of the well open.

'We're inside the mountain here,' said Albona 'This was once part of an old silver mine, now blocked off from the outside world and enlarged for this purpose.'

The air was cool and surprisingly dry. Some of the shelves were open. Others were covered in iron grilles. On each level as far up as Francis could see, two ladders stood opposite each other, one on each side, leading to the gallery above.

'A subterranean dove-cote,' he said. 'With knowledge nesting in the walls.'

He reached out to haul in and examine more closely a rope hanging from a pulley, one end counter-weighted and the other end tied to a basket.

'For letting down your chosen works, to examine in better light.' Albona was already climbing a ladder, robe tucked up between his legs, expertly hooking his lantern on the rungs above him. Francis followed him.

On the first gallery, instead of shelves there were diamond-shaped cubby-holes, each labelled with a number. These held books and scrolls in different numbers and varying sizes.

'Not yet my translations' said Albona. 'Though there is much here to interest you.' He touched a volume as he passed it. 'Here's History, with an account of the massacre at Udine – and the part played in it by an English merce-nary with an unpronounceable name.'

Francis took it without comment but considerable curiosity.

A shadow of movement slipped past Francis's line of sight.

'We may not have light but we do have cats.' Though he affected nonchalance, Albona's voice was vibrant with pro-prietary pride. 'Mice can be a ferocious enemy here. We offer them thirty thousand different temptations . . . Up once more.'

Looking down as he climbed up onto the third level, Francis had the same giddy feeling as when looking over the edge of the sea cliffs in Sussex on a moonless night. You knew that solid rock was there, and shale and water. But you had to take the existence of the world on trust and not let yourself swim helplessly out into nothingness.

'Here is where I keep my translations secure,' said Albona as he climbed onto the top gallery. He held up his lantern to show the locked grilles.

'I heard a rumour,' said Francis, 'that you have here in

La Spada some of the manuscripts saved from the great library at Alexandria.'

'"Saved" is a gentle way of putting it. Pillaged, raided, stolen, transported, and rescued . . . books suffer these fates just like people.'

'They can also be burnt.'

'Also like people.'

They shared a thoughtful pause in the semi-darkness.

'Only six thousand works in this entire library are so far entered in the catalogue,' Albona resumed. 'But I stopped the listing when I discovered the first desecration. Quite by chance. I knocked over my cup.'

He led Francis along the narrow gallery. 'Here are the Arabic works on Medicine. Here are Mathematics . . . with some very fine works on geometry and algorithms . . .'

Francis made note of the numbers above the cubby-holes. Secret knowledge. An urgent hunger filled him, to learn what might lie hidden here. Some strange new device waiting for him to find it. The secrets of how to swim underwater like a fish or fly like a bird. A different shape for the Universe that was nothing like an onion. Other gods. Unknown cures. The true location of the entrance to the Underworld. Proof of things he disbelieved and arguments destroying all that he held firm. His heart beat faster. Perhaps he might even find – a passing thought – a lost formula for producing red stars in a bursting rocket.

How could such secrets be dangerous? Why must they be proscribed?

'Geography . . . Navigation . . . Alchemia . . . the properties of material substances . . . Warfare . . .' Albona continued his listing with open pleasure. 'Only some are my translations, you understand. The rest are from Alexandria, where no one felt compelled to hide their wisdom under usurping words.'

'Who else knows what you have been doing?'

'Only you and the Sultana. Like you, she surprised me one night. But I've never brought her up here . . . imagine climbing those ladders in a farthingale.'

'Why have you trusted me?' Francis was suddenly aware of the long drop behind him.

'You wanted to know.'

Francis nodded. 'And I thank you.' He gazed around him at the treasures he must leave unmined for the moment. 'Please don't think me ungrateful if I ask you to trust me even more. I need to know some truths that aren't in books. About La Spada.'

'Would you settle for indiscreet rumour?'

'If it's rumour I can risk my life on.'

Albona tapped his teeth with a stained fingernail as he reflected. The sound seemed very loud in the semi-darkness. 'I must warn you not to trust me at all. I'm most unreliable.' He pushed the hanging basket out into the drop of the central well. 'My older sister, who is still a slave, served at court until the prince raped and infected her.' The basket returned to him and he gave it a second vicious shove. 'He has killed her. You can't imagine what relief it gives me to have said those words aloud.' He bent to re-tuck his robe and started down the ladder.

Francis found him waiting on the next gallery below.

'And Sofia Sultana asked her father for the gift of my freedom when she turned sixteen.' Albona's long face was a shadowy blur. 'Do you still trust me for information you can risk your life on?'

'I think you've just told me what I hoped to learn.'

42

The next morning, Francis found the prince sitting on a stool in his *scrittoio*, naked to the waist. His skin looked as if rats had gnawed at him. Lumps and craters covered his arms and back. His hair clung to his head in clumps. The royal physician stood over him, sucking on a thick roll of dark brown dried leaves and then blowing the smoke over his patient. The air in the prince's chamber was filled with a sharp sweet burning.

Francis knew the smell very well, had smoked it himself. Henbane of Peru. Tobacum. Sitting on the little terrace with his father at Powder Mote, with his back against the wall. In London, over a game of cards, where a certain lord, who was always keen for the latest cures had sworn that it relieved migrams, catarrhs and pain of all sorts. He had not mentioned the Great Pox.

'Breathe in, breathe in!' the prince ordered Francis over his shoulder, between puffs. 'Benefit from the virtues in any smoke that reaches you.' He waved the physician away.

'What have you to tell me?' he demanded, holding out one scarred arm for his new manservant to encase in a shirt-sleeve.

Francis waited until the prince's head reappeared through the neck of the shirt. The prince accepted the embrace of a long fur-lined robe, wrapped it around him and sank back into his heavy, carved chair. For a few moments, the only sound was the laboured pumping of his breath. Francis tried not to stare at the dog and bitch on the wall to his left. The princess was not there today, only the Jesuit and the royal physician.

The prince held out his hand.

'Here is your chariot, sir.'

The prince studied the drawing. 'And I am to recline there? Leaning backwards thus?' He gave out a wheeze like a leaking bellows.

'If it please you. It's the best position for flight.' But if the prince objected, Francis would change it at once. Draw a Heaven-bent galleon, a celestial dung cart, if that was what his highness wished. Francis could offer to send the prince off on a wooden tilting horse with wings for all the difference it would make in the end. His only urgent need was to satisfy the prince and leave the room alive one more time in order to try to find the bond.

Albona! he thought. Who better to ask about secret documents?

'It looks like a firework,' said the prince.

'On first sight, it may resemble a large earthly rocket. But here we come to my first invention . . .' Francis pointed to the front end of the rocket. 'A steel ram on the nose! Made of finest steel from your own mines, forged by one of your own smiths, then polished with my secret oil. It will pierce through the shells of the Spheres.'

He could not see the prince's face clearly enough to know his thoughts. He took his next step with the greatest care.

'The difficulty that I believe has never been solved in the past is the question of propulsion. Anyone can see that the

241

parts of any familiar sort of rocket will at last fall back to earth, no matter how strong the initial push.'

He lowered his voice and leant closer than he would otherwise have chosen, to keep his next words from the Jesuit's ear. He avoided all mention of fire. 'Your highness, by the application of mere science, through the manipulation of my family's secret formulae, I can lift you and carry you far beyond any distance ever before imagined by man. But these distances are nevertheless still finite. Measurable. And there is no agreement among even the wisest men as to exactly how far Heaven may be in measured distances. Here, we meet true uncertainty for the first time.' He glanced at the priest, who seemed lost in his book.

'So I must be damned without appeal then?' asked the prince dangerously. He sucked in a deep breath.

'Not at all!' murmured Francis. 'Look here!' He pointed to the many little arcs he had attached to the body of the rocket. 'I have harnessed the power of the angels. With these, I need lift you only to within their grasp. First the cherubs who inhabit the third sphere will take hold of these handles and carry you upwards into the realm of the seraphim. And these will convey you onwards to the archangels who are allowed to stand beside the very throne of God!'

Together they contemplated the detailed drawing of the ram-headed rocket with its numberless handles for an infinity of angelic porters.

This is when I learn just how mad he is, thought Francis. His reason will surely be shocked into returning.

'Build it,' said the prince.

With Yuri in mind, Francis said, 'Of course.'

He could not build it, of course. He saw himself earnestly carving out angel handles and offering them for the prince's approval. That charade might buy him a few days but not much more.

He realized that the prince was waiting for him to speak again.

Imagine that you're in earnest, he told himself. What would he say now if he truly meant to build the thing?

He tried to imagine this ridiculous chariot as a real rocket – a little larger than was usual, but a thing he truly meant to launch.

Then he saw a course that might help him a little farther towards the way out.

'To build it I need a *factorium*,' he said firmly. 'Above all, it must be secure from the prying eyes of the Inquisition.' Away from the Castello and that long, exposed causeway.

The prince nodded his approval.

'It must also,' said Francis with great authority, 'be remote enough from the town that accidental explosions will not kill any of the populace.'

Both of these statements, in themselves, were absolutely true.

It was beginning to seem to Francis that lying was not so much a matter of convincing someone else of a falsehood. To do it well, you first had to convince yourself.

At least I need only give the appearance of building his chariot, he thought.

Before much longer, the prince would be past caring. His death would leave Francis with a good many problems, but at least, not that of launching his highness to the foot of God's Throne.

'I know the place,' said the prince.

43

With excitement which they took pains to hide, Francis and Seaborn rode back down the causeway. The prince had ordered the Uskoks to take Francis to the hunting lodge at once. Da Monte was to make it known that Francis would prepare the funeral fireworks there.

'And it's dangerous work,' Francis had insisted to the *Camerlano*. 'Be sure to make it clear that the work is very dangerous! People must keep away.'

'I hope it will suit our purpose,' said Francis now, as their horses picked their way through narrow cobbled alleys. 'The prince is firm in his opinion that it will suit. And I haven't seen anyone disagree with him and live.'

'At least the place is off the causeway.' Seaborn gazed about him like a puppy let loose in a meadow full of rabbits.

They left La Spada by a gate in the city walls onto a muddy road leading north.

'And which purpose is that?' asked Seaborn a very long time after Francis had mentioned it.

Francis glanced back at the city walls behind them. 'Shall we make a run for it? We carry lunch in our saddlebags.'

Seaborn gave him one of his uncertain glances, then

snorted gently. Four Uskok guards rode ahead of them, four more behind, on horses with hard feet, bred for stamina and the harsh terrain. Seen in felt caps and riding clothes, without their glinting fish scale armour and straight-nosed conical helmets, the Uskoks lost their otherworldly menace. They looked smaller. Nevertheless, they were bred for harshness like their horses, stocky, with sharp dark angry eyes and black moustaches that hid their mouths.

And they were quick, Francis noted. Even when they were slightly encumbered by their light armour, their speed would balance his superior reach in a fight. They rode now in loose trousers like long slops tucked into their boots and bristled with knives – in belts, boot tops, sheaths. They all carried short curved swords. Two carried saddle maces. Their captain also balanced a long-barrelled pistol across the pommel of his saddle.

Studying their escort, Francis thought that he had never been anywhere so strange as La Spada, in spite of his years spent out of England, not even in the great sea-trading cities like Amsterdam. In the Low Countries he had shared the complexion and colouring of the Hollanders, along with their taste for cheese and beer. When he met Flemings, Germans, Spaniards and Portuguese, he had at least been able to name their language even if he did not speak it. In Amsterdam he had seen men and women from all parts of the world, but never so many sorts jumbled together at the same time, in the same place, as in La Spada, seeming to share more-or-less the same life. Thinking of Albona who took his name from a lost birthplace, he wondered how many of these people felt they belonged in La Spada or whether they merely existed here.

The muddy road narrowed to a track just wide enough to ride two abreast and turned up towards a cleft between two sharp peaks. Unfamiliar birds darted out of the trees to peck at the horses' droppings. Now Francis drew a deep breath that smelled of resin and horse and looked ahead with anticipation He had never before seen mountains like these, though Boomer had often spoken with longing about the wild, lonely mountains of western Scotland. Francis had imagined that these mountains in Friuli might be similar, if perhaps just a little higher.

'Aspetti! Halte!' A faint voice shouted. They heard the clattering of hoofs on stone as a horse came up fast behind them from the city gate.

The rider wore the prince's badge. 'His highness summons Signore Cointo. You must return with me at once.'

Without breaking rhythm, the Uskoks turned their horses and the procession trotted back towards the gate of La Spada.

44

At the door of the prince's *scrittoio* Francis felt an animal's urge to run. Reason told him that he wouldn't get far. With the blood thudding in his head, he entered. The prince, the princess, Father Daniele the prince's Jesuit confessor, and the royal physician all stood waiting for him. So did the Duke Da Monte and Prince Ettore. Both men eyed him with suspicion and distaste.

'Signore Cointo,' said the prince, 'I have decided to share my secret intentions with both my heir and my chief minister. I feel myself slipping. You will need their assistance both now and when the great moment comes. Explain to them all that you told me this morning.'

His legs turned watery. His head swam. He tried to think of an excuse.

The prince made an impatient gesture. 'Speak.'

There was no escape.

Francis explained to this audience who were not mad, not dying of the Great Pox, two of whom would control his fate when the prince had died. Under the urgent eye of the prince, with his face burning and tongue rebelling, he explained how the prince would achieve the foot of God's Throne, battering ram, angel handles and all.

When he had finished, there was a long silence. Six pairs of eyes stared at him, the prince in hope, the princess in veiled approval. The confessor and physician looked away, at the floor, anywhere but at Francis. Prince Ettore and Da Monte gazed in steady, implacable disbelief.

'Da Monte,' said the prince, 'you will give Signore Cointo however much he asks from the Treasury, and every assistance he needs. The resources of La Spada are his to command.'

'My suspicions fell far short,' said Prince Ettore. 'Do you think we're ignorant peasants, living a hundred years ago?'

No doubt, some people might still believe what Francis had proposed. He had merely drawn on a few outworn beliefs. But the heir apparent and the sharp-eyed *Camerlano* were not such people. Francis saw it in their eyes.

The next ruler of La Spada, the present Lord Chamberlain, and a representative of the Roman Inquisition had all heard him swear to fraudulent lies. Heretical fraudulent lies at that. He had sworn that he would help to challenge God's Will. He had even signed a contract saying as much.

'The man is a mountebank,' said Ettore. *'Impostore.* A fraud. Father, he's gulling you as surely as that carnival fool who claimed he could send you to Heaven on a flying carpet.'

'For shame, brother!' cried the *principessa.* 'Do you think our father can't detect a mountebank without your help?' Defiantly, she met her brother's murderous eye.

Ettore did know after all, thought Francis heavily. When I first met him, he knew what his father wanted, just as surely as he knows that it can't be done.

Francis had lost his gamble that the prince would keep his great plans to himself long enough for Francis to lay his hands, somehow, on the bond. That the prince would clutch to himself all the drawings and philosophizing and promises and then hand over the bond. The moment he had agreed to undertake the commission rather than flee empty-handed, Francis had set himself on course for this moment of crashing into reality.

'This "mountebank" as you call him can tame the fires of hell. I have seen it! He has sworn by contract to do it!' The prince rose to his feet and pointed at Ettore. 'You have always hated me!' he shouted. 'I made you my heir and you repay me with hatred. You are filled with evil. The lions tell me your true thoughts. You ooze evil like a toad. I know what you did to your sister . . .'

'With your agreement, sir! Don't deny it! You agreed that it was for the best!'

Even through the pounding in his ears, Francis heard the princess make a throaty sound, like a creature choking on its own blood.

'How dare you!' shouted the prince. 'Get out, before I change my mind and squash you back into the mud! So long as you wish to remain my heir, you will support me in every action. You will do as I wish!'

'Father.' Trembling so hard that the light shivered on the jewels sewn to his sleeves, Ettore bowed. 'Forgive me. I am yours to command entirely.' He raised his head and gave his father a winning smile. 'It's my hot Pirati blood, sir. Even though it may sometimes lead me to risk your wrath, I would never wish myself to be without a single drop of it.'

'Get out!' The prince extended his hand blindly. The *principessa* caught it and helped him back to his chair. The physician seized up the prince's other wrist to count his pulse.

'I look forward with great anticipation to the fulfilment of your contract,' Ettore said to Francis. He bowed again to his father and left. The look Francis saw him give his half-sister made him fear for her life.

'And you, Da Monte?' demanded the prince, when Ettore had gone. He yanked his wrist out of the physician's grasp. 'Do you believe that I'm a gullible fool who must burn in hell, like it or not?'

'Highness . . .' Da Monte raised both hands in disclaimer. 'I live only to carry out your will.'

'My will is that nothing hinder Signore Cointo in this great work. Give him whatever he asks.'

'Highness . . .' Da Monte turned on Francis a gaze that held both amusement and malice. 'No one is more agog than I to see this great work carried to a successful conclusion. Signore Cointo needs only to give me a list of his necessaries.'

Don't be trapped into sharing his knowingness! Francis warned himself. He had just begun to glimpse a faint but possible hope of a way out . . . forced on him but just possible.

Da Monte still held him in a challenging stare.

You're in good faith! Francis told himself. He must not admit to the lies. Not a mountebank. He believed everything he had said. At all costs, he must avoid the eyes of the *principessa* who knew better.

'I will be most grateful for your help, sir,' he told Da Monte. 'Shall I send my lists of requirements to one of your secretaries?'

'Best to keep this affair to ourselves,' said Da Monte. 'Wouldn't you agree?'

'Guided by your wishes.' Francis sketched a bow to hide his face. He didn't trust his ability to hold that look of bland eagerness for very much longer.

He decided to gamble one more time.

'Your highness, may I beg a word with you alone?'

'Are you mad?' asked Da Monte. 'To think we'd leave you unguarded with our prince?'

At that moment, Francis knew for certain that the ever-present Jesuit did carry a knife in his robes.

'Neither Cointo nor I is so mad that we can't exchange a private word,' said the prince. 'Withdraw, Da Monte. Stand over there by the door if you won't leave the room. I'm moved by such fervent loyal concern for my safety.' He waved away his daughter as well.

Francis watched her go to the window, not so far as Da Monte, where she seemed to ignore all that was happening in the room. He knelt close to the wrecked body, within the tomb reek of the prince's breath. 'Sire,' he murmured, downcast. 'I must beg your forgiveness for what I will now ask.'

The prince stiffened. 'A difficulty you haven't confessed?'

'No difficulty with the great work,' Francis assured him hastily. 'It's a matter of state, in which I have little experience. As a mere soldier I must stumble as best I can to do the duty asked of me.' He looked up in pleading. 'Highness, pardon the messenger . . .'

'Get on with it!'

'The English Secretary of State fears that during your highness's illness, the English bond may have been stolen. He gives you my services freely, bond or no bond. But for his own case, and no doubt that of his secretaries, he prays that you will show me that the bond is still in your possession.'

'Cecil would permit your work for me even if the bond were gone?' the prince asked suspiciously. 'You would complete the great work even if were not to erase the debt?'

'Even if Cecil did not permit – which he does – I would still do it. Your highness wills it. That is enough.'

He did not like the level assessment that had found its way into the prince's eyes. Francis told the truth, as far as he dared. 'I will be frank with you, highness. Your heavenly

251

flight offers me a challenge beyond any that I have ever faced. If you knew me better, you would know that I hunger for challenge above all else.'

'Then, you admit to having some personal ambition in my great work?'

'How can I not wish to complete this work? Your salvation spurs me on to achieve a thing no other man has done. You offer me rich resources that no other man has ever been fortunate enough to have. How can I not continue?' To his astonishment, he realized that what he had just said was almost true.

The prince clapped him on the shoulder. 'Well-spoken. I trust ambition. And now I trust your honesty. Did you think I'd swallow that clap-trap about my will? What can my will matter to an Englishman? But English ambition is as hungry as Venetian ambition, or German ambition or Turkish ambition.' He lowered his voice further. 'Signore Cointo, return after supper. I will show you the bond, let you sniff it – which is more than Da Monte has done. Then you can swear to your Cecil on seven Bibles and your mother's head that you have had the ocular proof that the bond is very much still in my possession.' The prince rested his head against the back of his chair. 'Come back tonight.' Abruptly, he fell asleep.

In the corner of his eye, Francis saw the *principessa* stiffen. Her hand shifted on the window edge.

Francis backed away and passed Da Monte at the door without meeting his eye.

Ettore was waiting, leaning against the big bed in the prince's grand *camera*. He straightened and stepped into Francis's way.

'You have only until my father dies to make good your promise.' He jabbed a finger into Francis's chest. 'Be certain of that. I will make no excuses for failure! But none will be needed, I'm sure, as both you and he are so certain of success.' His smile confirmed Francis's deep dislike of the young man. 'I look forward to witnessing this miracle for myself.'

'I will try not to disappoint you.' In spite of himself, Francis locked glances with the prince. Still, the damage was already done. Until he could lay his hands on that bond, he must turn true mountebank.

Richard was pacing the star-roofed chamber in his riding clothes. 'You're still alive,' he said with relief.

'I'll tell you whilst we ride back up to look at this Hunting Lodge,' said Francis. 'My head still spins. And trees don't blab. I need both your advice and help.'

He had learned at least that the prince seemed not to have told Da Monte about the English debt. And after the exchange between father and son, Francis suspected that Ettore did not know either. If neither the Lord Chamberlain nor the heir apparent knew, then most likely the prince had told no one yet. Therefore, stealing the bond before the prince died would destroy the debt. Suspicion without the paper would be worthless to Ettore, or anyone else who might rule instead – the *principessa* or Da Monte.

Not entirely satisfactory, Francis thought. But it was now his only course of action. It was far more possible than firing the prince through the seven heavenly spheres, with angel teams waiting like post horses to lift him on, no matter what he had promised.

Then he thought, this accursed contract of mine with the prince cuts both ways.

Sofia's hand held tightly to the edge of the window as her father and the Englishman leaned their heads close together. She half-turned her head and strained to detect the shapes of words in the low male rumbling of their voices.

'. . . back tonight,' she thought her father said. She heard the Englishman's murmur of assent, then her father's first gasping snore. Then she heard the Englishman leave. She couldn't look at him now that the time to act had suddenly come. But it did not matter. He would return tonight.

She must try to make her father swallow a second cup of his pain-killing tincture. He must sleep through the night! Just this once. She must risk stopping his heart too soon. Tonight, her father must sleep!

To Francis's astonishment, the day continued to unroll bright and undisturbed as if never interrupted. The same birds darted out of the trees. The same sun, a little lower, still sliced through the pines. The same Uskoks rode with them up to the hunting lodge.

A little above the town, the muddy road to the north climbed into a valley cleft and became a forest track with occasional rocky scrambles. Miniature rivers of snowmelt laced the sides of the track. Long spears of sunlight sliced down through the tall firs and pines. Fallen needles muffled their horses' hoofs. For a time, they followed a small frothing, tumbling stream.

This time, Francis confided in Seaborn as they rode close, side by side. Sucked into turning his fantastical comedy into reality, he explained his new, second possible course of action. How to make the promises cut both ways.

'I must now make it seem to happen.' He might still hang for fraud. But if, somehow, he could seem to act in good faith, and make it seem that the prince had been successfully sent to Heaven, in a way that no one could disprove . . . Then he might still be a heretic, but an honest one. By contract, the prince's heir would be bound to write off the English debt.

'I don't like the odds,' he said quietly. But he saw no

other way to prolong his life, and Richard's, for more than the few days it would take the prince to lose patience with still more cobbled-together promises. And then, there was Ettore. And Da Monte.

'But you don't have to send him to Heaven in truth?'

Francis shook his head. 'Merely to seem to do it.'

It might be possible for a man like himself, experienced in devising wonderful fiery effects. Even so, it was far beyond any devisings he had ever before attempted. Stealing the bond seemed just as possible.

'Whilst I play at mountebank trying to devise some semblance of a journey to Heaven,' Francis said quietly, after he had finished his tale, 'you must devise the prince's funeral fireworks. That work must be cover for the rest – just as necessary for my new purpose as it was for the prince's folly.'

Seaborn's face lit up. 'You'll trust me to design as well as to make? Give me full responsibility?'

'Why not?' Francis eyed him wryly. 'It can be your master piece, as my apprentice.' The young fool was so delighted that he seemed to forget the circumstances behind his happy chance. And it didn't seem to occur to him that he would almost certainly never have the chance to carry out his fireworks. 'We must disguise your true role for as long as we can, but the task is yours.'

In response to the sudden excitement of its rider, Seaborn's horse broke into a trot. In contrast, Francis was now sunk in gloom.

There was little in his experience to help him with what he must do now. He could not see how Catherine wheels, sky-rockets that spat out stars, or fire-breathing dragons, or even paper warships firing false shells at each other across a pond could help him. Even military fire master's cannon could not help him. The prince was a good deal larger than the largest cannon ball.

Everything hung on his visit to the prince later that night. Cecil should have sent a real fairground mountebank or playhouse manager who knew how to make a ghost appear to walk and heads seem to fall.

PART FOUR

45

THE WALLS, CASTELLO OF LA SPADA

From the battlements, Sofia watched them come out of the city gate far below her and set off up the muddy road.

Be patient, she told herself. But she felt as uneasy as a sack of snakes. Her hands would not stay still. Her shoulders wanted to twitch. Her feet wanted to jiggle and pace.

Her eyes followed them up the muddy road, in and out of the trees, until the tiny horses disappeared at last into the cleft of the mountain track. She waited until they reappeared briefly on the high bare knob of a bend. The Englishman was not wearing a hat and she imagined that even from this great distance, when horse and rider were less than a quarter the size of her little fingernail, she could pick out his hair catching the sunlight.

She imagined for a moment that she too was riding away from La Spada. She could see the road so clearly in her imagination, the dusty puffs raised by her horse's hoofs, the brightness she could glimpse through the trees ahead of her. But where was she going?

She could not think where she would rather be instead.

In the Republic of Venice, which she had always heard described as the jewel of Italy? She could not imagine trying to live like a mermaid in the watery city of Venice, her feet and hems always wet. Or moving only from side to side and never up or down, like the people living in the great flatness of the central Veneto, never able to climb or to look down into empty space. She could not imagine being able to see the clouds only from below and never looking down on the backs of flying birds. She did not want to leave La Spada but only to be safe here. To be safe, she must make it her own La Spada, not her father's, nor her brother's.

Shielding her eyes with her hand against the afternoon sun, she peered up into the mountains and imagined that she saw tiny scratches moving slowly against the distant rocks. From here, she could see part of the cliff scar that fell away below the hunting lodge. The lodge itself was too far away to be seen, even if a jutting shoulder of the mountain range had not hidden it.

She had not foreseen that her father would send the Englishman to stay so far away, out of her reach. How had she missed that possibility? She had considered several outlying estates where he might be sent to work, safely distant from the city. But she had never thought that her father would risk giving him such freedom to sleep away from the Castello, even under guard. In the Englishman's place, she would already be plotting her escape.

Urgency gripped her in a cold fist. Ettore had let his hatred of her show openly, his fury only just contained, not minding that their father saw it.

He might not wait until their father died to move against her. She saw clearly how many ways she might meet a fatal accident, just like Baldassare. Every torch, every slippery stair, every bite of food she ate . . . Glasses shattered and became accidental knives. Belts turned to nooses.

She must act first, if only she could.

Francis would return later. Surely, he would stay in La Spada again tonight at least rather than make that unfamiliar ride in the dark.

46

THE HUNTING LODGE

'It's impossible!' Francis prowled unhappily among the outbuildings behind the hunting lodge, accompanied by Venturini and the lodge steward. It might become possible, but not in the time they were likely to have. With the prince's promise of infinite resources, Francis could ask for as many assistants as he needed to make it possible, but that would invite in an army of spies.

But how he wanted to stay here! He liked everything about the place, except the fact that he and Richard would not have time to turn it into a workplace before the prince died. Escape from here would be far easier than from La Spada.

From the edge of the broad rock ledge where the hunting lodge stood, you could look towards Venice, where there was a safe house and an English ambassador to help them back to England. Almost an hour's ride from La Spada, the lodge was not only outside both the *fortezza* and the city walls, it placed them a very little bit closer to Venice. With Richard's gift for making friends in the kitchens, his nephew would soon learn which tracks and trails might lead them there.

Earlier, when they had set off for the lodge for the second time that day, the Uskok captain had nodded in recognition, not friendly, but at least admitting Francis to the fellowship of the living.

'What do you hunt here, from this lodge?' Francis called in Latin to the Uskok riding just in front of him.

'*Venat?*' the man asked or something very like it. '*Orsi . . . cervi . . .*' He pointed up .'*Kitz.*' Bear, deer and, perhaps, mountain goats. Or chamois.

'Wolves?'

After a silence while the man decided whether or not to respond, or else he was trying to translate his reply, he said over this shoulder, 'Once. Before our prince lost his strength. We hunted wolves with dogs.' He sounded wistful.

Francis lapsed back into silence, satisfied for the moment. If they were to make this ride very often, he hoped to lull the Uskoks into friendly carelessness. Perhaps.

They ducked and scraped under a fallen pine. While Francis was brushing green needles from the back of his collar, a deer flashed out of sight among the dark tree trunks below them.

Soon after they had climbed past the point where Francis was called back to La Spada, they emerged from green shadow into a sharp crisp sunlight. Gradually, the trees shortened until they no longer soared upwards but crouched on ledges with roots dug-in against the wind. The diamond-crusted snow on the tallest peaks crept closer. Francis's chest tightened and his breath thickened. They had climbed a long way up from the plateau floor in less than an hour.

Riding close to the shelf edge, Francis saw La Spada behind and below them to his left, impressive even from above. From here the sword shape that gave La Spada its name could be clearly seen. The abrupt tower of rock on which the castello perched revealed itself to be a final spur of the mountain ridge.

The beauty of this ride alone made Francis like the lodge. He would enjoy riding here for pure pleasure, when not in search of a place to do the impossible.

After levelling off and curving around the mountain shoulder along a narrow rock shelf, the track rounded a steep upward bend and met a gated wall. The wall ran between shelf edge and mountain cliff, blocking their way.

It wouldn't stop a serious assault with battering ram or explosive charge, thought Francis. But it did offer protection against the idle curiosity of the outside world. It was a second count in the lodge's favour. Unfortunately, the wall would not guard against the curiosity inside it. They passed through a high solid wooden gate onto a curved sloping forecourt of packed earth and stone.

The prince's hunting lodge stood with its back to the mountain, overhung by crone-like pines, looking out over a precipitous drop into the plateau. A stable-yard of wood and stone outbuildings crowded behind it, pressed against the mountain rock.

Three floors of dark wood rose from a base of stone. Interlocking wings projected from each side. Steeply sloped roofs, covered with rusty cedar shingles held down by battens, would shrug off snow. Wooden balconies jutted from the two upper floors. Heavy dark red shutters, now hooked open, protected windows already shadowed by the balconies. Smoke twisted up from the chimneys. The air smelled of pines and the wood smoke.

The Uskok captain shouted. As they reined in their horses, the central double doors swung open. These doors, made of heavy timbers reinforced with iron and as solid as the gate, were framed by a delicate, ornate escutcheon painted onto the wall. Exuberant curls and frivolous waves of reds, greens, cream and gold chased each other around the door frame. Painted pediments above each of the windows further imitated in a cheerful rustic fashion the carved stone and moulded plaster of the Jesuit splendour of the new *Magno Palazzo* in Castello La Spada.

A wide-planked wood floor creaked under their boots to announce their arrival. The air inside the lodge smelled of freshly cut wood and resin, a little mixed with smoke and dust.

In other circumstances, thought Francis, this would be a very fine place.

Centred on its great hall, the lodge was made entirely of wood like the alpine farmhouses they had seen on their journey to La Spada. Huge tree trunk posts soared upwards like columns in a cathedral nave to an intricate wooden fili-gree roof of angled joints and interlocking beams, braces and struts. Where a cathedral or church would have a side aisle on each side of the nave, the lodge had rows of chambers, with a second floor of lodgings above them. Each side was reached by its own wooden staircase.

At the far end of the hall in place of the altar stood a vast fireplace, holding a huge pair of ornate iron firedogs – two cathedral spires topped with brass balls the size of a baby's head. Hooks dangling on chains and spider-legged trivets of brass and iron announced that it could be used for cooking as well as warmth. Logs as large as a man blazed in welcome.

Francis advanced a few more steps into the hall and grunted with satisfaction. He shifted his weight from one foot to the other. The broad planks squeaked under him. The lodge creaked like a ship. This floor would serve as well as a pack of watch dogs.

As if to confirm this conclusion the creaking of the wooden staircase to the right announced the hurried descent of a dark stocky man, who might have been either a farmer or a cook but wore a hunting knife, sword, and the prince's sword-and-castle badge. He was their steward, he said in fluent English. His name was Ricco Smith.

'How did you come to be in La Spada?' Francis asked. Here, surely, was Cecil's man at last. Who could be better placed than an English steward to watch his back?

'I was born in La Spada,' said Smith. 'There are many Englishmen in Italy . . . came to fight for money, stayed for love. My father was English.'

'Do you often visit England?' Francis waited for the flick of an eye, the slight nod, anything to acknowledge their true relationship.

'Devout Essex farmers don't waste their hospitality on the bastards of foreign Catholic whores.'

Francis cursed. If he wasn't Cecil's back-watcher, then Smith was almost certainly someone else's spy. It was more than chance that the man's ears would catch every word that Francis and Seaborn said in his hearing.

'Come with me to the stable yard whilst I decide whether this place will serve.'

Smith found a tablet of paper and a lump of graphite wrapped in string and followed Francis outside. Silently, Venturini joined them.

This is impossible, thought Francis again, staring around the run-down stable yard. A derelict hen house, wood store, half-filled hay barn, a cowshed, a grain store, small cow barn, and the rumps of their two horses shifting in an open stable.

But he liked the tell-tale wooden floors of the lodge, the distance from La Spada, and the wall that blocked the track. He liked the ride up the track and the flash of the deer. He and Seaborn were far better placed here for possible escape than they were when locked inside the Castello at the top of that narrow causeway, with its steep drops and falconets.

And it was the prince's will.

They could use that dry grain store for their own non-explosive supplies, he decided. The wood store could be cleared to hold charcoal. The hen house was substantial enough and the right size for a mixing room. It had once been secure against foxes, stoats and wolves.

'Our most urgent need is for a safe, protected room for grinding our gunpowder . . .' Take care, he warned himself. Avoid 'we'. 'I need a secure mixing room.'

'We can make anywhere secure for you, sir,' said Smith. 'The Uskoks will guard you.' He jerked his head at Venturini.

'I don't mean secure for me,' said Francis. 'I mean for everyone else.'

He poked his head into the stone hen house and gazed at the broken perches and mouldy feathers. He would have preferred a wooden building to release an accidental blast, not to hold it in and throw it back at him. Fire masters differed on that point. He and Boomer had argued it for many years.

'This hen house will do for my mixing room, if it's cleaned and lined in leather against chance sparks.'

Unhappily, he judged the distance between the hen house and the lodge, not more than sixty feet. The mixing house at Powder Mote was several hundred yards from the house and surrounded by a thick bank of earth.

'I need two hundred full hides, stitched together in pairs,' he said.

'Two hundred?' Smith managed to sound both astonished and disapproving.

'I'm told that my resources are infinite.'

Smith raised his brows but wrote. 'Two hundred full hides, stitched . . .'

'Then stuffed to make mattresses.'

Smith exhaled. 'Stuffed with what? It's too early for hay.'

267

Francis felt his temper rising. 'Dried bracken, feathers, bombast, floor sweepings . . . what ever you use to stuff with in La Spada!'

Why did the first Englishman he met in La Spada, whether a spy or not, have to be a jumped-up inventory clerk?

Smith wrote again.

'Then I will want flat willow frames woven, one to fit and support each mattress.'

'How many feet of willow will that be?'

'As many as the men making the frames tell you they need.' He felt his fists clench. 'Have you heard of *vinea*? The moveable shields the Romans used to protect their men while attacking a castle or fort?'

Smith looked blank.

Venturini stepped forward. 'Do you mean *karwah*?'

'I don't know if I do or not.'

Venturini lifted paper and pencil from Smith's hands and drew a rough picture of a padded shield, with a handle to carry or brace it. Then he scribbled a little man to show that it was much larger than an ordinary shield, far too heavy to carry while actually fighting. Then he quickly sketched a square of them, close together, making walls and a roof around the man. Then, for good measure, he drew three flaming arrows shooting down at the roof.

'Yes!' cried Francis. '*Vinea. Karwah.*' He strode around the stable yard, stamping his boot. 'One to go here . . . and here . . . and here.'

Venturini nodded his understanding. 'We know *karwah*. We have used them.' He held up his hands to say, wait. 'We can make them. Leave them to us.'

'You find the hides to line the hen house,' Francis told Smith. 'And clear the other outbuildings.'

'Why are you doing this?' he asked Venturini as they left the stable yard.

'For our prince.'

Francis nodded. 'And do you think you could help Smith find a safer place for the horses?'

'We would never leave them where they are,' said Venturini. 'Even with *karwah*. Not so close to gunpowder.'

The man's English was even better than Francis had feared.

'And I need a secure gunpowder store away from the lodge. A dry cave perhaps.'

Again Venturini nodded.

Francis would have been overjoyed by his new allies, the Uskoks, if they had not also been the prince's personal guard.

47

Back in the lodge he told Richard and the steward to unload the horses. They would stay.

'Your bags are already in your room, sir,' said Richard. He seemed subdued, perhaps by the presence of the steward who spoke English almost as well as he did. 'There are mice,' he added.

Their sleeping quarters were as fragrant as the hall below. Francis looked out through two shuttered windows towards the valley. His bed here was a large semi-enclosed cupboard bed set into the wall. Instead of a pallet on the floor, Richard had a real bed of his own set up in a smaller antechamber, made of leather strips woven across a short-legged frame. Both beds had thick feather quilts folded at the foot into a high soft mound like whipped cream. Francis sat on his and sank almost to his armpits. 'We must take some of these back to England.'

'I have already begun to make a list of possible effects for the funeral fireworks,' ventured Seaborn, from the corner of Francis's floor where he was laying out the firework supplies they had brought with them. 'Shall I tell you my thoughts? If you truly welcome them.'

In other circumstances, Richard's eagerness to tread on his heels might have amused Francis. Now, given his own dark humour, his nephew's fervour grated slightly. But he must not discourage it. He needed Seaborn. Had he not already said as much, aloud?

'Shortly,' he said. He returned to his own thoughts. The *factorium* – if it could be made ready in time – was sure to be watched. Francis must permit the Uskoks to protect him. He must even seem to permit a certain amount of surveillance of the making of fireworks. Like leaving your door a little ajar.

He would be allowed his small professional secrets, the special powder mixes, the rare ingredients, but any attempt at true secrecy or hidden work would raise instant suspicion. Richard's true role would soon become known, if he had not already stirred suspicions. The young man's schooling had honed his keen mind but it had not taught him to be inconspicuous. Francis himself could most likely do some of his secret work in the *factorium* as if it were part of preparing the fireworks . . . when he had decided what this work must be. But where and how would he create his false tricks of theatre?

'You have until my father dies,' Ettore had said.

Even if Francis managed to seem to satisfy the terms of his contract with the prince, he was not at all certain that Ettore would honour his father's agreement.

Francis tried to take an interest in Seaborn's lists of what they had brought from England:

A dozen large shells, packed with coloured stars on delaying fuses, carefully wrapped in oiled paper and cushioned by sheep's wool. Two hundred paper shell cases, cut out but not yet folded into shape, light to carry and time-consuming to make. Francis and Boomer had debated about these.

271

'Yes,' he agreed now. 'It's as well we brought them.'

Seaborn set out and counted off the stoneware crocks of colourants – iron filings, mineral salts and precious Muscovy rosin.

With only half his attention, Francis inspected and re-coiled lengths of rope soaked in different saltpetre solutions, to make fast and slow fuses. He listened to Seaborn discuss possible choices from a sheaf of drawings for 'machines' or devices on which to mount the fireworks.

'Put carpenters, plasterers and gilders on our list of craftsmen.' Francis shook out his leather apron and his clothing that fastened entirely without metal for fear of causing a spark.

He opened the two small kegs of sulphur and saltpetre, otherwise called nitre. He inspected these two vital ingredients of gunpowder for moisture or other decay. They did not travel well when combined. The third ingredient of gunpowder, charcoal, could easily be found anywhere in the world that a man might go.

'Tell Smith to find us charcoal. You work out how much.'

How was he to carry off his deceit? It wasn't enough to devise the fraud. He must also execute it in a very short time. And in secret. Without being detected by intelligencers for either the prince or Ettore. Or agents for the *principessa*, for that matter. And don't forget Da Monte, and the Inquisition. All of them, except the prince and perhaps the *principessa*, were eager to prove him a deceiving rogue.

He unwrapped his 'lucky' pestle for the dangerous stage of incorporating the saltpetre with the sulphur and charcoal. After much debate, he had given in to Boomer and also brought his favourite mortar in spite of its weight.

'You'll have enough to distract you there,' Boomer had said. 'You'll need the feel of familiar things in your hands.' To avoid that heartbeat of fatal distraction, his father had not said. The blinding flash and the explosion you probably won't hear because you'll already be dead.

When both he and Richard were satisfied that nothing had been damaged either by the journey or by the search at La Spada, they began to draw up lists of what to buy. Among much else, they needed still more sulphur and salt-petre, more iron filings. They needed to have more shell moulds turned by a joiner. Any assistants would need purse-lipped powder spoons.

Francis did not know yet what he would need.

A revelation, he thought sourly. A real one this time.

The worst of it was that all of their efforts today might be to no purpose. Tonight, the prince would show him the English bond. Tonight, Francis meant to hold it in his own hands and decide what to do next. Tonight, they might have to make a run for Venice.

As they worked, they heard mice and other small crea-tures scampering noisily in the walls – an entire secret nation. Francis listened to them thoughtfully. Mice and their gnawing habits were a danger when you were making and storing explosives.

At last, Francis stood up and put on his riding cloak. 'I must go back down to La Spada before the track grows too dark.' He did not yet know how well they could be over-heard here at the lodge. 'Do you still wear your belt?' he asked. Seaborn always wore his money and any jewels around his waist.

Seaborn gave him a startled enquiring look.

Francis touched his sword, then mimed eating and pointed at his saddlebag.

Seaborn nodded. He rose and set his own sword ready near the door. Briefly, they clasped hands.

'Don't wait up for me,' said Francis. 'I'll find my bed by myself.'

As Francis gave his gelding its head to deal with steep rocky track, he realized that he also needed to answer a second urgent question – but only if they did not flee tonight. Not just how he would seem to launch the prince but where?

Dear God, what was he tangled in?

By the time he and his two escorting Uskoks reach La Spada, lanterns were being hung outside inns and candles were lighting oiled paper windows with a warm glow.

48

The prince was in bed. Francis had never before seen him in bed, but always in his chair under the wolf skin rugs in his *scrittoio*. The parade of rooms had been emptied of all but those who would sleep there or were on night guard. In the *antecamarilla*, the night ushers raised sleepy heads from their mattresses, or looked up at Francis from candle-lit huddles gathered around a late game of cards. As they scrambled to their feet, he waved them back down again. The new man-servant who had replaced Yuri waited in the prince's antechamber to admit Francis to the grand *camera*, the bedchamber itself.

'Leave us!' The prince waved a dismissing hand at the manservant and the two Uskoks. It seemed that he had already dismissed the princess. Besides the prince and Francis, only the priest remained, dozing slumped against the far wall with his black hood pulled low over his face. Francis looked at him again. It struck him that Father Daniele might be a little taller than before. With those hoods, you could never be certain if it was the same man, or not.

'Come closer, or you won't see what you came for.'

Francis approached the vast gilded temple draped with

silk hangings into which had been woven the sword and castle of La Spada. The juices in his belly seemed to curdle.

In this light, the prince looked very near to death. The two candles set on carved brackets inside the bed canopy painted hard black shadows under the bones of his face. His brows were overhanging ledges. Deep in their caves, his eyes showed only as tiny pinpricks of light – the candles reflected in the rheum. His nose was a craggy beak, his mouth a slit in the wreckage of his face.

Don't die yet, Francis begged him silently. Or you'll take Richard and me with you. Give me a little longer to devise a way out . . . or else give me the bond.

'I have it here.' The prince held a parchment in his hands. It was opened now but had once been folded to enclose its contents. On one ribbon dangled a circle of red sealing wax bearing the sword and castle of the Piratis. The other carried what looked very like the seal of Robert Cecil.

Francis reached out. The prince pulled the bond back.

'You may read it, but I will continue to hold it,' he said. The coverlet seemed to lie almost flat across his hips and legs. He drew a rasping breath 'I trust you, Cointo, but not that far. If I give it to you, you might thrust it into the fire and destroy it before Father Daniele could stop you.'

Francis stepped closer. A smell of urine came from the bed, and putrefaction. There was not going to be time to achieve any of his aims, he thought with despair. The man would not live long enough.

'Satisfy yourself and your master,' said the prince.

Francis leaned close enough to read the ornate copper-plate hand. As he did so, he noticed that one the carved panels in the ornate, gilded bed head sat at a slight angle, like a door that had not been completely closed. Then he saw what the bond said, in Latin, and forgot everything else.

'To James Stuart, King of England and Scotland the sum of . . .'

This is wrong, thought Francis. Cecil said that the king did not know about the loan. He began again, not trusting what he thought he read.

'To James Stuart, King of England and Scotland . . .' His eyes skipped onwards. *'Received by Robert Cecil, Viscount Cranborne, English Secretary of State . . . against the surety of the jewel known as the King's Great Pearl . . . said loan given by . . .'*

The signature of the party making the loan was 'Alessandro Hugo Piratii, *Princeps.*'

Francis read yet again, looking for explanation in the lawyer's Latin, which was only a distant cousin of the Latin that he himself spoke. What he read seemed to be nonsense. His own ignorance of how such things were done would explain his failure to grasp it.

'You've seen it now.' The prince pulled the bond away. But not before Francis read the signature that acknowledged receipt of the loan. 'Robert Cecil, Viscount Cranborne', which had been Cecil's title before the grateful king made him up to Earl of Salisbury. Cecil had not written 'on the part of' or 'under the seal of' or any such other lending of royal power. Just plain 'Cecil'. In that unmistakable swooping signature, always far larger than any others that shared the same page, as if Cecil asserted his true stature on paper. The world saw the small lopsided body. Statesmen, in their documents, were shown the true scale of his power.

It seemed to Francis that Cecil had borrowed more than money. He had usurped the king's authority to secure it.

Francis tried to remember the exact words he had read. The King's Great Pearl was the pledge, no doubt about that. But if the king did not know about the loan, as Cecil had said, then James most certainly had not offered his jewel in surety. It was to buy such gew-gaws, amongst much else, that Cecil had taken the loan in the first place. If he could be believed.

Then Francis's habit of suspicion towards Cecil gave way to good sense. Cecil had no reason to spin such a dangerous, self-destructive lie. He had been snared by the truth.

You seem to have bought your lordship dearly, Francis told Cecil. Unbelievably, he seemed to have caught Cecil, at last, in a reckless mistake.

Cecil didn't make reckless mistakes, but he did take risks, like all great men.

The king's jewel. Francis shook his head in protest. Cecil had no right to pledge the king's jewel.

Francis understood now why Cecil had been so urgent for secrecy. Now he understood Cecil's final words. 'I trust you, Quoynt.'

Cecil had trusted him with his life.

Francis glanced at Father Daniele, wondering yet again if the man carried a knife, and whether he was a priest at all or only a bodyguard.

'Da Monte knows that the money is owed,' the prince warned.

'Has he seen the bond?'

'Not yet.' The prince began to laugh but was seized by a fit of coughing, until it seemed that he might choke. He set the bond down on the far side of the bed.

'Da Monte,' said the prince with a hint of malice. '. . . Da Monte has taken quite enough power into his own hands already. I shan't give it all to him just yet. Nor to my son. They can both wait a little longer.'

Da Monte knew of the loan, then, but not the significance of the bond itself.

Francis also understood what Cecil would trust him to do next.

'Shall I call your physician?' asked Francis, eyes still on the bond, tantalizingly close. Cecil would trust him to seize the bond and burn it.

The dozing priest lifted his head.

The urgency of Francis's concern for his health seemed to amuse the prince, even while he waved away the question. In the last paroxysms of coughing, he felt amongst the bedclothes for a silk napkin, then spat into it. He wiped his mouth. 'I don't mean to die before you're ready for me. But you must make haste, all the same.' The napkin vanished into the bedclothes again.

'May I see the contract again?' Francis asked. 'You snatched it away rather sudden.'

'You've seen enough.'

Father Daniele stretched his limbs.

Francis remembered the weariness with which Cecil had said, 'A necessary for England, but a costly one.' He remembered Cecil fighting to retain his former influence with a new monarch, his reluctance to tell the king that tiresome word, 'no'. Cecil's refusal to press the prince further in negotiations. Cecil sending Francis alone, when he could have sent Francis merely to do the supposed fireworks and one of his smooth-tongued agents or diplomats to carry out the negotiations.

'I trust you, Quoynt.' It had not made sense at the time. Now, it did.

Cecil took the loan for the best of reasons, Francis was certain. But to seem to act on behalf of the king, when you did not, was treasonous fraud. To pledge the king's own jewel was both theft and treason. The excellence of your reasons made no difference.

The prince shook the bond gently. 'As long as I hold this bond, I believe Salisbury will parlay on anything I ask. I don't think he wants a dispute.'

Francis watched the prince fold the bond and hold it in both hands, waiting for Francis to go.

Briefly, Francis considered the risk of asking the prince to delay repayment until the date the money was due. But, even leaving aside the plundered ship and terrified cabin boy, he saw clearly that the prince had no reason to agree. His highness had matters exactly as he wanted them. He, or someone, might well have meant to catch Cecil in exactly this way from the start. In any case, in 1610 when the money was due, the prince would undoubtedly be dead.

Cecil had sent Francis alone because he trusted him to be loyal enough to hide the truth. The prince had blackmailed Cecil into sending Francis. It occurred to Francis now, that the prince might not mean for his heir to return the bond at all.

Francis stared at the man in the bed. The more he considered this last possibility the more likely it seemed. The prince, once happily launched on his way to the hope of Heaven, need not care whether or not his bargain was honoured on earth. Why surrender this unimaginable advantage? What ruler of a small European principality – even a mad one – would hand back, or want his heir to hand back, the secret power to make the English Secretary of State jump and dance like a pet monkey?

'Send for my daughter when you leave,' said the prince. 'Have the Uskoks summon the *principessa*. I need her tonight. I won't sleep, else.'

Destroy it now! Francis told himself. His muscles prepared. He must imagine only the sequence of his actions. He did not let himself imagine his dying.

Almost absently, the prince slid the paper deep under the bedclothes. Whoever was acting as Father Daniele that night leaned forward alertly, ready to leap to his feet.

I won't have time, thought Francis heavily. By the time he had overpowered the prince and found the bond amongst the bedclothes, and turned to thrust it into the fire, Daniele's knife would be in his ribs. He settled back onto his heels again. An act of pointless courage would be no help to Cecil at all.

49

After he had relayed the prince's order to the Uskok guard, Francis remembered his other purpose in La Spada. He took his time entering the House of Wisdom, deliberately rattling the key in the lock. By the time he opened the door Albona had already hidden his work.

'You,' the librarian said, with obvious relief. 'Back for more books already?'

'No. Tonight, I need something very different.'

Having got his cat, one of Albona's half-grown feral kittens, Francis first tried putting it into his saddlebag. Within an instant it had clawed its way out again through a gap that looked barely large enough to admit his finger. After catching it again with some difficulty, he buttoned it inside his jacket. It seemed a little calmer there although it clung to him with tiny needle claws.

If it didn't let go soon, he would leave the damned thing here and come another time with a stout sack.

But as Francis headed back up to the lodge once more, in the company of two Uskok guards, the rhythm of the horse seemed to lull the kitten. It settled inside his jacket against the beating of his heart and slept. It woke once when his horse stumbled in the near-darkness. The frightened claws hooking through his shirt again suddenly put Francis in mind of the princess. Though she was more mountain lion than mouser.

He laid a reassuring hand on the lump in his jacket until it settled again.

Think again, madam, he told her silently. I don't make tender prey. And I've learned caution from trying not to be eaten alive by my employer.

His surprising employer who deserved his understanding after all. Had Francis himself not signed a contract that was just as mad as the bond?

He let his horse pick its way up the dark track. He had never wanted to carry such weight, as either soldier or civilian. If he failed here in La Spada and the debt became known in England, it would be the block for Cecil, no escape. The little man's enemies would dance with delight. And the many people who might not have liked him in chilly person but nevertheless trusted his probity would now desert and turn against him. By the time Cecil lost his head, of course, Francis would almost certainly be dead.

But the question that kicked his heart into a gallop was what might happen if he should, by some miracle succeed? Once the bond . . . if the bond . . . was safely back in Cecil's hands, or else destroyed, what was the likely fate of the only other Englishman who knew Cecil's terrible secret?

His quickened breath and racing heartbeat disturbed the kitten again. The tiny needle claws scrabbled inside his jacket. Again, he soothed it with his hand while his thoughts still raced.

It interested him that while he could imagine Cecil having him killed, he had never questioned where the money had gone. He was certain that Cecil had used it to serve the king.

*

'If we need more,' he said a little later, when he showed Seaborn the cat, '. . . you fetch them.'

Seaborn pointed.

To his intense irritation, Francis saw a scrawny shape already crouched motionless in a corner of the room, eyes fixed on a tiny gap between wall and floor.

'Ricco, our steward found it,' Seaborn explained. 'Christened Henry, like the English king . . . the man not the cat. Or so he says. He likes to talk.'

'Just what we need.' Francis regretted his sharpness at once. 'That's good, Rich. Learn all you can.'

The level blue gaze told him that Seaborn, while younger and perhaps over-eager, was not to be patronized. It also reminded Francis how much this young man had survived in order to be here pretending to be his manservant. He was risking his life to help Francis.

'Oh, Rich . . .' He did not yet know how much they could be overheard here in the lodge, though Richard had undoubtedly learned by now. 'Come with me to see the outbuildings. I think I may have found our mixing shed.'

Outside, they dropped the pretext of the outbuildings and walked to the cliff edge, where they stood looking out into the night. A single tiny light from a distant farmhouse pricked the darkness of the valley floor. A layer of low cloud was advancing from the east, pale and luminous against the black sky and even blacker silhouettes of the mountains.

'I gossiped in the kitchens while waiting for you earlier.' Seaborn tilted back his head as if searching for stars. 'You need to watch Da Monte. It seems that he's the true ruler here, in day-to-day matters at least. Pretends deference to his cousin while helping to hide the true extent of the prince's madness from all but a very small circle of his friends at court.'

'Ambitious?'

'The general opinion holds that he's happier forging

another man's signature than standing by the consequences of his own.'

'You learned all this in the kitchens?'

'I've wriggled higher, as you asked.'

'Take care, Rich!'

There was a long silence. 'It may be,' said Seaborn at last, 'that I'm more at ease higher than lower, and better able to judge others. And therefore happier for you to risk trusting my judgement.'

Seaborn had never before referred to his birth. Now, it was a statement of relevant fact, not a boast. All the same, Francis took a moment to settle into the truth that his nephew was more at home in their new courtly world than he was himself.

'I'm grateful for what you judge to be the truth at any level,' he said finally.

'Trusting fool.' Seaborn spoke lightly but sounded relieved by Francis's reply. 'There's another wall and guarded gate farther up the track,' Seaborn went on. 'Beyond the gate, the track leads to a number of abandoned silver mines. If you keep working your way north past the mines for long enough you reach the Austrian border.'

'Just as the Austrian Hapsburgs can reach Friuli from the other direction?'

'More to the point, the kitchen grooms say that old herding tracks run all through these mountains. Those walls don't trouble anyone willing to do a little scrambling through the *sottobosco* and risk tearing their clothes on the scrub.'

Francis nodded. 'That's good to know. I must risk my clothes in the morning.' He stared towards Venice again and decided. He owed Seaborn full honesty. Whether or not Richard knew it, he was as tangled with Cecil as Francis was. 'Now I want to tell you what I have just learned tonight in La Spada.'

Seaborn did not seem altogether surprised. But he had the delicacy to nod and keep his mouth shut.

'The Englishman has gone back up the mountain to the hunting lodge, your highness. He did not stay in La Spada.' Isabella delivered the message with no hint of innuendo. Her manner was always quiet but straightforward. For that combination of restfulness and restraint alone, Sofia was determined, in time, to make the girl the chief of her women.

'Thank you,' said Sofia, without looking up from her writing.

The Florentines were laughing at a private anecdote in their usual places at a gaming table near the lion. They had been joined after supper by two hopeful suitors, neither of them wealthy or influential enough to gain royal approval.

Isabella waited a moment to see if the *principessa* wished her to sing tonight. Then she slipped away to her corner where she sat silently fingering the strings of a lute, which the *principessa* had given her, so that the Spanish girl could enlarge her range of songs.

Sofia resisted a fierce need to drop her head into her hands and weep with frustration. Now that she was so near her goal, it grew harder, not easier, to be patient. She yawned delicately and unclenched her fists, which would betray her to any sharp watching eyes. She did not let herself look around to see if any of her women had noticed. There was no need to look, she told herself.

No one could know what she meant to do.

One of the Uskoks entered and approached her. 'Our prince asks for you, your highness.'

As she rose with a show of willingness, she thought that she might still try to persuade her father to drink a double draft of his pain-killing tincture tonight, even though the

Englishman had gone. If she had to sit still on that stool for more than a moment, with his hand weighing her down, she would start to tear her own flesh with what was left of her nails.

50

In the first faint light of the following day, Francis found a long wooden shepherd's staff and a small billhook in one of the outbuildings in the stable yard. Wearing his oldest doublet and soldier's heavy leather jerkin, he worked his way up the steep slope behind the lodge. When he stopped to look back down, with one foot braced on a boulder, he saw a pair of Uskoks watching him from the forecourt. The head of a third Uskok vanished around a bend on his way up to the higher gate that Seaborn had mentioned.

Francis waved to the two men in the forecourt. One of them waved back. Francis waited a little longer but no one came clambering up behind him.

It would seem that, here at the lodge, he might not always have a watchdog at his heels. There was a chance that he might be able to carry out some secret work undetected if he could find a place to do it, away from the eyes of slaves, Uskoks and Ricco Smith.

Standing high on the tilting slope of the world, he breathed in cold clean air, listened to the drip and trickle of water all around him amongst the rocks, and snatched at the illusion of freedom. He ached to have a clear familiar purpose again.

To be looking down on La Spada with an attacker's assessing eye. Or to be in Sussex, driving a cart through muddy lanes in search of the purest saltpetre, or looking for light pine rods that were straight enough to guide rockets safely into the sky.

He thought again about Cecil's bond. Not England's bond after all, as Cecil had somehow led him to believe, but the little man's personal debt, negotiated on fraudulent terms. With this unwelcome burden of knowledge, Francis had also made one small advance – that panel in the prince's bed, slightly askew, out of line with the rest of the surfaces. Having just settled his mind on a playhouse version of the sham flight to Heaven, he almost wished that he had not guessed at the bond's possible hiding place.

In the last day, one absurdity and one suicidal endeavour had both become a little more possible.

He waved again and pointed to indicate that he meant to climb higher. The men in the forecourt did not respond. He took this as permission to move on. He flung himself up a steep scramble of loose rock. Somewhere above him, spotted from the track outside the gate, was a large dark shadow that might be the mouth of a cave.

A shrill whistle stopped him. Then he heard another, and another. At the edge of his vision, small rusty brown bodies scattered into burrows and under rocks.

Marmotta. One of the new words he had learned from Venturini. Marmots, who lived in large colonies in the mountain rocks.

They would make excellent sentries.

He found not a cave but an abandoned mine. The roof had collapsed. A strip of mountainside blocked the mine with a solid core of broken rock. Small fleshy plants like sea anemones had already formed mats among the boulders.

A little higher up the mountainside, he found a second

mine where the entrance was still clear. The roof props still looked sound. He explored inside, his hair collecting cobwebs and brushing crumbs of earth from the low ceiling. He passed broken machinery, hoists, ceiling props, parts of carts. Then he came to a solid rock fall blocking the tunnel.

Back outside, he waved down again to the now-tiny figures who had moved to the very edge of the cliff to keep him in view. Then he began to climb the side of the low saddle above him, ignoring what looked like signals from below telling him to stop.

From the ridge of the saddle, he looked down with a flare of excitement into a small natural bowl. On the far side of this bowl was the entrance to a third mine. An overgrown track leading to the bowl could still be made out in the scrub. Once it had been wide and level enough to allow carts to bring in tools, heavy equipment and miners and carry away the mined ore. With only a little work, it could do so again. The mine entrance was partially blocked by a small rock fall but even from here, Francis could see into the shadowed mine shaft beyond. What interested him most, however, was the dark eye of an old cistern or well near the centre of the flat base of the bowl.

He slid down the steep slope past a pillow-sized, lavender-grey patch of late snow lingering where the sun never reached. A crumbled stone wall had once protected this hole into the earth, which was roughly seven feet across. A thick ruff of ferns and other weeds obscured its depth. Francis dropped in a large stone. It ripped down through the ferns and landed at last with a faint distant thump.

Not a well, he decided, but a ventilation shaft for the mine. He glanced up at the skyline around him but saw no sign of a watcher. Thoughtfully, he dropped another stone into the air shaft. He did not have to lift the prince at all. Not if he could devise a way to sink him into the earth.

289

His neck crawled briefly as he considered what the prince would make of that idea – instead of a chariot ride to Heaven, a shove on the way towards Hell.

Nevertheless, he stood for a long time, staring at the dark opening in the earth that just might help him a little farther along his own way out. Then he turned to the mine.

In spite of the small fall of lichen-covered rock, the props around the entrance were sound. Francis worked for almost an hour to clear enough room to slide through. Then he set his teeth and prepared to crawl into darkness.

As a fire master, like Boomer, he had insisted on going anywhere he would send his miners. Often he went with his sappers to set the charges himself at the end of dark, zig-zag tunnels. Hardened or not, he had never relished this part of his work. Though he made himself do it, he was too tall and too broad in the shoulder to fit well into tight underground wormholes and *cuniculi* where you crawled farther and farther away from daylight, around the twists in the tunnels towards the blackness where you would plant death.

Beyond the fall, the passage was clear, wide enough for a small cart and high enough for Francis to stand almost upright. He reached up and carefully explored the roof with his hands. It felt solid. The props here were sound. He surmised that the entrance roof might have been deliberately brought down to close off the mine to sheltering bandits or anyone else who had no business being there. Somewhere in the darkness ahead of him, water gurgled faintly.

He wriggled back out and worked until almost noon to clear enough of the fall to let in both light and clean air. In that time, no head appeared over the saddle. No one came up the overgrown track. The marmots did not whistle in alarm.

Spring had arrived. A hot midday sun shone. The little bowl was protected from the wind. Soon he took off both jerkin and doublet to work in only his shirt.

At last, fully clothed again, he went back into the instant chill of underground gloom. There was now just enough light from the entrance for him to feel his way cautiously forwards. He paused to let his eyes adjust from bright sunlight then set off along the tunnel, testing the footing in front of him with his shepherd's staff.

At the same time he sniffed the air. Given the blocked entrance, he should not meet a bear. But wolves could have scrambled through the gap, and in a mine of this size there might well be other ways in. When he listened, he heard only the rustling and scuttling of small creatures fleeing from his advance, together with the sound of running water.

The walls of the tunnel disappeared and the roof over his head sloped sharply upwards. He smelled bats and their dung. He held out his arms sideways but felt nothing. Then he found the wall on his right and stroked it to judge the surface. He had entered a high wide chamber shaped by miners' tools but once, perhaps, also a small natural cave. Directly ahead of him stood a tall pale ghost wrapped in a misty shroud.

Still testing the floor with his staff, he advanced towards the ghost. As he drew closer, he saw that it was not a shape at all but the absence of shape, a column of faint light seeping down from above through an old air well. Judging by his estimated position under the mountain, it was a second air shaft, not the one in the centre of the bowl.

Back again in the startling intensity of light in the outer world, he pushed uphill through waist-high scrub above the mine, prodding at the hidden ground, sighting on the two dead tree branches he had stuck in the ground in a line with the entrance to the mine until he found the second air shaft.

With the billhook, he cut back the growth around the top of this second air shaft. Lying on his belly he cleared the weeds and seedling trees that grew on the walls as far down as he could safely reach. When he returned to the chamber the second time, much more light now fell from above. The stale air was already freshening through the natural chimney.

Now he could make out a broken pick handle, a tangle of ceiling props, a boot without its sole. As he circled the walls, listening for the source of the water, he bent to pick up a small rock fragment that caught his eye. He took it into the light at the bottom of the well, rubbed it hard against his sleeve and held it back to the light.

Silver glinted through black tarnish. Not an irregular pebble after all, but a small medallion the size of his thumb nail, in the shape of a *figa*, the ancient obscene gesture of insult and contempt, a hand with the thumb thrust up between the first two fingers. Worn as an amulet, it was thought to bring good luck and ward off the evil eye.

Francis rubbed it again on his sleeve and polished it with the ball of his thumb. He hoped that no harm had come to the man who had lost it, but the *figa* felt like a good omen.

Though he prided himself on being man of reason, no one in a trade like his ever failed to perform secret rituals before firing a charge. Without openly admitting it, he, like other fire masters, made small private prayers and promised offerings to whatever deity it was who controlled the outcome – whether this particular handful of sulphur, saltpetre and charcoal would offer success or death. Smiling a little to show that he did not really believe such things, he put the *figa* carefully into the pouch on his belt. He was growing as addled as the prince, welcoming a good omen for a mad task.

Perhaps by coincidence, modest good fortune followed at once. In one of several side passages leading from the large chamber deeper into the mountainside, he found the water he had heard, in a pool only eight inches below the level of the mine floor.

When he returned to the main chamber, it now seemed

almost as bright as the day outside. The air already smelled cleaner and was surprisingly dry.

Before leaving, he put three more small rock fragments into his pouch to look at more closely in the sunlight. Remembering bandits and bears, he blocked the entrance again. Water, a track for the carts needed to carry materials, curving tunnels to deflect an accidental blast, and that air shaft in the bowl. He had found a place that might serve his purpose in almost every way. All that it lacked was secrecy.

By the time he climbed back down to the forecourt of the lodge, the two watchers had disappeared, but Ricco Smith came out to meet him.

'Will you need labour to help you at the mine tomorrow?' the steward asked.

Francis shook his head, thanked him and went to the stable yard in search of Venturini. Back in the forecourt away from curious ears, he told the Uskok that he wanted to make a further workshop in the abandoned mine. 'We will say that it is for the fireworks.'

Their eyes met. Venturini's mouth flexed slightly under his moustache, not in a smile but to let Francis know that he deceived no one.

'For the prince's private purposes,' Francis added. 'Please mount a guard on the track to keep away the curious.'

Venturini nodded without further comment, silent or otherwise.

'I will be doing dangerous work there.' Francis would repeat this warning later to the steward, Ricco Smith. 'This work is very dangerous! Please warn everyone to keep away.'

Venturini nodded again.

'And the *vinea*?' The *karwah*?' Francis asked.

'Coming,' said Venturini in a tone that forbade all further questions.

Francis went to his new, airy *camera* and took his copy of

the *Liber Ignium* from a locked travelling chest. He turned the pages, his brain humming with black powders and balls of lightning that seemed to hover, and engines and rockets and the weight of the prince and how to make the human eye see one thing and believe it has seen another.

Since noticing that panel standing a little ajar, he must now also give urgent thought to how to lay hands on the bond and make for safe haven in Venice. Francis was certain that his surmise was right. Given the prince's physical state, a secret panel in the bed would be a perfect place for him to hide important papers.

He wondered again if he might have had time to burn the thing last night. He asked himself whether reason had excused him with 'no' only because his courage had failed. Courage or no, Francis must not let Ettore get his hands on that bond.

He tried but failed to imagine a confrontation between Cecil and Ettore, when Ettore was calling the tune.

Meanwhile, he must seem to satisfy the prince. He returned to the *Liber*, looking closely now at the loose pages at the back, not yet copied into the master book at Powder Mote – his own notes from the last two years at the English court. His new skills of showmanship might yet prove useful. If he could make the English king seem to appear, as if by magic in a flash of light, surely he could make a minor prince disappear.

Be patient, Sofia told herself, while Francis was studying the *Liber*. Dear God, try to be patient.

The smoky air in her father's *scrittoio* felt as thick as hot pitch in her chest.

She was so close now. It was all very well to think ahead, but she must not let her feelings leap ahead with her thoughts. She must not betray herself with a heightened flush or air of purpose. She must be a hawk, a cat, a coiled snake, still and unseen until she moved.

The prince's dinner had left tracks down the front of his doublet. It would have been dangerous to notice his growing clumsiness. Her mother had died for protesting when Ettore was set above her daughter in the succession. Sofia had no intention of being killed by her father now for daring to brush away a crumb.

In his post-dinner sleep, his hand lifted from her wrist to scratch under his cap. She pulled her hand away and waited, willing him to sleep on. When he did not wake, she stood up from her stool. She backed slowly from the room, then slipped into the walls to escape up onto the battlements and fling her knife again and again at a wooden door.

51

The next morning, however, despair again crouched heavily on Francis's chest. Not even the light caress of his feather quilt or the resinous fragrance of the air lightened his humour.

I can't play my own part in this alone, he thought.

There was too much to do and not enough time. He had begun to see what he must do. But for fear of betrayal, he dared not enlist the help he needed in order to work fast enough to do it. He needed an army of carpenters who could be trusted not to blab. He needed a squad of mute smiths.

He had found a possible site for the prince's supposed launch to Heaven but did not yet know how to launch him. He had found a hole in the mountainside where he might secretly construct a false chariot. But the old mine was no place for the precise, delicate work with explosives. Without the living flame of a lantern or candle it was too dark. Therefore, he would have to do all such work in the mixing house in the stable-yard.

Seaborn, too, needed assistants to help make the many hundreds of shells and other effects required for a royal funeral display. These assistants would serve well enough for grinding charcoal, or for making leather and parchment shell cases, even for filling them. The best of them could be trusted with sieving the lumps of dried gun powder and corning it into different sizes of grain, but the crucial mingling of sulphur, saltpetre and charcoal needed a knowing hand. And, however practised you might be, you could not hurry. If you hurried, you died. Lady Gunpowder did not forgive those who rushed at her. But, with outsiders at work in the stable-yard, any one of whom might be a spy, Francis would be able to do only that work which might appear to be part of the firework display.

The prince was weakening far too fast. Francis had seen his decline the night before. Again, he heard Ettore's voice saying, 'You have until my father dies.'

I need an angel to lift me up out of La Spada, he thought. At that moment, he might even have risked a flying carpet – so long as he could also take Cecil's bond with him. And Seaborn.

He dressed, said goodbye to Seaborn, who was already busy in the stable yard arranging their stores in the hay barn. Accompanied by two unfamiliar Uskoks, Francis rode back down to La Spada yet again, in pursuit of a thought which teased him, dancing just out of sight. Yet again, he breathed in the pine-scented air and steadied himself with the open stillness of the plateau valley. He listened with approval to the marmots whistling their alarm.

Leaving the Uskoks with the horses in the royal stables, Francis went alone up onto the walls. He found his way back to the tower where he had seen the remains of the mount, half-submerged in a puddle on their first morning there, after the storm.

Today, the stone walkway was dry. He could clearly see the arrangement of decaying beams and rusty bolts. With his eye, he measured the distance between the beams – too wide for any gun that would not slowly shake the stones of the walls apart with its recoil.

Francis tried to imagine the Castello under siege with the eye of a defender. The sheer cliffs meant that the Castello did not need the usual defences against close attack. Defenders would not need to counterattack against wheeled siege towers and battering rams, which could never reach so high and needed level ground to stand on.

He looked straight down. Here at the north end of the Castello, the base of the walls rose from a narrow strip of steeply rising ground, rather than sheer cliffs. A few *casones*, sending up the smell of wood smoke and middens, clung to ledges linked by steep zig-zag steps. The raw earth of early vegetable gardens darkened the thread-like terraces of the slope. A narrow dirt track ran beside the base of the walls.

You could manage to place siege ladders there, Francis thought. If you could first break through the lower town walls and fight your way up to that track. Castello La Spada did have a small chink in its armour, if you could get close enough to attack it.

He turned back to the rusting bolts and decaying wood of the mount. It was a relic of an older style of warfare than he had been schooled in. It might have supported the pivots for a giant caldron filled with burning hot sand, or glowing charcoal, or even turds, to tip down onto attackers trying to climb siege ladders to the battlements. It might have supported a small throwing machine.

He felt a sudden surge of the excitement, the beginning of an important thought. Not forcing it, trying not to snatch and frighten it away, he walked on to the next tower, where he found another mount. Just beyond this tower, the strip of land ended. The wall-side track descended steeply in a series of steps cut from the rock. Anyone on that end of the track, or trying to climb the steps, or gathering on the flat rocky field below them waiting to go up, would be exposed to side attack from the next tower beyond the one where he stood.

Sure enough, when he got there, Francis found a different arrangement of rusting bolts and decaying beams. It might have held a small early form of gun. But it might also have held an engine to shoot flaming arrows, or a throwing machine, one of many possible sorts. La Spada had once been heavily protected by the engines of outmoded warfare. Francis remembered his grandfather's meticulous drawings in the *Liber Ignium*.

Where were those caldrons and those engines now?

He began to see the shape of that elusive idea.

Past the next tower, he turned a corner, trotted down eight steps and found himself above sheer cliff again. Ahead of him, the walls snaked onward in tight curves following the contours of the peak, rising and falling as the rock beneath it rose and fell.

In one place, the raw rock of the mountain thrust itself up through the line of the walls. A large cannon stood on this rock, aimed at the valley below.

Guns and mining – La Spada would have a large gunpowder store somewhere safely distant from the Castello. Venice had moved its gunpowder to an island three miles away.

Around another twist in the walls he found another culverin, aimed at the nearest mountain behind La Spada. He added it to the two culverins over the gatehouse, which protected the causeway.

These guns were the new warfare. Armoured knights and spear charges were finished. Longbows had lost their dominance. Gunpowder now ruled the battlefield. Siege engineers were no longer the wizards who were the sole masters of the deadly force of Lady Gunpowder, like Catholic priests who alone could speak with God. The Lady had turned whore and now gave her favours to the lowliest militiaman who could manage to load a musket or set a spark to the fuse of a grenade.

The *principessa* flicked into his thoughts. The royal whore. He had her measure now. She was as purposeful as gunpowder, though the purpose of gunpowder was honest and clear while hers still eluded him. She was ruthless, where Lady Gunpowder was simply impartial. As wanton as Lady Gunpowder had become, and almost as dangerous.

He threw himself into a furious walk, head forward, long legs slicing the air. But painful thoughts clung like Greek Fire and would not be shaken off. He also owed her an almost unpayable debt for introducing him to the House of Wisdom. Without Albona and his books, Francis was certain that he would not have known how to survive even this far.

Be honest! he told himself. You know that you want to bed her, as ruthless, wanton and openly purposeful as she is. The touch of her cold fingertips still marked the skin on the back of his hand. The image of those fingers stroking his belly stiffened his cock.

The wind was rising. The swift slide of clouds through the plateau below him reminded him that time passed. He pulled his thoughts back to his present purpose. Where were the old engines of war that once sat on those mounts?

Most likely burnt, he warned himself. Or taken apart to hold up the roofs of barns. Or eaten by worms.

He heard a faint scream. Not from the Castello, but from beyond the wall.

The appearance of his head over the wall startled the ravens. They flew out of the cage, protesting. One perched on the wall a little way from Francis, tossed its head and swallowed whatever it held in its beak.

In ordinary circumstances, Francis would have studied the system of chains and pulleys devised to allow easy raising and lowering of the open iron cage. But now he could only stare down while the wind that galloped through the plateau valley snapped the loose edges of his cloak. He had seen similar horrors before on battlefields when the battle was done, or amongst the dusty smoking ruins of a citadel he had helped to bring down. Beastly scavengers – rats, dogs, wolves and ravens – were always quick to follow the human body strippers. But when the human scavengers had finished, whatever they left was dead.

The man in the barred cage was alive. Francis had heard his scream. He lay awkwardly, carelessly, as still as if already dead, shrunken like a mummy that had been buried in dry sand. Then Francis heard him moan. He stirred, painfully, barely alive. His head turned as if he had heard Francis above him. His eyes were empty sockets, one crusted and black, the other a bright fresh glaring red. The raven on the wall dropped down onto the roof of the cage again.

'Get away!' shouted Francis. He saw himself in such a cage, knew what he would want done. He left the walls at a run, to his saddlebag in the stables. But by the time he found his way back to that distant part of the walls with his pistol, the man was already dead. This time the ravens ignored Francis. He hid his pistol under his cloak again. The man was theirs now, fair enough.

'The worm will do its kind . . .' The phrase had stuck in his mind even though the new play where he heard it had made his head ache with trying to listen to all those words. The reluctant fop Francis had been then, forced to sit still in that playhouse against his natural bent, had entirely sympathized with the worm.

Often as he had seen it on the battlefield, he could not bear to watch the ravens feed now. His two years at court had softened him. Then he shook his head in silent scorn. How could he think he had softened when he was working night and day to devise how to murder a sick, mad, old man, while at the same time lusting for his daughter and lying to his son?

Whether he liked it or not, and no matter what Cecil had promised him, he was back on the battlefield. He must begin to think like a soldier again, while still costumed in a courtier's rig. A dancing bear in a ruff, but with claws still sharp, he prayed, and teeth not yet pulled.

Above all else, he must try to stay alive. A dead soldier is of no use but for filling defensive ditches. A dead man can no longer do his duty, however well he served before his death. Dead men can't turn hero. Dead men don't pretend to do the impossible, although at least two men now dead seemed to have tried.

He shouted once more at the ravens and watched them rise. He left before they could settle on the cage again.

The two Uskoks had disappeared from the stables. Francis found them at last in the bake-house in the under-castello, a village in itself, holding the kitchens, the lodgings for the servants, and the other offices and service rooms for the Castello itself.

At first, blankness greeted his request, made in English, rough Italian and Latin. Francis led them to the locked armoury in the old *fortezza*, which he and Seaborn had found on their first morning of exploration. The two Uskoks consulted intensely.

'*No sono spia inglese!*' said Francis impatiently. I am not an English spy. A phrase a soldier learned to say in every language.

One of the Uskoks disappeared and returned after some time with their captain, who unlocked the door.

There was something to be said for being given infinite resources by the ruling prince.

'Tell me what the English man takes from the Armoury,' said Sofia. 'Does my brother also know of his visit there?' She slipped the question in casually.

'Not from one of us.' 'One of us' meaning an Uskok. Venturini sounded indignant.

Sofia gifted him with a warm smile. 'Thank you for bringing me word.'

Venturini bowed again and left.

Thoughtfully, Sofia watched him go. Her chances of surviving to rule La Spada improved if the Uskoks thought her worthy of intelligence that they denied to Ettore. But then, she was Uskok too, like them, not a watered-down mix like her vicious half-brother.

52

THE ARMOURY, LA SPADA

Francis marched briskly past rank after rank of spears, bill-hooks, maces of different lengths and ferocity, spiked axes, racks of swords. He passed stacks of full shields and small round leather targes, and still more ranks of engraved steel bucklers with riveted steel cross-bars for carrying into battle.

It was a wasted opportunity for a non-spy.

He opened inner doors onto boxes of lead shot, racks of muskets and pistols, bundled ramrods and ammunition belts. With no more than a quick curious glance, he passed cannon laid side by side, ranging from somnolent giants larger than ancient tree trunks down to dainty *moschette*, little flies. Cecil would have wait for a report on the military resources and readiness of La Spada.

A giant mortar slept on a fat-wheeled frame that was for transport only. A single recoil from that beast would crush the wheels and drive the frame into the ground.

None of what he passed was what he wanted.

Francis mimed the act of releasing the throwing beam of a trebuchet.

The captain nodded, called for a lantern, and unlocked another door that opened into a high vaulted undercroft. Francis saw what looked at first like a giant's woodpile.

Then he began to detect the order. The massive beams, planks, poles, levers, wheels, ratchet wheels and frames to hold counter-weights were organized into separate stacks. All the parts of each stack were painted with the same number. Each pile wore a large label.

'Onager,' Francis read. A throwing machine used when laying siege, named for the wild ass because of the power of its kick. Terrifying in its time, before gunpowder tilted the odds. This undercroft was a graveyard of old siege engines.

With growing excitement, Francis spent some time moving among the dismantled war engines, some of which his great, great-grandfather, the first Francis Quoynt, might have used. His great grand-father and even his grandfather would also have known how to deploy and fire these monsters to throw missiles at the enemy long before cannon and gunpowder were used in European warfare.

He recognized almost all of them from the *Liber*. Most worked by releasing a beam that had been put under tension. Some of them were set by human strength, others by turning rachet wheels. Some were counter-balanced, some were not. They might project stones, grenades, cannon balls or barrels of blazing pitch. They had been used, in at least one siege against stubborn defenders, to fling barrels of offal and decaying horses in order to set off a plague of infection in the resisting city. There were also several different types of giant crossbow for shooting multiple arrows at the same time, or a single large bolt, flaming or otherwise.

Francis wandered, testing one alternative, then another, letting his imagination play around the image that had begun to form when he saw the two mounts rising out of a puddle on the walls. He remembered the prince's fear of fire. He began to see another possible step towards the way out.

'I'll take that,' he said, pointing to a heavy wheeled frame. 'And those beams. And that.' He pointed at a giant crossbow. 'To the lodge.' He gave the order twice, once in English, once in Latin. He made a show of lifting, carrying and pointing up towards the hunting lodge.

'Can you do it?' He could not think how they could carry those heavy, unwieldy engine parts up the steep narrow track to the hunting lodge. On the other hand, he had infinite resources, even if he did not yet know them all.

'We can do it,' replied the captain in Latin . . . or perhaps it was Ladin.

'When?'

The captain held up his finger, dropped his head forward and snored loudly. '*Un. Uno. Ein*. One.'

Tomorrow.

He knew the Uskoks too well by now to risk the insult of insisting that the siege engines be moved at once. If the captain said, tomorrow, then tomorrow was the earliest possible time. Nor did Francis insult the captain by asking, how?

By the time they left the armoury, the abrupt mountain darkness had already fallen. Francis felt suddenly very weary. His two years at court had softened him after all, if a simple mountain scramble and shifting a few rocks could tire him so much.

He realized then that he had not eaten all day and was ravenously hungry. In the absence of a manservant, he found his way back to the kitchens and begged some bread, cold meats and wine.

Instead, a place was made for him at a long table and a bowl of steaming stew arrived in front of him, made of maize meal, pork skins and beans. He sat eating contentedly, listening to the babble around him, trying to pick out the different dialects and tongues and smiling back at a pair of dark-eyed flirtatious kitchen maids.

Hunger satisfied, Francis returned to the palace stables. While waiting for him, his Uskok guard had fallen asleep in the corners of stalls beside their horses, slumped against the walls. Their dismembered armour hung from bridle hooks and the top of the stall doors – hands and arms, heads, shins and feet. He imagined waking them, then riding up to the lodge in the dark yet again. He felt again how weary he was. He shook one of the Uskoks gently, pointed up into the Castello, held up one finger, then dropped his head and snored.

He found his way back up the tower staircase from the stables and into the old *fortezza*, to the starry-roofed *camera* that was still kept for him. After he had passed the watch at the heavy door at the top of the tower, no one stopped him.

As he pushed open the door to the *camera*, he smelled a freshly blown-out candle. Still blind from the torches in the passageway, he drew his dagger.

'Close the door.' It was the *principessa*'s voice.

53

Francis closed the door but did not sheathe his dagger.

'Madam,' he said levelly. His ears strained for the grating of feet on the stone floor or whisper of shifting fabric or faint metallic clink. He turned his head, reading the air like a dog, seeking the feral whiff of a man about to attack. Willing his night sight to return, he peered into the shadows in the corners. A ghostly thread of smoke twisted up from one of the candles in the stand by the bed, spreading its telltale scent.

'There's no one under the bed neither,' she said.

Slowly, his eyes adjusted to the darkness in his room. A slight pale shape sat on the foot of his bed, just visible in the light of the night sky that slid through the narrow window. He stepped closer to the bed and stopped abruptly. She was naked. The dark pool of a discarded fur robe lay on the bed around her hips. Embroidered slippers sparked in the faint light as she moved her feet.

'You'll be damned if you do and damned if you don't,' she said. 'In your place, I'd take the pleasure. 'There was an edge to her voice that did not sound like seduction.

Get out now, he told himself. This isn't a game you can win. He swallowed. 'Is that advice or an order, madam?'

'And is that anger I hear?' She sounded strained but triumphant. 'The growl of wounded male pride?' She widened the angle of her thighs, proving beyond doubt that she was not wearing even a night shift. 'What ails you, Cointo? No Italian or Turk would refuse such an offer. Perhaps not even a German.' When he did not reply, she added, 'Are you a man? Or merely an Englishman?'

'You needn't provoke me to taking you in a rage. I'd take you happily enough in a good humour.'

She drew a deep, sharp breath. 'Then what stops you?'

'You must know very well, madam! Your brother. And I'd be a fool to take your father at his word . . .' He stopped, suddenly uncertain how her father's offer to give her in payment had touched her.

He heard an angry impatient breath. 'My father may kill you at any time, with or without reason if his wits curdle that way, just as he may kill me. My brother doesn't give a fig what I do, so long as I don't conceive a male threat to his succession.' A tiny crack opened up in her voice.

'Harsh words, lady.' But this time he believed her. He had seen both princes in action. Desperately, he fought off pity. Remember Cecil! Remember her performance with the cabinet of poisons.

'I've led a harsh life. But it suits me. I've grown teeth and scales. I don't blame you if you run.'

With every shred of his reason screaming 'No!' Francis crossed to the bed and sat beside her. Her body tightened and she closed her legs, but he could still see the dark hair between them. He imagined stroking it. Sitting next to her, he could smell her different scents, from her hair, her skin, the parting of her thighs.

Lest she imagine that he was giving in to her game, he hardened his voice. 'You're a princess. At the very least both your father and brother must want to protect you as a commodity.'

'I'm also a widow. Why else do you think I always wear black? Didn't you hear what my father and brother said?'

'Yes,' said Francis quietly. He also remembered the sound she had made when she learned of her father's role.

'I'm already spoilt goods. I may have some value to my father and brother, but it doesn't lie in what I'm offering you.' She wrapped her arms across her belly as if she were beginning to regret being there.

'How old are you?' He knew before he finished speaking that she would not like the question.

'One hundred and ten . . . more. Lady Methuselah. I feel too weary even to be angry that you don't want me after all.' She looked away. 'I thought I read desire in your eyes. I was mistaken.'

Francis groaned. His cock was stiff.

He could overrule lust. He had done so before now, in the past. It was a simple matter of will. Like holding your hand steady to the fuse on the battlefield.

Her hand lifted uncertainly into the night air feeling for some invisible hold. Francis caught it as it fell back towards her lap.

They sat for a moment, uncertain what to do next. Then she slipped off the bed onto her knees in front of him and began to pull off his boot.

'Don't! Stand up!' His voice was harsher than he had meant. 'I'm not your father!'

As he yanked his foot away, she pulled the boot the rest of the way off. He stood up, then bent to lift her back onto her feet. 'Get up from that stone floor!'

'What do you want me to do?' she begged. 'Tell me.'

He stood holding her in front of him, feeling her tremble with cold. He tried to remember how to be wary but contact with her bare skin blurred his thoughts. His hands – treacherous rebels against his reason – slid down her arms to her elbows and back up to the sweet curves of her shoulders. Goose bumps roughened the silky smoothness of her forearms and the soft backs of her upper arms. His right hand dropped to the beginning swell of her breast. He snatched it away, wondering if she knew that he was erect.

'Get into the bed before you freeze.' His heart was beating so hard that he could scarcely get the words out.

'It won't make any difference. I'm cold all the time.' But she obeyed.

He watched the beautiful pale curve of her haunches in the darkness as she climbed onto the bed, and the folding and stretching of the lines of the slim legs. His eyes were drawn helplessly to the black shadow between her buttocks and the mysterious diamond of darkness where it disappeared towards her belly. The way in.

'Oh, God!' he groaned. He should turn on his heel and leave the chamber at once. He pulled off his other boot and then his stockings, then struggled to undo the tiny silver buttons of his doublet.

She watched in silence as he undressed, the coverlet and fur robe pulled up under her chin.

He yanked off his lace collar and hauled his shirt over his head, in a blind terror now that she would suddenly sit up and laugh at his urgency, pull the fur robe around her and leave him.

She continued to watch him in the darkness from far away inside her own thoughts.

When he found her bare skin again under the covers, he exhaled with delight, still braced for her to say she had changed her mind. Now that she had proved to herself that she could bend him to her will, she would pull back and say that she had been toying with him and never had any intention of satisfying the lust she had worked so hard to arouse.

He bent and kissed her hard. Then waited for her to scream, to push him away, to cry 'rape!' and call for men-at-arms.

She permitted the kiss but gave nothing back.

Still in disbelief but beyond stopping, he stretched his length out beside her, skin to skin, then raised himself over her, just as he had wanted to do since the minute he saw her.

'How can you be so warm?' she asked. 'What are you waiting for?' She threw her arms suddenly around his neck and lifted her head to press her mouth on his.

It had been too long since he had last visited his woman in the Paris Gardens in Southwark. He must make haste, or else disappoint her.

Then he froze, in confusion and disbelief, holding back his first thrust.

'How long were you married?' he asked.

'That's no concern of yours.'

His urgency, with its cold edge of anger vanished. Into its place rushed a startled but infinite tenderness, still tinged with confusion.

'Sweet girl, I believe it is my business now.' He pushed again, gently, to be sure. Again he met resistance.

'Don't leave me!' she said desperately. 'Don't leave!' With her hands, she tried to hold him in place on top of her.

'Sofia, hush. I'm going nowhere but where you want me to go. I just want to go there a little more slowly.'

'I was married a very short time,' she whispered. He bent and kissed her again, this time gently, reining back the soldier hot to march briskly into action. He felt suddenly old and coarse.

How had he done it with Kate for the first time, all those years ago, when they were both so young? His first time.

Kate, his only other virgin. It seemed impossible but there it was. He could not let himself begin to think of the possible consequences of this madness.

'Are you quite sure?' he murmured.

Her face was turned away from him now, partly covered by glinting hair, but she nodded.

He did not just want her now. He felt a passionate need to give her joy, to force into a crack in her existence the possibility that men might be a source of happiness as well as of disgust and fear. How had he managed to misread her so badly? How, with all his worldly experience, had he managed to miss the signs?

He kissed her eyebrows, her nose, her ears. Slowly, he instructed himself. Slowly.

'I know it will hurt,' she said. 'You don't have to do all that.'

'I serve here voluntary,' he said. He felt the lift of a half-smile under his kiss. He moved on to her neck, to her breasts, to her belly. When his steady gentle pressure finally broke through, her back was arched as she offered up her nipples to his eager mouth.

What have I done? he asked himself a little later. He kissed her hair, then lifted away a strand that had caught on his chin and was tickling his lip. They lay still wrapped together, not yet admitting the first drafts of reality. Sofia had tucked her head beneath his chin like a puppy.

'Did I please you?' she whispered.

'Dear God!' he said. 'Yes.' He kissed her hair again, as that was all that was on offer. 'Did I please you?'

There was a long silence. She pulled her head away to look at him. 'You've made love to a good many women, haven't you?'

'You're my first princess.'

313

'I should think so. The ones in England are still children. The French ones are cows.'

He felt her fighting for distance again, studying him in the faint light. 'I never looked to see.' He cupped her cheek in his palm and tried to kiss her again.

'You can still run,' she said. 'I meant what I said about teeth and scales. I helped to kill my husband.'

Francis used every fibre of his will to keep from pulling back and what little was left of his wits in trying to think what best to say. This girl was not Kate. His tenderness sat side-by-side with a new coldness. He waited in suspense like a man hearing a chilling story told around a fire.

'I helped Count Baldassare to cheat the sheets,' she said. 'We both cut our thumbs to share the act that way if we couldn't the other.'

'Count Baldassare was your husband?'

'If I had let it be known that he was incapable of playing the man's part, he'd still be alive. Above all else, Ettore feared that I might conceive a son.'

With a rush of relief that he did not like to examine too closely, Francis kissed her again. 'You protected his pride. Ettore killed him, not you.'

He was delighted to find that, old and coarse as he might feel, he was not yet too old to make love to her again.

Back in her own bed as if she had never been anywhere else, having slept for only three hours, Sofia surfaced shortly after dawn. She swam up through a dream of a momentous event that she could not quite define. People spoke urgently with their heads close together, and ran whenever they thought they were unseen. From the battlements, she watched men marching outside the city but could not identify them nor their purpose, because their shining silver armour flashed in the sun and blinded her.

314

She prowled, miraculously invisible, and listened at the lions, trying to overhear a snippet that would tell her whether to rejoice or flee. She might have asked, but she knew that the sound of her voice would change everything. Until she knew what was happening, she must stay silent.

Then she felt the bowl of down pillow under her head and her night smock twisted around her thighs. She remembered.

She opened her eyes and lay for a few moments, breathing quickly, staring up at the canopy. Then she pulled her closed fist from under the covers and opened it. Even in fitful sleep she had held on tightly to the linen scrap, which she had cut from the sheet before leaving Francis's bed.

She had done what she had set out to do. Undone the damage of the day that she showed him the House of Wisdom. She drawn him to her, attached him, just as she had planned. She should be feeling triumph.

She sniffed the bloodstain and the marks he had left on the sheet. The curious odours made her feel either sick or ecstatically happy. Whatever she felt, it wasn't triumph.

She wasn't ready yet for this particular day. She needed solitude to think over what had happened. She listened for sounds of her women stirring in the next room.

Silence.

She curled onto her side and closed her eyes, trying to slow her heart, her thoughts swooping and circling like bats. She blew out a long unsteady breath. The sheets felt icy cold around her.

Everything had changed, just as she had intended, but not in the intended way. She recognized the subject of so many conversations among her women, and its symptoms.

She had caught the infection. She knew the symptoms – like the vivid way she could still feel and hear him.

He had called her 'Sofia'. Not *'principessa'* or *'sultana'*.

'Sofia, Sofia . . .' murmured again and again. Her name on his tongue had made her feel more naked than anything he had done with his hands or mouth or cock.

'Francees.' She tried to whisper his name aloud now in the English way. 'Quoynt' defeated her entirely. With one hand, she touched the faint soreness between her legs and sniffed her fingers. The odd new smell – salty, sweet, mysterious – twisted something in her chest. She curled more tightly and wrapped her arms around her knees.

Beforehand, it had seemed straightforward. Nothing in the friendly conspiracy of her wedding night with Baldassare had alerted her to her danger with this Englishman. For most of her life, she had overheard both father and brother discussing different profits to be made from her maidenhead. If her virginity could be given to pay for treaties, new lands or a seaport for La Spada, why could it not buy her an assassin?

If only he had not suddenly stopped and begun to pay real attention to her!

She wasn't an ignorant child. She had expected to feel different after having her first man. She had prepared herself, braced herself for pain and disgust. She should have been warned by her feelings the night she had spied on him in the bath chamber.

'Dear God,' she whispered. 'Help me!' She burst into tears of angry helplessness.

Where was he? Why wasn't he here with her now? She could not bear it! If he were here, she might, by some miracle, look into his face and see safety after all.

She sat up, intending to go to him at once. She had to see him at once . . . any excuse would serve. Then she sank back again onto her pillows.

Only his arms could hold her steady in her tumbling confusion. But his arms were the cause of the confusions. Her thoughts were curdled by desire.

Trust no one, she reminded herself. Not even him. Not even now. Particularly not now. Think ahead. Take particular care when things seem to go well.

She was in danger of breaking her own most important rule of all – do not attach your heart. Even the brief friendly companionship with Baldassare had opened her to paralysing misery after his death.

Where was the physic for the frightening infection of love?

Now, even while reason shouted, 'danger', her skin tingled, her lips wanted to smile, her nipples tightened. She wanted to hear Francis's voice, to feel his breath against her neck. It would be enough just to lean against him like a friendly hound.

How could she ever think clearly again if she permitted herself to have so much to lose? She had come this far. She must not lose her grip now.

Weak! Fool! Worse! If he were to come to her now, she knew that she would do anything he asked. A *principessa* would become the slave of a foreign mercenary soldier.

Distrust your own desires. Distrust your desires.

But she had never felt desires like this before. She yearned for him from the centre of her bones. She must reason herself out of this unforeseen danger.

She heard the footsteps of her women in the antechamber and quickly wiped her face with the hem of the coverlet.

I may have been buying an assassin, but Francis was making an exchange too, she told herself. The sham of his passion in exchange for her favour.

He needed her favour to advance in the game he was playing with her father. He knew that she saw what he was doing. He needed her influence. Her silence. She could voice her suspicions at any time – to her father, to Ettore, to Da Monte, to the lions. Without her silence, Francis was lost.

This truth of her power over him eased her misery a little.

But then the next step of reason made her want to shred the coverlet with her nails. A man of such quick wits would understand exactly what he must do to gain her protection. A man of his courage would not hesitate to take action. A self-deluding virgin was no challenge if you were accustomed to handling gunpowder. And looked as he looked.

She groaned. He had somehow tricked her into thinking that she was making the first approach. He had seduced her with tricks of gentleness learnt from long practice with those bawdy Englishwomen one heard of, who showed their breasts to everyone and exchanged kisses as freely as they stroked their lapdogs. He was laughing now at her pitiful self-deluding bravado.

She felt a scalding rush of shame.

But he had refused at first, she reminded herself. His hesitation argued for his sincerity.

Then she thought, in an unwitting echo of Cecil, that there is no deceiver more dangerous than the honest-seeming man. How could she judge? She had known so few honest men.

Her door opened to admit one of the Carnians with an embroidered jacket, closely followed by a maid carrying her breakfast.

54

Francis awoke with a jolt and stared up at the stars on the deep-blue vaulted ceiling. Whilst his body insisted on an intense and languorous well being, his reason took an inventory of what he thought he knew. He was in an alien place called La Spada . . . true. He was in the Castello, not the Hunting Lodge . . . also true. The *principessa* had come to his bed in the night. He had taken her maidenhead.

He turned his head to the hollowed pillow beside him, uncertain. He buried his face in the pillow and smelled a faint delicious hint of the perfumed oils she put on her hair. He wanted her back, there now, again. Now that she . . . He could not say exactly how he imagined her to have felt before he took her. But now they could truly share delight. At the very least, he must see her, to confirm, even if only with their eyes, what they had discovered together. He must see that she had not now finished with him, having achieved what she had clearly set out to do.

No, he decided. There had been no coldness or calculation in her in the end. Not as there had been when she embraced him after showing him the poisons and the snake. Last night, she had trusted him with her true secret self.

And he must protect that secret young woman, help her survive and shed the scales and claws she had grown in order to survive.

Then his fingers caught on a raw edge in the middle of the under-sheet. He threw back the coverlets and sat up. He remembered how she had insisted on cutting out the stains. He fingered the ragged hole she had left in the sheet. Even now, she did not trust him enough to leave behind the evidence of their coupling and the proof of her virginity.

He drew up his legs and hugged his bare knees. Perhaps she had some other devious purpose entirely and wanted to keep the proof to use herself.

I don't care, he thought. He wanted her again. Now. Devious or not. She was lovely, lovely, lovely! Infinitely desirable, eager, surprising . . .

And a terrifying complication.

The mountebank must not fall in love with the daughter of the man he meant to gull.

He laid his hand in the hollow her head had made in the pillow. Francis did not lie to himself any more than he found it easy to lie to others. He knew the difference between lust and this new hungry desire to possess and protect. He also knew that he was not a match for a princess, however minor the principality. He was a tradesman – of a very special sort, it's true. But the Quoynts had turned gentleman only through royal gifts of land. They were rough soldiers who had profited from close service to great men.

There too much danger for them both.

He laid his face in her pillow again for a few moments, then rose with decision. He would dress, ride back to the lodge with the Uskoks and take a few hours to clear his head. Here was one danger proved already. He wanted only to relive their love-making in his imagination, not bend his thoughts to the best use for those old engines of war.

55

Sofia believed that she was done with surprises. But her bath, the humble process of cleaning the sweat and grime from her skin, changed everything yet again, just as a moment of divine revelation can shake a hermit, or the sudden imagining of a new formula awakens a mathematician to the sense of living in a larger world than before. She had been asleep, dreaming a chilly dream of transactions and shame.

Suddenly, now, she was truly awake. Her body was telling her a truth that her reason denied. When she stepped into the tub of hot water, every inch of her skin took on a life of its own, each with the capacity for separate delight. Toes, palms of her hands, ear lobes, the sides of her neck, backs of her knees. She was a whole world of delights, a universe of sensations. The delightful prickling of her shoulders as they slid beneath the warm water – why had she never before noticed that exquisite meeting of water and flesh? Or the sudden announcement of pleasure by her shins, those silent sulkers, overlooked until now. She had never felt that crimping at the top of her buttocks, nor the flooding delight of submerging in warm water the new centre of her being. She had never before regretting washing away its smell.

Though the bath maid could not possibly have read her thoughts, she covered her face with her hands while she examined the sensations of this part of her that had mysteriously usurped her reason. That warm, vital, insistent, comfortable, hungry, friendly, yearning place between her legs, where all her being now seemed to reside. She had scarcely noticed it before except during the messy nuisance of her monthly flow. Now Francis had been there.

Why had no one warned her? Why had none of her women explained, in those endless conversations she had overheard? Or had she missed some truth they were hiding with giggles and shafts of cutting wit?

Why had no one warned her that giving yourself to a man was like inviting the enemy through the gates to sit at your table and letting him eat from your fingers? That you handed over power along with your body and that a new ruler, benign but autocratic, would usurp control of that very same body, from within. She had felt no tremor of warning even when Baldassare had turned to her on their wedding night to set his lips hesitantly against hers. She already knew that Baldassare would not have made her feel as Francis did.

She had split into two Sofias. One was familiar – wily, patient, ambitious and still living with fear as if it were the air she breathed. She could not remember living without fear, not since her mother had been killed – by her father, she was almost certain. This Sofia could think coldly about such things. Or perhaps killed by Ettore. But in spite of his undisguised ambition, not by Da Monte, who was too soft. Da Monte was an eel, quick to withdraw under his stone and watch for his next strike with sharp wily eyes. She had watched him and become certain that he was a scavenger who would always let others do the killing. She was still that Sofia.

The other, newly awake Sofia was filled with astonished

joy and a sick giddiness at the same time. This Sofia found that a bath made her whole body feel as if it were singing. She was impatient with fear. She saw the morning dew trembling on grass blades like countless tiny suns. The chemise of this Sofia brushed the skin of her arms so that every hair pressed up like a purring cat. Her nipples kissed the inside of her bodice. The greatest pleasure the old shift had ever given her had never been more than a whispered promise of what she felt now.

 She accepted the soft embrace of the towel. Her feet slid into her slippers as smoothly as fish. Her hands . . . she held them up for study . . . things of beauty, not shame. She let the maid dry them for the first time without wanting to hide her fingers inside her fists. Francis had kissed every one of those bitten nails. 'Like the insides of shells,' he had whispered. 'I can look through them like tiny windows and see a little deeper inside you.'

She imagined her own face now looking back out through those windows, nose pressed against the other side of the pane. Looking back at him from inside herself.

Absently, she raised her arms to allow the maid to drop a fresh chemise over her head. She had kissed his fingers in return, beside herself with astonishment and pleasure to know that such things were done, were allowed. That he had wanted her to do it. His fingers had tasted salty, and a little like freshly toasted bread, with a tang of musk that was partly hers.

She closed her eyes and endured the tugs and jerks of lacing with more patience than she had ever shown before. His tough fingertips had resisted her gentle bites. To tease her, he had stretched out his thumb to tighten the plain at its base so that her teeth could not catch the skin. Her head moved slightly from side to side as she remembered how, instead, she had taken the side of his hand in her mouth and shaken it gently, wanting to bite harder, wanting to eat it, wanting to give him pleasure and learning, learning, learning as fast as she could.

This Sofia felt like weeping when she had to tear her arm away from his, leaving the warmth of his skin for a cold that seemed unbearable. This Sofia was already listening for his voice and knew that when she heard it, she would instantly forget whatever she was thinking, would throw down whatever state document was in her hand. This Sofia would give whatever was needed to keep him here with her forever, no matter what the cost. How could this Sofia also govern La Spada?

By the time this Sofia was dressed, she ordered her maid to undress her again and bring different clothes. This Sofia would forget to see what the lions had to say today. This Sofia knew only that she had to see Francis again, as soon as possible. A Pirati to the core, she went to face her chief obstacle. Unlike her former self, she went at once to see her father, thinking ahead only for the time it took her to arrive at his *scrittoio* door.

56

At the lodge, Francis found Seaborn and Venturini in the old hen house, trying to explain to three labourers that the stone floor and walls must be lined with leather, without using metal nails or tacks.

'Do you need a glue that will fix leather to leather?' Ricco Smith was asking, 'or leather to stone?'

'We should already have shoemakers and saddlers here to stitch the hides together,' said Francis. 'I thought I made that clear two days ago.' He looked around with despair. The floor had been swept. A pile of hides was stacked to one side. Two hides lay loosely on the floor like hearth rugs. Almost no progress in preparing the *factorium* had been made while he was absent.

A glance at Seaborn's unhappy face made him swallow his furious oaths. Also, he would rather not have to explain what he had been up to when he should have been here to push things onwards.

Smith went away to requisition the necessary shoemakers and saddlers. Venturini simply went away.

'I'm sorry, France,' said Seaborn. He glanced at the two labourers. '. . . sir.' He corrected himself.

'Much as I dislike it, I must speak with Da Monte,' said Francis. 'We need more help than Smith seems likely to find for us.'

The stable bell rang for midday.

'I did have some good fortune yesterday,' said Francis. To his irritation, he blushed. 'I think may I have advanced my own devising,' he went on quickly.

'And Venturini has found me a family of basket weavers,' said Seaborn. 'They've already begun making the frames for two dragons and a pair of ships.'

'Splendid,' said Francis absently, wondering suddenly whether he had made the right choice from that giants' wood-yard yesterday . . . and where he would find silent, incurious labour to help him assemble his imagined engine.

To guard their privacy, Francis had asked Smith on the first day to dismiss as many as possible of the servants who had been sent up to the lodge to look after them. As the Uskoks fended for themselves, only a single meat cook and a pastry cook remained in the kitchen, with one kitchen groom, one house groom and one serving maid. Francis intended that he and Seaborn would look after their own horses, but then Venturini said that, as the Uskoks would have to look after their own horses, two more made no difference to them.

Now Francis and his nephew went to the kitchen and took plates of cold meats, bread and cheese up to his big airy *camera* on the middle floor.

'Did you hear that?' Seaborn demanded around a mouth full of *prosciutto*.

There was a second roar. Then they heard shouts. They went to the open window. The roars and shouts continued, joined by hideous grunts, as if all the demons were climbing up from hell. They grabbed their swords, then ran down the stairs and out onto the little terrace at the top of the front steps.

Around the bend of the track up from the gate came a swan-like neck supporting a head of comic ugliness. The head pulled back then reappeared. They now saw that the neck was attached to a body carried on long, splayed ungainly legs. Or rather, Francis assumed the body. What he saw was a structure of padding onto which were lashed two of the heavy beams from the armoury. The beast grunted and lurched forwards into the forecourt, led by a Turkoman driver. Another creature followed behind it, then another, all protesting loudly.

'Camels,' said Francis in awe. Like those in the market. 'I never thought to see one live outside the king's menagerie in the Tower.'

Still the camels kept on coming. Some carried pieces of siege engines. Others almost disappeared under mountains of what Francis recognized as complete *vinea*. Still others wore vast carapaces of bundled cowhide mattresses and folded sailcloth. The drivers shouted, hauled on the lead ropes and brandished sticks with which they struck the camels on the neck to couch them. The long legs crumpled at the knees. Beasts and burdens settled majestically like buildings brought down by mines. The forecourt was filled with weaving heads and a ferocious stink.

There was no help for it. Francis called to Venturini and told him to have the siege engine beams carried up to the abandoned mine. He could see no other way of moving them. The man nodded. Then he pointed out a group of men huddled on the edge of the forecourt.

'Slaves,' he said. 'From Slovenia and Croatia. The prince ordered them for your secret work. We'll kill them when you're done with them, so they won't talk. There's a smith, six carpenters and a rope maker among them, as well as your leather stitchers.'

Francis had not yet recovered from this information when

327

another camel appeared around the bend in the track. This one carried a rider instead of a load. The rider tapped the beast on the neck with a long stick, swayed fluidly as the camel settled to the ground and smiled at Francis. Sofia was wearing a wide brimmed hat, full white split riding trousers and dark red boots. She swung one leg over the top of the saddle and allowed the Uskok captain to offer his hand to ease her slide to the ground.

57

'I'm here to represent my father's wishes,' she had said after dismounting from her camel. 'He sent me to report back to him.'

With her presence added to Francis's orders, the Uskoks set to work as readily as the eleven slaves. At some point, more Uskoks arrived.

Here was true power in action. Francis had only to ask for it to happen. The miracle began to take shape even before Sofia returned to La Spada again that evening.

Throughout the afternoon, Francis felt suspended with her inside a bubble of waiting to make love again, even while he dashed from one place to another, answering questions, showing what he wanted done.

For a long time, Sofia stood at the top of the steps above the bedlam of unloading the camels, watching the camels being led away, the loads being carried into the stable yard, a pair of ship's sails being partially unfolded. From time to time, Francis met her eyes. Once, recklessly, as he passed her, he even managed to touch the bare skin of her hand. Before he could see her response, someone called him to come and say which saddles and bridles should be moved from safe-keeping in the barn to join the horses in a new temporary stable being built below the gate. As he turned to go back down the steps, he saw Ricco Smith watching them from the forecourt.

His fervour chilled. Here was the other truth of power in action. As he headed for the barn, he wondered who would shortly be told that the English mountebank presumed to aspire to the favour of the princess. By now, he was certain that it would not be Cecil.

A little later, Sofia vanished from the steps. Then he saw her looking out over the valley from near the cliff edge. Relief that she was still there warred with an unreasoning feat that she might jump.

By the end of that afternoon, Francis had his mixing house, leather-lined and sheathed on the outside with a second layer of hides to absorb fragments of exploding stone. Sofia left without saying goodbye, after all, while Francis was inspecting this new workplace.

By noon the next day, a staggered wall of *vinea*, stuffed cowhide mattresses on willow frames, had been built around the mixing house, each giant shield braced by a post driven at an angle into the ground. Ship's sails had been hung slackly across the back of the house, with further leather mattresses lashed to the balcony rails and over the window shutters, which would be kept closed once the mixing of gunpowder began. Francis and Richard were a little safer in their rooms at the front of the lodge, but the servants' sleeping quarters, behind the sails, were also given padded protection against a blast.

By the end of the second day, Francis had his drying room, his storage room, and a second buffered room for soaking fuses in solutions of saltpetre and filling shell cases with gunpowder. A forge had been set up in the forecourt, well away from the *factorium* in the stable yard at the back. A small rope-walk for twisting lengths of fuse ran parallel with the edge of the cliff. A second hay barn had been turned into an atelier for stretching paper and vellum on the firework frames, for painting, varnishing, gluing and gilding. Near the forge, carpenters already worked under an open-sided shelter, making six-foot Catharine wheels out of pine, while Seaborn explained his drawings of a giant flaming sword.

Francis had asked Venturini to make it absolutely clear to every Uskok, servant and slave that in the stable yard there were to be no weapons, no pipes, tinderboxes, candles, or lanterns. No metal of any kind. No light but daylight, no matter how urgent the need.

He saw that he would have to give up the pretence that Seaborn was an ordinary manservant. Through Venturini, he explained that Seaborn was in fact Francis's apprentice and was to be treated as his second-in-command.

'You have achieved miracles,' he said to Venturini as the sun sank behind the teeth of the mountains. The forge and carpenters' shed were both now silent. The slaves had been taken away to sleep.

'We do it for our prince.' He looked away as if listening to the first night insects. 'We remember him as he once was. A very strong ruler. The first prince, his father, was Uskok. He gave us back our arms.'

Francis made a decision. He must choose to trust someone, to a degree at least. 'Now I need a second miracle. Your prince needs it.' He watched closely to try to divine how much the Uskoks knew of the prince's madness. 'I need a second workplace.' He would not pretend to himself that it could be kept entirely secret, but it could be made secure. And his life would depend on whether or not he could trust the men who must keep it secure.

'Show me where,' Venturini said.

The two men set off for the abandoned mine in the

thickening dusk. Francis took a lantern so that he could show Venturini the inside of the mine and explain exactly what needed to be done in the morning. He did not mention the air shaft, which he had covered over with broken planks and loose rock.

'We will begin tonight.'

'My work here must be secret.' Francis shifted the lantern to throw more light on Venturini's face. 'The prince has a purpose beyond mere fireworks. There are those who would prevent him.'

'We know.'

'You know what he wants me to do?'

Venturini nodded. He cast his eyes briefly skywards.

Whether or not they believed it possible, the Uskoks seemed to accept without question their prince's desire to attempt his flight. Therefore, they would assist Francis in satisfying this desire. He did not have to try to hide the prince's true commission from their sharp eyes.

But this relief brought with it a new fear. If he did not want to paralyse himself with terror, Francis must not let himself think what they would do to him if they ever learnt that he meant to gull their precious prince.

'The work here will also be dangerous,' he said. 'Even more than the work at the lodge.'

'I understand.'

Great Mars, let him not truly understand, begged Francis.

A letter was waiting for Francis in the lodge. It was addressed in a delicate schooled hand. He snatched it up. From Sofia! He broke the seal.

It was indeed from the *principessa*, but it was not a love letter, nor a renunciation of love. Nor even a verse into which he might read either. Her father wanted to see the fruits of the two days of great labour, she wrote. As his highness could

332

not travel to the lodge. Francis was ordered to come to La Spada.

With those fruits of labour.

She wrote nothing more. It was a secretary's letter. Why had he expected anything more?

Exhausted as he was, he penned a reply. Then he looked into Richard's room. Seaborn lay sprawled with his long limbs overhanging the edges of his short narrow bed, snoring gently.

Francis went back into his own chamber, lit four candles in addition to the lantern Seaborn had left burning, in hopes that the light might help to keep him awake. Sitting at his table again, he stared at the blank paper in front of him. The fruits of their great labour refused to take material shape to show the prince. The leap was too huge from imagined teams of angelic porters to a physical reality that could be acted out on a mountainside. He was falling into the chasm between them.

He considered what he already had.

The air shaft. The significance of his greatest discovery, the air shaft in the mountain bowl, must continue to escape everyone else.

The Uskoks would have recognized the body of the giant crossbow, now at the mine. Therefore, the prince very likely knew of it. Francis meant for the prince to know of it, – the fireless launch – but not to understand its full purpose.

Francis saw that he had absently stripped the last barbels from the shaft of his writing quill. He stood up and went down the creaking stairs to the dark kitchens at the back of the lodge, where he waved the startled kitchen groom back down onto his pallet then found a jug of wine and a flat bread roll coated in sesame seeds. He creaked back up to his chamber and sat at his table again.

It had been surprisingly easy to build an imagined reality

with words. Turning those words to solid matter was a different challenge altogether. He paced the room. He looked again at the drawings he had shown the prince of the proposed chariot to Heaven. He remembered the flash of brilliant light, and King James's almost supernatural appearance in the swirling smoke and torchlight.

Air shaft, crossbow, flash of light . . .

Suddenly, he saw how to do it. Scattered fragments of thought came together. He sat and scribbled furiously, leaving sprawling rusty brown inkblots as the footprints of his fervour. There were still one or two difficult problems to solve, but he could see how to begin. Excitement rose in him. He forgot his weariness. Details swooped in and landed like a flock of birds. His pen could not write or draw fast enough. He forgot the bread, the wine, his body, even the princess. The entire universe lay concentrated in that tiny bubble of space where he worked, where the imagined turned real.

At last, he slowed. His final drawing was meant for the carpenters in the morning. A simple diagram of what looked like the rims for two Catharine wheels and a number of narrow, shaped timber poles – nothing there to raise suspicion of any sort. Returning to the rest of his work, he burnt his rough sketches and early trials, destroying all but the best and most finished of his notes and drawings. He fell soundly asleep in his cupboard bed, under the cloud of feathers, still wearing his shirt and stockings, with the saved papers inside his shirt. Even the thump of the kitten leaping onto the foot of the bed failed to wake him.

58

Late the next morning, he set off yet again for La Spada. With him he took Seaborn to assist him, the two finished wooden wheel rims, both still a little tacky with fresh gilding, and the bundle of rods, now shaped and newly painted a heavenly blue, with gilded stars. The fruits of their great labour. At the last minute, he added a rolled-up drawing.

The prince was again seated in his chair in his private *scrittoio*, with the wolf skin rug across his knees. The air was a fog of sharp gamy smoke from herbs burning on the brazier. The censored frescos looked more than ever like people who had been hit by an explosive shell. Francis noticed a pair of coupling squirrels that had escaped him in the past.

'At last!' The prince turned his beak of a nose towards Francis like a thirsting man to the smell of fresh water. He waved away the steaming cup his physician was offering him.

Sofia sat on a padded stool at her father's knee, one of her hands held prisoner in his grip. Francis looked away. The sight of her subdued like that made him feel queasy. He wanted to grab the prince by the front of his robe and shake him until his neck snapped. In unspoken agreement, she and Francis did not look at each other.

The prince scowled. 'What have you been doing at the lodge? What progress?'

'I shall tell you as we work, your highness,' said Francis. 'My time here is short and we have much to do, you and I, to advance our great work.'

Father Daniele sat in his usual place against the wall at the side of the prince's private altar. He was so still that he seemed to be one of the prince's holy statues, a black statue, joining St. Ignatius carved of black marble and St. Elmo, made of fiery-veined grey.

Francis signalled for Seaborn to set down his load.

The prince leaned, intent. The wolf skin rug slipped from his lap and lay in a heap at his feet like a huge sleeping dog.

Francis held up a delaying hand. 'I shall show you what I've brought you in a moment, but you must be weighed. Until I know exactly what weight is to be propelled upwards, I can do nothing more.'

The same information would serve both truth and lie.

Sofia looked at her father for permission, then stood and disappeared in search of a scales fit for weighing a prince.

'And now, your highness,' said Francis, 'I must confess to a small deception I have practised on the world.'

The prince's hands tightened on the lion heads of his chair arms so that part of a lion mask snarled at Francis between the royal fingers.

Hastily he continued. 'In order to serve you as well as possible, I brought with me to La Spada my most gifted apprentice, disguised as my manservant to avoid tedious explanation on our journey. As an English fire master and pyrotechnician I wanted every possible advantage while working here in this land of master pyrotechnicians.'

The prince glared without seeming to understand. Either the intelligence of Seaborn's true role had not yet reached him, or his madness gripped him fiercely today. In truth, the smoke from the herbs was making Francis's head swim.

'My apprentice serves as my hands and multiplies my achievements as if he were a magic ring.' Francis bowed, grimacing at his kneecaps in spiritual pain. 'I see no reason to hide the truth from you any longer now that we're hidden away at the Hunting Lodge . . .' he couldn't resist adding '. . . safe from spying eyes.'

The prince did not smile drily, as Francis had expected.

'Now that I understand your true wishes, I praise God that I had the unwitting foresight to bring him.' Francis waved Seaborn forward from the shadows and smoke. 'This is he.'

The prince studied Seaborn with an unfriendly eye. 'He's very like you. Same bold stare.'

'I forgive him the occasional impertinence.' Francis dared not look at Seaborn. 'He's family, the bye-blow of a distant cousin. I value the loyalty that comes with blood. In my trade, I must trust the men who make my explosives.'

To his relief, the prince nodded, dismissed Seaborn from his thoughts and returned his eyes to what they had brought with them.

'That is a model of the frame for your chariot.'

Francis gestured to Seaborn. 'I must be certain that it will fit. Would you be so kind as to stand, your highness? Now step into the centre of this ring.'

With the prince standing in the centre of one of the wheel rims, Francis and Seaborn assembled around him a delicate cage of sky-blue starry bars. The shaped rods lodged neatly into holes cut into the wheels. The upper wheel looked very like a halo close above the prince's head.

'It's too fragile!' protested the prince from inside the cage.

'This is only the pattern,' Francis explained. 'It's not the thing itself. Your true chariot will be made of silver. But it must fit you neatly, as I don't want to lift more weight than absolutely required – all the more important if we are to propel you upwards without fire.' He made some marks on the bars. 'I will make a small window,' he assured the prince. 'To give you the rare chance to observe the glories of the Heavens as you pass through them.'

The air in the room was heavy with the pungent burning herbs. Each excited breath forced out of the prince's labouring lungs thickened the air by another degree. But speaking these words made Francis more queasy than any other cause for feeling ill.

A rumbling approached through the next room. Quickly, they dismantled the cage again. Relieved that Sofia had not had to witness that piece of mummery, Francis nodded to Seaborn.

'After you have been weighed, my apprentice will measure you for your suit to protect against the heat of sun and stars.'

The door opened. Two grooms hauled in a handcart carrying a large beam scales from the customs house, designed to weigh bales of silk. Sofia followed.

While the prince stripped down to his under breeches and shirt, Francis reminded himself of all the reasons not to pity him.

He was a man of barbarous cruelties and ruthless appetites. His guilt fuelled his terror of hell. He exacted an unnatural attention from his daughter.

But the eagerness with which the prince now climbed onto the scales and the hunger with which he locked on to every preposterous word Francis uttered made Francis writhe with his own guilt. You could not help but feel a little compassion for someone so fallen . . . once so powerful, now so reduced. You could not help but imagine your own eventual decline . . . your second childhood. With someone like himself making an ass of you.

Don't be a fool! he told himself sharply. It's bad enough that you were tempted to pity Cecil. You're tormented with pity for Sofia. You'll lose your wits altogether if you're mad enough to pity the prince. In any case, few fire masters lived long enough to reach their second childhood.

When the prince had been weighed, measured and returned to his chair, too befuddled to ask more questions, Francis came to the first true purpose of his visit – no more visible fruits for as long as possible.

'Your highness, with time so precious, I must work day and night at the lodge. If we are to achieve our great work, I must stay on the mountain. Can you not send someone daily from La Spada whom you trust to bring you my reports?' The second true purpose of his visit he must now leave to Sofia.

Later, he could not remember what the prince had replied. As the scales rumbled out of the *scrittoio* again, Sofia passed close to Francis. 'Don't lock the little door,' she murmured.

59

Sofia breathed gently at his side, one slim arm thrown above her head. The toad stone ring she wore to protect her against enemy poisons threw back a tiny slice of light at the candle on the bed head shelf. Pieces of ribbon lay tangled in the coverlet, although the lengths she had carefully rolled up were now tucked under her pillows.

She had brought with her to his room a pocket full of ribbons. While Francis laughed and protested that he felt a fool, a naked Sofia had tied ribbons around his neck, ankles and wrists, like a little girl adorning her lapdog or pet monkey. He watched the movement of her breasts, the turn of her shoulders and let her lay other ribbons along his legs, across his chest and waist, while he laid his hand on her thigh or the top of her hip.

'Quid nunc?' What are you up to? He sat up obediently and let her tie another around his head like a laurel wreath. In a flash of uneasy memory he saw himself measuring the prince.

'Is this how you treat your lapdog?' he asked. This is how it is for an ordinary pair of lovers, he thought. Seeming care-free and delighting in each detail of the other's presence.

Propped on one elbow, he watched her sleeping now. A strand of gold hair rose and fell gently near the corner of her slightly parted lips.

She had been up to something, of course, but at this moment he didn't care.

He lay back against his pillows again and stared up into the dark canopy. What he was feeling was dangerous, unsoldierly and as inarguable as a fist in the belly.

He wanted to be Sofia's beloved. He was sick with a hunger to be both loved by her and free to love back, without caution or reserve. He wanted to let himself glow with Richard's new radiance. He remembered Ricco Smith's dark triumphant gaze, looking up from the forecourt. He and she would never be free of such watchers.

He turned to look again at Sofia asleep beside him – or was she feigning? With her, he must always remember to question appearances.

She was beautiful. (Oh, God, yes!) So quick-witted that he often felt he was scrambling to keep up with her. Sexually passionate and, for some reason, interested in him. She was a pretender to the throne of an Italian principality. She was untrustworthy, devious and ambitious. She came from a deadly family.

He turned his head against the pillow, thinking about the father and brother, who both misused her and wished to continue doing so. Even if he were to throw away all reason and let himself feel as he would like . . . if he let a dangerous compassion presume to detect a more fragile, more tender creature inside that poisoned rose . . .

He'd end up floating face down in the Adriatic. One way or another. Or else feeding the ravens in a cage hung over the void.

Nothing in La Spada had been simple before. But now . . .

If he were honest, he had at first liked the edge of danger

341

with her. It had stirred him. The edge had suited the hidden brutality of the secret anger he still carried about Kate but could not admit – not after being shamed into behaving well at Powder Mote. That anger had gone now, melted away. It no longer seemed important. If he were honest, he had also hidden behind impossibility. Now he ached for the ordinary, the possible . . .

He leaned and kissed the end of her nose.

She smiled.

'Aha! Caught you,' he said.

'What were you thinking about?'

'About how beautiful you are.'

'No, you weren't.' She offered him her mouth. 'What were you truly thinking?' she asked after the kiss. 'Don't lie!'

'I was wondering what you wanted from me when you looked up at me, a stranger, on the day I first arrived in La Spada.'

She made a little sound as if he had punched her lightly in the belly. 'What did I want from that stranger?' She was silent for some time, then turned her head to him with reckless decision. 'Before I knew he would turn into you, what I wanted from that stranger was an assassin.'

60

'I wanted that stranger to kill Ettore,' Sofia had said.

'And now?'

'The need has not changed.'

He had known from the first moment that she wanted something but had not guessed the magnitude. 'I know,' he said.

She waited.

'Ah, Sofia . . .' he said miserably. 'I'm not a cold-blooded killer.'

'You're preparing to kill my father.'

'I'm praying to avoid the need.'

'Ettore has already killed my husband. He will kill me, as soon as possible after he comes to the throne.' She began to extract the coiled ribbons from under the pillow.

'I won't let him,' said Francis.

She stopped midway through pulling her sleeping shift over her head. 'And how will you manage that if you don't kill him?' She finished putting on the shift and reached down with her feet for her slippers. She stood up and put on her fur-trimmed velvet night robe. 'I'm not angry, Francis. Don't fear that I'm angry with you. You're not that stranger any longer.' She looked down as she stuffed the coiled ribbons back into a pocket of the robe.

'Sofia!' Francis stretched out a long arm and caught her by the wrist. 'Look at me. I swear that if the time comes when I must kill Ettore to protect you, I will.'

She looked at him searchingly but did not speak.

'I will not let him kill you!'

In the candlelight, he could not tell whether her eyes now held the same intense question that he had first seen in them. She nodded. 'I believe you, Francis.' She slipped into the wall and went back to her own *camera*.

You should have asked her to steal the bond, thought Francis.

After a sleepless night, Francis rose with the first Castello servants before dawn, roused from a restless torpor by the distant canonical bells. He forced his thoughts away from Sofia at last. He then spent the next hours before daylight in studying his copy of the *Liber* by the light of seven beeswax candles – why else did a man have infinite resources at his command, if he could not use them to read easily in the hours of darkness?

He read every note made in the *Liber* by three generations of Quoynts, on secondary fuses, the carriers of the tiny secret flame that sets off the explosion of a rocket at the peak of its trajectory, releasing stars. He had not expected his present mountebank shamming to bring him back to the concerns of his former skills, but here he was.

Neither prince nor shell would easily survive the violent explosion in the mortar or gun that gave the first upward push. The shell often exploded too soon, frequently in the breech. The prince, made of soft flesh without iron or steel casing, if truly projected, would be scattered in so many pieces that the angels would have trouble collecting them to reassemble for the Resurrection.

The giant crossbow solved this first difficulty. The prince would also see that he could be propelled upwards without the fiery hazards of either being shot from a gun or riding on top of a rocket's burning gunpowder charge. It would not matter whom the prince then told. Francis believed that he knew how to make this initial propulsion seem to happen.

The second challenge was to seem to make prince, alive or dead, seem to disappear. Francis now believed that he knew how to do it.

The third part of Francis's challenge, also shared to a degree by prince and shell, was easy to see but impossible to put into action. He must make a rocket-like shape seem to climb past the top of all known trajectories and keep climbing towards Heaven. He still did not know how to do it.

As soon as the sun had leaked into the eastern end of the valley, he let himself into the House of Wisdom.

'Quoynt!' exclaimed the librarian. 'Just in time to share my breaking of night's fast.'

To Francis's surprise, Albona seemed pleased to see him. He offered Francis some flat bread, dried dates and a bowl of curdled milk flavoured with honey. When he saw Francis glance curiously at a small glass of a murky black-brown liquid, he took another glass from one of the shelves and filled it from an enamelled metal jug shaped like a bird.

'Is this for drinking or for destroying books?' asked Francis.

'For both,' the librarian replied cheerfully. 'It aids me most wonderfully in my work.'

The glass was warm in his fingers. The smell was nutty and enticing. Francis took a cautious sip and winced at the bitterness.

Albona had also poured for himself. He raised his glass to

Francis and tipped down the contents. Francis hesitated for three heartbeats, then did likewise. Almost at once, his heart jolted in his chest and began to race. He had made a terrible mistake and let himself be gulled by sleight-of-hand into swallowing poison! He started to rise to his feet.

'Steady,' said Albona, looking alarmed. 'I forget how sudden you men of action always are. I haven't poisoned you. Please sit down again. I wager you'll soon begin to find the sensation quite pleasant.' He poured himself a little more from the enamelled metal bird. 'I thought you would have enjoyed the sharpening of your wits and senses. I shouldn't have lured you into drinking it so fast.'

Francis continued to breathe freely. His heart still raced, but no faster than before. Deadly cold did not begin to overwhelm him. He sat down again on Albona's spare stool.

'*Kavah . . . Caffea*,' Albona explained. 'Sofia Sultana is very fond of it. It also stimulates the bowels and brings on the need to piss.' He rose and took a heavy Latin herbal from its shelf. Francis sipped more slowly at a second glass while Albona showed him the shiny dark-green pointed leaves, clustered white flowers and red double-seeded berries of the plant itself 'From a province of Abyssinia,' he said, 'but the Arabs now supply the world.' He returned the herbal to its place. 'The tree will grow to a great height, but is kept cut short for easy picking, just as men are reduced to make more docile slaves.' He smiled to underline the lightness of his tone.

'My present work may interest you,' he said in an abrupt change of subject. He showed Francis the latest pages he had retrieved, but not yet translated.

Francis paused over a picture of what looked like an engine for blowing fire across great distances. As soon as civility allowed, he showed Albona his copy of the *Liber Ignium*.

'Have you any like this amongst your thirty thousands works?'

Albona led him into the shadowy tower of books and up a ladder. After trying several places, he lifted out a book and offered it to Francis. 'I fear that it is in Arabic, but there are some fine diagrams.'

As Albona held his lantern over the book, Francis leafed quickly through it, looking at the diagrams. 'May I take this down into the light for further study?'

They went back out to the little ante-library. Francis sat on the sleeping pallet with his back against the wall below the window, studying the book until the bell rang for midday.

'How long would it take you to translate these pages?' He showed Albona twenty or so that he had selected. 'I warn you that your own quick understanding may burden you with more than you want to know.'

'Sofia Sultana mistakes both of us from time to time.' Albona counted through the pages. 'Tomorrow?'

'No messenger,' warned Francis.

Albona nodded. 'Only the two of us. I assumed as much.'

It occurred to Francis only as they rode together back up to the lodge to wonder where Richard had spent the night. The young man had an air that was both shifty and excited. He also had dark circles under his eyes, and a cautious bearing that suggested a sore head from too much wine.

Francis almost said that late nights and too much drink did not lead to a long life for a fire master. But he held his tongue. Who was he to give such advice?

Then he wondered if Seaborn were in love.

A few weeks earlier, he might not have noticed, let alone been able to diagnose the ailment.

61

Bad news waited for them at the lodge. An intruder had been nosing around both the *factorium* and the mine.

'He must have climbed in over the mountains,' said Venturini with indignation. 'No one got past either of the gates. We had guards on the track to the mine.' His handsome leathery face flushed. 'There was also a guard at the mine.'

Francis felt the back of his neck go cold. Before leaving for La Spada, he had hidden his drawings and notes for the false launch in the mine.

'That man fell asleep. He says that his wine was poisoned.'

'It may well be true,' Francis said. 'He may not be at fault.' That was as far as he cared to interfere with the internal discipline of men who killed slaves to keep them from talking.

An insider! he thought, who could approach from the least guarded direction. Placed to meddle with food and drink.

Leaving Seaborn to examine the evidence of disturbance in the stable yard, Francis ordered a lantern and set off at once up the track to the mine. Venturini followed.

'We have doubled all the guards,' he said. 'It won't happen again.'

Trying to hide his urgency, Francis lit the lantern. He left Venturini at the mine entrance and went in alone. The new footprints in the dust of the floor were easy to see, with flurries of disturbance around shelves and cupboards. The searcher had gone a little way down the first side tunnel, following tracks left by Francis and turned back as Francis had done, when stopped by a broken beam braced at an angle against the fallen roof. Francis studied the floor here, where they had both turned. Then he bent and studied the lower half of the fall.

There was another blur in the dust below a large waist-high shelf, which formed the floor of a deep alcove where the miners had explored a possible side vein of silver ore. Francis held his lantern inside. The searcher had climbed up and ventured the fifteen feet or so to the end of the false tunnel.

The searcher had also gone as far as the water pool in the second tunnel. He seemed not to have entered the third tunnel, which led to a ventilation hole in the sheer cliff face.

Francis went back to the entrance and looked out. Venturini leaned disconsolately on a broken mining cart, staring at his feet. The two guards stood a distance away, also not speaking. He went back into the first side tunnel, to the fallen roof brace. He knelt and dug out a gap in the rock and earth beneath the beam, just large enough to admit his arm and the top of his shoulder. Stretching through, he felt the papers. Beside them sat the *Liber.* He pulled the papers out into the lantern light, just to be certain that they were not replacements, but relief was already washing through him.

He sat on his heels thinking. It had been a thorough search but a hasty one. And it was incomplete. If he were that intelligencer he would return. And with more time, he might even think to test the solidity of this apparent fall. He returned the papers to their hiding place, rebuilt the fall, and left the mine. It did not matter whether the spy worked for the prince, for Ettore, for Da Monte, or for the Inquisition. Francis was dead no matter which of them learned what he was really doing in the mine.

'Keep the double guard,' he told Venturini, 'but withdraw them to a greater distance. Today I begin very dangerous work.'

'Withdraw them?'

'Or risk their lives,' said Francis. 'Tell everyone who lives or works here at the lodge that today, I begin my most dangerous work. Tell them they must stay below the top of the saddle, on the far side. Outside the rope.'

After a long moment, Venturini gave his usual curt nod, but his eyes said that he understood what Francis was up to.

Francis had four slaves mark out a large perimeter around the mine with rope, on the outer slopes of the bowl, too far down to see into the bowl. He took gunpowder, flints, a few paper shell cases and lengths of different fuses from the stable yard. After consulting briefly with Seaborn and admiring the numbers of rockets already prepared for launch, he worked alone inside the mine for the rest of the day.

The explosion woke them all well before dawn. Francis and Seaborn joined the swarm of lanterns racing up the track. Francis had not undressed to sleep.

The entrance to the mine was destroyed, shortening the tunnel behind it by several yards. The Uskoks flung themselves at the rubble as if to atone for their lapse of the night before.

Francis heard a shout. One of the Uskoks held aloft a severed hand and forearm skewered on the point of his sword. The object was dark with charring. He left them to the search. He had lost any stomach he ever had for such work. It had been almost four years since he had last had to face the effects of his military skills.

When they found enough to identify, the man was burnt almost past recognizing. But the shape of what was left of his torso, his remaining hair and the remnants of his clothing were enough to confirm the uneasy suspicions Francis had held since very shortly after meeting the man. It was Ricco Smith.

'*Bighe*!' Venturini spat on the remains of the steward. Prick!

Francis turned away towards the sound of the Uskok captain shouting. One of his men stood with blood running down his neck from a scalp wound.

'The fool stood too close,' explained Venturini. 'On the top of the saddle. He says that he wanted to see down into the bowl, to guard the mine better. He'll know next time to keep low on the other side, outside the rope.'

In the end, Ricco Smith and his master, or mistress, might have done Francis a favour. That day, once the Uskoks had finished clearing the entrance, Francis was able to work at the mine unobserved.

Several times after the midday dinner, he went out into the bowl and looked up at the mountain above him but he never saw the glint of a spy glass. The Uskoks doubled their guard, but stayed outside the rope. Then, just as the mountains were beginning to pull down the sun, the marmots whistled.

62

Francis went out into the bowl.

'Signore!' 'Signore!' The shouts came from the track below the mine. He climbed up onto the protecting ridge and looked down. The Uskok guard stood exactly at the rope barrier, waving to catch Francis's eye. He pointed back down the track at a white-robed figure mounted on a mule.

It took Francis a moment. He had never seen the man anywhere but in his library. He looked implausible here on the rocky mountainside, with his long legs hanging nearly to the ground on either side of his mount.

'Albona!' shouted Francis. With the pleasure of seeing an old friend, he went down the track to greet the librarian.

'I have your translations,' said Albona.

'So soon?'

'I worked through the night. Your time is short.'

They walked together down to the lodge.

'I should warn you that I had an escort up from La Spada.'

'Vranghi?' asked Francis unhappily.

'No one like that. Someone you will want to meet.'

Francis was still not entirely reassured.

As soon as they entered the forecourt, Seaborn took

Francis's arm and led him across the pounded earth to the lodge steps, towards a young man wearing very elegant and costly riding clothes. Jacket of turned buckskin embroidered with silver threads. Fringed riding gloves. Black boots as shiny as an obsidian mirror.

'Francis, may I introduce you to Count Niccolò Schiavoni?'

Francis had seen him at the court. The broad shoulders and dark, handsome face with its slightly heavy brows had often stood amongst Ettore's waiting gentlemen.

'Signore Cointo, I am very happy to meet Zebbo's hero, at last,' said Schiavoni. 'His Odysseus and his Aristotle rolled into one.' He sounded entirely sincere.

Francis gave Seaborn a sharp glance. Seaborn's face looked merely happy. His eyes were bright and completely free of irony.

'I have had the impertinence to bring a few necessaries to ease the Spartan life you lead up here,' Schiavoni said lightly in fluent Latin, giving no offence.

Francis noticed the hampers on the top of the steps. Schiavoni opened them and offered the contents. Cheese from his estates to the west of La Spada. Wine and olive oil. Sweet pickled pumpkin and sugared almonds. An entire salt-cured boar's haunch from San Daniele.

'It will make a change from pork skin and beans.' Schiavoni exchanged quick smiles with Seaborn. He had also brought an oiled coat for Seaborn to keep him dry, *caffea*, to help them both stay safely alert while working such long hours, and five pounds of silver leaf from Schiavoni's mines for use in the fireworks.

How does he know about the Spartan life and long hours? Francis wondered. But the answer was already clear. He hoped that Seaborn . . . 'Zebbo' . . . had not been mistaken in his trust.

He watched the two young men together, one tall and

fair, the other a little shorter and dark. Here was the source of Seaborn's new light-heartedness. Francis listened to the nimble ease of their conversation, the shared impulse to laugh. Niccolò Schiavoni was quick to smile under his slightly forbidding brows. His nature seemed far gentler than his looks. He was more polished than the Uskoks, a little taller, and infinitely more finely dressed, but shared their look of dark ferocity. Watching Schiavoni with his nephew, Francis saw an earlier courtly life as a noble bye-blow begin to reach for Richard Seaborn. With a pang of loss, he felt the modest country grip of Powder Mote beginning to loosen.

'So this is where you teach fire to fly,' said Albona at his elbow. 'I mean to stay here until you have read through the translations. You may need me to explain some term, or have some necessary you decide to have sent up from La Spada. May I see a little more of what you do here whilst I'm waiting?'

Francis recognized a shared curiosity. 'With pleasure. But be warned, it could be dangerous.'

Albona laughed.

While Albona, at his own risk, watched the firework makers in the stable yard, and Schiavoni talked quietly with Seaborn at the lip of the cliff looking out over the plateau, Francis took Albona's notes to his *camera* and read them hungrily. As so often happens, the solution simply arrived. It was waiting quietly for him to notice it. Then offered its hand. Hello. Here I am, if you happened to be looking for me.

'I need a glassblower to make me some vials,' Francis told Albona before the librarian and Schiavoni returned to La Spada. 'A great many of them.' He gave Albona a letter for Da Monte.

'I hope I may be a witness to the fruits of your labours.'

Francis leaned closer to the dark face with its glinting spectacles. 'As a colleague, you'll be very welcome. If I live so long.'

63

'Sir!' Seaborn knew better than to touch Francis when awaking him, but his low voice served better than a slap on the face. Francis sat up fully alert, his hand reaching for the dagger under his pillow. Seaborn stepped back. 'You'd best come at once and see what the night brought us.'

It was the day after they had found Ricco Smith at the mine. Through the open front double doors, Francis saw a huddle of backs, two Uskoks and several slaves. The men stepped away to let him through. A dead man lay at the bottom of the steps on the packed stony earth of the fore-court. His throat had been cut. There was almost no blood on the ground, even though his clothing was black with it. He lay with his spattered cloak twisted around his body and one arm trapped under him.

Killed elsewhere and dumped here, thought Francis. The hard earth disguised the tracks of whoever had delivered him.

One of the Uskoks was already squatting beside the corpse, feeling through his clothes.

The grey-white face looked familiar to Francis. Any hair not bloodied was sandy brown and fell below his ears. He had a sparse moustache like a thousand others and a beard darker than his hair. Francis searched his mind for the plump, snub-nosed face, trying to imagine it a healthy pink, with the grinning mouth in the correct place instead of under his chin. It had not been a smiling face . . .

The Uskok grunted with satisfaction and held up a scrap of parchment. '*Franji.*'

'That's "Frankish", I believe,' said Seaborn. 'An all-purpose local word for western foreigners.'

'It's that uncouth Englishman,' said Francis. 'Who glowered and belched when we first met in the Sala, as if I wanted to steal his bone.' About whom he had wondered, through whom he had hoped to send urgent word to Cecil about the prince's true madness. But the man had never given him a sign. Francis took the piece of parchment, which was far too clean to have been on the man when he died.

'Have him taken down to the Castello and tell me who claims his body,' he ordered the Uskok captain.

He and Seaborn watched the efficient bundling of the dead Englishman into a kindling sack.

'I had suspected he might be Cecil's man,' said Francis. 'This message confirms it. Or at least, it says that he has suffered the inexorable fate of all English spies and intelligencers.'

'I stand warned,' said Seaborn.

Francis folded the parchment and lowered his voice. 'A prompt retort to my own message yesterday.'

He wondered again whose man Ricco Smith had been. Prince Ettore? Or the prince himself?

Sofia? Reason said that he must make himself continue to think such things. Then he remembered Smith's dark look as he watched Francis and Sofia together on the steps of the lodge. With relief, this time at least, he felt safe to discount her.

The Inquisition?

As Albona had said, there was no room to squeeze one more intelligencer or agent into La Spada. They should join together and set up a bourse for information, thought Francis. Trade openly. Perhaps fewer people would then get their throats cut, or walk into explosive traps.

He tried to think like Cecil. The Ottomans were in uneasy alliance with England against all Catholic powers. The Hapsburgs were holding the Ottomans balanced in a fragile treaty and looking to the west. Both powers had a stake in La Spada as a gateway to the west. It was possible that this man's death had nothing at all to do with Francis himself. It might simply be a way of warning England against an alliance with La Spada. 'Stay out of La Spada!' If Cecil had told him more, he might be quicker to judge.

He had no appetite for breakfast. He did not feel ready to work in spite of the urgent need and his discovery of the afternoon before. When the dead Englishman had been removed, he turned in the opposite direction, up the track, and left the lodge compound by the upper gate. The Uskoks on guard wished him a curt good morning and locked the gate behind him.

'*A bon riviodisi,*' Francis replied in one of his new phrases in Friulan. *Au revoir.* Until we meet again.

He set off on foot up the track. He could feel their eyes on his back. But after their shared labour, the Uskoks seemed to decide that Francis was here to stay. He wished to encourage this belief. If they let him roam unguarded, escape from the lodge would become much more possible.

The track climbed a little then began to descend. He had missed his ride from flowers into snow. All the snow now raced downhill in ribbons and rivulets of bright cold water, joining into tiny streams, splashing over ledges in miniature waterfalls, twisting together in a small river that he could just see through the trees below him.

He scrambled up the mountainside to sit on a boulder, setting off a panic of shrill whistles and burrow-diving bodies. Far below, he saw the Uskoks spy him, consult and return to their posts by the gate. He stared out.

This morning, a lake of lavender cloud still lay in the valley. The sun came and went, leaving him first warm, then chilled. Francis had thought that he loved the Sussex Downs, with their soft female curves where pale chalk gleamed through a smooth pelt of bracken and grass. Now he felt an unexpected stirring of passion for this abrupt landscape, all teeth and elbows, with sheared-off cliffs and boulders the size of palaces. Sheer terror in mineral form plunged down into tranquil pools and rivers of green space. Narrow defiles called out to be explored.

He sat so still that a pair of what he now knew to be chamois began to feed among the rocks a little way above him. He watched a small grey lizard pretending to be part of the lichen-covered stone. He sighed and stood up to return to the lodge.

In the end, it made no difference to Francis who had killed Cecil's man. He must now assume that his back was no longer being watched. There would be no intervention. He and Richard were on their own. He had not admitted to himself how much the possibility of English aid had comforted him.

'*A bon riviodisi,*' he said again at the gate.

'*Grüss Gott,*' replied the Uskok.

In spite of his dark humour, Francis smiled. He was now quite certain that they were playing with him. '*Salve.*'

Their eyes flickered. He walked on towards the lodge, unaccountably cheered. He might even be ready to attempt his next step, which he had found waiting quietly in Albona's translation of the *Liber Ignium Missilium*. The book of fire hurled into the sky.

PART FIVE

64

FRANCIS'S *CAMERA*, LA SPADA

Time was his enemy. As finite as a single heart beat, as impossible to pin down as fog.

Was it a substance? A property? A current? Do we breathe it, swim through it? Do we let it pull us like a rope through our lives and let go when we die? How the devil do we measure it precisely?

Francis had been stopped dead by time. He sat at his table in his *camera* in the hunting lodge, cursing time.

He saw now how to step from the idea to the substance. With luck, that substance would seem to meet the terms of his contract with the prince.

The picture was clear in his head. The prince – enclosed in his gilded silk capsule, solid-looking but as fragile as a butterfly's wing, mounted on the giant crossbow, a bolt ready to fire. The blinding flash, a thunderclap. Whoosh! A missile rising . . . soaring upwards, on and on and on until out of sight. And on the ground, nothing was left but rubble and the giant crossbow shattered by the force of its firing, a few ashes. Almost possible, almost within his grasp. His illusion was almost complete.

He must make it happen! The need now gripped his soul with more than just fear. He needed to know that he could succeed.

Francis closed his eyes. He was almost ready. The prince's capsule was made, the giant crossbow stood assembled in the bowl outside the mine. He believed that he knew how to make the prince vanish as if by magic. The first soaring missile that would seem to carry him was being varnished even now in the stable yard, lost among the many hundreds of very similar rockets.

He also saw what he could not yet make happen. Behind his lids the soaring missile seemed to rise and rise. Never seeming to fall back to earth as every rising earthly body must in time begin to fall back to where it began.

That was the effect he must achieve.

That diffident idea that had been waiting quietly for him in Albona's translations, told him how he might, just, achieve that continuing rise into the heavens.

But to put that idea into practice, he needed to measure time into tiny parts, which remained always the same. His pulse would do for less precise calculations, but its rate changed subtly. The thought of Sofia's naked breasts, for example, could double it.

He leaned his elbows on the table. Yet again, he stared down at Albona's translation of the Arabic *Liber Ignium Missilium* with its diagrams of fusing devices, some familiar, some unfamiliar. All for the mechanical triggering of an explosion, many without a burning fuse. Devices for striking sparks, variations on flint and steel, some of them very like those he himself used in his small percussion stars, and ground rats for frightening enemy horses in battle – both of these thrown onto the ground, where the shock of landing struck the igniting spark.

He was certain he had chosen the best of the devices or

rather, that it had chosen him. As if it had known about Boomer's gift of vitriol for unknown purposes in an unknown land, which Francis had forgotten until now.

He turned his head sharply to the sound of a small thump behind him. The half-grown kitten he had brought from La Spada stood with its nose pressed to the base of the wall, tail twitching angrily.

'Missed?' asked Francis.

The cat ignored him. After a few more angry twitches, it folded itself neatly to wait, never taking its eyes from the slim crack between the boards. Francis thought suddenly of the veiled purpose he felt in Sofia. He watched the cat's intense stillness. Waiting. Teeth and claws hidden. The cat was like a held breath. It was the mouse's death waiting to uncoil in a flash. He stared absently at the cat for a little longer, imagining that sudden unleashing of power. He could imagine Sofia unleashing a hidden power.

He could imagine her in his bed. She must surely have understood his purpose in suggesting that her father send an agent to report.

He hauled his thoughts back to the notes.

For that missile to seem to keep rising, far enough to disappear from sight, he needed to give it a second push. The first push would come from the crossbow, the second just as the missile reached the top of its arc. He thought he knew how that might be achieved, but to achieve it, he must measure the exact time it took to reach the top of that arc. And reproduce it, exactly. Again, and again, and again.

He had worked with different forms of water clocks and watches, but they were unreliable or bit time into mouthfuls that were too large for the delicate timings he must make.

He stared at the remaining glass vials. He stared at Boomer's gift of vitriol. He stared at the giant crossbow. With the help of two slaves, he had fired the bow and made a rough calculation of its maximum range, at different angles of fire, with different sizes of bolts. But that was only half the story. He needed an absolute marriage in time between loosing the bow and the firing of his second charge.

He pulled a blank piece of paper to him and copied his proposed firing device, adapted from Albona's *Liber Ignium Missilium* into the Quoynt *Liber Ignium*. At the very least, this device would be a novelty to show his father.

He could make no more trials without a way to count those very small precise bites of time.

He sank down onto the edge of his cupboard bed and dropped his head into his hands. His head weighed him down like a stone cannon ball. It was so crammed and jammed with undone tasks, untested devices, and possible dangers that there was not even the tiniest crack for reason to wriggle through in search of a way to measure time.

The wooden stairs began to sing their night creature song of creaks and squeaks. The floor yielded noisily to a weight that stopped just outside his door.

'Tell him to go away,' said Francis. He flung himself back against the pillows. More than sleep, he wanted oblivion, just for a short time to be without constant fear and speculation. The previous night's sleep had been filled with dangers that he could not remember in the morning but which had left him feeling awry.

Seaborn opened the door. Francis heard muffled conversation. Seaborn laughed softly and crossed back to the bed.

'A messenger from La Spada, sir. Who wishes to deliver a gift.'

65

'Tell him to leave the gift. I'll send thanks in the morning.' He lay back on the bed and threw his arm across his eyes.

'Francees.'

Francis lurched upright.

'I would like very much to stay to be thanked in the morning,' said Sofia, 'but alas, I must be back in my own bed before dawn.' She bent to set a large basket on the floor.

'Sofia!' His heart hammered. His weariness vanished. 'How the devil . . .?' He took the hands she held out to him. They were cold from her ride. He closed his own around them. 'You shouldn't take such a risk!'

'But I am that trusted agent you told my father to send,' she said. 'Who else? Just as you intended.' She tossed him a wicked smile. 'He can't trust Da Monte not to use information for his own ends. He can't trust Ettore at all. As far as the rest of them know, I'm safely tucked up in my bed – or so the charming Isabella assures everyone.'

She wore a man's hat and cloak over the split trousers of a Hungarian horseman and heavy riding boots. 'Build up the fire to make a good bed of coals,' she ordered Richard. 'How sweet this room smells – like a forest!' She took back her hands and strode around the chamber with open delight, listening to her feet. Creak, creak, squeak.

'Listen! You can play this floor like an instrument.' She stepped suddenly sideways and drew a deep baritone groan from the wooden boards.

Her open delight made him remember how young she really was.

She's also dangerous! She's dangerous! he reminded himself. Remember that she wanted an assassin. She still does. You have promised not to let Ettore harm her, without knowing the cost of that promise.

But the warning of reason made not one bit of difference. Francis felt his face smiling helplessly. Delight filled him at the sight of that slim body pacing his floor, her legs moving crisply in the flow and rustle of the trousers. The dance of her words.

'What are you doing here?' He glanced at Seaborn's back, bent beside the fireplace, his elbows flapping as he worked the painted bellows to fan the flames.

'Don't fear Signore Zebbone,' she said, following the direction of Francis's eyes. 'Our secret is safe with him. He has secrets of his own that we can threaten him with – don't you, my *polpettino*?'

Francis was torn between astonishment at this new familiarity between the *principessa* and his former manservant . . . '*polpettino*'? . . . since when had Seaborn become her little meatball? . . . and an absolute need to kiss her lips. And her eyelids.

She took pity on him at last and came into his arms. But only for a quick kiss. Then she was foraging in the basket and handing Seaborn eggs, an earthenware jug, a muslin-wrapped cube, a dark-green stoppered bottle.

There's a conspiracy here, thought Francis. He had never seen her quite like this. Animated, happy, but a little feverish.

When Richard disappeared with his treasures, Francis took her hands again. 'Sofia.' He tried to gather her up into a shared stillness in this fragrant room. Whatever this unexpected moment was, he wanted to know it, to taste it. It must not rush past. What was waiting for them all would not allow many more such gifts.

'Sofia . . .'

She nodded gravely. 'Yes, I know.' They hung balanced for a moment in this extraordinary new space they occupied together. Then she added lightly, 'You may sit down again.'

She had to look away, to break the moment and regain control of herself. You can't prevent the future from taking its course. Sofia knew that truth better than most people. But you can try to shape it. She needed this time tonight. Whatever they would take onwards with them into the future depended on her now, and on what she did in the next minutes, the next hour or two. She had never been so terrified in her life.

She looked at his beautiful face and the open pupils of his eyes, which were beyond the control of will. He truly liked what he saw. She leaned over to kiss him gently. Then she sat beside him on the bed and leaned her shoulder against his strong warm one. The sensation was as complete and satisfying as if they were making love, but more peaceful. She closed her eyes. This peace was a new feeling, one that she wanted to have forever.

Remember this. Remember this.

'I don't want to move,' he said, pressing back. 'Ever again.'

'I was about to say the same.' She turned her head, pressed her nose into his shirt, then brushed her face slowly back and forth against him. 'I can smell gunpowder on you.'

'And I wager that's not all.'

She smiled. Her terror was beginning to ebb. It might be all right. Their present stillness fed her courage in a way that remembered hunger did not.

Seaborn came back into the room a little awkwardly, as if he expected to interrupt a tender moment. He was carrying, very carefully, a Chinese porcelain bowl. 'Highness!' He held up the bowl to show her, then set it down beside the fire.

'Now!' said Sofia, with a slight return of her earlier over-brightness. 'Now I will introduce you to one of our old customs.' She exchanged a look with Seaborn. 'You may leave us now. Thank you.'

They listened to Seaborn's feet creaking outside the door. He went a short distance along the gallery, then stopped.

'He will stand watch,' said Sofia. 'And now, I have a wizard trick of my own to show you. But my magic is real.' She shot him a look to be certain that he understood that she was only teasing him. He smiled wryly.

She made herself busy to hide her uncertainty. She carried the basket closer to the fire and knelt, an act which was delightfully easy in trousers and almost impossible in petti-coats with hoops. Even that simple sense of physical ease fed the bubble growing under her heart.

Remember this.

From the basket, she took a pair of round iron plates each a little less than a foot across, which had been hinged together on one side, with a pair of long straight handles on the open sides opposite the hinge. She felt his eyes on her as she held the utensil in the fire to warm it. Then she greased it with what was left of the muslin-wrapped butter. Opening it to lie flat on the hearth, she carefully poured a thin layer of batter from the bowl onto one of the iron plates. She closed the hinge, pressing the two plates together and stretched to hold it over the fire at just the right height above the coals.

'What are you doing?' he asked.

'Don't distract me!' She flipped the iron over to heat the other plate over the coals. Francis crossed to the fireplace to watch over her shoulder. She felt his nearness behind her as warmly as the fire on her face.

She withdrew the iron, opened it and lifted out the finished wafer with her knife. Then she stood up and faced him. 'We must look into each other's eyes as we eat it.'

'I must read it first.' Francis lifted it carefully in both hands. 'To know what I'm subscribing to.'

The plates were engraved with decorations that printed themselves onto both sides of the wafer. Turning it in his hands, Francis read on one side, printed around a central device of a pierced heart, the words, *'Gioia, camerlano cuore'*. The other side bore the same words in Latin intertwined with garlands. *'Gaudium, camerlingus cordibus nostris.* 'Joy, the chamberlain of our hearts.'

'Will you eat it with me?' She managed to keep the tremor out of her voice.

'Why am I put in mind of Eve?' he asked lightly. Before she could flinch, he added, 'Sweetest Sofia, I will eat any apple you offer me, with the greatest joy.'

Gravely, she took a bite, then offered the wafer to him. He put his hands on her wrists to steady her while he ate, very carefully, the word *gioia*. Joy.

In the end, it was she who had to drop her eyes.

'Do you know how many wafers I burnt whilst learning how?'

'As many as I would?'

His answer pleased her immensely for reasons she did not understand.

'Now we must speak in earnest,' she said. She held up her hand to silence his protest. 'I mean, we must speak with steady purpose. Not merely exchange words in place of kisses.' She took his hand and led him back to sit on the bed again, as her knees threatened to give way. Once seated, she clung to his hand.

'You know that we can never marry.' She felt his hand jump but did not let it go.

'I would never presume to such a thing,' he said at last. Her ears strained to detect either regret or relief.

'But I also know that I will never give my heart again as I give it now to you,' she said.

'Nor I,' he said after a brief pause.

She thought that he sounded more startled than anything else. There was a longer silence while he seemed to be thinking.

'You're right,' he resumed in the same tone of discovery. 'We are a match, you and I. Who would have thought it?' He shook his head wryly. 'I don't know what that means about either of us. But I fear that you are right.'

'Fear?'

'Forgive me, I'm not being sufficiently earnest.' He lifted his hand and kissed hers that still clung to it.

She frowned slightly, trying to judge his tone. Only a little farther to go. She wasn't entirely certain of the ground, but this chance might never come again. With her free hand, she felt into the hanging pocket on her belt. She opened her fist to show two rings made of heavy twisted gold wire, each set with a single square-cut ruby.

'We have a custom called the "marriage of hearts". When there cannot be formal marriage, two people can still pledge themselves to love forever, just by saying so and exchanging a gift of rings.' She was speaking too fast. In spite of her resolve, the hand with the rings trembled slightly.

'Close your eyes.'

'Why?' she asked, startled. He meant to abandon her!

'Close them. And give me my hand for a moment.'

She obeyed but gripped onto the hem of his jacket, lest

he slip away. She felt him shift as if searching amongst his clothing. 'Open them again.'

She raised her eyebrows, both relieved and curious. He was still there. Nothing had changed.

'Look!' He pointed. A tiny explosion flashed on the floor a short distance from their feet.

She laughed, half amused, half irritated. She did not understand. And he had not answered her about the marriage of their hearts. She could not think what she would do if he refused. 'And now?'

He held up a ring. 'Now I have a ring that I can give to you. How else can we exchange?'

She looked down. Only one ring remained in her palm.

'We make a fearsome pair,' he said quietly. 'Locked into a fearful partnership, forever. Are you quite certain it's what you want? I can't do such things from cold purpose nor for empty show.'

'I once believed that I could.' She laid her palm against his and looked at their two hands. 'I even believed I could give my body for cold purpose. I never before thought to include my heart.'

Without separating their hands, he slid the ring down over her finger. Then she placed the other on the little finger of his left hand.

66

'As your father's agent, can you find me a means to measure time exactly?' he asked Sofia before she left him later that night. 'Ask Albona. Tell him I need the intervals of a sleeping heartbeat, but precise and consistent. He may be able to help us.'

'"Us?"' She smiled at him with delight. 'There's the first outward symptom of our conjoined hearts.' She repeated the word, 'Us-us-us-us!' She was dressing again in her riding trousers and boots. 'I shall have our master of music write us a cantata – the words "us" and "we" and "our" set to the musical creaking of floorboards.' She looked up from fastening her belt. 'I can hear the *castratto* now – "Ahouuuuuuuuuuuuuur!"' Rising up on her toes and clasping her hands as if in prayer, she imitated the plump little man Francis had heard singing after supper in the *sala*. 'With occasional explosions of gunpowder in place of cymbals or drums,' she added.

Francis laughed with sheer delight.

She took the basket, repacked for her by Seaborn. 'I ache to sleep one whole night beside you, *caro*,' she said. 'I shall do it soon.' She felt giddy with joy and relief. She had never heard herself rattle on like this. She closed her fingers around the warm weight of the ring. But then, she had never thought to find herself in such a state of happiness. Outside this room, the world was very different. But here, just now, she felt as light and reckless as when she had kicked her mare up slope of the mountain meadow.

The memory of what had happened then sobered her now.

'I must not test my father's tolerance too far, all at once. You were very clever to suggest a trusted agent. He must feel only the gain of my breathless reports and not the loss of my presence.' She laid her free hand on Francis's arm, not because it was politic, not as a calculated gesture but because she would die if she could not feel the warmth of his body touching hers, however innocently. She touched him only because she truly wanted to, because she had no other choice.

'Tell me what I must say to him. We can trust each other now.'

When she arrived back in La Spada, she used the entrance in the wall. Most of her women would be asleep or chatting drowsily in the *antecamera*. But Isabella was waiting near her bed, aquiver with urgency.

'Thank the Lord, you're back,' said the young waiting woman. 'The royal physician doesn't know what to do. He says that only you might be able to calm the prince. Please come at once!'

Sofia ran, still in her riding clothes.

67

Her father crouched in one corner of his *camera* wearing only a thin silk night-shirt and night cap. He had pulled the bedclothes off the great canopied bed and dragged them across the floor behind him. The air was thick and sharp with burning herbs.

'ABRAHAM! ABRAHAM!' The prince's voice rang out, huge and hollow, not his own. 'BEHOLD! HERE I AM!'

Jaw wobbling in terror, he then shrank farther back into his corner. 'Do you see Him?' he asked Sofia and the physician in his own voice. 'The Lord speaks to me. Do you hear?' He pointed with a shaking hand at the opposite corner.

'Here I am!' he repeated in the great hollow voice, standing straight again. 'Allessandro, you once scorned Me. How dare you presume to crave My Mercy now?'

The royal physician made a helpless gesture to Sofia.

The prince stared into the opposite corner. 'Lord,' he cried in his own voice again. 'Have mercy on me. *Miserere me*! I have repented.'

His body straightened. 'Dost thou respect Me?' he boomed. 'How will you show repentance?'

'What do You ask of me?' The prince stared at the corner with the eyes of a terrified child.

She could not breathe. The smoky air caught at her throat and made her head swim.

The prince resumed the hollow voice. 'Alessandro, take now thy son Isaac, thine only son Isaac, whom thou lovest and offer him for a burnt offering upon one of the mountains which I will tell thee of.'

The prince turned to Sofia. 'Do you hear?' he whispered. 'Before I go to meet Him, I must give Him sign that I fear Him and that I truly repent. Like Abraham, I must not withhold my lamb.'

The hair rose on her nape.

He turned his eyes back to the empty corner. Still staring at the corner, the prince suddenly said, 'Gone!' He placed a hand over his heart as if holding it in place while it tried to jump free of his ribs. Sofia could see the upright collar of his shirt quivering against the cords of his neck. After a moment, he crossed back to the bed, sat on the edge and tried to drink from his gold lion-headed beaker. His hands still shook so hard that the physician's brew slopped into his lap.

'What have you dosed him with?' she whispered.

'Only a decoction to kill his pain, your highness! Forgive me! He was beginning to scream with the pain!'

'Come, girl! Soothe me. Calm me.' The prince extended one long leg. 'Stroke my feet.'

At first, Sofia could not make her frozen limbs move.

I'm not a son, she told him in her head. Not an Isaac, merely a daughter. But she didn't say it aloud, for fear of giving the thought any further shape. For the first time, she thought to look for Father Daniele. The priest had prostrated himself towards the corner where her father had just seen God and still lay flat with his arms outstretched, a large black cross spread on the rush matting.

'Did you hear me?'

Silently, she dropped to her knees and lifted her father's left foot into her lap and began to rub at his sole with her thumbs. Her fingers had learned how to land between the ulcer scars like gulls on broken river ice.

'I can't feel your fingers on my foot! Stroke my head!' He fell back askew against his pillows, leaving his foot in her lap. Whatever the physician had given him now sucked him towards sleep.

The physician helped her lift both of the prince's feet onto the bed, then to retrieve the strewn bedclothes and cover him. She pulled her padded stool to the bed head and ran her fingers lightly across his brow, the gulls still seeking clear ice.

'You're my best medicine,' he said. 'Ahhh. Yes! You're the only one who knows how to soothe me.'

Once, when I was younger, I would have been pleased to win his approval, she thought with astonishment. Before my mother. Before Baldassare.

She would have flushed with triumphant warmth that he preferred her to her half-brother Ettore in all things except the succession. Now she wished only that her father loved his bastard son better, that he doted on Ettore as Abraham had loved Isaac. But the prince had legitimized Ettore from dynastic desperation, not fondness.

The prince's thoughts may in some way have paralleled her own. 'Where was your brother just now when the Lord visited La Spada?' he demanded.

'Sleeping off his supper wine, I believe, my lord father.'

'In the dark, in the dark, that one. A night prowler using whores!' The prince was looking thoughtful. 'At least, you saw Him, my dove. You heard what He asked of me. It's a pity you weren't born a boy.' He turned his head to her. She dropped her gaze but felt the weight of his eyes on her head pressing down like a cold stone.

376

She kept her own eyes lowered. Her thumbs moved with gentle care on his temples, but her thoughts raced. It was time to put more words into the lions' mouths. And she had a new urgent use for the partner of her heart.

She wondered if she dared to test him and the limit of their bond.

She had learned her lesson, just as she had learned many other things about him. She must continue to be open. Francis knew when she was not. He saw her clearly, just as she saw him. Remembering their evening just now at the lodge, she could almost forget that she stroked her mad, dying father's head.

She shook herself back to cool thought again. She must never lose all her claws and scales. Her deepest danger in loving Francis Quoynt . . . her beloved, unexpected Francees Cointo . . . was that she might grow fatally impatient with dishonesty.

'You press too hard!' her father said angrily. His eyes drifted closed again.

Take a pillow and smother him, she thought. Her whole body went hot with the desire to finish him, this creature who was no longer her father, who had killed her mother, colluded in the death of her husband and now seemed very likely to kill her too, out of love for her.

But she had not studied, nor spent so many hours, days, weeks, months and years in thinking ahead, twisting the future first one way and then another in her thoughts to throw it away on the impulse of a moment. She stroked more and more lightly. He drew several irregular gasping sighs. Then his breathing grew shallow and steady. She lifted her fingers away like the last wisps of a cloud. Waited.

He did not open his eyes.

Carefully, she stood. Waited again, then left the bedside,

walking lightly in her riding boots. She nodded for the physician to follow her from the room.

'You know that my brother means to kill you if our father dies.'

The physician dropped to his knees. '*Principessa*, you know that he will surely die no matter what treatments I give him!'

'But my brother will rule La Spada after the prince's death, not I,' she said. 'What I know or don't know may be of no importance.'

'Tell your brother! Make him understand that I am no regicide! Intercede, I beg you!'

'We must help each other, *signore dottore*,' she said. 'Who can tell what might happen then?'

She saw from his appalled and terrified expression that he read the most extreme meaning into her words. 'I mean only that you must always bring news to me first of any changes in my father's state. As you did tonight.' She softened her tone. 'That was well done, and earned you my gratitude. Please continue in this well-chosen course.'

She went back to her *camera* and scrubbed her hands with her purifying potions while Isabella laid out her night shift. As she replaced the jars on the shelf of her *restello*, she leaned close to its reflecting glass eye and inspected her face. Her skin was still smooth and unblemished, without hint of a taint. In truth, she looked exceedingly well. She asked Isabella to bring a candleholder closer to the mirror. Her eyes only seemed to glint more brightly. Her cheeks glowed with health and joy.

The doctor had been quite wrong to think she was suggesting that he poison her father. If the prince died of obvious poisoning, then she, who spent so much time caring for him, would be the first suspect. Did the doctor imagine that Ettore would not blame her as well as the prince's physician? Nevertheless, she had chosen the wrong enemy to fear most. Just now, her father was more dangerous than her brother.

68

Francis began the next day after God had visited the prince by ordering, on Seaborn's instructions, ten pounds each of gold and silver leaf, pounds of Muscovy resin, copper salts, iron filings, silk threads, varnishes, enamels, gold wire, linen threads, more paint brushes, more turpentine. He ordered pigments – scarlet, terra cotta, ochre, and blue, including rare and costly lapis lazuli (why not, with infinite resources to command?). He ordered bundles of arrow shafts, without tips or flights, to use for rockets. For himself, he had the rope makers twist another thick bow-string for the giant crossbow. He ordered another two barrels of mid-grain gunpowder, only some of which was for the funeral fireworks.

At least Seaborn was making legitimate use of the unlimited resources. What could Francis not achieve if he could always snap his fingers and simply ask for what he needed?

He ate the last of his bread, swallowed the last of his *caffea*, brought by Niccolò Schiavoni, and climbed up to his workshop in the mine. The Uskoks by the rope barrier had wearied of their game of tongues and merely lifted their hands in greeting.

Da Monte had found glass-blowers for Francis at a glass furnace on an estate a short ride from La Spada. The men, father and son, had both served their apprenticeship on the Venetian island of Murano. They had blown two hundred glass vials of different sizes, with walls of different thickness, as Francis ordered.

While the prince was still sleeping off his encounter with the Lord, Francis began to smash the tiny vials made for him by the glassblower, which ranged in the thickness of their walls from that of a wine goblet down to the fragility of spun sugar. He pushed them, dropped them, threw them, threw things at them, testing how easily they broke. He nested them in sawdust inside a parchment shell case and repeated his assaults.

In the early evening, he heard the marmots whistle, then Sofia calling to him from the track below the rope. He assumed that her father wanted another report on the progress of the Great Work. Her arrival also reminded him of his vow to her about Ettore. Nevertheless, he rinsed the glass dust from his hands in a basin filled from the underground pool and ran eagerly to meet her.

'You must kill my father.' She spoke against his bare shoulder, a movement of warm breath over his skin, so softly that he wasn't certain for a moment that he had heard. But the words hung in the air just above his chest, waiting for him to let them land and sting.

They lay together in his cupboard bed, his left arm under her neck, his left hand slipped under her arm to cup her breast. He had been breathing slowly, half asleep in a delicious haze of remembered pleasure. Their time was short. Two Uskoks were waiting to escort her back to La Spada. The lodge creaked gently around them. Tiny feet scuttled through the nearest wall.

After a long while, he said, 'Why?'

'Because he will kill me if you don't.'

'Oh, Sofia . . .' He removed his arm and sat up to think without the distraction of her warm skin against his. All sense of unthinking pleasure fled, replaced by a cold, alert urgency of thought. 'Have you decided to raise a rebellion after all?'

She told him of God's visit to the prince's bedchamber. 'No one dares challenge him, mad as he is. His confessor, who might have calmed him, pretended himself to be struck by awe.' She sat up too, pulled up her feet and hauled the coverlet up to just below her chin. She kept a gap of chilly air between them. 'What else could Father Daniele do? He's too far mired in lies to turn honest now.'

He felt her waiting for his reply. She would not ask such a thing more than once.

'I don't despise him for it,' she said. 'We're all as bad as each other – creatures trying to live with fear, hissing and biting. If I become the next ruler of La Spada, I will be merciful. I will kill no one but my brother, unless they have done me a vile wrong.' She inserted the heart of her meaning into their conversation as neatly as a stiletto.

Francis felt it enter his heart. The next ruler. Of course. He had always known, but chosen to ignore.

Bed your potential allies! Seduce the man you intend to have murder your father, the ruling monarch. All his confusions fell away, leaving behind a profound, icy disappointment. He had truly thought that she might love him.

'You're quite sure you don't want your father dead so you can take the throne at once?' He braced himself for rage and indignation. He had a further chilling thought. How merciful could any new monarch be to the assassin of the old one?

'I am merely being open with you,' she said. 'I find it

381

frightening, but you will grow angry with me otherwise, so I am trying to tell you the entire truth.'

She sounded in earnest. He could hear no trace of that over-dramatic tone that betrayed her earlier performances. But. All the same . . . He groped for his reason, which he had ignored so shamefully for the sake of his pleasure.

Reason told him that the assassin of the prince would most certainly not stand a chance of negotiating the settlement of a debt with his successor. Reason also asked how much Sofia knew about the bond.

'You see how I trust you?' She still did not look at him. 'Yes, I mean to become the next ruler of La Spada. At the very least, even if I die this time, I will prevent Ettore.'

'"This time"?' he asked, buying a moment or two longer.

'I gave Ettore those scars on his face the day he snapped Baldassare's neck between his hands.'

From the ferocity in her voice, Francis would have said just then that the *principessa* was very able to kill her father herself. Whether or not that would win her the support of the people, he could not say. She would not like what he was about to say.

'Sofia, I can't do it.'

'Don't tell me that you have scruples about killing a poor old sick man?' Her low voice turned icy. This was a Sofia he had not seen before. 'You saw him slice off poor Yuri's head. Do you imagine that Yuri is the only one he has killed on a whim? Do you imagine that any of us are safe?'

'I do, in truth, have scruples about killing a sick, mad old man in cold blood, no matter what he has done. But that's not my reason to refuse.' He looked at her profile, aimed away from him, looking straight ahead above the silk mound of her bent-up knees.

'Sofia,' he began. Then he decided to address the new young woman in the bed. '*Principessa*. I'm not ready for his

382

death! It's safer for you not to know more of my reasons, but no one can kill him yet. You must make his physician keep him alive. The prince must not die yet or I am exposed. You might as well kill me now.' He heard an intake of breath. 'You see how I trust you too.'

He heard a small snort of what might have been derision.

'My father will die in any case, when you fire the rocket?'

'Yes.' He reminded himself that it would be as if the prince had chosen to fall on his sword to end his torment. But the argument still did not satisfy his conscience. He had killed enough men. Why did this one trouble him so?

'Your scruples have limits, then.'

He took a deep unhappy breath. 'Also, yes.'

'If he dies now, you are dead. If he doesn't die soon, I am most likely dead.'

'You've caught it exactly.'

'So, Francis-the-man-to-whom-I must-not-lie, what are we do to?'

He wanted more than he could say to trust the small cold hand that found his hand amongst the bedclothes and gripped it tightly.

'Neither of us can die now,' she said.

69

That same week, Lutz, the prince's fortune-teller and physi-ognomist, was arrested by the Inquisition and removed to Rome for trial. Venturini, who brought the news to the lodge, seemed chiefly indignant that the Inquisition had dared to touch one of the prince's own people.

'His highness welcomed the Jesuits here, even after they had all of Venice excommunicated.' This had been two years earlier. 'No one is safe when the Roman Church begins to attack its friends.' Venturini gave Francis a direct look.

A shiver of alarm spread from the back of his neck into his limbs. The arrest of Lutz read to Francis like a warning political shot across the bows of a weakening ruler. The Inquisition, as an arm of the Papal States, was growing more aggressive, now that the Catholic Hapsburgs had been freed by their treaty with the Turks to turn their atten-tion to Europe. La Spada lay squarely between the two Catholic allies – Hapsburgs to the north and the Papal States to the south. This time it had been Lutz. Given Father Daniele's knowledge of the prince's plans, Francis himself was an obvious candidate for the next warning shot.

'We must work even faster,' said Francis.

Venturini nodded fiercely.

Meanwhile, Richard Seaborn ordered the rope makers to twist two lengths, each as long as the causeway up to the Castello. His stable yard slaves finished binding seven hundred packed fountain cases to the giant sword, which now lay flat and bristling with fuse ends on the floor of the largest barn. More than eight hundred packed shell cases were wrapped in oiled paper and stored in the former stables, along with four hundred sky-rockets of different sizes. A thousand paces of twisted fuse cord soaked in barrels of various salpetre solutions. The slaves walked in bare feet. Everyone moved with great care.

Niccolò Schiavoni brought two more hampers to the lodge, including more coffee for alertness.

'I listen all the time for the sound of an explosion,' he confided to Francis.

Along with tiny artichokes in cream sauce and delicate swirling *biscotti* made by his pastry cook, he brought the latest poetry from Florence and Venice. He repeated the news of Lutz's arrest by the Inquisition.

'A wizard, they said.' He curled his lip. 'That tedious, earnest little man? It's an insult to wizardry! And everyone's as fearful now as a hen house with the smell of fox in the air.'

He also brought gossip from the court and good wishes from the *principessa*, who regretted not being able that day to take advantage of his offer to escort her to the lodge. He brought Francis a curious device sent by Albona.

'He said to tell you that it's called "an alchemist's balls".'

Five steel balls the size of cherries hung in a horizontal row, each suspended on a V of heavy linen thread from a wooden cradle. At rest, the balls just touched each other. Their magic was that if you raised an end ball and let it fall, the ball at the opposite end jumped free whilst those between them seemed not to move at all.

Francis swung the ball at one end. Tick. The fifth ball leapt out and fell back. Tick. The first ball leapt out and fell back. Tick. The fifth ball jumped.

Tick, tick, tick, tick . . .

If you started counting each time from the first swing, the time for three clicks, or for the first six clicks remained absolutely the same.

With the alchemist's balls, Francis began at once to time how long it took for Boomer's vitriol to eat through different thicknesses of wire, silk cord, and linen thread.

Tick-tick-tick-tick-tick-tick-tick.

He timed the firing of a weighted bolt from the crossbow, from thud to apogee.

Tick-tick-tick-tick.

He tested springs of brass and steel that brought together flint and steel spark striking devices, of different shapes and sizes.

Secretly, he began to clear the tunnel that led to the air-shaft in the bowl outside the mine, shifting the rubble far back into the third tunnel leading off the high-roofed main chamber.

Without explaining why, he ordered the slaves to build the stand for witnesses to the prince's launch, a platform raised six feet above the ground, large enough to hold Prince Ettore, Da Monte, Sofia, the physician, and a priest or two. He had to accept the possibility that a spy for a foreign power might also be among them. And he did not forget the Uskoks, whose sharp eyes would also be turned on their ruler's last moments on earth and who must be penned into the correct place. If the stand could pass as part of the planned fire-works, so much the better. If not, he must rely on the Uskoks to guard the prince's secret. He had the slaves build a berm, a bank of earth across part of the bowl.

He felt sucked into a world of mad purpose, a little adrift from the rest. Even though Cecil in London, and the extravagant English king, were the reasons that Francis was trapped here in this madness, they both seemed slightly unreal. As he set the dropping charges in the air shaft under the crossbow, the splashing surge and slapping sails of the English merchant ships for which he had hoped to find safe haven also seemed unreal, like their outward cargoes of good English wool and guns and their return cargoes of cardamom, cloves and silk. The only reality was his absolute need to succeed in his present purpose.

Francis fell into bed each night, too weary even to wash the dirt or silvery powder dust from his hands.

70

A page discovered Prince Alessandro in his nightshirt, velvet gown and coronet, marching, through the *antecamarilla* with his high-footed syphillitic walk shouting for a true priest to listen to his confession. The page ran to tell the physician, who sent at once for the *principessa*. Unfortunately, she was at that time riding back down the track from the hunting lodge, where she had visited Francis briefly in his mine. She had seen his wild look and the urgent preoccupation in his face, and left again, primed to tell her father that his chariot was now only a few days from completion.

'I will find you a priest,' the physician told the prince.

'Not that false priest Father Daniele!' insisted the prince. 'He lies and tells me all will be well! He is a bad shepherd who will let me fall into hell!'

The physician gave his master a calming draught and went in search of the two Jesuits whom he had often seen talking together and studying in the *saleta*.

Sofia stopped abruptly and pulled back into the shadows of the door of her father's *camera*. The prince was on his knees before the little altar, between St Ignatius and St Elmo. The priest on the chair at his side was not Father Daniele. This man was taller and broader, with a rim of salt-and-pepper hair around the shaved dome of his head. She had seen him talking with other Jesuits in the *camarilla*. He was Father Bernabo, a member of the congregation of the Inquisition in Rome.

She listened as hard as she could, but the thud of her heartbeat in her ears was louder than the low murmur of her father's voice.

Her father spoke on and on, his voice rising a little with urgency.

Damning himself with every word, she thought desperately. And any of us thought to be in his confidence. She could not tell if the priest knew she was there. If he had not heard her, she could pretend to interrupt by chance, apologize prettily and bring her father's confession to a speedy end.

The priest turned his head slightly. He had heard her enter after all. 'I absolve you,' he said to the prince, 'but your penance will be heavy. God asks true repentance of you and firm intention not to sin again.'

'Yes, father,' said the prince. 'I will do His Will! I must be forgiven!'

The next morning, Sofia heard the moist grating sound as soon as she entered her father's *scrittoio*.

The prince sat in his big armchair, sharpening his knife. He held the whetstone across his knees, knife handle in his right hand while the fingers of his left hand pressed down on the steel blade. Father Daniele again sat motionless on his stool against the wall beside the prince's altar. The faces on his walls, rising up from behind their clouds of modesty, seemed to stare at him in alarm.

Around and around, the tip drew little circles on the stone. The rhythmic grating scraped fingernails up her spine.

'Why do you do that, father?'

'To be ready for my enemies.' He gave her a crafty look. 'My end is close. I feel hot ambitious breath on my cheeks at night. But they must all wait. Including you, my dove.' Her eyes met sudden malevolence and chilly assessment.

'Put it on the altar for the saint to bless.' He offered it to her, handle first, daring her, challenging her.

'Of course, father.'

Smile with blank, eager eyes!

She must not seem to understand the challenge. If she understood, it meant that she recognized the thought. If she recognized the thought, she was a traitor.

But it was tempting. Not easy, but possible. Not in the body, the prince wore too much padding. She would never find the space between his ribs. The throat? The eye?

Behind her, Father Daniele stood up from his stool by the wall.

She must not even think it! The thought would leak out through her eyes. The muscles in her hand would tighten and denounce her. In any case, it would be an unthought, disastrous gesture. Not part of the future she had devised for herself.

Father Daniele stepped back to let her approach the altar. She placed the dagger on the white linen cloth where it lay in the embrace of the gilt and enamel altar-piece looted from Byzantium, like a malign reflection of the jewelled cross standing upright above it.

Then her father began to cry for something to relieve his pain.

Francis woke that same morning deserted by the fever that had driven him for the last week. The stand for the witnesses was now complete, set a little way down the track, outside the bowl, just inside the rope perimeter. Close enough to the eventual site of the giant crossbow over the air shaft, so that the people seated on the platform could see that something did indeed head for Heaven. Close enough so that they would be affected by the smoke, deafened by the thunder clap and blinded by the flash. Far enough away that they would not be able to see details.

His body refused to move. His thoughts had jammed solid. He could not think about the prince's flight nor about the complicated subject of Sofia.

He didn't dare risk working in this state. He held up his hands and thought he saw a slight tremor in his fingers.

After lying for some time, staring up at the painted wooden ceiling of his cupboard bed, he got up, dressed and sent for his horse. He left the lodge compound by the upper gate.

'*Bon jour.*' The Uskoks on guard nodded good morning. '*Salve.*'

He was right, it was a game. '*Grüss Gott,*' Francis replied.

Though he was now mounted and might have made his escape, they had stopped watching him by the time he reached the first bend.

No saddle bags, thought Francis. Of course.

Where he had climbed before, he now turned his horse down the slope through the pines, where the fallen needles muffled his horse's hoofs. They moved in and out of patches of sun. At last, he dismounted, tied his horse to a tree beside the track and slid down a steep slope through the trees to the little river he had seen from above. He sat on a boulder above the tumbling white water with his head in the green shade and his boots catching a shaft of sun.

The wind sighed high above his head. He listened to the startling, noisy progress of a falling branch. The river rumbled and splashed above a deep occasional thump. He let go of all thought, just for a short time.

He felt eyes on him and looked up in resignation. He heard his horse whicker uneasily up on the track. He was not trusted after all.

On the far bank of the little river, a wolf was regarding him with calm interest. Francis looked back. A she-wolf, he judged, but not nursing cubs. They sat for some time. Between them, a small arc of white water scrabbled constantly and fruitlessly at the side of a damp green boulder. Finally the wolf turned and trotted away, with the impression of a shrug.

Homo lupus homini, thought Francis. It's man who is a wolf to man. For some reason, his spirits had lifted. His hands felt steady again.

That afternoon, for the first time, he fitted together the pieces of his new device. First he rigged a small billet of wood to swing at the end of a short length of fine rope from a twisted root that stuck out from the wall of the bowl about ten feet above the flat bowl floor.

He looked around for observers, but it did not matter. His actions might seem mad but they gave away nothing that mattered.

Then he packed a small trial parchment shell with gunpowder and set it against a sheer rock in the wall of the bowl, near the suspended billet. Into an opening at the top, he placed a steel spring, held compressed by a net of fine wires above a flint striker. Around this, he nested, with great care, three of the tiny glass vials and filled them with Boomer's vitriol. Carefully, he backed away.

From inside the entrance of the mine, behind another of the *vinea*, he tugged a length of rope to release the billet of wood. It swung down through its arc. As it struck the shell case, he released the end ball of his alchemist's cradle.

Tick, tick, tick . . . he ducked behind his cover . . . tick, tick, tick! Explosion! Yes! After exactly six ticks. Small fragments of earth and rock rattled against the shield and flew past him into the mine.

He wanted to leap and shout with triumph. Instead, he walked over through the black smoke and settling dust to inspect the results of his blast. The glint of a spyglass appeared higher up on the neighbouring peak, trained on the haze of smoke. But no watcher would now learn more than that a fire master had set off a trial explosion. He set up a second trial against the wall of the bowl nearest to the watcher, where the drop would hide the swinging billet and his actions in assembling the device.

Tick, tick, tick, tick, tick, tick. Exactly six ticks of the alchemist's balls.

I've done it! he thought. With Albona's help, he could measure time into tiny, accurate bites. He could now pursue his illusion of infinite upward flight! He must make several more trials before he could begin to claim true certainty. But his gut knew, after only two trials. He had done it! Now he could make his final preparations.

He closed his eyes and saw the first rocket reach the peak of its climb, saw the small burst of flame as the second rocket climbed onwards. Up, up, up, up. Scrambling up towards Heaven.

It's a sky monkey, he thought. Climbing the tree of Heaven whose apples are made of stars.

Then he had a thought that weakened the muscles in his legs. He sank down on the crossbow frame. He entered a moment of realization so enormous that it pushed the world away leaving him suspended in a bubble outside time. He blinked rapidly. Rubbed his mouth with the fingers of his left hand.

He backed away from the thought, came at it again, half expecting it to spin away. It stayed, lodged now, already on its way to becoming substance. He felt a little confused, after travelling for so long to reach this spot, to find himself suddenly here. Excitement begun to bubble up under his breastbone. The confusion cleared like early fog, exposing a solid landscape of truth.

He had not thought closely enough about the similarities between the prince's launch and the problems of timing an exploding shell. If he could time the firing of the second push for the prince, he could apply the same principles to time the firing of the explosive charge in a shell. It seemed – he still questioned it – that he had unexpectedly achieved a thing that had eluded three generations of Quoynts. The way to time explosive death, not too soon, not too late, but so as to tear out the exact heart of a target.

The Sky Monkey. A playful name to disguise its true dreadful nature. His Sky Monkey had suddenly grown scales and claws. It would tip the scales of war to favour whoever had it.

He must risk working with powder in the mine. What he needed to do now would not pass as funeral fireworks to the eyes of men, like the Uskoks, with military experience.

That afternoon Sofia escaped without her father's permission and rode up to the lodge. She did not care if her father called for her. She told Francis about the knife.

He tried to listen but his head still racketed with the Sky Monkey

'He grows worse daily,' Sofia said. 'Both in body and wits. I fear that Ettore may make a move soon to protect his succession. The Vranghi were on manoeuvres again today, at full strength.'

Her urgency reached him. 'The prince must live just three or four more days! I'm almost ready but can work no faster.'

'It doesn't matter how fast you work!' She gave him a desperate look. 'We are deceiving ourselves, *caro*. We both know that what my father wants is impossible. What difference does it make whether he dies tonight or the day after tomorrow? You can't do what he wants. We both know that. You won't survive Ettore. He made his threat quite clear. We must think how to save your life.'

'Do you truly not know what I intend?'

'To try to fire my father to Heaven?'

'You haven't guessed?'

She shook her head.

Trust her.

He wanted to trust her. And, if she was telling the truth about not knowing, his security precautions against spies had held far better than he had dared to hope.

Trust no one, said his reason. Not even the woman you adore.

Trust her, argued his heart, his cock, and every sinew in his body. Her love for you is open in her face. How can you fear her?

The internal battle went on for so long that Francis saw Sofia's eyes begin to cloud. He reached back for the internal stillness and peace he had felt that morning beside the little river, while he returned the gaze of the wolf.

'I have devised a way to seem to satisfy Ettore,' he said at last. 'And Da Monte. I have found a way to cheat my contract – to seem to meet its conditions.'

'Just as I cheated the sheets?'

'That's what I must finish making ready – the seeming, not the reality.'

'And will you tell me how you mean to do this?'

Francis let out a shaky breath. Did he love her or not? If he loved her, did he trust her? Suddenly, he could not tolerate the half-trust and the half-truths a moment longer. He needed the relief of speaking plain at last.

'I can do better than tell you, my sweet. You can do me a service. I need your fresh eyes to tell me what they think they see. Will you act as a witness to a rehearsal?'

If he were wrong, he would pay the price. Having thrown away caution, he careered onwards. 'How much do you wish to save my life?'

'As my own. More!'

Careful, Francis told himself, even now. This is the cliff edge you can't climb back up again. He jumped.

'Your father has hidden a bond that is the true reason I came to La Spada. If I could lay my hands on it, I could go at once, before your father dies. I wouldn't have to gamble that Ettore will honour your father's agreement.'

There was a long silence. 'And leave me to Ettore's mercy?'

'I swore I would not let him harm you. I will keep my vow.'

'How?' she asked coldly.

'If I can launch a prince up to Heaven, I can deal with Ettore.' He did not know how, at this moment, but he would devise a way. 'Remember what I said the night we exchanged rings. When I make a pact, I mean to keep it.' He searched her face for any sign of guilty discomfort or evasiveness. 'If you accepted me on those terms, you must believe me now.'

'Would you return to La Spada?'

'As soon as Cecil permits me,' he said unhappily.

'Stay and kill Ettore. Help me take the throne!'

'Will your people welcome a fratricide as their next ruler?' he asked harshly. 'And what would be done to me – the assassin of the legitimate heir?'

'Tell me how else I am to survive!'

'I can't, now, but I will devise a way.'

'Then I suppose I must help you to run away.' She would not look at him. 'First, of course, I must find this bond.'

'I suspect that the prince may keep it behind a panel in the head of his bed.' Forgive me, my lord, he told Cecil. Your secret is as safe in her hands as in either those of the prince or Ettore. 'Your father left the panel a little ajar when he showed me the bond. Search above the candle ledge to the right of his head when he lies in bed.'

71

Sofia went to the chapel that evening. It was time for her twice-weekly confession, but she also needed to think. She rehearsed her usual list of small sins and harmless misdemeanours: snapping in anger at one of her waiting women, greed that made her drink too much coffee. Today she would add the sin of despair at her father's failing health – a nice touch that one, to boast of virtue while appearing to repent of sin. She was almost certain that Father Daniele violated the confidence of the confessional and reported to her father anything the priest thought he should know.

She went into the small side chapel and knelt on her *prie-dieu* in front of the small altar and the tiny gilded altar piece, which she had put there. Not booty from Byzantium but carved from local pine in a workshop in La Spada *di sotto*. The silver leaf on the stars had been beaten from silver mined in the nearby mountains. In the wall above her, a single narrow stained-glass window threw pale broken patches of rose, blue and gold onto her face and folded hands. She bowed her head and thought unhappily of her last conversation with Francis.

She began to tease at the frightened tangle of her thoughts.

Little by little, she began to pull them free and to straighten them out, to lay them side by side in order.

She heard the priest close the chapel door and take his chair at her side. A triangle of his black robe cut across the side of her vision, striped with the fringe of his purple shawl.

'Father, give me your blessing, for I have sinned.' She trotted through her list, eager to be done and for him to leave her alone with her thoughts again.

'I grant you absolution.'

Startled, she turned her head to look at him. She did not know his voice. He was the wrong shape, too tall and broad. His accent was not Friulani but Florentine.

'You're not Father Daniele!' She dropped her hand to feel secretly in her skirts for the hilt of her little dagger.

'I am a priest like him. I can grant absolution and impose penance just as he can.'

She stood up and backed away. 'What are you doing here?'

'You've often seen me in the *camarilla*,' he said. 'I asked Father Daniele to let me take his place here today. I want to speak with you.' He gestured at the *prie-dieu*. 'I assure you that you're in no danger from me. Please kneel again so that I may speak quietly.'

She obeyed, but without letting go of her dagger.

'I think you're troubled,' he said.

Now she looked at him closely. This was not the usual way of confession.

'I will help you. If you are ever in despair, come to me. Daughter, listen to me.' He leaned closer and lowered his voice even further.

After listening for a moment, she said, 'You're trying to trap me. I won't hear another word.'

He leaned back and made the sign of the Cross. 'So long as you remember my words in your hour of need. *Pax tecum*. Go now in peace.'

'I shall stay and pray for strength,' she said. She felt him stand and heard the door of the chapel close behind him. Here was another tangle to tease out. If she could trust him, she had a new ally.

She bent her head again over her clasped hands. Save Francis. Make Cecil send him back. How?

72

Francis's need to test his intentions for the prince's flight with an unsuspecting witness was now urgent. Until he was certain that his chief illusion would convince, he dared not begin the most dangerous work that remained. Exposed, out in the bowl, in full view of anyone who might still ignore his warnings and come past the rope. Or who found a spot to watch with a glass where he could not see the light reflected from the lens. For a time, he would have to uncover the concealed airshaft. He would have to drag the crossbow into place over it, then conceal it again. He would have to make at least one trial that would betray him to any watcher.

Sofia neither came nor sent a message. The last scraps of reason persuaded Francis not to involve her further, for her protection and his own. In any case, she now knew too much. Her quick wits might anticipate and see more than other eyes. They might not be fresh enough. He sent for Albona.

When two Uskoks escorted his mule up the track at dusk, Francis went again to meet him. He gave the mule's rein to an Uskok and led Albona past the rope into the bowl.

'You asked to witness the fruit of my labour,' he said to the librarian. 'Would you like to sample it while it's still sour and green?' More seriously, he added, 'I also beg you to refuse at once and return to La Spada.' He explained the risks of becoming party to what he was about to do.

'If my true purpose is detected, I'm dead,' he said. 'And my witness will be as guilty as I am. My friendly Uskoks would slice me finer than a San Daniele ham.'

'They were never my friends,' said Albona. 'The Uskoks have never forgiven the Turks for pushing them north out of their homelands.' He removed his spectacles and polished them, revealing fine brown eyes and astonishingly long lashes. He replaced the spectacles.

'I feel all of our lives running out along with his majesty's.' His tall stooped frame reminded Francis a little of a heron as he peered curiously around the bowl at the remains of shattered glass, dangling ropes, the giant crossbow on its wheeled mangonel frame, now strung with its new bowstring, tightened and set.

'I will be your witness only if you promise to explain everything,' said Albona. 'I would far rather die in knowledge than in ignorance. Explain what you want me to do.'

'Just watch. But look for fault. Try to see with Prince Ettore's eyes.'

'What exactly will I be watching?'

'That is what you must tell me.'

Francis felt almost as excited as when he had fired his first gun or carried out his very first firework display in Brighthelmstone in Sussex, which seemed a very long way from La Spada. His pulse raced. His mouth dried.

He sent Albona to sit on the witness stand. The sun had gone but there was still enough light to see to work. Light enough for the witnesses still to trust their eyes. This was

401

the time he preferred. He must insist that the prince flew at dusk.

He made a note to himself to instruct the prince that he must not fly when there was still a danger of hitting the sun. Not at mid-day. Not while the sun was still in its zenith.

This is only a trial of the part, he reminded himself. The greatest part is still to come. The part that no one must see until the launch itself. Nevertheless, the success of the whole depended on what Albona did nor did not see now.

He loaded a rocket-shaped bolt onto the crossbow, inside a lighter coat of paper and wood. He opened and closed a hinged flap at the bottom end of this overcoat. He made a final careful check of the charge lashed to the massive frame – the charge that the prince did not know about.

'Make ready,' he called to Albona. He released the bow and dived behind the bank of earth. He saw the sides of the bowl flash white, heard the roar of the explosive charge. A lightning strike. Debris spattered against his shield. Black smoke boiled around him. Lifting his head quickly, unable to breath, he watched the bolt rise. Tick, tick, tick, tick, tick, tick.

A perfectly ordinary-looking sky rocket burst and scattered a few stars.

He heard distant shouts of approval from the Uskok guard.

He wanted to dance and shout. Yes! Yes! Yes! That ordinary skyrocket had broken exactly at the peak of its trajectory. Tick, tick, tick, tick, tick, tick. The stars had scattered innocently at exactly the moment the Sky Monkey would begin its climb. That ordinary skyrocket had not had an ordinary fuse. It had no fuse at all.

He ran to the crossbow. The flap had dropped and hung down, now badly charred. He called to Albona.

'What did you see?' he demanded breathlessly.

'Not very much,' said the librarian crossly. 'You've blinded me for the next two days with that flash of light.' The bite of the smoke made him cough.

'But what did you see?' Francis insisted. 'A rising missile? A rocket? A flying horse?'

Or a posturing, glittering, costly king?

'I could not swear to it,' said Albona, 'but I believed I saw a large skyrocket. Then I saw the stars and concluded that I was right.' He shrugged in apology. 'I'm sorry to be so unhelpful.'

'On the contrary! You tell me just what I want to hear.'

'Have I earned my explanation?'

'Here is what will happen,' said Francis. 'Or so I devoutly hope.'

He paused to launch a small skyrocket to support the impression that he was merely trying out pyrotechnics. Again, the Uskoks cheered in the distance.

73

Albona climbed down from the stand and came into the bowl.

'First, the witnesses arrive,' Francis said. 'They take their places on the stand from which you watched.'

Looking at it now, Francis thought that it had unfortunate overtones of a stand for the official witnesses to an execution.

'How many know the prince's intent?' asked Albona.

'Prince Ettore, Da Monte, the *principessa*, the prince's confessor, Father Daniele . . .' Francis was still not certain how many men the priest truly was. 'And the prince's physician. I hope to bribe him to swear that the prince died at the last minute before he flew or else I may become a royal assassin.

'The Uskoks will most likely want to attend their prince's Ascension.' He looked at Albona. 'You, if you still wish.'

'How many of those witnesses know that the show is a counterfeit . . . for that's what it is, is it not?'

'None, I pray!' said Francis fervently. 'Except the *principessa*. And you, now.'

He turned back to the crossbow hunkered down solidly on the rock. 'I will have moved that engine to the centre of the bowl, where it will stand ready, aimed steeply upward, straddling the opening of an old air shaft, invisible both then and now. The prince's chariot capsule will be ready on it.

'The prince's litter arrives. I dismiss the porters and send them away to a safe distance. Then I lift the prince into his chariot, dead or alive.' He grimaced. 'An act of tenderness I don't relish. I do all this urgently, as no authority I found seems certain how long the soul lingers after death.'

Albona nodded.

'I close the side of the rocket,' said Francis. 'I bow, I release the crossbow. Then I hit the ground, crying "God speed His Highness!"'

He raised his brows at Albona. 'Am I plausible thus far?'

'I've read worse.' But he was listening as intently as a child to a fireside tale.

'Now comes the blinding flash you saw, and the explosion, but magnified three times. Too late for the prince to object to. A thunderclap that breeds a cloud of dark smoke and fire. Out of the smoke, a silver shape streaks up into the sky. It will rise and rise and keep on rising. A small burst of flame is seen and just when you expect it to begin to fall, it climbs again until it disappears from view.

'On the ground will now be a blaze as intense as I know how to set. When those flames subside, which they will quickly do, and the smoke begins to clear, there remains only the crossbow, now broken and burnt, and a shallow pit in the earth dug by the explosion. Nothing is left of either the chariot into which I placed the prince or of the prince himself. No charred bones as there would be if I had tried to incinerate him. No fragments of burnt robe. The prince has vanished. Left us for a better place.' Francis smiled briefly. 'Where he means to stay.'

'So, where is he?' asked Albona intently. 'You can't have lifted him as high as you describe. He would fall back to earth, even if at a distance. His remains could be recovered.'

405

'He's gone, from the surface of this earth, I tell you.' Francis laid his hand on his heart.

'You cheat me of my full explanation.'

'Are you not convinced? Do you, like Prince Ettore and the duke, now want to probe the ashes? Please feel free to do so, though you will find them very hot for a time. You won't find the prince.'

He launched another rocket, a flight of serpents this time. More distant cheers.

'Quoynt!' said Albona in a friendly warning tone.

'*Concedo*.' Francis grinned and held up his hands in submission. 'The prince simply slides through the bottom of his chariot into the air shaft. I once saw this done very well at the Bartholomew Fair. And that false wizard didn't have the advantage of so much smoke when he made his confederate disappear.

'The only trace of the prince will be under the earth, beneath the rubble brought down by the small dropping charges I mean to set in the air shaft walls. The missile everyone sees rising from the bow will ignite with that distant flash of fire and scatter itself across the mountains. The royal chariot will have burnt to ash – or else I will have wasted those oceans of saltpetre in which I have soaked every part.'

'Is there a chance that the dropping charges won't cover the corpse?' asked Albona. He leaned to examine the ground beneath the crossbow.

'There's a chance for everything to go wrong,' said Francis. 'But I may have no choice but to make the attempt.'

Albona pursed his lips and nodded. 'It's plausible.' Then he looked up as if following the course of an imaginary rocket. 'I don't think you've told me yet how the rocket keeps climbing when you expect it to begin to fall.'

'As your translations first showed me the way . . .' Francis then explained about the Sky Monkey.

74

'I must make inventory again today!' Her father, newly dressed, walked carefully to the locked cabinet in his *scrittoio*, placing his feet as if uncertain of the ground.

Sofia wondered yet again if his departing wits had not been replaced with another animal sense that could hear unspoken words and feel the textures of other people's intentions. He had not made an inventory for four days.

With the key he kept on a chain around his neck, he unlocked the cabinet. 'Thieves will have to wait until I'm dead,' he said yet again. He stood before the open cabinet and handed her jewel cases and caskets to set on one side.

Weary with standing, he took a large embroidered pouch to his chair and sat to continue his inventory.

'Bring my casket of Treasury papers.' He kept his eyes on her as she crossed to him. She stood a little behind him while he counted through the documents inside. Several of them could have been the document Francis had described.

'If only you were a son,' he said. 'You could share this task with me.' He did not open any of them today but merely riffled through with his thumb.

'I could help you in any case.'

He shook his head. 'Affairs of state, my sweet. Not for you, more's the pity.' Satisfied, the prince closed the casket. 'Put this back and bring me the scrolls.'

When he was done with those, he pushed himself up and walked into his *camera*, closing the door behind him. She had always wondered what he was doing in there. He had always forbidden her to follow him. Now she knew that Francis was right. He had other papers hidden in his *camera*, ones too precious to risk keeping with the others, even in a locked cabinet.

She replaced the scrolls and waited patiently on her stool in the silent company of Father Daniele, staring idly at the pair of copulating rabbits on the wall, the butterflies mating on the wing, the distant stag, seen dimly through the painted leaves of the glade, mounting a hind. Then she studied the faces of the nymphs and satyrs, whose pleasures had been painted over. Their wild, fixed eyes, open mouths and splayed fingers spoke more of pain and fear than of joy.

She dropped her head into her hands.

Her father returned. She waited until he knelt in prayer at his altar in the *scrittoio*, Father Daniele at his side, their backs to her. Silently, she rose and went into the prince's *camera*. His manservant had gone to empty the chamber pot and bring fresh wood for the fire. She looked back through the door, saw her father still at prayer and closed the door the rest of the way.

Above the candle ledge, to the right of his head.

She ran her fingers over the panel, pressing gently. It felt solid and unmoveable. Then she felt around the carved garland swag above the panel. One of the laurel leaves wobbled slightly. She paused. This was her last moment of possible innocence. She listened. She was assuming that her father had finished whatever he had been doing alone in here. She pushed down on the leaf. One edge of the panel jumped out of line.

She felt inside, pulled out a bundle of papers tied together with a linen string. With unexpected certainty, she identified the bond Francis had described. There was no mistaking the double ribbons and the two seals of La Spada and the English lord. She eased it out of the bundle.

She replaced the other papers, closed the panel and slipped the bond into a slit in her full parchment-coloured sleeve.

It went in neatly with a small twist and without catching on the fabric. She felt it lodge securely in a nest above the slash where the lining was tacked to the outer sleeve – just as she had practised again and again the night before with a letter folded as nearly as she could estimate to the size and shape of the English bond. The red seals were only a little darker than the red lining of her jacket sleeves. She had chosen the jacket for that reason. She slammed the door of her thoughts firmly in the terrified face of Yuri just before her father had beheaded him. Her danger now, when guilty, was no greater than it ever was, she told herself, if innocence gave no protection.

She must now return to the *scrittoio*. She had merely seized the chance to go relieve herself. She forced the thought into her head until it began to seem true. She laid her hands on her cheeks. They were icy cold. She feared that her teeth would begin to clatter together.

'Where did you go?' the prince demanded.

'Modesty forbids my answer, sir.' She smiled prettily. 'Shall I put some *lignum vitae* on the fire?' Scarcely waiting for his nod, she slowly arranged the pieces of heavy dark green wood, famous for its efficacy in treating the pox. She turned and fussed at it until the pleasing smell of the burning resin began to fill the air and her hands were warmed.

'Come sit by me.' As the prince's hand fell on her wrist

like an iron lock, she tore her thoughts away from the bond, and thrust them out into a half-remembered sunlit road. She imagined herself walking, skirts tucked up like a farmer's wife. Her feet kicked up little puffs of dust. Someone was walking at her side, not a little behind like a waiting woman or a guard but beside her, shoulders almost touching. If she did not turn her head, she could imagine that it was Francis.

He father was staring at her.

Keep walking. Keep walking.

She imagined tilting her head back to watch a golden eagle planing overhead. A chamois balancing on a crag looked back at her.

This distraction worked. The last of her trembling disappeared. Her hands rested quietly in her lap. For the rest of the morning, she sat at her father's side while he dozed and woke, cursing his pain. She stood only to refill his beaker with the physician's decoction of *lignun vitae* resin, and to make room for the physician to take her father's pulse and examine his tongue and eyes. She sat and watched the prince's hand where it lay on her wrist, inches away from the bond in her sleeve. Again and again, she had to force her thoughts back out onto that road, for fear that he would feel her heart racing under his fingers.

When the bells rang at midday, she asked his permission to go and dine. She forced herself to curtsey, to walk slowly out of his *scrittoio*, to walk steadily through the *enfilade* of rooms, nodding from time to time to men from whom she had hopes of support.

In her own apartments, the ladies surrounded her, chattering, pinching cheeks and smoothing hair before entering the market place of the great *sala*. Maddened with impatience, she forced herself to smile. She allowed the owner of one of the two voices that did not drip poison into the lions' ears to unpin her hair and rebuild it into a plaited knot on her nape.

All the time, the bond seemed to pulse against her skin, as clear to see as an ensign on a flagstaff. She finally snatched a moment of solitude when she moved the bond from her sleeve to a safer home inside her shift, against the skin over her ribs.

'Are you ready, your highness?' Her waiting women hovered in the *antecamera*, waiting to go down to the great *sala*. She must wait to learn why this ordinary-looking piece of paper seemed to carry such power. Enough to force compliance from the English. Enough to force Francis Quoynt not only to come to La Spada as the English envoy but then to stay and carry out a hideously dangerous charade.

Alone in her *camera* at last after dinner, whilst her ladies walked in the gardens or were busy with their own affairs, she finally was able to read the bond. She read through it several times. She stood very still for a long time, with the parchment in her hands. She read it once more. It seemed straightforward enough, but before she did anything more Francis must confirm what she believed.

She had only the rest of the day and the night, until her father's inventory the next morning. She called Isabella, who had remained in Sofia's *antecamera* to practice a new song on her guitar, and told the young waiting woman to arrange for a messenger to ride to the hunting lodge at once.

75

Sofia stepped out of the wall between the scratched plea *'miserere nobis'* and the tally of days made by ghostly soldiers who had once watched the plateau from the long passage between the inner and outer walls of the *fortezza*. Francis had ridden straight to La Spada in his work clothes. As he reached for the bond, his fingertips seemed dipped in liquid silver from the gunpowder dust.

She had done it, just as she had said she would. Here was the same piece of parchment, folded curiously so that the words written on it were completely enclosed by folds. The same two ribbons carried the seals of the Piratis and of Robert Cecil.

She gave it to him.

Nothing in the content had changed.

The loan made to the king of England, with one of his most costly jewels proposed, but not given over, as surety, and signed by Cecil, was still a fraud. It would still be the block for Cecil, condemned for treasonous fraud, however good his reasons might have been. The many people who did not like Cecil personally but who trusted his probity would now turn against him. Francis imagined the glee with which Sir Francis Bacon would seize on this weapon for bringing down his hated little cousin who seemed to best him at everything.

He glanced at Sofia, trying to gauge whether she understood the full power of that parchment. Whoever held that bond controlled Cecil. And Cecil controlled England.

Francis felt odd holding so much power in such dirty hands. He also held a choice. He heard his boots grating on the cold stone floor, saying, 'Take it and run!'

'Lord Salisbury seems to be liable,' said Sofia. 'Not the king of England.'

Francis nodded unhappily. Cecil had never actually said that it was a Treasury debt, or the King's debt, but he had made Francis believe those words had been spoken. He still had the impression of hearing them alive in the air. Now, with the bond in his hands at last, he must choose whom to save, Cecil or Sofia.

Sofia stood close beside him, also reading the bond, her shoulder touching his arm. Even in his turmoil, he breathed in the smell of her hair, sweet in the damp musty air of the passage.

'When my father made this gesture of "future amity",' she said dryly, 'he was also trading with the North African corsairs of the Barbary Coast to buy the cargoes of raided English ships.'

'And Cecil was nursing hopes for safe haven for those same ships among the Uskok islands of Dalmatia.' That long, eastern coast of the Adriatic was otherwise controlled by the Turks and their new, uneasy Catholic allies, the Hapsburgs. There was no safe route through to the east for English merchant ships.

'Is this Robert Cecil so very important then, that the king would lend him such a valuable jewel as a pledge?'

Francis looked down at her sharply. She did understand

413

the significance of this piece of parchment. 'He's powerful enough that your father, not yet completely without his wits, accepted his pledge of a royal jewel.'

Take the thing now. Flee La Spada. Abandon your attempt to reach Heaven.

Abandon Sofia.

She nodded. 'I can see that he must be very highly placed. But I'm ignorant of England and her politics. In La Spada, Da Monte would hang in a cage on the walls if he pledged one of my father's treasures to a foreign power as surety for a personal loan.'

'I think you grasp matters very clearly.'

He could not do it. He could not bear to leave her. He saw Ettore cutting her throat.

He saw Cecil on the scaffold steps, because Francis had failed to act.

Sofia took back the bond and seemed to study it. 'What will happen if Ettore finds this contract amongst my father's papers?' She stepped away from his side.

'He must not find it!' He took a step after her then stopped. 'Do you mean to give it to me, Sofia?'

She shook her head. 'I must put it back.'

He inhaled sharply.

'My father makes sure of his papers every day. If this is gone, he will suspect me first of all.'

Overpower her now and snatch back the cursed thing, thought Francis. Then destroy it . . . no, flee and take it to Cecil, so he can see for himself that he is saved.

His muscles tightened.

As if reading his thoughts, Sofia backed away, tucking the bond deep into her bodice.

Did she imagine that he wouldn't still take it from her there? He must decide now. This was his true purpose in coming to La Spada. Such a chance would come only once.

Still, he could not do it.

'Whatever you're thinking, I don't like it,' she said. 'You must understand, I stole it for only a few hours, to show to you, to be sure that it's the right document. But tomorrow my father would see that it's gone.' She pressed both hands against her breasts. 'Then, I am dead, along with who knows how many others!'

Francis dropped a half-raised hand and stepped back. He had vowed not to leave until she was safe from Ettore. He could not desert her. Could not let her be harmed.

Forgive me, my lord! he begged silently. 'Don't get caught putting it back!'

Sofia held his eyes. 'I swear to you, by the marriage-of-our hearts, that the moment my father dies, before Ettore can find it, I will steal it again.'

He snatched up her hand and kissed the wrist.

'Don't do that!' she cried. 'That feels as if you're saying farewell to my hand.' She opened the small wooden door and disappeared again into the walls.

I have it! thought Sofia in triumph. Francis had confirmed it, whether he meant to or not. At last, she had the weapon she needed. Leverage against Cecil, leverage against the English through Cecil. She had never imagined having so much to offer in exchange for support in her succession to the throne of La Spada.

She now knew how she might save Francis's life and how to make Cecil send him back to La Spada. All she must do now was to survive her brother.

She had not lied to Francis. She had only the hours of the coming night before she must return the bond to the secret compartment in her father's bed.

The thought of what she must do to return it caused only a tremor of agitation, not the wash of terror she had felt while stealing it. She slipped into the walls and climbed narrow stone stairs up onto the battlements. The wind snapped loose strands of her hair. She leaned on the wall between two of the towers and looked into the space above the plateau.

The Uskoks were on cavalry manoeuvres this afternoon, in place of the Vranghi. Everyone was getting ready for change. She must make them all into her men. Just as it was her plateau. Her city. Her mountains. Her people.

It was possible. The strands of the future were almost twisted as she wished.

Don't think of the rabbit holes, don't think of what might bring you crashing down. Keep your eyes on the crest of the meadow slope.

She went back into the old *fortezza* and spun around and around down the long spiral staircase leading to the House of Wisdom and to Rabac Albona. Tonight, he would at last repay her for the gift of his freedom. And then, she would write to Robert Cecil, Lord Salisbury, the English Secretary of State.

PART SIX

76

THE PRINCE'S *CAMERA*, MORNING

Sofia made herself sit still. Something felt very wrong. Her father pretended to sleep, but his hand did not lie on her arm with its usual unthinking weight. This morning his fingers felt like snakes coiled around a mouse, secure in the capture, free to devour at leisure. He did not snore and gasp. Instead, his breathing was shallow and tight with thought.

What frightened her most was that they were entirely alone. For the first time since the prince had begun to keep to his *scrittoio*, Father Daniele was not there.

'I have spent a night of torment,' he said suddenly, without opening his eyes. 'I am already in hell now. But it's bitter cold there . . . my heart is ice . . . Oh, God, what must I do to please You? What gift will move You?'

He opened his eyes. 'What can I sacrifice that is most precious to me after my own soul?'

Her heart began to bang at her ribs.

'I see by your face that you understand,' he said. 'I knew you would. Tell me, am I to show myself less firm of purpose than Abraham, or Agamemnon? Like Abraham, I am a ruler. Like Agamemnon, I am a general.'

She began to rise. He stood up, pulling her the rest of the way to her feet with an unexpected surge of strength.

This sudden action took her by surprise. Although alert, she had misjudged and waited too long. She should have struck first, when he had handed her the knife.

He began to drag her towards the altar. She flung her weight backwards and clawed at his fingers with her free hand.

'Why do you fight me? God waits.' He was already panting with the effort of holding her. 'You must be obedient in this as in all else . . . do your duty to me as a loving daughter.' Once very strong, he was still a head and half taller than she was, with the weight of his bones and the last of his muscles still giving him a small advantage while he was possessed by this fervour.

His sharpened knife still waited ready on the little altar. 'Come, kneel in front of me,' he said gently. 'I will stand behind you, stroking your hair. You will not even know the moment. I will make it so quick. My hand still remembers how to cut a throat cleanly . . .'

'No!' She clenched her teeth and braced against him. Her shoes slid a little closer to the altar. He reached out his arm towards the knife. She hauled backwards against his pull. Her feet found purchase on the rush matting on the floor. They hung poised, both gasping for breath. He seemed to have called up all the strength that was left to him in this life to explode in this moment. He took a step closer to the altar, off the mat.

The mat began to slide. She rode it helplessly, closer to him, inch by inch.

'You must obey me! I am your father and your lord.'

Her eye measured the distance between his hand and the

knife. When he thought to reach for it again, he would have it.

'Forgive me, father.' She stopped pulling, summoned a smile of submission and reached for him with her free hand as if to embrace him. Then she lunged. They collided in a desperate embrace. He fell backwards with her clinging to him like a cat to a falling tree.

Sobbing for breath, she rolled off, yanked her skirts from under him, scrabbled across the floor to find her feet again. She stepped back over his feet to snatch the knife.

He groaned and stirred on the floor but did not open his eyes. Still alive.

Do it now!

She stood by his head, with the knife in her hand. How could one tell when someone was feigning the loss of his senses? He had deceived her so often before.

His chest seemed to tremble. Then it rose in a ragged breath. It fell, then rose again. His eyelids flickered. Beyond doubt he was still alive.

Do it now! You missed one chance. You'll not get a third one. If he regained his senses, he would now have her killed for certain. He would never trust her again. She was as dead as her mother.

She stooped warily, then stood again. Her bent knees shook too hard to support her. Why didn't you die when you fell? she screamed silently at him. Why didn't you die?

She tightened her grip on the knife. The handle slipped in her damp hand. She shifted the knife to her other hand and wiped her palm on her skirt. Her father's head lay turned a little to one side, exposing the tendons in his neck.

Do it! She closed her eyes. Tried to steady her shaking, her breathing, her thoughts. She felt for that cold still place that had allowed her to survive this long. She must step into that place, draw in resolve like a breath of winter air.

Become cool and steady and inexorable. She was a Pirati. And she now had more reason than ever to want to survive.

After so much waiting, it was time to act. From too much waiting, she had nearly lost the knack for action.

It must be done exactly right. There was no room for the least mistake now. After thinking for a moment, she set the knife aside on the far side of the room well out of her father's reach.

She laid one of his wolf skin rugs on the floor beside him, fur side down, and rolled him onto it. He did not open his eyes.

One foot at a time, she hauled him back across the floor to his chair. Here she stopped to regain her breath. The weakness of terror was beginning to pass. A ferocious purpose took its place.

She swung the rug around, climbed onto the big chair and hauled her father into a sitting position with his back propped against the front of the seat. She climbed down and watched him for a moment. He still seemed to sleep. Still alive.

Swallowing against her rising gorge, she stepped close, straddled his legs, took him in both arms and heaved his dead weight up onto the seat. She kept her face tight against his chest so it would not touch his face, but the smell of his decay was thick in her nostrils. He rose half way into position then slipped. She grunted with effort and gave another heave. The gold lace on his doublet sleeve scoured the skin off her right cheek as she lodged him at last in his chair.

She studied him again. Was it possible that he was still feigning, waiting to see how far she would go?

She must take the risk.

She fetched the little basin that she used for scented washing water and set it in his lap. Then she lifted his left arm and the wrist across the rim of the basin. When she let go, his arm stayed in place. She went back for the knife.

All she needed to do now was to slice each wrist cleanly. The act seemed far less horrible than cutting his throat. And far more likely as the last desperate act of a man who wanted to choose his own death. People would excuse him – they would see why – even while they muttered piously of suicide as a mortal sin.

She still could not believe that he wasn't feigning. The part of her that had played the obedient daughter for so long still feared that he might be waiting to trap her in her next hideous intent. Reason tried to insist that he had already risked his life much too far. If he were suddenly going to open his eyes and shout in furious triumph, he would already have done so. But a terror of him, lodged in her since childhood, and the habit of obedience, however reluctantly learned, made it hard to believe that she truly, at last, had total power over him.

'I'm sorry, father.'

He seemed to have shrunk, as if his burst of strength had sucked out the last of his vital force.

You hate him, she reminded herself. And beyond doubt she did. So why this present holding back from an action she had imagined again and again with such dark, sinuous delight?

Francis would not do this one thing for her. He had made it very plain. She still had to decide whether she was angry with him for that refusal. The action was now hers to take, alone. And it was too late to wait any longer. She would think about Francis when this was done.

One wrist would be enough, she decided. If the cut was deep enough. He was right handed. She tightened her grip on the knife and lifted his left hand. It hardly seemed possible that blood still flowed through that shrivelled glove of skin.

His pulse brushed faintly and unevenly at her fingertips. She stood a moment longer looking at him.

His lids no longer fluttered but seemed to have closed as firmly as winter shutters. She leaned a little closer. From time to time, his breath drifted in and out across his lips, seeming to stop for eight or ten thuds of her racing heartbeats. She leaned closer, still watching the jerky rise and fall of his chest. After so many years of fear, it was hard to grasp such a different new shape for the truth.

She frowned slightly. The world shifted around her and began to take on a new unfamiliar shape. The people in her dream stopped whispering and running. She could open her mouth and speak at last. She felt a pressure in her chest that would soon uncoil into a complex elation. The longer she watched him, the more certain she grew that her father was never going to come to his senses again. He was beyond hurting her, would never hurt her now. She must do nothing rash. She watched him a little longer.

He had already begun to slip away, at last, far more gently than he deserved. She would not have to murder him after all. She and Francis would both have a few more hours to prepare for the final battle.

She took the basin from his lap and set it on the floor again. She pressed her father's head gently into the corner of the chair back so that no sudden accident of movement might rouse him. She tucked another wolf skin robe around him so that the evening chill would not trouble him back to waking. She went silently to the altar to replace the knife but then found that she could not make herself leave it with him, even now. As she had learned to do so well, she slipped soundlessly from the room.

'His Highness will sleep in his chair tonight,' she murmured to his new manservant who was drowsing on his pallet in the antechamber. 'He has taken a pain-killing draft and will now sleep through the rest of the afternoon and evening until morning. I settled him. You need not attend him at bed time.'

'Thank you, highness.' The man could not hide his relief that he did not yet have to go back into that dangerous room.

There would be rumours as always. But though she had grown hardened to the poison vomited out by the lions, she was glad, all the same, that she could treat any whispers that she had killed her father with a clear conscience. The more truthful she could be, the more convincing she could make the rest.

She must warn Francis that his time had run out. He had only a few hours, a day at the most.

She decided to return to her own apartments through the *enfilade*.

'Your highness. Sultana . . .'

She acknowledged the bows with a graceful nod. Sometimes, she also bestowed a smile. Da Monte was in the *antecamarilla*, near one of the windows in the last of the daylight, holding a document close to his eyes while a man in Turkish robes watched him. She met Da Monte's eyes directly, held them and was gratified to see a flush blossom once again above his high collar and beard.

This one will declare for me, she thought, with the right inducement. She would need him and his experience of ruling.

She moved on through the post-dinner recreations, disguising her haste, still assessing. Another for me, she thought. And that one's Ettore's creature.

With relief, she saw Richard Seaborn in the *saleta*, where the higher sort of petitioners still lingered, deep in conversation with Niccolò Schiavoni, a distant cousin of Baldassare.

She beckoned to him. 'You must both accompany me to the hunting lodge, now!'

77

THE HUNTING LODGE, AFTERNOON

Francis was working urgently in the mine, trying not to make mistakes in his haste. He heard a horse whinny on the track up from La Spada, and his own horse reply from the lodge stables. He locked his work away and slid down the short-cut track without stopping to set his traps. By the time he reached the stable yard, the visitors' horses were in the forecourt. Francis entered the lodge from the stables and rushed to meet Sofia as she came into the great hall. Schiavoni and Seaborn remained in the forecourt.

He took her hand to lead her to a seat by the fire.

She pulled her hand away. 'I have just left my father,' she said softly. 'No one yet knows it, but I think he is dying.'

'I'm not ready yet!' exclaimed Francis. 'I told you that I needed more time. I've also had to try a new discovery.'

'Do you think more of new discoveries than of saving yourself, and me?'

He shook his head, trying to think how to make her understand. 'Sofia, I have my exploding shell. I have my Sky Monkey! You must give me more time!'

Sofia stepped back and stared at him. 'You think I tried to kill him, don't you?'

Francis shook his head uncertainly.

'If you will not help me, I do what I must.' She leaned close so that her words were no more than a fierce breath. 'But if I had tried to murder my father, I would have succeeded.' She turned on her heel and left the lodge again.

The sound of horses disappeared back down the mountain track. Francis saw the porter staring at him from the door. Seaborn came in and went upstairs without speaking to change into his work clothes.

It begins to unravel, thought Francis. He walked towards the right-hand staircase, trying to imitate a carefree man. He stopped with his hand on the newel post. The ring Sofia had given him rang faintly against the wood. He had trusted her then, against all reason. For that short time, he had believed that she truly loved him. He had seen with absolute clarity and joy that, in more ways than he wished to look at too closely, they shared a common heart as well as hunger.

He tapped the ring gently against the newel post, then saw what he had just done. She had ridden up here to warn him and he had insulted her for her pains. If the prince died, Ettore would seize any chance to denounce his half-sister. He would see the act of warning Francis as what it was – knowledge. He might argue that it was proof she had murdered the prince herself – how else would she know with such certainty?

Francis half turned to go mount his own horse and ride after her, to beg her forgiveness. Then he turned back, climbed a step, still hesitated. He ran up the rest of the stairs, setting the whole lodge creaking like a ship in a storm. He must not insult her further by wasting any advantage gained by her warning.

Instead, he went to his chamber.

'Is all well?' asked Seaborn as he passed the door.

'The prince is dying.'

'I'd best work fast, then, in the light that's left.' Seaborn gave him a troubled looked and creaked down the stairs.

As swiftly as pen and ink would allow, Francis wrote down all he knew about the Sky Monkey and how it could be used to time an exploding shell. To the knowledge that had been locked into his head, he added clean copies of all his notes and drawings. From time to time, he looked at the fading light outside the window.

He wrote, he blotted, he wrote again to include a detail he had forgotten. He looked at the sky. Time to stop, whether he had written everything or not. He read through it all one last time. It must serve!

He parcelled his work inside a larger sheet of parchment, then folded and sealed the parcel. With the parcel inside his jacket, he scrambled the short way up to his secret work-shop in the mine, touching the papers from time to time to be certain that he had not lost them in the scrub and rocks.

Thanking Mars that he had not taken time to set his traps, he now re-entered the mine without the need to disarm them. The dust he had taken time to strew on the iron chest in the side tunnel still remained undisturbed. The two models of the Sky Monkey firing mechanism were still safely locked inside. He wrapped one carefully in sheep's wool and put it into a soft leather pouch. He put the pouch into his own hanging pocket. He touched the papers yet again to be certain they were still safely lodged over his heart and left the mine for the lodge for a second time. Again, for the sake of speed, he decided not to set his snares.

Seaborn was now in the stables, working half by feel in the dusk, with the shutters thrown wide to catch the last light. When Francis touched his arm and jerked his head towards the door, Seaborn set aside the wooden mould into which he had just shaped an empty shell case and took off his leather apron.

Francis led the way to the open lip of the ledge and stood as if taking a last look at the lurid flare of the falling sun, out of sight too soon behind the jagged screen of the mountains. A chilly evening breeze brushed past them into the valley. A distant dog pack barked at a passing excitement. Francis put his hands on his hips and arched his back as if stretching it. 'Richard, I want you to leave tonight for Venice.'

Seaborn did not turn his head. He seemed to gaze placidly out over the valley.

Francis clapped him on the shoulder in a friendly way and passed him the small parcel of papers and leather pouch. 'Then on to England as soon as it's safe. Take your time. You must not be caught.'

'This is more than fireworks.'

Francis nodded. 'A thing that must not fall into the hands of England's enemies.'

'Your fusing device?'

'Applied to warfare.' Francis explained very briefly about the device and how it could be used to time the explosion of a shell.

'Read what I have written when you have time. A new dangerous Sky Monkey lives there. Ahhhh . . .' Francis sniffed the cooling air appreciatively. 'And in my head. I might not make it back to England. One of us must.'

Seaborn slipped the pouch and papers inside his jerkin. 'You want me to take these to Cecil?' He laughed lightly as if Francis had made some inconsequential jest, but Francis could hear the strain.

'I trust no one else.'

'You trust me?' He looked back out into the dark space above the plateau.

'Why not?'

'Nuncle, you're a fool.'

Francis said nothing. Seaborn was most likely right.

'It's a fearful responsibility,' said Seaborn, after a long pause in which Francis still did not speak.

Francis nodded. 'I'm sorry to lay it on your shoulders. I've been tempted more often than I can say, just to burn it all and forget what I now know. But Albona's books and manuscripts still lurk waiting to blab to the next inquisitive fool. If these thoughts came to me, more or less by chance, they could come to someone else. Therefore, England must have what you carry, before any other power.' He began to turn as if heading back into the lodge. 'I want no trace of it left in La Spada.'

'Tonight, you said? But how will you carry off the launching of the prince's chariot without my help?"

'I'll have to risk the Uskoks. Which of your assistants would serve best?'

'Use Venturini,' said Seaborn at once. 'For his English. You can't risk any misunderstandings. And, with him to interpret, you can also trust Rossi. He has a steady hand and a true passion for Lady Gunpowder.' He paused. 'He was to be my chief assistant if we had been able to bring off those funeral fireworks.' There was real regret in his voice.

'You'll find another assistant in London,' said Francis.

'Can't you come tonight too?'

'There's something else I must bring safely out of La Spada.'

'She won't leave.'

Francis ignored this last remark. 'Go at once but without seeming to leave. If you reach London before me, I grant you the pleasure of telling Cecil just what he sent us into.'

'I shall visit Nicco.' Seaborn sniffed the air in his turn. 'We are invited to join the *die Rehe* tonight.' The Deer, a group of Schiavoni's friends. 'Carlo has imported a troupe of dancers from Slovenia to his estate. Nicco will help me get away from there . . .'

Francis nodded. 'I had hoped he might.' He handed Seaborn a small piece of silver-veined rock. 'Give this to Cecil with the other. Tell him to turn his acquisitive eye away from the Americas.'

They walked together towards the lodge.

'. . . If I have your permission, sir?' said Seaborn clearly.

'All work and no play,' replied Francis. 'Just don't make me have to kick you out of bed in the morning.'

'Sleep well then. And thank you, sir.' Seaborn bounded away as if let off his leash, back around the lodge towards the stables again. A little later, Francis heard his horse clopping towards the lower gate. Then Seaborn's voice greeted the guards on the gate in a reasonable imitation of the local dialect. 'What shall I bring back – blonde, brunette or redhead?'

'One of each,' called back one voice.

'Keep it in your breeches,' said another. 'For me, a pot of *polpette* and a skin of Moscato . . . Safer.'

The gate clanged. Seaborn was gone.

Francis calculated that their chances of meeting again were small. Here was another one who had come into his life and then gone again, who had surprised Francis pleasantly and showed his mettle as a true Quoynt. Seaborn was kin after all. And now gone without a proper farewell.

He turned back to snatch one more look at the mountains beyond the plateau. The raw rock had softened to a misty lavender. A single tall peak in the distance still caught the last sunlight and shone like a beacon fire. Things were unravelling. His time here was now short, one way or another. He savoured the chilly resinous air like a man mounting the scaffold. Then he trotted up the steps of the lodge to the ornate double doors.

Seaborn had wished him a good sleep. Francis no longer had time to sleep. He ordered bread and some leathery slices of wild boar ham. Then, with these in his pouch, he slipped out the back of the lodge and went yet again to the mine.

'No one else yet knows it,' Sofia had said. And she had warned him. Even if she had tried to kill her father, as he suspected, she had risked warning Francis.

He must trust her now, he thought. There was no other choice.

'I would have succeeded,' she had said. That he believed.

Trust her! Decide to trust her so that you can clear your mind and use the time she has given you.

The Sky Monkey to Cecil and the bond destroyed. Sofia, Richard – stay fixed on those two stars.

Sofia will steal the bond again. He remembered her anger as she left the lodge and felt a quiver of uncertainty.

Richard will escape to Venice. If he can. If he chooses to take the risk.

Dear God, he thought. Battle at its most ferocious was simpler and less terrifying than this untried terrain. Though his animal being balked at dying, his reason told him that he needed to survive only long enough to take the bond from Sofia and destroy it. Cecil might suffer some uneasy days or weeks until he realized what had happened, but sooner or later the truth would become clear to him. To live just long enough to destroy the bond was almost a reasonable aim, if he had not vowed to protect Sofia from Ettore.

78

Later that evening, Sofia sat at her table, with pen and ink. Her meeting at the lodge with Francis still made her tremble. The over-solemn voices of her women would have irritated her if she had not been concentrating so hard. Who was she to be this time? A simple anonymous betrayer was not enough in this case. She must see clearly in her imagination the person whose words she would write down. She could not risk a slip. This person must be plausible. This person must be in a position to know.

She nodded her thanks to Isabella as the girl placed a small red and gold glass of coffee at her elbow. While she waited for the young woman to sit down again to study her book of German songs, she inhaled the scent of the Turkish brew and took a bitter, refreshing draft into her mouth. Then she gulped down the rest – nutty, a little sour, with an undertone of burnt bread. After a moment, her heart jumped like a kicked horse. Her thoughts sharpened. She began to write, in Latin not Friulan, in a hand not her own but schooled all the same.

'In his ambition, a certain lofty duke aspires to climb the highest peak. He dares to hope that the princess will help him ascend.' She did not sign a name.

She looked up. Her women had broken into smaller groups, subdued by new rumours from the prince's quarters. A few were sewing, three seemed to be composing a letter. Isabella was silently mouthing songs to herself. One woman slept with her head dropped forward onto her chest. The others chatted in a listless way. They were killing themselves with tedium because their ruler might be dying, thought Sofia. All of them terrified of taking pleasure in anything, lest they be misunderstood. If only they knew how little she would reproach them.

*O, pie pelicane,*she told herself wryly. Self-sacrificing pelican daughter. To be mistaken for what you are not is the price of giving a convincing performance.

She imagined the prince sitting in his chair, head back, mouth fallen open, the wolf skin rug tucked around him, just as she had left him. No matter how much she ached to run back and learn if his heart still was beating, she must not let herself return to his chamber. Must not risk stirring suspicion. She must wait. She knew how to wait. But waiting grew no easier with practice.

With the *denunzio* folded and safely tucked away, Sofia began to write again. This time, she used paper that was her own, with the Pirati emblem at the top.

'Brother,' she wrote, '*I entreat you for an audience. I have lately learned . . .*'

On the outside, she wrote '*Principe, Ettore Ferdinando Uskoki di Pirati*'. She folded and sealed it and gave it to Isabella to deliver. Then she rose, told her women that she wished to walk alone in the gardens before going to bed, and set off to find a lion with its belly in the right place. If Da Monte did not already aspire, this *denunzio* would put it into his mind.

79

THE NEXT DAY

The prince's manservant looked in on his master once during the night but noticed nothing wrong. All was just as the *principessa* had said. Just before dawn, he tried to rouse his master for his first herbal tisane. He sent for Prince Ettore and Princess Sofia. Then he woke the physician who was asleep in a nearby chamber.

'Revive my father or I will hang you for his murder,' Ettore told the physician. He ordered two of his Vranghi to stay to watch with the Uskoks.

The prince did not revive. He slept on, slipping deeper every hour. The desperate physician bled him, burnt more tobacco under his nose, applied a freshly killed cockerel to his chest. When he next felt the royal pulse, he began to tremble, from head to foot. Every limb quivered.

'All he needs now is a dose of . . .' His hands refused to obey him when he tried to pour a tincture. The murky liquid slopped onto the tops of his shoes.

'He's dying, is he not?' said Sofia quietly.

'Highness, I do not despair . . . I do not. No! Never! There's still hope, I swear!'

'You fill my heart with joy.' Under her breath she added, '*Signore dottore*, don't lie to me . . .'

'Your Highness, I beg you . . .' He threw himself onto his knees before her.

With a glance at the Vranghi, she knelt beside the distraught man. 'Hush,' she murmured. 'I will pray with you,' she said more loudly. 'Let us bow our heads together and pray that His Highness continues to mend.' She felt the wretch juddering with terror at her side. 'You've no need to hide the truth from me,' she murmured again. 'I am not my brother.' She waited until she saw that he had finally caught her drift. 'If you are wise, and do as I say, I believe we may be able to save your neck from my brother's vengeance.'

He had the crossbow in place over the airshaft, strung but not set. The prince's chariot was hidden in the mine. It seemed to be made of beaten silver but was really parchment over a wooden frame, all of it soaked in saltpetre solution and then dried. The Sky Monkey waited ready to be primed with vitriol – the harmless one, not the dangerous new Sky Monkey that would make walled cities as vulnerable as wooden barns. Francis had only the last dropping charges in the airshaft walls left to put into place, for which he needed daylight and to uncover the shaft.

Dirty and red-eyed with lack of sleep, he was trying to decide between early breakfast or an hour in his bed when he heard a rider in the forecourt.

With a lurch of his gut, he thought, the prince has died! This mummery is about to turn real. He washed quickly and rode back with the messenger to La Spada.

Sofia was waiting for him, white-faced, in the *antecamarilla*. Two of Ettore's Vranghi were posted at the door. 'He died just before breakfast,' she said. 'And Ettore knows.'

Francis gathered himself, snatching at fragmented thoughts flying off in all directions. 'What does Ettore say?'

'Nothing yet, but to promise death to the physician.'

Francis could see only one possible course of action. He lowered his voice enough to bring frowns to the faces of the Vranghi. 'How far can you trust the Uskoks?'

'They will do whatever they believe my father wished.'

And Ettore might not wish to confront them so soon by openly ignoring his father's wishes. The new prince had nothing to lose by honouring them. Or so Francis thought he would decide in Ettore's place.

'Will you dare do a thing that might still save us?'

'I see little left to lose,' she said.

'Tell Ettore that I still mean to attempt the flight and fulfil my contract. The soul lingers in the body for a time after death.'

'You mean to attempt it?'

'Who knows what chances to redirect the future might present themselves.' He watched a gleam enter the peaty depths of her eyes.

'I will try.'

'If Ettore agrees, call for the litter in your father's name,' said Francis. 'Let the Uskoks help him into it. I must now make haste back up to the mountain. If you travel without too much speed, there may just be time for what I still must do.' It was not his chosen time of day, but the clouds were low. He bent over her hand, which was icy cold. 'Have you stolen the bond?'

'How?' she breathed. 'When? Ettore has had guards on me ever since the manservant raised the first alarm that his Highness had begun to slip towards his final sleep. He himself is in there now . . . here's Venturini.'

Francis heard the name 'Ettore' and knew, even though the man spoke in an urgent flurry of his own tongue.

Sofia gave Francis a desperate look. 'My brother orders you to attend him at once, in my father's *camera*.'

80

Prince Alessandro's body lay stretched on his bed, the mountain ridge of his large frame draped stiffly with a black and gold brocade coverlet. Candles burned on either side of his head. Two Uskoks stood either side of the bed as guard of honour. Branches of rosemary crackled on the brazier to purify the air. Prince Ettore stood beside the bed, looking at the papers in his hand. Behind him, the secret panel in the bed head stood ajar.

Francis felt his guts lurch. 'Highness, you sent for me.' He dropped onto one knee. His throat tightened so that he could not swallow.

Prince Ettore ignored Francis, left him on one knee, making him wait. He read a letter and threw it onto the brazier with the rosemary. Still ignoring Francis, he turned a jewelled dagger in his hands, gave it to a servant to set beside a casket on the prince's table. He threw an old map onto the fire, then two more letters. He opened a small enamelled box, curled his lip, tipped out what looked like locks of fair hair and crushed the little box under his boot. He reached into the secret compartment and pulled out another fistful of documents.

'Take those wolf skin rugs from the chair and burn them,'

he ordered. When they were gone, he sat in the prince's chair to study the papers.

Grimly, Francis watched Ettore working with what looked like intense purpose, opening documents, scanning them quickly, burning some and laying others aside.

'Aha!' Ettore waved a document at Francis. 'I believe I have just found your ill-judged promises.' He set that paper aside with the others.

Francis could never blame Cecil entirely for the loan bond. Francis had signed an agreement that was just as mad.

Another paper went on the fire.

Francis was certain that he knew what the new prince was looking for. The English bond he had been told of but never allowed to see. He had to know about it. He was taking too much pleasure in making Francis watch him find it.

Ettore let out a sigh of satisfaction. He opened the intricate folds of a parchment document from which dangled two shiny red seals.

Francis knew those folds and those seals.

I should have overpowered her when I had the chance! he thought in a fury of despair. Sent it with Richard and risked his being captured. I should have trusted him not to tell Schiavoni. He should have listened to reason, not to his heart and cock, and abandoned Sofia to the wrath of her father and the bile of her brother. Now, because he had done none of these things, Cecil had fallen into the power of an Italian prince who would happily sell England to either the Hapsburgs or the Turks – whichever bid the most. Cecil would have only two choices: to co-operate under blackmail with a hostile power or to hand himself over to the English crown as guilty of treasonous fraud.

Ettore read the document.

Francis could now see the familiar swooping hand that had written the address on the outside. Cecil's hand, exactly as Sofia had shown him. How many other letters to La Spada was Cecil likely to have written himself?

Take it from him now and put it into the fire – as you did not the last time. A quick soldier's death if you make the guards think you're attacking the prince.

Francis calculated how many heartbeats he would be allowed before the nearest man could give him a mortal wound. Even bleeding to death, he could snatch the bond from Ettore's hands and hold it in the fire. There might be time for it to be destroyed.

Ettore frowned and turned the parchment over to look again at the name on the outside. He returned to the contents and read once more. Then, with a curse, he threw the bond onto the fire.

Francis gaped. The fire flared. The parchment turned to a fragile shiny sheet like beaten metal leaf. He watched it crumble. He stared at the new ruler of La Spada.

Surely Ettore had understood what he was holding! Francis felt suddenly unmanned by relief. Relief loosened his limbs, made him waver on his knee. He touched the floor with the fingers of one hand to keep his balance. The bond was destroyed.

He did not have launch himself to certain death, not just yet. Even a few moments more of this earthly life felt like all the treasures of Heaven. He was so giddy with renewed life, so aware of the blood still thudding through his body, so drowned in sensuous joy at occupying his husk for a little longer, that even the hard marble floor beneath his kneecap gave him joy. He leaned forward to brace both hands on the floor.

Was it possible that, by one of his devious miracles, Cecil had already struck a deal with the new ruler and failed to let Francis know? Or had been unable to let him know, given the dead agent on the porch of the hunting lodge.

Hope flared like the fire. Francis's own freedom might,

just possibly, be one of the terms in such a deal. He straightened, still on one knee.

Ettore looked at Francis at last. 'You're a thief, Cointo!' he said. 'Stole money from the Treasury of La Spada by fraud – a capital crime, I believe.'

Hope of any unknown deal by Cecil died. Francis bowed his head. He thought that he had been prepared for this next turn of events but now fumbled for a grip on his argument. His thoughts would not let go of the extraordinary fact that the bond had been destroyed. Ettore himself had cast it into the fire. Whatever happened next, if he himself were about to die, Cecil was saved, and English diplomacy with him. That had to be consolation enough. But he was no longer certain.

Cecil was safe. Francis was not.

'What do you say, Cointo?'

The speech Francis had just asked Sofia to make was his part now.

'Your Highness! There's no fraud! I can still achieve your father's wishes. You will be able to witness for yourself that my promises have been successfully met.'

Ettore listened with ironic attention. 'The comedy is over, Cointo. Stop play-acting. You know very well that you are a mountebank and that my father is already dead!'

'God rest his soul in peace,' murmured Francis. 'Alas, so I have just learned.'

He had entered that fire master's nightmare, the infinite pause between lighting the fuse and the misfire that would kill him, knowing what was coming, knowing that he was helpless to change anything.

'And so his physician has said.' He looked up boldly. 'Highness, take heart! There's still hope. The wisest religious authorities still differ on how long the soul lingers in the body after death. If you will permit me, now, without a moment's further delay, to make the last arrangements, we

441

may still carry out your father's wishes to fly to Heaven before his soul leaves his body. If we don't waste one more second, he might still reach Heaven in time. You will witness for yourself that I have stolen nothing but worked only in his interest. Succeed or fail . . . and I warned him from the start that it would be difficult . . . my purpose was always honest.'

He poised eagerly, ready to leap to his feet and leave the moment Ettore gave the word. If he could get back to the lodge and his workshop in the mine, his chances of escape, though not large, would be infinitely greater than they were here inside the *fortezza* at the top of that long, narrow exposed causeway, in daylight.

Ettore rose and came to stand close above Francis. Even with Francis kneeling, the difference in their heights was not great. Ettore spoke just loudly enough for Francis alone to hear.

'My father can go to hell for all I care. Do what you like with him. Light him like a firework or roast him like a pig. Carry on with your sleight-of-hand and fairground tricks . . . Did you think you had kept your deceiving a secret from me? Play any tricks you like with his corpse. If I dared, I'd have it dragged around the Castello by horses, but my new subjects might think me an ungrateful heir. By all means, play out your comedy. That's not the fraud I meant.'

Francis knew what was coming

'I refer to the money you spent secretly, meaning to steal away with the result.' Ettore bared his teeth in what could never be taken as a smile. 'You meant to deny your generous patrons the fruit of their patronage. In La Spada, theft is made worse by ingratitude.'

This time Francis could think of nothing to say.

'There's only one way to save yourself. Give me your Sky Monkey.'

81

'All formulae and drawings,' said Ettore, 'as well as the thing itself.'

Francis stood up without permission before he toppled over, dizzy with treachery. Who had betrayed him? He stamped his foot to restore feeling and tried to collect his thoughts.

Ettore was hanging so intently on the reply that he let this incivility pass.

And what would you do with the Sky Monkey? Francis wondered. Threaten your neighbours? Use it to jeer at the Hapsburgs? Or sell it to them? Or to the Turks? Or to one of the other ambitious jostling powers that hunger for new territories – Russia, for one, or Spain. He imagined Ettore controlling the precarious balance between Hapsburg and Turk and ruining Cecil's hopes for an alliance in the Adriatic. Ettore could trade the Sky Monkey for alliances of his own, for trading privileges, for reductions in taxes and safe passage for ships, for mercenaries and weapons, for a grand political marriage.

The question Francis most needed to answer, but could not, was whether whoever had betrayed him had seen and described the Sky Monkey itself.

'Your highness . . .' Francis tilted his head to indicate that he wished to draw Ettore away from the Uskoks by the bed. He limped after the prince to the window embrasure.

'I can't give you the Sky Monkey,' said Francis. 'But that is not to say that I won't.'

Ettore frowned. His mind was devious but not agile.

'I must first make you one,' Francis explained. 'At the moment, I carry it only in my head. Your Sky Monkey does not at this moment exist. It is merely the possibility of itself. I exploded the last one in a trial last week.'

'I must have it,' Ettore insisted.

'There is no difficulty. You will have it.'

Ettore looked more suspicious than gratified.

Francis saw where he was going wrong. He was being too straightforward. 'But I must ask for a small sign of your favour.' He allowed a market trader's pause to let mutual understanding to arrive.

'I thought we might come to that,' said Ettore.

'Imagine,' said Francis, 'you will be able to project accurate exploding shells at an enemy whilst still far out of their range. Imagine that you would not have to move your siege cannon forward to . . .'

'How much do you want?' Ettore interrupted

'Your pardon and safe passage back to England.' He must drive a hard bargain, or Ettore would smell a rat. 'May I remind your highness, that your father's funeral fireworks have been costly . . .'

'And so have your mountebank deceptions,' said Ettore. 'Never try to run a market stall, Cointo. How much money do you demand beyond that you have already stolen?'

Deceit was indeed easier when the deceivers wanted to believe.

'Only enough to buy a small country estate of my own in England.'

He watched suspicion, calculation, speculation and gratification jostle for a turn in Ettore's eyes. Francis still did not understand about the burning of the bond, but he was gambling that it had now been destroyed.

Ettore gave a small private smile. 'Take him to his workshop,' he ordered his men. 'But I want his legs fettered. And keep three men on him at all times.'

They tied his feet together under his horse and shackled his wrists. As they set off up the track to the Hunting Lodge, Francis now had time to wonder who had been the traitor.

Who had known? After the 'accident' no watchers had come close enough to understand what he had really been doing. Or at least, he had detected none.

He could see how Ettore might have learned that the prince's flight to Heaven was to be a false piece of theatre. There were too many physical signs. Too many props, even though the air shaft had been hidden and the crossbow was plausible for its supposed purpose in sending the prince to Heaven. The false rockets had been made in the mine and successfully hidden there, so far as any of his markers and traps showed. Even so, any one of the many watchers might have noticed something a little wrong or questioned an inconsistency.

Given the absurdity and danger of the prince's request, a reasonable man might simply have laid far higher odds on a deception than on a sincere attempt. Father Daniele, for example, the prince's confessor, who had been told of the proposed Heavenly flight. And the physician who had been bribed but might have been doubled by a higher bid and a desire to curry favour with the next ruler of La Spada. Any of them might have sniffed out and betrayed the intended sham.

But they could not have guessed the Sky Monkey!

The sudden heave of his mount up a steep step in the track almost unseated him.

'Sorry,' he murmured to the unhappy animal, which expected better horsemanship from him than the painful shackles allowed.

After Albona brought him the translations, he had kept all his work carefully hidden in the mine. He was almost certain that he had done nothing in public that could not be explained by either the funeral fireworks or the prince's Heavenly voyage.

His betrayer, therefore, must be someone he had trusted with the truth. There was no escaping it. Albona, who hated Ettore. Sofia, who loved Francis and hated her half-brother. Neither seemed likely. Venturini? Perhaps, if the man had sniffed more closely than Francis had thought, and did not share the fierce loyalties of his fellows. Venturini might have been able to search the workshops, or overhear a fragment of conversation between Richard and himself.

Richard Seaborn. Francis made himself look squarely at this possibility. Richard Seaborn, recently acquired nephew, foreign born, who had found a new allegiance here in La Spada. He had the papers and the models of the device. Perhaps he had offered to sell the information to Ettore, who had decided to seize it instead. Was it the influence of Schiavoni?

Although the thought made him feel sick, Francis allowed himself to weigh this possibility. He had never thought to fear Schiavoni because he had never before questioned Richard's loyalty. He shook his head in protest, then asked himself why it was not possible. Richard was ambitious. He had successfully passed himself off as Francis's serving man, and then proved to be a keen intelligencer amongst both the servants and the nobility in the *Castello*. But the young man had also seemed open and unswerving in his loyalty to Francis, and even more importantly, to Boomer.

But then, thought Francis viciously, some people believe me to be an honest open man.

He shook his head again and thought of the slaves, and of the Uskoks whom he had begun to trust almost as much as they seemed now to trust him. Perhaps there was another Ricco Smith who had escaped Francis's notice. With so many greedy eyes and ears on the alert, there must be someone else altogether whom he had overlooked. There's no need to suspect friends when you live amongst the Lions.

82

Back at the mine, his hands were freed. The shackles on his feet were removed when he told the guards that the metal cuffs might create a fatal spark. The Vranghi chose to defy Ettore's orders to watch Francis at all times and stayed outside the mine entrance. But even if they had stood at his side, he knew that they would not understand what they were seeing, or know whether or not it was the new dangerous Sky Monkey with scales and claws.

He was now prepared to die, but meant to choose his own time and his own way. His chief purpose in coming to La Spada was achieved, by bizarre happenstance, but achieved nonetheless. It was a pity he wouldn't be able to tell Cecil in person. On the other hand, he was not entirely ready to give up without making one last attempt to shape the future and keep his promise to Sofia. Ettore had given him a chance he had never expected.

He took the second Sky Monkey device out of the padded chest. Once he had gathered all his tools and materials beneath the light well and donned his leather apron, he forced himself into slow deliberation. Every move must now be unhurried and absolutely precise. He sat for a time, breathing softly, letting the last tremor seep away, leaving his hand steady.

The Vranghi delivered Francis to Ettore's *camera* in the old *fortezza*, not to one of the larger public rooms in the *Magno Palazzo*. With satisfaction, Francis noted the thick stone walls and small windows, which would contain and compress any explosion. Ettore's desire to escape witnesses would help to kill him. Francis set the cushioned crate beside the table set in the centre of the floor. The Vranghi stayed as far from him as they dared without actually leaving the room. He had had little difficulty persuading them to leave him unshackled so that he could carry the device himself.

He laid some folded papers on the table. Then he lifted an explosive shell onto the table from the crate. Into the little chamber at the top, he inserted, very carefully, the delicate glass vial, nesting it into the compressed spring mechanism already there. He took from his pouch the last of Boomer's final gift. He opened the vial and stood ready to pour.

After this, there was no going back. He poured the vitriol very, very carefully and, with infinite delicacy, closed the shell. Now all that remained was to choose the moment to begin the count-down to death.

He heard the Uskok drums. Marching feet crossed the next room. Eight of Ettore's Vranghi entered. Then came eight Uskoks, including Venturini. Ettore entered next. Beside him walked Sofia.

Ettore lookd curiously at the shell. He picked up the papers from the table and leafed through them. 'Is it all here?'

'It is, your highness.'

'Take the English mountebank away and hang him,' said Ettore.

83

'What are you waiting for? Take him away and hang him.'

Francis stared at Sofia in horror. She should not be here in Ettore's chamber! It had not occurred to Francis that she might be. He had imagined her locked in a cell, on the way to a distant convent, even dead, anywhere but standing calmly at her brother's side gazing down at her folded hands. He willed her to look up and meet his eye.

Ettore put down the papers and reached to pick up the Sky Monkey.

'Don't touch it yet!' shouted Francis wildly.

Look at me, Sofia! he begged.

Startled, Ettore stopped.

'I must warn you of the dangers.'

At last, she looked up.

'Your highness,' said Francis. He let his eyes flick to hers for an instant then fixed on Ettore. 'Hold my hanging at least until I can show you how to take care.'

'The ruse won't work, Cointo. If you carried it here, I can carry it away.' Ettore turned to the Vranghi. 'Seize him!'

One man grabbed Francis's hair and yanked his head back. Two others gripped an arm each.

'Search him. Who knows what tricks of fire he may carry?'

They sliced open doublet, cut off his pouch, and ripped his sleeves to feel inside his shirt.

Ettore examined one of the small exploding stars that Francis always carried in his pouch.

'It's merely to entertain,' said Francis. The words struggled thinly through his over-stretched throat 'Throw it on the floor.'

Ettore hesitated suspiciously.

'Here, brother. I'll do it.' Sofia took it from his fingers and tossed it. There was a 'paf' and a small bright flash.

Ettore flinched, then smiled. 'I've heard it said that you're a wizard, but you're a mere mountebank, are you not, who has a little knowledge of matériel?'

'I claim only great knowledge of rockets and explosives,' croaked Francis, 'and a desire to let them serve you.'

'I won't give you a chance to play any tricks in a cage,' Ettore told Francis. 'Take him and hang him at once in the piazza. Show the people of La Spada what their new ruler does to thieves and frauds.' Ettore turned to Sofia. 'Aren't you going to beg for the life of your leather stretcher?'

Francis swivelled his eyes. He could see her blurred in the corner of his vision.

She was looking steadily back at the new prince. 'His life is of no importance to me, brother. You may do as you like.' She turned and left the chamber.

'I'll send you his cock and balls,' Ettore called after her. 'The parts of him you'll miss the most.'

She has some plan, Francis reassured himself. He could . . . would not let himself believe that apparent serenity at his imminent death. But time was short for putting any ruse into action. The Vranghi quivered with eagerness to get on with the day's unexpected excitement of a hanging.

Face still forced to the ceiling, hair about to be torn out by the roots, a stout soldier locked onto either arm . . .

Stay calm. You've just lit a fuse. Enter that stillness. Slow time down . . . think. What can you do to save yourself?

The Uskoks . . . was there any hope of help from them? Sofia, departed, who could not be depended on . . . he was unarmed. If he moved suddenly, his neck could be broken . . . Ettore would soon pick up the Sky Monkey with death coiled at its heart, straining at its bonds, needing only the jolt of a footstep to set it free. The Sky Monkey, which Ettore himself had asked for, could not be stopped now. Very, very soon it would show its true terrifying, lethal nature disguised with a playful name.

The Uskoks had not moved. They might have helped him once, Francis thought. But only to serve the prince. Now they served the new prince.

There was nothing he could do. It was almost a relief to accept the truth. If he had a chance of escaping death, it lay with Sofia.

You're giving up, he told himself. Keep thinking . . . you're not on the steps of the gallows yet. Perhaps in the holding cell . . . it will take a little time to build the gallows . . .

His captors turned him and forced him through the door into the buzz of the curious crowd in the antechamber.

'The English fire master!' 'What did he . . .?' 'Who is it? I can't see!'

He heard more voices, in the chamber beyond. Loud, angry, commanding. A single protest. Then a Jesuit priest ran towards them, hood thrown back, his face as grey as a corpse. He pushed past Francis and soldiers into Ettore's chamber.

'Highness!'

'Father Daniele,' exclaimed Ettore angrily. 'I don't believe I summoned you.'

Francis's captors paused in curiosity. With his head still hauled back, Francis could only hear Father Daniele's urgent voice.

'Highness, there was no warning . . . I beg you, tell them how I guided your father towards God in his final days, tell their envoy that I am a faithful servant of the Holy Church of Rome!'

'What are you babbling about?' demanded Ettore.

Francis heard the tread of marching feet. Peering down his nose, he saw two soldiers wearing the Papal livery of Rome, then two more, followed by the tall Jesuit whom Francis had seen from time to time in the *antecamarilla*.

'Stop there where you are!' the Jesuit ordered Francis's captors. 'By the authority of Rome.'

The grip on Francis's hair loosened enough for him to take a good sideways look as the priest walked past. Tall, lean and imperious, the man had thrown back his black hood to reveal a long skull, the scalp shining above the tonsure, and the nose of a Roman general.

'Prince Ettore?' The Jesuit turned his long thin face and vulture beak towards the new ruler, the very image of a prosecuting agent of the Inquisition. 'I have an order to arrest the heretic Francis Quoynt, said to be taking refuge here in your court.'

'I am the new ruler of La Spada, Father,' Ettore said after a moment. 'And I welcome you to my presence now, as I welcome all Jesuits to my court. I understand your stated purpose but do not know either your identity or your authority.'

The priest skewered him with a look combining scorn and threat. 'I don't understand your purpose in pretending ignorance. My authority is the Inquisition. You don't need my name, but I offer it from a surplus of civility – Father Bernabo. We met once before when I first arrived in La Spada, invited by your late father.'

453

Francis could still only listen.

'I also arrest that heretic priest.'

Father Daniele shouted in protest.

'No heretics find refuge in La Spada,' said Ettore. 'I am as keen as you to smoke them out.'

The Vranghi, absorbed by the scene behind them, loosened their grip on Francis enough for him to turn back too.

Father Daniele, on his knees in front of Father Bernabo, pointed through the door at Francis. 'That's the man you want! Out there. That's Quoynt, the heretic! I have been watching him. I can testify to his crimes!'

'I have anticipated you in cleansing my new domain,' said Ettore. 'There he is already snared. You passed him on the way to me.'

The Jesuit turned to study Francis with cold eyes. 'Indeed, that's most convenient. So timely that I'm tempted to call it God's Will.'

'I mean to have him hanged shortly,' said Ettore. 'Allow me to serve God and save you any further inconvenience at the same time.'

'I claim his living body for our punishment. Secular crimes, even treason, must give way to crimes against God.'

Ettore made a sound of protest.

He will let me go, thought Francis. He has his Sky Monkey.

'Do you set yourself above the Inquisition?' asked Bernabo. 'Like the oligarchs of Venice?'

Ettore sat back in resignation. 'No, Father. I am its devout servant. But leave me my confessor at least. I swear that he is a most faithful servant.' He stared at Father Bernabo in challenge.

'I will testify against the English heretic,' cried Father Daniele as one of the Jesuit's men-at-arms hauled him to his feet.

'You will,' agreed the Inquisitor. He studied them all. Then he nodded curtly. 'For the moment, priest, I accept your worldly master's assurances. But you will indeed testify against the Englishman. And I am also curious to know exactly how you endeavoured to save the prince's soul for your Heavenly Master.'

He turned to leave. 'The Englishman will be tried in our courts, and if found guilty, he will burn.'

A shameful weakness turned Francis's legs to water as they led him away. He could not have resisted the Inquisitor's men-at-arms even if he chose to try. Reason told him that the work of worms was no prettier than that of flames . . . but . . . to die in a fiery explosion was at least fast. He knew how long it could take to die at the stake. This time, he had finally lost.

84

Sofia had read the warning in Francis's eyes, but she did not know how long she had. A quick exchange of glances could not tell her whether a tiny flame was already burning in the heart of the Sky Monkey. It could not tell her whether something else might have to happen first.

She stood aside until Francis had been led away. She dared not chance even the slightest contact with him lest she give herself away. But she must go back into Ettore's *camera*, no matter how great the risk. She now looked her stark choice directly in the eye – rule or die. No more time for thinking ahead. The next moments, and her own courage would decide her fate. With the help of Francis.

Daniele was kneeling before Ettore. 'The blessings of God be upon you, your highness. I thank you!'

Ettore scarcely noticed her return. He had eyes only for the Sky Monkey. He picked up the papers again and put them into his embroidered pouch pocket. 'My own fire master shall have these. What a surprise I will give some of our threatening neighbours.' He turned to the Vranghi.

'Two of you take my sister to her apartments and keep her there safely. Keep all her women under guard as well.

Let no one see or talk to her until I return.' To Sofia, he said, 'We will discuss your future later.'

Sofia nodded meekly,

'And you . . .' He pointed to another of his guards. 'Pick up that shell and bring it with me to the Armoury.' He pointed to two others. 'And you come guard us there.'

The first man hesitated by the table.

'The Englishman carried it here, did he not? asked Ettore impatiently. 'Do you fear to do what he did? Such shells must first be fired to be dangerous.'

Sofia was not so certain. She held her breath as she watched the man pick up the shell, gingerly. She fought the useless urge to squeeze her eyes closed.

Nothing happened. Holding the shell in front of him like a pudding on a dish, the guard followed Ettore from the room, with two more Vranghi behind. The door closed behind them.

Now, thought Sofia. The absolute moment had arrived, the pivot on which the future swung.

The two Vranghi ordered to escort her were hesitating, uncertain whether she was still the *principessa* or now a mere prisoner.

She had only a few heartbeats before they decided. She stepped away and turned to face them all, both Uskok and Vranghi, like a player on a stage facing her audience. This would indeed be the prologue to her play. If she spoke it well, she would carry the day. If badly, she would be driven from the stage forever.

She looked at the two private mercenary armies, the Uskoks and the Vranghi.

She was ready. She was astonished that she felt no fear. On the contrary, she felt as if all the different Sofias had stepped into the same skin at once, each doubling and tripling the force of the others.

With one ear still listening for the end of all her troubles, she turned first to the Uskoks.

Her words were ready, with the help of Rabac Albona and many hours of practice in her bedchamber. She had found her cadences in his books of oratory but couched them in her own words. The speech must now seem to spring *extempore* from her heart, to flow freely from her tongue as if she were set on fire by the passion of this moment.

'It is now time for you to choose,' she said. 'La Spada must now choose who will rule her next.'

The Uskoks exchanged glances. They had been prepared for this moment. Sofia knew from the lions that one of them had been overheard arguing for a move while her father still lived, lest Ettore try to speed his end.

'Will you declare for me, or for my half-brother?' She held up one hand. 'Say nothing yet. Take a moment to reflect.'

She turned to the five remaining Vranghi. 'And what will you do? Has my half-brother earned your love and trust? I will pay you just as well.'

She looked from one group to the other. The two Vranghi ordered to take her to her *camera* seemed for the moment to have forgotten their task. Nevertheless, the entire group stirred uneasily. She would not be given long.

'I am my father's true blood. An Uskok, like him. You see his true spirit in me. You will see his rule as it was before he grew ill, but softened a little by a woman's love for her people and natural sense of justice. I will care for my people as even he never did. I will not shed blood without good cause.' She turned to the five Vranghi again. 'I will not punish men for loyalty to anyone before me, so long as they serve me with the same good will. I don't think my brother will offer the same leniency.' A glance at the Uskoks showed her that they had already considered this.

Father Daniele stared at her in astonishment. 'For shame!' he cried. 'Serpent in your brother's bosom! Overweening Eve!'

Sofia ignored him. 'What do you say?' she asked the soldiers.

Father Daniele started towards the door to follow Ettore.

'Stay!' Sofia stepped into his way. He was taller and broader than she was. She turned all the force of her will onto him. Above all else, Ettore must not be called back. He must not return to this room. He must keep walking farther and farther away. He must carry the Sky Monkey as far as possible from this room, though she did not know how far was far enough.

Father Daniele looked at the Vranghi, then at the Uskoks, weighing their relative numbers and likely sympathies. He seemed to gather courage from what he saw. 'The new prince must be warned that his own sister is a traitor.' He stepped towards her to push past.

Sofia put out her hand to the nearest Uskok and felt a dagger arrive in it.

'Stand aside,' said Daniele.

She smiled and shook her head. She stepped closer to him.

Daniele's eyes widened. He tried to step back but an Uskok blocked his way, tight against his back. Sofia found the soft place just below his ribs, leaned with her whole weight behind her hand, and slid the blade up under his ribs into his heart.

The room dissolved into chaos around her. One of the Vranghi, trying to push past her like Father Daniele was tripped and killed by two Uskoks. Another of the Vranghi turned on one of his fellows just as the man opened his mouth to give a warning shout, and changed the shout into a grunt with a blow to the head. 'I'm with you!' he shouted. 'I'm with you!'

Sofia stepped away from Daniele's body and waited,

panting, the knife still under the priest's ribs, until she could see how matters would settle.

'Your highness!' Three of the Uskoks dropped to their knees, then five, then six. The two surviving Vranghi joined them. The explosion came before the last two Uskoks could declare themselves.

85

Francis was thrown blindfolded and bound into a cart. He had only one clear memory from the time after his eyes were covered, lying on the hard floor of the cart while the horses still carefully descended the causeway along the blade of the sword. Behind him, in the bowels of the old *fortezza*, the exploding Sky Monkey made the horses shy. He had heard distant screams begin, far-off shouts.

'Steady!' he heard Father Bernabo say. 'Don't turn back.'

Francis was almost thrown from the cart as it accelerated, jolting viciously over paving stones ridged to give purchase to horses' hoofs.

He might never know whether Sofia had been killed. Or whether Ettore had examined the Sky Monkey and triggered the explosion, or without Francis there to guide events, whether he had ordered it removed just too soon by an unsuspecting servant.

Francis tried to remember whether he had seen a flicker of understanding in her eyes when he had voiced his warning. He decided that he merely wanted to believe that she had understood. Then he asked himself how she had come to be there with her half-brother, who was her arch enemy, or so she had made Francis believe. Blind and lost, he was easy meat for the serpent of suspicion.

His captors guarded their words in his hearing, but he thought they might be Florentines. One of them might have been Venetian. After a time, when his ears told him that they had left La Spada, they put him on a horse and tied his legs together under its belly. From time to time, they freed his hands and gave him bread, which he ate blindly. They put into his hands meat he could not always identify while spitting out tiny bones or mysterious lumps of gristle. They allowed him to drink water and to relieve himself. Then they tied him back on his horse.

For the first day, to hold off fantasies of burning, he tried to imagine step by step that they were retracing the route he had taken with Seaborn. But the remembered landmarks did not arrive. When they stopped to make camp the first night, they replaced his blindfold, which could be nudged upwards to allow glimpses of the world, with a firmly tied hood.

On the second day, when they never reached the settlement with the waterfall and forge, he felt dizzied by these disappointments and gave it up. He smelled firs and pines. They were still in the mountains. Though the blind awkward journey seemed endless, he was in no hurry to arrive wherever they were going. He would not be able to talk his way out of this one. He was guilty of their charge of heresy. He had known that risk before he began. He had warned Cecil. He would die as a heretic.

He tried not to dwell on Rome as England's most implacable enemy . . . he was going mad in the darkness.

I haven't heard them pray yet, he thought one night as he rolled carefully onto his other side, trying to find a comfortable way to lie in shackles. But there would be enough

462

praying over his soul when they reached Rome . . . or whatever other city in the Papal States they were headed for.

He smelt himself beginning to stink.

The painful lurching of his horse up and down steep tracks turned to the easier ride of flatter ground. One night, he slept once again above cows in a farmhouse but with only the mournful cowbells to disturb him, not the waterfall.

Then, even through the hood, he smelled the sea and heard the cries of gulls.

He was transferred to a small craft. Someone pushed his head down to clear an awning or door. They rose and fell on gentle waves for a very long time while the sun grew hotter and the air inside his hood seemed to thicken. He had the impression that the boat was only a little larger than a wherry. He felt the repeated surge of an oar or oars. This did not feel like a ship bound down the coast towards Rome.

The voices of a city began to bounce off walls and out of the funnels of streets. Always, he heard the slapping of water. He could still smell the sea. He made out the occasional shouted word.

Venice after all, it would seem. The world had turned mad enough . . . why not Venice? He didn't understand Venice . . . if it were indeed Venice, but he liked it better than Rome. He had meant to come to Venice.

But he had not heard the shouts and whistles and flapping rigging of the ships' pool at the bottom of the Grand Canal.

The boat turned into cool silence, leaving the voices of the city behind. All sounds were closer now, bouncing off nearby walls.

'On your feet!' He was shoved up some slippery stone steps. The sun stabbed bright pinpricks through the black fabric of the hood. Heat banged on his head, stifling inside the hood. His raw bare wrists burned with saltwater.

463

His feet crossed hollow wood. Up a few more slippery steps. Then the stillness of a walled courtyard. Someone removed his hood. His eyes squinted in the pain of the sunlight. Only two men now guarded him, neither of them a priest.

'Where are we?' He asked in soldier's Italian, then in Latin. '*Venezia?*' They pushed him up the wide stone steps of a villa.

On the heavy double wooden doors, two lion-head knobs stared malevolently. Inside, the villa seemed occupied though bare of furnishing. Through open doors, he saw vast tracts of black and pale grey marble floor. In the entrance hall were only an intricately inlaid stone table and a few gilded stools. In one corner, a swift's crumbled mud nest lay where it had fallen from the meeting of the ornate plaster ceiling with the wide band of carving at the top of the walls.

They climbed a double sweep of curving marble stairs to the *piano nobile*. At first, because he was looking straight into the light that poured in through the tall windows running from floor to ceiling along the length of the room, Francis could not see who else was there with him.

'Your need for a bath is painfully evident,' said Cecil's voice. 'But we must speak first.'

'My lord!' Francis felt an absurd desire to seize the English Secretary of State in his arms and hug him. 'I did not expect to meet you here!'

I won't burn! he thought. I'm not in Rome! Not in England neither but back among friends. Against all odds, all expectations, I am saved! He found himself grinning at Cecil.

'I said that I would watch your back,' said Cecil tiredly. 'I kept my word, though it's more than you deserve.'

'No, my lord!' Francis felt drunk. At any moment, his head would float up to join the angels on the painted ceiling. 'I've done what you asked. It's done. All is resolved.' He could begin to see Cecil now. The little man's face looked oddly unfriendly and strained. Of course, he could not know all that had happened, not even Cecil could know everything. 'The bond is destroyed, my lord. You're safe.'

'You've never lied to me before, Quoynt. Why begin now?'

86

'I swear, my lord, I swear that I saw the bond destroyed, with my own eyes.'

'And I swear that it still exists.'

Seeing the chill in Cecil's eyes, Francis wished that he had had the delicacy to say, 'England is safe,' not 'you are safe'.

'My lord, I beg you, don't toy with me. My wits have been beaten to pulp in the last weeks.'

'Why would I toy on such a subject?'

'I saw the bond burnt!' cried Francis.

'Her highness, the new ruler of La Spada, swears that it was not.'

Francis stood open-mouthed. There was too much matter in that speech to begin to take it all in.

Cecil gazed briefly out of the window again then walked to his writing table. He looked ill and tired. His shoulders drooped beneath his heavy black robe. 'Do you know, Quoynt, that whilst you've entertained me in the past by your variable attempts at evasion, this is the first time I've caught you in a bald lie. What I don't understand is why.'

Cecil picked up a silver-mounted goose quill, turned it absently in his stubby fingers and laid it down again. 'I feel I should be able to read a reason for your deception, but I can't . . . and that frightens me. You have a choice. You must go back to La Spada to finish what you have begun, or you go to the Tower.' He set his right hand palm up on the desk on one side. 'La Spada.' He set his left hand on the other side. 'Tower. You choose.'

'My lord, I don't understand the *principessa*'s game, but she's lying to you. She cannot still have the bond.'

'What are you trying to do to me?' Cecil demanded, suddenly ferocious 'Have you gone over to my cousin Bacon's side after all? I have trusted you far more than reason advised. You're no fool! You know what it means if the new ruler of La Spada still holds that bond.'

'The new ruler? Did you not say just now, that the *principessa* is the new ruler?' Then, Ettore was most likely dead.

Cecil stared at him in cold assessment. 'Could I have been so wrong about you for so long?' He grimaced, as if in pain. 'If so, you're the first man or woman to gull me so completely. You could teach Cousin Bacon a thing or two about deviousness. I congratulate you.'

'Will you listen to me?' shouted Francis, provoked beyond control. He was also growing terrified that Cecil meant what he was saying.

Cecil's pupils had contracted to needle points.

'Sir . . .' With difficulty, Francis calmed himself and dropped onto his knees. His face and Cecil's were now almost on a level. 'Forgive me, my lord. I have spent too long in a mad house. I thought I had left it behind. Now I find that the madness has followed me here. I don't understand, but I swear . . .' He threw up his hands. 'Never mind! Give me my sword to fall on and I'll save the hangman the trouble.'

There was a long silence.

'Don't play the ass,' said Cecil. 'Clearly, someone is lying. The only way to resolve this conundrum is for you to go back to La Spada as I have ordered and learn the truth.'

Francis climbed slowly back to his feet. 'Do I assume then that you've decided to believe me?'

Cecil rubbed his forehead in a gesture that spoke of controlled irritation. 'I know most of my envoys to be liars but I still send them abroad. If I insisted on dealing only with honest men, I might as well go searching for a virgin in Southwark.' He picked up his pen again and smoothed the barbels between finger and thumb.

'I can't hope to survive La Spada a second time.'

'If I fall, you fall with me, Quoynt. Don't you feel that La Spada is worth the gamble?' Cecil set the pen down yet again 'The princess, who succeeds her brother, is not entirely your enemy from what I hear. She's willing to settle the debt on very reasonable terms but insists that you be my envoy.'

Francis felt his own eyes narrowing. 'How do you know this so soon? Her father died barely a week ago, and, I must also assume, her brother.

Cecil smiled, back on the familiar ground of devious statesmanship. 'Your wits are as curdled as you say, Quoynt. A messenger on fast post horses can ride to Venice in a day and a half. But such mistreatment of man and mount wasn't needed in this case. The *principessa* has written to me more than once. And most insistently, now that she holds the bond.'

And since I confirmed its worth to her, thought Francis.

He held up his hands in submission. 'I'm yours to command, my lord. First, however, I'd be grateful for a wash, a meal and a night's sleep free of fetters.'

'You'd not be welcome in La Spada without the first,' said Cecil tartly, 'and I'm not so cruel as to deny you the rest.'

'With good wine and a feather bed?'

'Don't over-stretch my good will.'

They both spoke lightly but the tussle was real enough. Cecil needed Francis, and Francis was almost past caring. 'And a brief visit to the Arsenale before I again leave Venice would buy my heart entirely,' he said.

Cecil stared chilly-eyed while Francis vowed never to press his advantage, ever again, however playfully. He must never even seem to know that he had Cecil at a disadvantage.

Then Cecil decided to smile. 'I've already agreed with Sir Henry that one of his men will take you there tomorrow. Your whole heart is cheap at the price.' It was a small victory but one that Francis thought politic to grant him.

87

Church bells woke him the next morning. The air of his room felt dense with their clanging and pealing. A delicate quartet of bells slid down their mournful scale again and again almost directly overhead. Remembering the closely-packed churches and bell towers he had seen from the deck of the galley, he threw open the wooden shutters of one of the two arched windows.

Outside the window was thick fog, alive with the sound of bells. The mournful quartet were just above his head to his left, but he could not see them, only the hazy shadow of the campanile. A row of leering stone faces peered half-seen through the fog from a wall facing him. If he looked straight down the stained, peeling stucco wall below his window, he saw the blurred dark grey stripe of a small canal. The wake of a vanished boat slapped wetly against the house walls. The smell of sewage reached him even here, two floors up. Though it was late summer, the marble floor chilled his bare feet. He shivered and got back into bed.

Back under the light feather quilt (yes, indeed . . . as well as a very fine wine at supper) he allowed himself a moment of unexpected well-being. He was still astonished to find himself still alive. He no longer needed to suppress the paralysing terror of being burnt alive. Whatever duty Cecil exacted from him now, it was nothing compared to the little man's gift of continuing life.

He stretched his naked limbs, feeling the linen sheets brush sweetly against his skin . . .

Sofia.

He dropped his forearm across his eyes. His other hand reached for her.

He clenched his teeth and let out a long deep breath. He couldn't bear not knowing if he would ever make love to her again. He would almost rather be certain of the worst.

He heard her voice saying again, 'His life is of no importance to me, brother. You may do as you like.' Which of them had she been deceiving, Ettore or himself? He should be able to answer that by now. But reason told him that his longing for her shaped the reply.

He turned her ring on his little finger. The ruby disappeared behind his finger and rose again like a small red sun.

Pull it off and drop it into the canal, he told himself. Make a clean break.

Instead, he pressed the ring to his mouth, feeling the stone hard against his lips and teeth, tasting the creamy metallic tang of the gold. He could not believe that she had been dissembling the night she put it on his finger. And yet . . .

To distract himself, he felt on the floor for the one unambiguous pleasure of his return to Venice. Cecil had brought a letter from Boomer. Even whilst tangled in his own troubles, Cecil had thought to send to Powder Mote and offer to serve as messenger. The little man could indeed be kinder than he knew.

Though you'd best not rely on it, thought Francis as he unfolded the letter to read yet again.

The world of Powder Mote, which had begun to seem

471

unreal in La Spada, leapt back into vivid life through Boomer's jagged scrawl and familiar dry words. All was well there, though both Francis and Richard were much missed. The boy, named William, was still there, talking again (though not of the past) and proving himself useful with the animals, poultry and fish.

'However, Petty France now crawls as fast as a puppy can run, and we brace ourselves against the day that he grows large enough to lead William's good-natured willingness astray . . .'

Francis lowered the letter onto his thighs and tried to imagine ever going back to Powder Mote to stay. To rest, of course. To be warmed and feel loved, always. But his familiar old bedroom against the chimney and under the tiles no longer belonged to the man who lay here in a vast gilded bed in an echoing, plaster-walled chamber in a Venetian *palazzo* with water slapping at its feet. Powder Mote had very little to do with a rescued mountebank waiting to return to an unknown fate in La Spada.

His well-being began to slide into melancholy.

Though he had brought news of Powder Mote, Cecil had had no word from Seaborn. Nor had Sir Henry Wootten, it seemed. Seaborn and the Sky Monkey had disappeared. Rather than think about what that silence might mean, Francis threw back the feather quilt and looked for his clothes. Fog or no fog, this time he would explore Venice before leaving it again. But his shirt, trousers, stockings and linen had disappeared. He entertained himself briefly with the image of walking the streets wearing only his doublet, hat and boots.

'*Giorno, signore.*' Greeting, knock and breakfast arrived together with a manservant. Francis was delighted equally by the smell of freshly baked pastries, the sight of his clothes, miraculously cleaned and ironed, and the smiling sideways glance of the laundry maid. Even the message from Cecil

472

that they must call on Sir Henry Wootten later that morning, at his house near the Jewish Ghetto in Cannareggio, did not deflect a renewed rising of his spirits. He poured himself a small cup from the pot of *kave* and waited with interest for his heart to begin to race.

By midday, fog lifted and duty done, Francis was headed for the Arsenale, down the Grand Canal in Sir Henry's private gondola, in the keeping of a man called Sir Walter Markworthy. Markworthy, whose exact diplomatic role had escaped Francis, was clearly a man of weight in the English Embassy to Venice, far grander in dress and manner than Sir Henry, who had seemed a cheerful, rather dough-faced man of quick wits and self-deprecating speech. Markworthy soon demonstrated his impressive fluency in both the Tuscan and Venetian dialects. He also delighted in facts and took even greater joy in imparting them.

As they turned right out of the Rio della Misericordia and then left from the smaller canal into the Grand Canal, Markworthy pointed happily and informed. 'You will never see such delicate tracery on any London house,' he declared, pointing to a lacy façade on the left bank. 'Nor such extravagant use of vermillion, gold and lapis lazuli . . . built for the procurator Marino Contarini . . .'

Watching Markworthy in his dark coat in the shadow of the gondola's awning, Francis was suddenly reminded of his last journey on the Thames with Cecil – another moment of suspension, a similar brew of anticipation and fear. But now, in place of cool English night, a hot sun thumped at his head if he leaned out from under the awning. And Cecil had not talked so much.

'The Fish Market . . . *pescheria*,' said Markworthy, savoring every syllable. '. . . the Rialto, which is the Venetians' chief commercial district, where . . .'

The water of the Grand Canal was not dark and muscular like the Thames, or lit by tiny lanterns. Instead, it seemed to crackle and jump with a fierce broken reflected light that dazzled his eyes. Where London held its river firmly in place between solid banks, Venice on its low flat islands felt to Francis like an interloper into the world of water, precariously awash and likely to be swept away. But until the sea claimed it, glorious.

'. . . and that adjoining pair are the *Palazzi Giustinian* built for two brothers . . .' said Markworthy. '. . . and, of course, you can hardly miss the renowned basilica of San Marco . . .'

There was too much to take in. Francis stared hungrily, half listening to Markworthy, half listening to the cries of the boatmen and the conversations that passed them on the water. To his astonishment, every fifth boat seemed filled with English visitors.

They reached the ships' pool at the bottom of the Grand Canal.

'. . . two miles of walls encircle it, with a single opening for galleys to pass in and out . . .' Markworthy pointed.

But Francis was already staring in anticipation at the tall pink brick walls topped by the square gap teeth of crenellations – the Arsenale, a small city in itself, where the Venetian fleet of sailing galleys was built and equipped down to the last gun, rope and ship's biscuit.

'It's name is from the Arabic,' Markworthy announced with relish, '*Dar sina'a*, or "house of industry".'

Their gondola slid between the two towers that guarded the gate. Francis gazed in amazement around the huge internal basin and peered into the roofed sheds where carpenters and caulkers were building dozens of hulls. Even the busiest shipyard in England offered nothing like this mammoth Venetian house of industry. He breathed in the scents of raw oak and boiling pitch. He had never seen so much making and devising going on at the same time in the same place.

He asked a squad of oar-makers if he could watch them working their long planks of Croatian beech. Then he would view the making of the gunpowder, and the giant rope walk, and the sail factory.

'. . . reported to be able to install in a mere six hours, ten masts, ten sails, ten rudders, 500 foot braces, 1,500 oars, twenty spars . . .' Markworthy rumbled on happily.

Listening to the shouts and clangour of the Arsenale foundries where all the guns for the Venetian war fleet were forged, Francis knew that he would have to survive La Spada and return again. To see it all, he would need at least a month. But Cecil had begun well in the purchase of his whole heart.

88

'The Englishman is back!' the boy shouted. He ran into the barn of the isolated farm. 'The man who killed Prince Ettore has come back!'

A man stepped out of the barn to stare at the glittering, jingling procession. A woman leaned from an upper window.

'Is that what they say here?' asked Francis in alarm.

Venturini shrugged. 'You just heard them.'

'And will they string me up or buy me a jug of ale?'

Venturini leaned down in his saddle to cut with his quirt at a farm dog that barked too close to his horse's feet. 'It depends who you ask.'

Francis thought that there was a slight possibility that the man had made a joke, though it was impossible to be certain.

And what would Sofia offer him? He tried not to imagine them in bed again. Must not let himself . . . too many questions still to be answered.

He was accompanied from Venice by Markworthy, who carried gifts for the new *principessa*, and a letter from King James (very possibly forged by Cecil) congratulating her on her accession. This letter also expressed a larger good will and the fervent desire of England to arrive at a mutually helpful amity with the principality of La Spada. Obliquely, it mentioned a shared distrust of the major powers to the east, the spiritual and territorial aggression of Rome, and the joint advantages of a flourishing English shipping trade in the Adriatic. Cecil had also sent a personal letter deeply regretting his own urgent need to return to London but expressing his great pleasure in satisfying the *principessa*'s wishes for his choice of deputy.

Francis had not read this letter but carried in his head a further message, expressed by Cecil as good will and hope for mutually fruitful negotiations, but which Francis knew was nothing more than the English Secretary of State flat on his back, with his tail wagging hopefully, belly up in submission. The vision almost made him like the little man. Looking down at his ring, he wondered what to expect from that delicious, terrifying young woman who could see her brother murdered, seize a throne, and get the better of Cecil at the same time.

As they travelled northward from the coast, Francis had remembered his moments of surprising joy on his first journey to La Spada. This time, at the forge where he had bought his knife, he had ordered a sword with engraved flames dancing along the blade, to be collected on his return. He knew that he was leaving this commission as a hostage.

Riding onwards now from the riverboat, he thought how much he would like to return with a lighter heart. He would ride far up into those mountains, look for lynx, swim in the natural hot springs he had heard praised for their soothing properties. Hot water from the earth intrigued him, being somewhere between water and fire, the two opposing extremes of his trade.

Francis wished he knew whether Sofia was more likely to welcome him with open arms or cut off his balls. He tried to keep a tight rein on his own expectations but still kept imagining her coming secretly to his bed again.

Once again, a guard of silver-scaled Uskoks had ridden out from La Spada to meet him. This time, he had known the silver river for what it was and called out greetings to Venturini and Rossi and the others who had worked with him.

'*Bon di! Bon di!*'

He had seized the chance to learn what he could from Venturini while the Uskoks escorted him to La Spada for the second time. As ever, extracting information was a slow painful process, but the Uskoks seemed to be still at the heart of things at the court, still the ruler's personal guard.

Francis detected satisfaction, and perhaps the faintest hint of pride, in Venturini's voice.

Sofia had indeed taken the throne, as Cecil had said. After the death of Ettorc in an explosion in his armoury, the succession had been straightforward and bloodless. The new ruler declared that her brother's death had been a soldier's accident. There was no mass execution of her brother's followers. True to her promise, Sofia had not arrested nor executed her enemies, although a few had chosen the precaution of leaving La Spada.

Some fled altogether to live in Venice. Some, like most of the Vranghi mercenaries, went east to fight for the Hapsburgs. A few military men went south through Dalmatia to join the Great Turk. Signore Bembo had fled to Venice to rejoin his relatives there. Some of the titled landowners had left the capital city for distant country estates where they hoped to be left alone to produce hams, oil, guns or wine. A few of the resident English had also thought it wise to visit Venice, where they would be out of judicial reach, until they could be certain of the *principessa*'s political intentions.

'And the slaves who worked at the lodge?'

'Freed,' said Venturini. Francis hoped it was true.

He gathered from Venturini's lean reporting that the rest of the inhabitants of La Spada were happy enough to welcome the old prince's daughter to the throne. The madness had ended. She seemed a reasonable young woman. In fact, she surprised and reassured a great many fearful citizens when she provided a fitting royal funeral for what was left of Ettore as well as a much grander one for her father. She decreed a suitable but not excessive period of public mourning for both of them. She was still busy accepting oaths of loyalty from many of their followers.

She gave great joy to the trades people and merchants, Venturini had said dryly. To meet the intended luxury of the celebrations for her coronation, the jewellers, silk merchants, apothecaries, barbers, butchers, bakers, confectioners, shoemakers, bookbinders, were all, at this moment, working feverishly and profitably whilst praising her name.

'No more forged signatures,' Venturini now offered in reply to yet another question from Francis. 'The *principessa* is like her father, as he used to be. No more decisions taken by Da Monte alone and sent out with the royal seal.'

'What will become of Da Monte?' asked Francis. 'Did he manage to keep his head down enough to survive?'

'Her highness will marry Da Monte soon,' Venturini leaned forward to rearrange the mane of his horse. 'Very clever.'

Jealousy punched Francis in the stomach like a fist. 'Wed Da Monte?' he asked tightly. His face seemed to burn. Sofia to wed Da Monte? That smooth-tongued perfumed little bear of a man? That consummate courtier who had stood with his eyes on the floor while the prince sliced off Yuri's head. Sofia in bed with Da Monte! He felt a revulsion almost as fierce as when he had thought she was a creature of the prince. Surely not!

'Her highness is clever to make the duke her consort.

After her half-brother, he was her greatest threat. He's a cousin of Prince Alessandro. He knows how to run the country. And now I think he will do it her way.'

'Indeed,' said Francis. 'Who would not?' He swallowed. Anything he said now would betray his sick rage. But a glance at Venturini told him that his secret was already out, among the Uskoks at least.

Da Monte? he thought incredulously. Da Monte, the *principessa*'s consort!

Did Cecil know? Francis now felt a burning fury. If Cecil had told him that Sofia was to wed Da Monte, he would have dug in his heels, at no matter what cost. Of course, Cecil knew! Sofia had called him back in order to taunt him. And Cecil was permitting it.

Francis remembered the girl in his bed. Her eagerness, her hunger . . . Devious, ruthless . . . yes . . . all of those. But she had been a virgin, he was certain beyond doubt. She could not have learned so quickly to act so falsely . . . Or could she?

'The duke is old.' This time, Venturini slid his eyes sideways to meet those of Francis, man-to-man.

Francis could not summon up a response to the invited male collusion. 'Thank you for telling me,' he said, when he regained control of his voice.

Venturini acknowledged the debt with a short nod. 'It's always better to know what to expect.'

'Is that possible in La Spada?'

'We know.'

'Who? The Uskoks or the people of La Spada?'

'We . . . The Uskoks. We learn to know. Pay attention. That's how we survive to earn our name.'

'Then the *principessa* is truly clever to have won your loyalty.' Francis could not keep the edge off his voice.

'She always had it. She's of us, like her father. Of the clan.'

Then must I believe that she too always knows what to expect? wondered Francis in fury. Unlike the rest of us who stumble from guess to guess? He remembered the night she had sworn that she would steal the bond when the prince died.

Like a fool, I believed that she then meant to give it to me!

She had never said as much, but let him assume she had said it. She was very like Cecil. They deserved each other as allies.

Now, there would be a match! he thought. How well they both read him! Sofia had known he would tell her what she wanted to know. Knew that he would not attack her to take the bond back, would not put her life at risk by taking it too soon.

As they climbed onto the plateau, he looked at Castello La Spada in the distance, crouched on its sword-shaped peak.

I'm almost ready to take you, he thought fiercely. I need only a little longer, a few more attempts. He imagined a flight of Sky Monkeys climbing into the sky and dropping down behind those walls, the explosions, the flying stones, the smoke and flames . . . what was he thinking?

Was he still a child, dreaming how he would land terrible punishments on someone who had damaged his feelings?

He was a grown man, who should be in control of his thoughts and emotions. But the older he grew, the harder it seemed to become to behave well.

The wide plateau distracted him with a sense of familiarity. He had never expected to gaze eastwards again along that open route leading onwards towards the Hapsburgs and the Hungarian plains. It was both odd and pleasing to feel such fierce recognition for mountain shapes and for a city that his imagination had not known to exist such a short time ago.

Nevertheless, his stomach tightened with dread as they rode up the steep causeway in the sudden dusk of the mountains. Once again, he climbed surrounded by a clattering Uskok guard. This time, however, he was without Richard Seaborn. He still did not know what had become of him. Cecil had heard nothing. Venturini, when asked for news, had shifted his eyes away and replied to some other question entirely.

Dead, then, thought Francis heavily. He prayed that Venturini simply did not want to admit to ignorance. Having to tell Boomer that Richard was dead seemed far worse than Richard telling Boomer that Francis was dead.

This time after arriving in La Spada, he was allowed to go straight to his old *camera*, where a new manservant waited to help him wash away the smell of horse.

I seem to have come full circle, thought Francis wryly as the man helped him into the court clothes provided by Sir Henry Wootten, of the fineness that the ambassador decreed for any English envoy to a foreign court. Back in starched lace and jewelled buttons.

All the same, he studied himself intently in the looking glass and changed his collar twice.

89

Keep your hand steady, he told himself. He stepped through the door of the great *sala*. For a moment, he saw Gloriana amongst her courtiers, the English queen Elizabeth, alive again and young, and much more beautiful.

'Advance. Signore Cointo, come sit by me,' said the *principessa*. 'We keep an easy court here.'

But what he saw contradicted her words. She seemed taller than before, even sitting on the throne. She still wore black – for had she not just lost both father and brother? – but a golden haze lay over the black silk of her skirts. To Francis, she seemed all black and gold and shimmering lights. Her jewels caught the torchlight when she moved. A star glimmered at the corner of her jaw as she bent her head to speak quietly to Da Monte.

The Lord Chamberlain bowed his head and left. Francis glared after him. The fortunate consort-to-be, who knew how to rule, how to keep things in order. She had what she wanted now and meant to hold onto it!

'Francees!' She was looking at him in question.

Francis collected himself, bowed, only half-aware that she

had just addressed him by his first name in front of the court. He glared at the floor.

Wolf bitch. Deceiving cunny! And just where did she mean for him to fit into her ruling? She might have persuaded Cecil that she wanted Francis merely as an envoy. Francis was certain beyond all doubt that her reasons were far more complex.

He raised his head and inhaled sharply. She was magnificent. He felt that odd dislocation of meeting someone you know well in a dream, who is not quite as you remember. The pinched watchfulness had gone, making Sofia seem in some ways even younger than before. Yet her bearing held new authority. The weight of power seemed only to buoy her up.

She smiled into his eyes. He stared coldly back. He would not let that smile touch him.

Her smile cooled though her lips held their pleasant curve. She lifted her hand to point to one side. He looked past her and drew a sharp breath.

'Come meet my newest waiting gentleman,' she said.

Francis, moving forward, had already seen him.

'Signore Riccardo Zebbone.'

The young man stepped out of the shadows of the throne, looking almost as splendid in gold and white as he had done when Francis first met him, but much happier.

'Richard!' Nephew and uncle gripped hands. If they had not been at court, at the foot of the throne of the new ruling monarch, Francis would have whooped and pounded his nephew on the back. He forgot all earlier suspicions.

Richard smiled and smiled. 'We all thought you dead. It took two days for Sir Henry's pigeons to bring word that all was well.'

'I thought you dead until just now,' Francis replied. 'What the devil have I missed?'

'I hope you'll forgive the missing of a manservant,' said Richard.

'As gladly as your sudden elevation.' But his nephew's manner had already turned more certain. The grip of Powder Mote on Richard Seaborn had slipped almost entirely. Another loss in the waiting. Niccolò Schiavoni, Count of Alte Terme, waited smiling for Richard to return to his side.

Richard turned prettily to the *principessa*. 'He is surprised to see me after all, your highness, when you vowed that he would not be. I believe that you owe me one gold angel.'

'Not yet,' she said. She looked at Francis with an expression he could not read. Did he imagine disappointment there?

Disappointment at what, dear God? He was the one who had just learned that she meant to marry a pusillanimous old fart.

'There's another surprise to come. I hope it pleases you as much.' She nodded, setting off a ripple of instructions that flowed out of the room. A moment later, Francis heard the tight insistent beat of the Uskok drums, like a multitude of marching feet.

The Uskoks entered two-by-two, full armour gleaming, a slow river of silver that curved from the door across the broad floor towards the throne where Sofia sat and Francis stood near her feet. The courtiers fell back to let them pass. Mysterious behind the shining nose guards of their helmets and the dark holes of their eyes, they advanced as if no wall, no rock cliff face could stop them. Even Francis, knowing them, having unloaded camels and shared work with them, had to steel himself now to stand facing their steady advance and not to move aside.

They reached him. The river split into two streams and flowed to either side of him. Francis found himself looking up the still-advancing river at a silver giant who lurched forwards, with an Uskok supporting him on either side.

'For you,' said Sofia.

Then Francis saw that the giant was an empty suit of armour, supported on a wooden frame, riding on a low, wheeled cart.

'It's made of silver from our mines – my second gift of welcome to you.' She was watching him intently.

'Ahhhh.' A breath of awe rose from the assembled courtiers.

The silver armour looked to him as he imagined the skin of an angel might be, reflecting God's glory. A man inside its flashing shape would become more than human, turned both beautiful and terrifying.

Francis took refuge in a courtier's civility. 'Your highness, I am both overwhelmed and unworthy.' In truth, he was both overwhelmed and confused.

Richard and Niccolò began to clap. One by one, the rest of the courtiers joined in. Francis saw Da Monte clapping like the rest but with a thoughtful look on his face.

Sofia raised a hand for silence. 'Leave us now. I want a word alone with Signore Cointo.'

The room emptied except for two guards, the waiting woman Isabella, Da Monte, Richard and Niccolò, who all withdrew to the door at the far end of the chamber.

'Do you like it, Francees?'

'Sofia . . .' He looked to see whether he was still permitted this familiarity. He did not know how to act with a former lover, turned ruling monarch who would shortly marry another man.

'Answer me!' She was smiling but urgency lurked in her voice. 'It will fit you exactly.' She led him closer. 'Look. Hold your arm against it . . . there. And see, the length of the thigh. It comes exactly to your knee.'

'How did you manage that? Did Richard steal my clothes for you?'

'Do you remember the ribbons?'

Oh, yes, he remembered those playful ribbons, twisted around his ankles and wrists, laid along his legs. Stretched from nipple to nipple, wrapped around his palm. He had known she was up to something, but had never imagined such a wonder as this armour.

'Why are you giving this beautiful thing to me?'

'I give it to my general,' she said. 'I need my own army to keep a firm hold on power. I have my father's Uskoks but they are not enough. I want a complete fighting force, my own White Army, like Sir John Hawkwood gave to the Florentines. And I want you to lead it.'

'But I'm not a general, not even an officer. I'm a fire master.'

'You know guns and explosives?'

'Yes.' I told you, my lord! he said silently. Not a simple envoy after all.

'I want you to train my army, in the modern ways of warfare. The Uskoks are cavalry, and skirmishers. They're raiders, the sons of corsairs and bandits. They can't field a large force and march against cities. They don't know how to defend against such a force. I will find you tacticians and strategists, if you wish. You have a library to consult for ancient wisdom. Albona will be delighted to help.'

'You want me to do this for you in exchange for a suit of silver armour?' he asked cautiously.

'England will also provide and pay for two hundred men for one year, as mercenaries. If any wish to stay on after you have trained them, then La Spada will become their pay master.'

'All this in exchange for a suit of silver armour?'

She shook her head. 'In exchange for the bond.'

90

'I never replaced it,' she said. 'That night when you were so tempted to snatch it from me.'

'I should have . . .' he began. Then he understood. 'Who made the forgery? It was too good to have been dashed off at a writing table.'

'Signore Albona. He copied the look but not the content.'

He didn't know whether he wanted to clout her or kiss her. 'I swore to Cecil by every oath I know that I had seen the damned thing burnt!'

'That was merely a tedious account of an old trade dispute.'

They were being watched now from the far end of the room. Da Monte, pretended to talk to Niccolò and Richard but was poised like down caught on a blade of grass.

Francis was afraid to speak lest he say the wrong words. The future hung quivering ready to blow this way or that with their next breath.

She had Cecil by the nose, and through him, England. Through Francis's loyalties to both Cecil and to England, she had Francis by the nose. This did not feel any longer like a marriage of hearts. He frowned at her hand, where she still wore the ring he had placed on it, just as he still wore his own. There was nothing she would not twist to her own use.

A deep shudder of rebellion rose up from his feet to engulf his heart and head. Against both of them, Sofia and Cecil alike.

'*Principessa*, I can't accept your commission. I will find you another fire master, a far better general, a dozen excellent drill masters. No doubt Cecil will agree to give you your mercenary army in exchange for the bond. But I can't stay here in La Spada. It's not a comfortable place for me.'

She went rigid.

'Too much remains unanswered here.'

'Ask me for the answers, then.' Her gaze reminded him again of that first searching look up from the floor at her father's feet. 'I have learnt that I must be open with you. If I can answer you to keep you here, I will.' She swallowed. 'I will speak as Sofia, the partner of your heart. Not as the *principessa*.' She held out her hands as if falling.

He caught them. They were icy cold. 'Above all else, I must know who betrayed the Sky Monkey to Ettore,' he said.

She made a little face as if struck by a passing pain. 'Ah, Francees . . .'

'Was it Father Daniele? The physician? Did Da Monte guess? Albona?' Deep breath . . . 'Was it Richard? The truth. I must know.'

Please don't lie to me, he begged her silently. He didn't know how he would tell, but she must not lie.

She tightened her grip before she spoke. 'I betrayed you to Ettore.'

91

'You didn't guess?'

He shook his head, not trusting speech.

'But it was the only way! How else could you have killed him if he had not asked you to hand him the weapon? How else would he ask for his own death unless he learned of the Sky Monkey? I know you, Francees. I have studied you so closely, paid such attention to your heart, to the dance of your wits. You had promised me that you would not let Ettore harm me. I knew what you would do.' She held onto his hands, would not let him pull away. 'Don't you see?'

Her words came in a fierce torrent. 'Do you think either you or I would have survived the first day after my father died? I knew my brother too well even to hope. I knew you would not let Ettore have the Sky Monkey. I knew you would now kill him, even though you refused when you did not yet judge it to be the time. I knew you would devise a way to do it.'

Was he truly so ruthless? Or so ingenious? Francis stared back at the self she was reflecting.

'I read that warning in your eyes and knew you would risk your own life, thinking to save me, and thinking that your Cecil was safe. I staked everything on what I believed of you – my life and all of La Spada. I thought that you surely must have guessed what I had done to help you.'

'How did you know exactly what to tell Ettore?'

'You told me the gist yourself. Albona explained the rest.'

She had indeed twisted it all to her use, but how magnificently.

Though he had not known it, they had flown together like a pair of birds. Without having to speak, in parallel, in the same direction always, turning together on shared impulse, knowing without speech where the other would fly. Sofia knowing, he unthinking. He saw the shared pattern now, the interweaving of their wills.

'You took a very great risk, to trust me so far,' he said.

'I trusted both your honour and your wits. And your true ruthlessness.' She paused, as breathless as if she had run up stairs. 'You see how I trusted you while you were still suspecting me.' She shook her head at him. 'Don't deny it! I saw that in your eyes too. But why do you think I left the room? Who do you think alerted Father Bernabo?'

He bowed his head and held out his arms to the side in submission. "Lady, you have humbled me.'

'Still not "Sofia"?'

He looked at her in desperation. Why were words so hard? 'Now I will follow your example. Be open with you.' He nodded as if urging himself on. First of all, he must be open with himself. 'Your words make me want to weep with shame but I still don't see how I can stay here.'

Her face tightened again. 'What else is left for me to answer? For what reason do you still fear and dislike me?'

'Not dislike ' he cried. 'Nor fear.' He could not bear the signs of retreat in her face, the return of the guardedness that had once ruled her life. 'Not at all.' He swallowed. 'On the contrary. Sofia . . . I felt . . . I feel . . .' In his mouth, waiting, lay coiled the word he had never managed to spit out at Powder Mote when eyeing Boomer with Kate, and Petty France . . . 'Jealousy,' he said. 'Ignoble, red-eyed jealousy.'

At once, he felt relief, not a happy relief, but the lightening of a sick man who has just voided the poison in his belly. 'I know that I have no right to feel jealous. I can make no claim on a princess. I expect nothing from you. We agreed on that. But, still . . . the marriage of our hearts? What will become of that when you are wed to Da Monte?'

'You are jealous of Da Monte?' She leaned closer to search his face. 'Is your jealousy of Da Monte behind all this?'

'If I stay to see you wed, I fear I will kill him.'

'Truly?' Her face began to lighten but she still studied him. 'But my marriage to Da Monte is mere policy, a marriage of state – I will never bed him – and it serves both of us, you as well as me.'

'Serve me?' He glared at her incredulously. 'Never!'

What a feeble word! He wanted words that would bring down walls, throw out fire, shake the earth.

'Indeed, it does most surely serve us both,' she said. 'I want you to undertake this commission, not only for me and for La Spada but for your unborn child.'

She could not have spoken the words he thought he heard. 'My child?' Then his breath grew thick in his chest. He forgot how to breathe. A waterfall roared in his ears. His head seemed to fill with blood, or sap, or honey. He wanted to laugh. Tears came to his eyes. He looked at her to locate a steady place in the shifting world.

'My marriage will make the child legitimate, and heir to the throne of La Spada.' She smiled, but with another flash of that look he remembered from his first sight of her. That intense searching question. Would all be well? Was he to be the answer to a question he did not know?

'A child?' he repeated. 'My son?'

But he knew it. He knew her too, as she knew him. But, unlike her, he had twisted the truth that he saw. Reason and caution had prompted him to twist it for the worse. She was in truth wily and devious – just as he was ruthless and ingenious. But she loved him. He believed her now. He still felt astonishingly uncertain of his footing. At the same time, absolute joy rose up from his knees, a warm rush that bubbled up through his belly into his chest. It rose through the still-clogged spaces in his throat and drew the corners of his mouth into a grin that had nothing to do with his will. It kept rising and turned to water in his eyes.

His own child. His seed, his boy, his flesh, growing inside Sofia's belly, inside that delectable curve of satin skin. Nothing more than a promise yet, but growing as surely as an unseen acorn uncoils and reaches for life with its first pale, fragile finger of a root.

'It might be your daughter,' she said. 'I won't make promises I can't swear to keep.'

A girl? He felt a lurch of tenderness, then excitement. He imagined the fascination of seeing the woman Sofia wound back to her beginning. To watch the skein unroll again. What would her beauty look like in an infant? How did courage and quick wits and wiliness and ruthlessness and sweetness first show themselves? At what age could you see the first marks, the first signals of what was to come?

A great clumsy lolloping joy began to thump around inside him.

'You must speak soon, France, or those people waiting over there will imagine something amiss. They already think you mean to refuse my commission.'

'Sofia . . . *Principessa!*' Francis dropped to one knee and took her hand to kiss. A last treacherous thought tapped at his awareness.

493

'If you still wonder whether to trust me,' said Sofia, 'you won't doubt me after the birth. Da Monte could never father a long, lean blue-eyed babe with duckling hair – which I'm certain this one will be.'

She couldn't repress a small gleam of pleasure at having read him right yet again. 'Don't fear. His grace already has his heir, by his first wife. And he feared exile or death under Ettore. I assure you, lending the name of paternity is a small price for him to pay if he can continue to help rule La Spada, together with a rise in station to royal consort.' She gripped his hand and pulled him to his feet. 'As I'm a widow, we won't even need to cheat the sheets. Try on your armour now.'

'I already know, beyond all doubt, that it will fit exactly.'

She leaned closer. 'Da Monte's far more obedient than you but lacks your fine legs.'

Poor Da Monte, thought Francis. As a man, perhaps not so content with his bargain as Sofia imagined. But the duke had struck a splendid bargain nevertheless. He would keep much of his former power. He would be clever enough to profit from his new elevation. However, he was not an Uskok.

And poor me, not an Uskok neither. Francis found himself smiling helplessly again.

Sofia called Richard and Niccolò to help Francis put on the armour. 'Behold my new general,' she said, watching Francis test the flexibility of his different joints. 'We shall do such things together, he and I.'

92

Sofia stood on the battlements with Francis and others of her court, gathered to watch the fireworks. Her investiture had taken place that morning. She was now *Principessa* Sofia Serafina Santa Catarina Adorata di Pirati, the anointed ruler of La Spada in Friuli. Though the main feasting was done, the celebrating continued. For some, it would run on until heads hit the table and men toppled from their benches. Francis stood on one side of the *principessa,* sniffing the night air. Da Monte stood on the other side. Francis looked sober but elegant in the restrained court garb of a soldier. Though the duke was not yet consort, he had already swollen both in dignity and in the grandeur of his dress.

The two of them will have to sort out the terms between them, she thought. Old stag, young stag. Though the horns would be the duke's, he professed himself content with her terms. Marriage in name only. He knew how much she would rely on him for help in governing La Spada and already took pride in her need for him. She had no doubt that her gift to him of three of Ettore's estates, including both a vineyard and a small silver mine, had soothed any last bruises to his male pride – particularly as he meant, with Sofia's

495

permission, to install his long-time mistress in one of them.

Amongst the others who had joined her up here on the walls were envoys from England, Florence, Rome, Venice, Vincenza, Vienna and Constantinople. She had invited them all, Catholic, Lutheran and Muslim alike. Like her father, she had made it clear that all were welcome, so long as they left hostilities at home and greeted each other civilly here in La Spada. Sooner or later, she would declare her alliances, but not yet. For the moment, the Hapsburgs, Spanish, English, French, Romans, Venetians, Florentines, Milanese and Turks all wooed rather than threatened. Meanwhile, the lions listened and digested.

She walked forwards to the edge of the battlements. The town below her was alight with bonfires and avenues of torches. She could hear singing and drums and the thin voices of distant strings. Her people, celebrating. The *Piazza Herbe* was as dense with fires as an army camp.

In her thoughts, she let a scrap of paper fly off into the night. Being Sofia, she would never let go of all her rules, but one, at least, must be rewritten.

Do not attach your heart. She glanced sideways at Francis. That rule was truly broken.

'What is it, *cara mia?*' he asked with a small frown of concern.

In reply, she closed her fist and mimed the act of flinging something into the night. 'An old fear,' she said. 'Gone now.' One day, she might even tell him about her rules. 'The spell is lifted,' she said. 'We live in the reasoning world again.'

Seaborn had set the first flights to soar up from the piazza in front of the *Magno Palazzo*.

'What is that?' Francis pointed down into the piazza at a large crossbow set almost vertically amongst the paper castles, garlanded posts and gilded leather monsters that bristled with rockets, fountains, Catharine Wheels and squibs. Smaller than his monster bow, but larger than that of a human bowman, it was loaded with a bolt in the shape of a giant rocket, almost large enough to carry a small man.

'You'll have to wait, France.' Seaborn grinned in teasing delight. 'Sir' had gone forever. In fact, Seaborn would have a title of his own after tonight's services as fire master to the *principessa*. He dashed away to signal to his men.

By next week, I'll be calling him 'sir,' thought Francis, watching his former apprentice disappear. It had always been only a matter of time. To his astonishment, he found that he did not mind in the least.

The fireworks began. Rockets climbed into the sky. Castles burst into halos of flame. Dogs howled. Cats shot into dark crannies. Babies woke and screamed. In the stables, the grooms stroked and soothed the stamping horses.

Suddenly, Seaborn reappeared. 'Your highness, France . . .! Watch closely now! Keep your eyes on the bow.'

Only the three of them, Francis, Seaborn and Sofia, knew what they were seeing. Albona was not there after all as he was at the bedside of his sister, now freed by Sofia. The bow thumped and rocked on its moorings. The rocket shot up out of a billowing skirt of white fire. Just at the peak of its climb, when an ordinary rocket must either explode or begin its fall back to earth, there was a small burst of flame. A second fiery shape leapt on upwards, barely visible amongst the falling stars from other ordinary rockets.

'You would have succeeded,' said Seaborn.

Francis tamped down a rush of elation. 'It's better that there was no need to try.' Ettore had proved well enough that the fusing device worked. He felt a sense of uneasy pride all the same. 'Thank you for that.'

All three stared up through a renewed frenzy of falling stars at the dark space into which the Sky Monkey had vanished.

'I haven't destroyed your notes and drawings,' said Seaborn. 'What would you like me to do with them?'

Francis was caught off-guard. The notes should be destroyed. He must force the genie back into its bottle, if he could. It must not be allowed to roam at large in a world so precariously balanced on the edge of new war. But he couldn't say the words that would destroy it. He had tracked it, stalked it, snared it, pounced with triumph and fierce delight. The Sky Monkey was his creature, his doing, the child of his thoughts.

'Give the papers to Albona, to hide,' he replied at last. 'He will know where. Tell him – where it was born and belongs.'

'Didn't you offer it to Cecil?'

'Not until England needs it.'

'Or Friuli,' said Sofia, missing nothing.

'Or until some other inquisitive fool stumbles on it, or on something very like it.'

'Cecil will just have to be content with the cancelled bond,' Sofia said.

Sofia heard the edge of regret in Francis's voice. Unbelievably, he was still here at her side, to stay, for a time at least . . . she still did not dare to trust this new sense of joy entirely. Only time could make her feel safe. She could let him run when he wished, to follow his curiosity and use his skills in new ventures. He would always return. If she herself ever failed to please him enough, their child would pull him back to her. For a third month, she had not bled. She had not been nudging the truth with Francis, after all. Her pregnancy was confirmed beyond all doubt.

There he stood, truly there, not just in her imagination. The husband-of-her-heart, tall, beautiful, wily, ruthless, amusing, loyal, restless, and kind. Smiling at her, suppressing a belch from the rich feast, thinking about all that he had not achieved. She could already see . . . was already mapping out . . . such a glorious future for him, and for them all.

She would never fling that rule away – always look ahead.

What is real in *The Principessa* and what is not?

La Spada is invented. The mountains of Friuli are real. By setting *The Principessa* in Friuli, I was able at my computer to relive my passionate love of mountains and to give to Francis my own joy in walking and climbing in the Italian Dolomites and eastern Alps. Like Francis and Seaborn, I have slept above those methane-producing cows and stood on those edges looking out over violet, cloud-carpeted valleys.

La Spada, though imagined, stands in a real and plausible place, and resembles any number of real medieval and renaissance Italian city-states before the Unification of Italy. The significance of its position on the Val Canale (now the route of a major road) is based on historical reality, as are the political pressures from the Ottomans and Hapsburgs. The awe-inspiring outer walls of the ancient *fortezza* recall my sightings of existing Italian hilltop fortresses, such as Runkelstein near Bolzano. However, the baroque *Magno Palazzo* inside my Castello La Spada is entirely imagined, as are the prince's erotic frescos. Venice, its Lagoon, the Arsenale and the coast of the Veneto are all real, of course, and shown as lovingly and truthfully as I could manage.

Robert Cecil was appointed Lord High Treasurer of England in May 1608, but Francis would not have known this because he had left for La Spada in March. Like his father, Lord

Burleigh, Cecil was indeed the most powerful man in England after the monarch. In *The Firemaster's Mistress*, I propose a possible early incident which threatened his almost absolute power but which he managed to suppress. In *The Principessa*, set three years later in 1608, I give him a further nudge towards his final fall from grace, and death in 1612.

Prince Ettore's tall, blond, moustachioed 'Vranghi' are imagined but plausible descendants of the historical Varangian Guard – themselves descendants of Britons and Danes – the ferocious mercenaries who helped defend Constantinople against the crusaders in 1203. The formidable but delightful Uskoks existed and may live again in a further book.

The presence in the House of Wisdom of manuscripts rescued from the Library at Alexandria is based on many scattered rumours of smuggled documents, in both classical and modern sources, as well as on a touch of common sense about human nature.

In 1608, Galileo, then a professor of Mathematics at Padua, had not yet enraged the Inquisition by publishing his support for the sun-centred Copernican model of the heavenly 'onion'. However, fellow scholars and other educated men would have known about and debated his astronomical investigations into Copernican theory.

History is not a distant place we visit like tourists peering through a glass museum case. Our life this minute is turning into the history of the future. I want the life of my historical characters to feel just as vivid and real to them (and to us, reading about it) as ours feels now. To try to understand how life was different in the seventeenth century, I cook from old recipes. I try on the clothes. I visit old buildings and walk to learn how long it takes to get from one place to another on foot – and try to learn whether I would have been walking on stone or through mud. Vivid truth lies in getting the details right.

I'm even more fascinated by what doesn't change. Neither emotions nor dirty politics, for example, seem to have changed much in Western Europe since the seventeenth century. For me, 'historical' fiction can shed fresh light on our own concerns by seeing them through the filter of the past. *The Firemaster's Mistress* dealt with both terrorism and government spin-doctoring in the context of the 1605 Gunpowder Plot, as well as the problems of a love affair across religious lines. In *The Principessa*, we get a different view of the troubled politics of the Balkan region, most recently in the news because of the conflicts in Kosovo, Serbia, and Croatia. Francis, with his explosive Sky Monkey – an early super-weapon – faces the same confusion of intellectual ambition and moral dilemma as the inventors of the H-bomb. Both he and Sofia face the still-current problem of how far you will go in order to survive. And laughter doesn't change, even if comic styles do. Francis, with his dry humour, would appreciate the awful ironies of modern politics.

The modern heavens are liberally dusted with real-life examples of the human desire to be fired for all eternity into space. This rocket-powered yearning upwards of the human spirit has even been dramatized on prime-time television in The Rocket Man, the story of a modern man who tangles with local council bureaucracy when he tries to fire his wife's ashes into the sky. The prince of La Spada begins to seem a little less mad and his problems a little less bizarre.

> Some suggested Reading Group Questions can be found at both www.christiedickason.co.uk and harpercollins.co.uk